ZIPHALIE AND THE SKY HUNTERS

LAUREN LOGAN

*This one is for me
because I am Ziph
and Ziph is me…*

DISABILITY NOTICE

The thoughts and feelings of my character with Attention Deficit Disorder with Hyperactivity are a small part of what it means to be ADD/H. The disabled community is not a monolith, and our experiences vary significantly.

CONTENT WARNINGS

Content warnings for Ziphalie and the Sky Hunters are listed on www.authorlaurenlogan.com

Ziphalie and the Sky Hunters is strictly for mature readers of 18+

Please protect your mental health.

CONTENTS

CHAPTER 1
ALMOST NORMAL

Ziph stood confidently, knowing she located the correct door when she knocked just seconds ago, but now this creepy, pale skinned human man in a white lab coat and surgical mask towered over her, and she was not so sure. *Why am I always so confidently wrong? Why can't I ever be confidently right?* "I'm here to donate plasma, but I think I may have the wrong address." Her painted face was white with black stars decorating her light green eyes and an exaggerated black smile covered her mouth, the designs from her shift at work. Unease wriggled inside as Ziph adjusted the waist of her black leggings and yanked her blue shirt down in the center where there was always a misshapen spot from her pulling on it incessantly. *Maybe I wouldn't be so fucking broke if I wasn't always replacing my shirts.* She recalled her cluttered bathroom counter, stacked with baskets of makeup, and she cringed internally. She knew exactly where all her credits went.

She just needed a few more credits right now though to make her rent payment on time. If she were late again, her landlord would kick her out, and her mom didn't have room anymore since she had moved to a smaller, cheaper apartment in the Venus District. Venus, that name which once gave her peace and hope, now stung like a wasp. *Speaking of that bitch- hey Venus, some fucking help right now would be nice. You more than owe me.*

Feeling the overwhelming urge to run, Ziph started to back up as she brushed her golden blonde hair from her shoulder, but the man seized her arm in a bruising hold and jerked her into the building. "What the fuck do you think you're doing?" She felt a sharp prick at her neck, and a thick, heaviness quickly overtook her nerves. *What the fuck did this asshole just inject me with? It better not be drugs! Oh, no, it's definitely drugs.* The world shifted under her feet as the cocktail of sedatives pumped through her veins.

"It looks like we don't need to search for a test subject, a Rubus showhouse acrobat just stumbled upon our front door." He was an older man and his voice was raspy. His speech seemed like his vocal cords had been damaged, or he was a heavy smoker.

Another man approached, this one was much younger, and without a mask. "She's perfect. No one will miss her. Strap her in the pod and move it, she weighs a ton so she will process the sedative quickly, and her eyes are already starting to flutter."

I absolutely do not weigh a ton, Halitosis Hans! They didn't even need the sedatives with that breath. She begged her nerves to allow her to move so she could turn away. *Why in Pluto's hell did Poopsicle Breath have to carry my front half? Ick! Stop breathing on me!* Ziph wondered as they moved her to a modified drop pod. She could barely see under her long, false eyelashes as they set her down in the seat and strapped her in. *What the fuck did they mean by test subject? Oh, gods! Now my fucking tail is smashed!* She prayed to Venus nothing permanent happened while she was drugged and at the mercy of these two nefarious lab researchers.

Prying one of her eyes open at a time, she blinked a few times to clear her vision and truly wished she had just remained with her eyes closed. This was an underground First Human research facility. Their symbols were all over the lab, and she tremored with terror. It felt as though her heart sprouted wings and tried to flap from her chest. The two human men closed the top of the pod as they chuckled at the fear growing in her eyes.

Why are they laughing like that? What are they doing to me? Fuck! Being paralyzed is a horrid feeling. If I can't regain my body control soon, I will be having a grade A temper tantrum, even if it is just on the inside. She watched in horror as the two men moved to an instrument panel and began plugging away at the keys.

In seconds, the pod began to warm and true dread set in. A bright white beam of light engulfed her inside and out, and she tried to stay conscious as the light lifted her with a wave of heat. It went on for what seemed like hours as the waves penetrated her every cell and carried her along like she was riding an endless current. The boundless warmth caused sweat to pour from her and soak through her clothing.

A calm fell over her, comforting her and sending her into a deep slumber. Gentle thunder in the distance, with the warmth surrounding her, made for the best sleep she had had in years, and she wasn't moving an inch. The relaxation she felt dipped down to her bones and was euphoric. It was almost like she had been drugged. *Did I take some kind of drug, and forget? I don't do drugs though. I really don't know if I care right now.*

A mechanical sound caused her to stir awake and an annoying clicking from a drop pod window hatch opening filled her ears. *Who the fuck do I know has a drop pod?* Droplets of cool water fell against her face, and she startled awake, but her chest was strapped down too tightly in the pod's seat, and she struggled to take in a full breath. Reaching down, she released the mechanism holding the straps together, and they rolled away into the seat, allowing her to inhale fully. As she did, she closed her seafoam green eyes and tried to calm the rage inside before she attempted to figure out where in Pluto's hell she was. The freshwater falling against her skin could never have been from rains on Emendo. All the rains there slightly burned when they touched exposed flesh, and this water felt cool and refreshing. She darted her tongue out catching a droplet, the taste was almost sweet it was so clean. Ziph groaned internally. *Where the fuck am I? I know I'm not on Emendo anymore.*

Her vision continued to blur, so she squeezed her eyes shut for a few more moments trying to clear them on their own. She didn't dare rub them because she knew how much makeup was still applied to her face, and the last thing she wanted was big grey smudges. Finally feeling the fog of sleep slip from her eyes, Ziph blinked a few times as she peered over the side of the pod and around the rocky ledge. *Um, wait just one fucking minute. Where in Pluto's hell am I? This place doesn't look familiar at all. Was that transport technology? Pluto's flaming nut sack! I could be in a whole other galaxy!*

From the rocky cliffside where her pod perched, she could see the planet she landed on had caught another smaller sized, dead rocky planet, but it must have been slow enough to catch the celestial body and hold it in place instead of both planets merging. The area between the planets appeared to not have any gravity. Although they were hovering, she could tell the planets were spinning as one from a balanced center point between them. As she was close enough to the low gravity area, she felt the gravity only gently as she moved, and she held her arms out to explore the floating sensation which was fascinating. *The acrobatics I could do here will be spectacular. I hope I live long enough to find out. Shit, I don't know if complex life even exists here.* She could see green patches in various places, but most of the terrain was rocky plains with deep cracks and slopes with random jutting cliffsides. *This planet has some fucked up geology.*

She noticed an instrument panel in front of her, which was recording data and sending it back. The fried instruments where the engine controls were told Ziph she was not returning home, and that's when she noticed a little blinking dot on the screen. It was green and on the edge of the map showing her location. Her stomach twisted as she realized she was not even in the same galaxy anymore. She was in a satellite dwarf galaxy adjacent to her own. *Are these First Humans really transporting people off to other galaxies and collecting the data? Oh gods! Are they trying to invade this planet? If I'm going to be stuck here, there's no way I'm going to help those fuckers reach this planet. Not today!* She knew exactly what the First Human goal was, domination and exploitation. Finally unseated in the galactic center, they were looking for worlds in other galaxies to exploit. The thought made her shiver with disgust, even if this was a planet on the line of being habitable, it did not belong to the First Humans.

Ziph balled her hand into a fist and slammed it into the controls, sending sparks flying out from the pod as she smashed a dent in the panel. *I'm glad I just spent the last three years working out, and as sure as Pluto's hell, I need it now.* She climbed from the pod, and something crunched under her boots, when she peered down, she could feel her world slow as time seemed to crawl to a stop.

She was standing on the freshly shed skin of a snake, one which could have swallowed the transport pod she arrived in. Ziph loved snakes, but if this was the typical size of serpents on this planet? She fought nausea as she tried to locate somewhere she could hide and regain her frazzled wits. Thunder cracked behind her as a bolt of lightning struck nearby, and that was her cue to move her ass.

Nothing but her own heartbeat drummed in her ears as she scrambled away from the snakeskin and took off running down the slope. As she squinted in the bright system starlight to survey the terrain, she could see what appeared to be a city in the distance with a tall, ominous wall around it. *Well, I'm sure as fuck not going that way yet. Giant walls around cities can never be a good sign.* Ziph studied civilizations in private school on Keru before her father ditched her and her mother, and she knew better than to march into a city where you don't know what point of evolution their society is in or what direction their politics have taken. The outcomes ranged from the inhabitants considering you a god, all the way to being on the menu, or worse, experiencing gruesome torture while a curious inhabitant dissects you for science. Besides all the basic fears, an alien arrival to an unprepared society could topple an entire civilization or dominate religion. *Venus, help me. I don't want to fucking do that.*

It's only Tuesday. Civilization toppling is more of a Friday activity.

She stumbled a bit on some rocks, slowing her a bit, but when she looked out in front of her, she discovered a low area ahead. As she neared cautiously, she watched as the crack in the rock opened into a narrow canyon with a deep crevasse on one side, and a ledge that dipped down and curved toward a cave opening. *Oh, please, please don't be occupied with giant snakes.* As she tiptoed down to the cave entrance, she sniffed the air, but didn't detect any signs of life. *Look at me, sniffing the air and acting like I know what the fuck I'm trying to smell.* Allowing her guard to slip a bit, she peaked around the corner and discovered a perfect little cavern to hide in. It had a small opening but a larger space behind it, so she slipped inside and brushed little stones out of her way so she could sit. It was deep enough to hide in, but shallow enough to still be well lit.

Ziph wiggled her voluptuous rear on the rock underneath and giggled a bit, thanking her Rubus mother for her thick thighs and round ass. It was coming in quite handy right now. *My mother.* Ziph blinked a few times as reality set in, and emotions welled in her eyes. *Oh, my sweet mother, I'm never going to see my mom again.* Tears burst from her eyes, and she tried not to make a sound, but her mom had been her best friend, and they had spoken daily at least. Sometimes they talked the entire day away. Her mom was the best part of her life. She's who Ziph clung to when she was scared or needed help. Saelly, her mom, never became annoyed when Ziph would talk endlessly about her various crushes at the showhouse, fully aware Ziph would never dare to make her desires known. Or how Ziph had found a new white foundation for her performance makeup, it stayed on her skin so well it would take her kitchen oil and a rag to remove it. Now, she was alone on a snake pit planet, still wearing the new makeup she had raved to her mother about. *My makeup probably still looks great even with the tears.*

A sorrowful hissing came from somewhere outside the cave, and Ziph froze. *I know I did not start crying aloud. What in the fuck did I just hear?* The painful cry was closer now, and Ziph began profusely sweating and pressed herself into the stone at her back. *Do I run, or wait and hide? What if it's mean?!* An ominous shadow appeared on the ground outside of the cave opening, and Ziph wanted to come unglued from her own skin. She desperately held back a laugh as she imagined herself running away with no skin on her body. *Stop it! That's so fucking gross! I cannot die because I'm laughing about something disgusting.* Again, Ziph's form streaked across her mind in only her meat suit with her arms flailing, and she snarled at the imagery. *Oh gods, don't laugh!* Ziph slid her hand over her mouth and pressed with all her strength to hold in a boisterous laugh.

A snake much wider than her, and a viper to be exact, peaked around the corner and looked directly at her. It tilted its head, studying her and deciding if she was a threat as it jut out its tongue to taste the air. The animal made another pitiful hissing cry, but this time soft and gentle, and Ziph softened. Whatever this creature had been through, she wasn't sure, but it was grieving, and that was clear.

"It's alright. I won't hurt you." *Please, just don't bite me, please, please, please!* The snake straightened with her calm words and slithered toward her. *Oh, gods here it comes. Just breathe.* She braced for the worst, but the snake seemed content occupying the space and curled up before resting its head by the opening. That's when Ziph noticed it had eyelids with fine eyelashes, and instead of just having regular scales alone, the snake had fine, imperceptible tiny hair all over its long body. *It has hair like a sea mammal. How strange. Wait, does that mean it's warm blooded? How infinitely interesting.* Its light grey color matched the rock so well that if she unfocused her eyes, the snake blended in perfectly with the background rocks.

When her new snake friend's eyelids shut, and she felt as though she could take a full breath again, she decided she would name the snake Lashes. Ziph finally relaxed and lay back on the rock, trying to figure out how she would deal with this preposterous situation. *My life was almost normal a few hours ago.* She could see her mother, staring at her in disbelief, with her eyebrows raised in shock at Ziph trying to claim her life was normal. *Fine. My life wasn't normal, but it could have been. What in the entire fuck happened Venus?! I gave that bitch of a goddess way too much of me and look what she allowed to happen.*

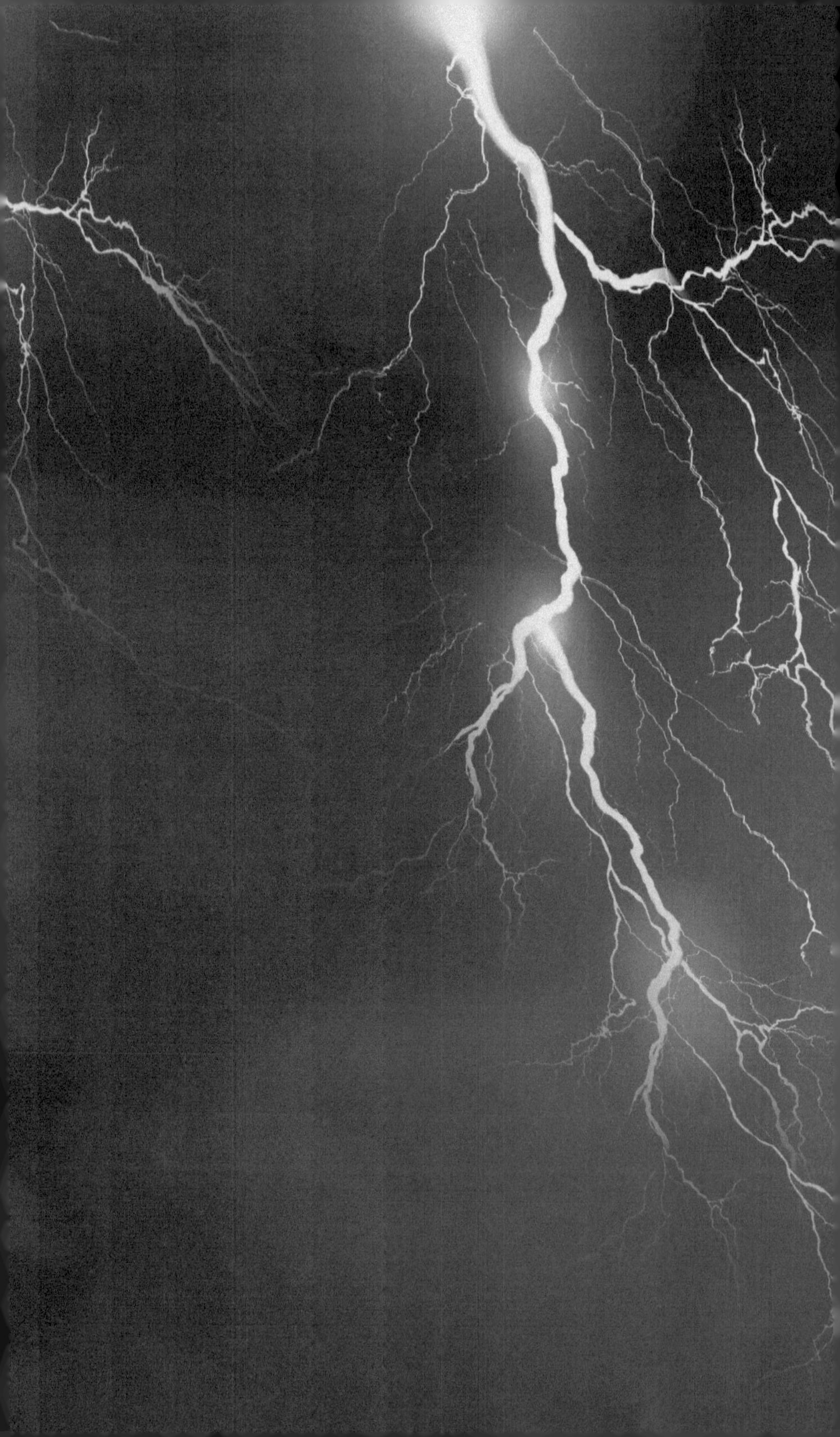

CHAPTER 2

MAKING FRIENDS

After fully disassociating and staring at her snoozing slithery friend for several hours, Lashes finally woke up and bashfully reacted to Ziph. As her new friend had slept, she noticed the temperature in the small space had risen, and she realized it was the snake who was emitting quite a comfortable amount of warmth. She had become so cozy, in fact, she had nearly dozed off herself. She yanked on the middle of her shirt and moved her tail behind her as she readjusted her position.

Lashes held Ziph's gaze for an extended time before inching forward and jutting her tongue out to sniff the air around her. Ziph held still, not from fear, but out of curiosity, and Lashes moved their face even with Ziph's, seeming to study her. They carefully watched Ziph as they pulled their long, warm body over to Ziph and nuzzled up to her. When Ziph could see Lashes tail, she bet the snake was a female because of how it tapered quickly to a point.

"Lashes, what do you want to do today?" Ziph reached out and stroked the serpent's back, and Lashes leaned into the touch. Ziph held in a giggle. Thunder rumbled outside and the sky seemed to darken by the minute as large droplets landed on the rock, turning the light dusty stone into a dark slate. "I guess we're stuck here for a while, aren't we? Does it rain here a lot?" *Did I really just ask a snake a question? Can I play this off like I'm talking to a pet? I guess I'm the only one here, so it doesn't matter.*

The droplets turned into a downpour, and Lashes gently wrapped herself around Ziph, and she was thankful for the snake's additional warmth with the temperature dropping and wind increasing. Even inside the little cave, Ziph could feel the winds spinning around her. Within a few minutes, the rain was so heavy it began rushing over the top of the cavern, and they watched as it poured down into the thin crevasse on the other side of the ledge. After the rain slowed a bit, and there was a steady stream of water coming down in a curtain in front of the cave, Lashes nudged Ziph and slithered over to put her face near the water. Ziph watched as Lashes sipped the water daintily before she joined her in having a drink.

Ziph cupped her hands and collected a handful before slurping it down, appreciating how good it was. "Lashes, this water is delicious. It tastes like rain on Keru." *Yes, that's what I'm doing. I'm talking to a pet, not to myself.* Ziph held her hair back away from her neck before she angled her face to drink directly from the stream. Lashes watched intently as Ziph tried not to drown as she filled her inflatable cheeks with water. Ziph sat up with her overly filled cheeks looking as if they were water balloons threatening to burst, and Ziph slapped a hand over her mouth as Lashes eyes widened. She came in close to investigate Ziph's bulging face.

Desperate not to laugh and spew her water, Ziph sucked it down her throat as quickly as she could. Ziph couldn't help but burst with giggling when Lashes shook her head in shock at Ziph's deflating cheeks. *I love this snake, and I want to keep her forever!* Ziph rubbed the makeup on her face and could feel it smearing with the water soaking in her skin. Lashes seemed hopelessly enthralled with Ziph as she removed her misshapen shirt and wiped her face clean with it. Her pierced nipples chilled in the cool air causing Ziph to shiver.

Ziph stared at the fresh grey mess on her soggy blue T-shirt with the overly stretched out spot in the center. Huffing, she wrung it out and slapped it to the rock wall, making Lashes roll around while she released a "Tststs" sound. "Are you laughing at me slapping my shirt on the wall?" *Can snakes laugh? Is that a fucking thing?!*

Lashes nuzzled her arrow shaped face against Ziph's thigh, and Ziph crossed her arms over her ample breasts, wishing she had worn something under her shirt. Even an undershirt would have been nice. "I guess we are both girls, so it doesn't really matter, does it?" Lashes looked up to her and promptly rolled over, showing Ziph her entire underside.

Lashes was most definitely a girl, and Ziph sat down, crossing her legs, before she reached over and stroked her hand under Lashes chin. The snake moved close and snuggled up to her, and they sat together as darkness fell. Lashes wrapped around Ziph gently as the chill set in, causing their breaths to turn to frost in the air.

The rain steadily fell into the crevasse as Ziph put back on her damp shirt. *It's too damn cold to have my tits out and flopping around. One of us is bound to end up with a cut from one of my frozen nipples.* Lashes had carefully moved to wrap around Ziph like she was before, but she made sure to give Ziph plenty of room to move around.

Before long, Ziph was curled up around Lashes too, and they were both sound asleep. Ziph awoke sometime later lying on her side on the ground in a huddle with her knees up against her chest as Lashes slithered away from the cave. It was light out, and Ziph rubbed her sleepy, sticky eyes. *Where in Pluto's hell are you going?* Ziph stumbled as she followed Lashes from the cave and out onto the open ground above before she watched Lashes move several yards away. Lashes began raising her tail, and Ziph turned abruptly. *Oh wow I followed you out for your bathroom break. I'm going back in the cave now.*

Ziph was thankful in that moment she wouldn't need to eat for at least a few weeks. Rubus were ravishingly hungry for six months out of a year, and for the remaining six months they would fast and not even need to use the restroom. Normally Rubus would become exceedingly exhausted during their fasting period within their hibernation cycle, but Ziph was different, and she had a rare condition which led to her retaining her energy during her cycle. That was part of how she ended up with the nickname Ziph, which was her favorite of all her names. There was her full name, Tarephine Ziphalie Arkwright. The nickname her mother called her, Ephine, and what everyone else knew her by, which was Ziph. The only person to ever call her by her first name was her father when he cared enough to speak to her. *Fucking Jupiter obsessed asshole.*

Lashes finished relieving herself and returned to the cave with a bit more vigor as she curled up in front of Ziph and raised her head to Ziph's eye level. Ziph grinned at her, "You are a gorgeous snake. I know you can't understand me, but I just can't help telling you." She swore

Lashes understood her as she acted as if she was smitten with the compliment.

Her mind raced and somehow ended up on what the people here might be like. She almost liked the idea of it just being her and this sweet snake. Remembering her recovery from the translator implant surgery she had before she went to school on Keru as a child, Ziph rubbed her throat where her scar was, and she wondered how well it would translate the language of the people who lived here. She guessed at what kind of species would have built the city in the distance. She hoped they were kind, and she could make a life here where she didn't need to hide. She knew there was a possibility she could die, but she would try and stay positive. *I just had to take all those classes on primitive civilization development, the perfect recipe for nightmare kindling.* Ziph sat down and crossed her legs facing the cave entrance and Lashes moved to curl up next to her.

Honestly, if I can just find a way to survive this disaster, I will do my best to be thankful. Do you hear that, Venus? I spent years praying in your temple when my father left us. Please guide me to safety, I stayed pure for you, dammit! Ziph knew her inexperience in the bedroom was her own fault, but either way she was using those untouched lady bits for all they were worth spiritually. Venus apparently took great pity on untouched maidens, and Ziph gagged a little at the sentiment. She hated the Venus church services on Fridays even though the message was from a human woman with the most unreal, gravity defying breasts she had ever seen on the front of a body, and they honestly were just magnificent. Easily some of the prettiest boobies Ziph had ever seen, and working in the showhouse as an acrobat, she had seen plenty of breasts.

She would miss the showhouse nearly as much as her mother. Ziph wished she could send her performance team a message telling them she was alive. Reality set in as she wondered if they would even miss her as she remembered the last time a teammate disappeared. The show had simply gone on like Urita had never been there at all. *I guess those ghostly pale human men at the lab were right after all. No one will miss me, except maybe my Mom.* Her old friends from school had even stopped talking to her when her father decided to stop paying for her school in the middle of her final year of upper level basic. She would have gone on to earn an upper-level advanced degree in biology before she went on to attend the Keru medical and biosciences academy. She had been interested in research for environmental recovery and terraforming systems. The K'hornibus had job listings for terraforming specialists, and she had been on course to snag one of those highly sought after positions. All she had needed was acceptance into the advanced program and, of course, the money for tuition.

Her heart ached thinking about her father. She loved him once. It was long time ago when she just saw him as her dad and not some sleazy criminal pharmaceutical developer who was always scheming with her piece of shit uncle. Her father, led by her uncle Shell, had tried to poison a whole planets worth of off market antibiotics with an addictive substance, but thankfully they were caught. Her uncle Shell had been killed while her father had been carted off to prison. She and her mother had not received anything from him in months before that, so, when she saw he had been arrested, she and her mother had themselves a little celebration with a bottle of bubbly wine Ziph had bought with some extra UTC credits she earned from her showhouse tips.

Lashes seemed to notice her shifting feelings and moved her head to nudge Ziph's elbow up before wiggling her head under her arm. Ziph hugged Lashes, and the sweet snake seemed to embrace her back. "It's nice to have a friend right now. I feel silly talking to you, but it feels right. I think somehow you do understand, at least a little bit." Lashes leaned up and closed her eyes before she lay her head in Ziph's lap. *It might be slightly delusional, but I swear this snake comprehends what I'm saying.*

This snake's affection was holding her together, and she could not have been more thankful. Ziph rubbed the loving snake's head, and Lashes leaned into her. She had always wanted a snake as a pet and thought it silly the universe had granted that specific wish at such an oddly trying time. She giggled to herself, thinking about all the posters of stunning jewel-colored snakes from all over the galaxy in her dorm room at the academy. The neon vipers of her home world Vidar were by far her favorite. Her planet had some of the most interesting reptiles and amphibians in the galactic center. She missed the sounds of the Vidarian tree frogs singing for mates with deep, long belches far below her grandparent's home in the top of his great oak tree. The soothing sounds of the forest spilled over from her memories, and she grinned remembering the symphony of creatures.

I would give anything to be back there now. She wanted to be in her grandmother's lap drinking warm peppermint and honey tea while they sat front of a gentle fire burning in the fireplace and her grandmother read her a story about two young squirrels falling in love. Her grandparents were no longer alive, but when they were, they and her mother had been her whole world, but that was all gone now. *I lived such a privileged life full of love, I don't think*

I ever appreciated it enough. I would do anything to be able to tell my grandma that I love her one more time. Now my mom is gone, and I have to wish to say I love you to her, too.

Looking down at the large arrow shaped head of the snake in her lap, she felt an incredible need to protect her new friend. "I care about you, and whatever happens, I promise you I won't let you down." Ziph rubbed her fingers along the ridges of Lashes face, and she lazily fluttered her eyes in response. *I love you pretty snake, and I mean that.*

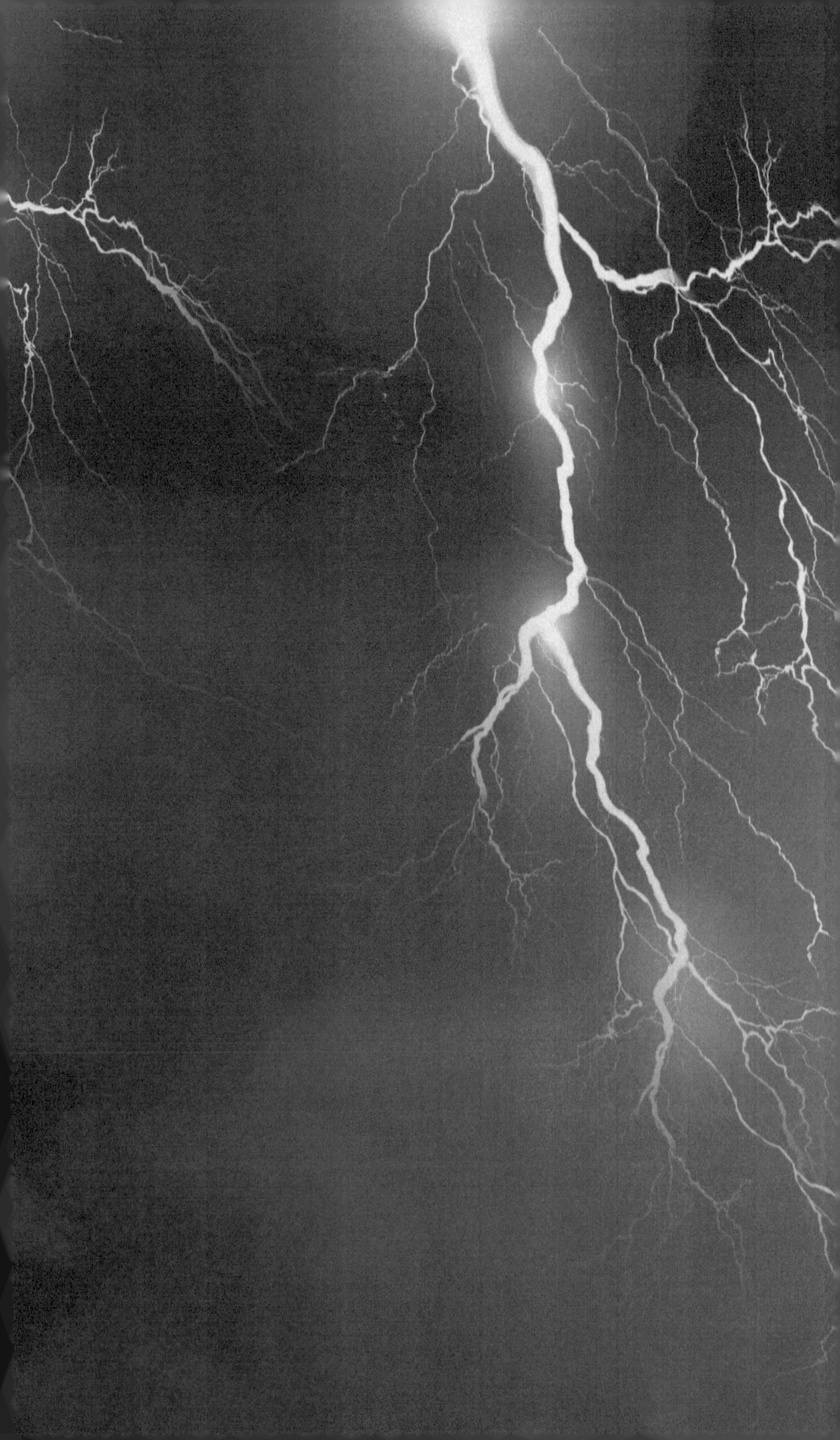

CHAPTER 3
SCENTS ON THE WIND

A worried look spread on Lashes as she and Ziph rested together in the cave. She slithered over to the cavern opening to take in the scent of the air with her tongue. Lashes seemed exceedingly uneasy, so Ziph came over to comfort her. "What do you sense? Is something up there?" *Pluto's fucking hell, she has no idea what I'm saying. There are no speaking beings around, and I'm still managing to talk too much.*

The snake cautiously rose up and peeked over the sprawling rocky plains above them before ducking and turning to Ziph in distress. "Someone, or something, is coming? Shit, we can run!" Ziph pointed to the sloped ground leading up and out of the small canyon. Lashes clearly understood as she darted up, only pausing to check behind them before she moved quickly toward the hill Ziph's pod landed on.

Ziph looked behind them as she ran but couldn't see anything coming after them. *Lashes must have picked up a far-off scent the breeze carried in.* She was diligent not to be disruptive as she followed the snake moving toward the hill. They hid behind it before Lashes looked back toward the walled city, which had to be at least a day's walk from where they were. Ziph and Lashes pressed down against the rock trying to remain as flat as possible as they kept watch toward the city. Lashes smelled the air with her tongue and again seemed increasingly nervous as she backed away while Ziph kept her eyes on the city.

Wanting Ziph to follow, Lashes tipped her head and moved toward an open area on the other side of the mound they had been hiding behind. If they kept going, the flat area would eventually lead to the place where the two rocky planets nearly touched. She could now make out a giant forest of greenery growing upward from the planet they stood on and downward from the otherwise desolate and hovering rocky world.

She could feel the gravity lessening as they moved forward. After almost thirty minutes of walking, Ziph noticed herself feeling lighter as she moved toward the place she wanted to call 'the gap,' and she knew as she closed in, she may even begin to float. *I better not come too close then. I am entirely too fantastic to just float away.* Ziph jumped and clicked her heels, and she rose much further from the ground than she intended as she released a "Whoop!" As she landed on her feet, it occurred to her how useful her acrobatic skill would be in an area like this, and she wanted to test it but knew right then was not the best time. Lashes was still moving quickly and didn't seem to have a place she was intending to stop.

Several more minutes past before Lashes finally slowed down, and Ziph grabbed her chest in horror as she realized what Lashes was showing her. Lashes was just a baby, and this must have been where her mother was killed. *Ooh fucking gods. There is dried blood and giant bones covered in beetles scattered everywhere here.* Lashes turned back to Ziph, terrified and frantically checking behind Ziph every few seconds. Ziph turned and looked back where Lashes kept focusing, and that was when she saw a small flash, like the bright daylight above had shone on something reflective. It happened again. *Oh gods, someone is coming, and if they killed Lashe's mother, they could easily kill Lashes and me.* Ziph was terrified of floating away, but she faced Lashes, and put her arms out, trying to ask her where they could go.

Lashes dipped her head. *There is nowhere we can run and hide, so, we will just run.* Ziph pointed directly away from the walled city as an option, and Lashes darted where she pointed. Ziph followed as closely as possible, sometimes having to jump over random crevasses and deep fissures in the terrain. It was as if the rock was splitting and raising up where the gravity wasn't holding on as tightly. As she moved closer to the gap, the crevasses grew in frequency and width.

Spotting what looked like a cave opening, she whistled, "Lashes! It's a cave!" Lashes whipped around and looked down at the cave opening before wrapping her body around Ziph and diving in. *If I had any question about this snake liking me, my answer is clear. This lady snake could've squeezed me to death at any point.* Ziph ducked to avoid hitting her head as Lashes carried her through the tunnel, not slowing when the tunnel opened up as they passed another crevasse. *How the fuck is she moving so fast while carrying me too?! she's going to knock me out on these rocks!* After a long journey through the tunnel being carried along by Lashes, they finally ended up in a larger cavern area with light streaming in from a long crevasse opening above them.

Lashes set Ziph down and curled up tightly next to her

before poking her head up and desperately checking all around confirming they were both safe. Ziph hugged Lashes as she slowed down enough to breathe normally again. Ziph saw a way to climb up and look behind them to check for any more flashes of light, but when she did, she realized all she needed to do was jump, and she flew straight to the top. Gravity here was low, and she acclimated quickly, using leverage and anchoring herself on stationary rocks. Any other time this would be some ridiculous fun, and it almost hurt to be fearful in this unusual setting.

Ziph peeked at ground level toward the walled city, and waited a while for any sign of company headed their way. What seemed like an hour passed when she finally saw a flash, and it was *much* closer. *Fuck, I have no idea what point in the industrial development these people are. What if they have vehicles?! What if the vehicles are what Lashes and I are seeing reflections of? Oh, fucking gods. What if they have simple technology, too? Oh, this is so fucking bad. If these are semi-primitive people, and they end up religious, I could be royally fucked.*

Sensing how unnerved Ziph was, Lashes knew they were still being hunted. Lashes slithered up through the air to the same spot Ziph had looked out over the terrain, and she remained there for a long while. Eventually, Lashes saw the little flash of reflected light, and her sorrowful eyes moved down to Ziph. The snake darted to wrap her long body around Ziph and hug her close. Ziph was at a loss at what to do until she had a harsh realization, the hunters were after the snake, not her. *I'm so fucking stupid. I've been looking at this all wrong.* Her heart broke. She knew she could have a devastating decision to make soon.

When the hunters arrived to kill or capture the snake,

she could even be rescued in a sense, depending on how well they accepted outsiders. Was that something she was willing to risk though? Lashes had been nothing but kind and loving to her. Tears formed in her eyes for she knew she could never betray the sweet snake she had fallen in love with.

No, Ziph was a moral and ethical being. She would remain with her snake friend until it was no longer safe for Lashes. Ziph's thoughts shifted again when another realization struck. *I will need to give myself up, or act as bait to save Lashes, but how do I explain that to her? Oh gods! I hope she understands! This is fucking hard enough!*

Ziph huffed and made her way up to the top of the cave to peek out from the crevasse to see if the flash was any closer. She frowned as she strained her tall, tufted ears, trying to listen as she tugged on her shirt. *Oh gods, I can hear gear filled clicking engines. We would never be able to outrun them. I must find a way to save Lashes.*

Ziph racked her brain, trying to think, not knowing where to start, she peered down at Lashes. The beautiful snake looked like she could have been a pristine model for the biology posters she once had on her walls. *Wait, biology, that's it!* "Lashes, you might not like this, and I know I won't, but it might be the only way I can save you."

Lashes tipped her head to the side as Ziph approached her. "You're such a sweet thing. I just can't bear the thought of something happening to you." Ziph hugged the snake and kissed her on her head before crouching low and pointing to where Lashes scent glands were found. Lashes trusted Ziph and quickly showed Ziph her underside by her tail, offering it to Ziph without hesitation. Ziph gently pressed on the area where she knew she would find the scent sac, and Lashes' gland released the liquid onto

Ziph's awaiting hand. Lashes watched closely as Ziph spread the snake's foul scent all over her exposed skin. After repeating this several times and emptying Lashes' scent gland, the action eventually caused Lashes to understand what Ziph was doing. Lashes squeezed her eyes shut and made a hissing whimper as she coiled herself up. Ziph was careful not to touch anything as the snake's scent absorbed into her skin, even though all she wanted to do was throw her arms around Lashes and comfort her. This snake had a big heart, and Ziph was devastated for her.

Ziph moved to the top of the crevasse but turned back to face Lashes who had followed halfway. "I'm so sorry I have to leave you, Lashes. I promise I wouldn't be leaving if I could have it my way. Damn it, now I'm crying, and you can't even understand me!" She sobbed to Lashes and Lashes curled up in front of her before she closed her eyes. "I love you, too. Please be safe and go far away from here where there are other giant snakes. Somewhere you can grow up."

Lashes lay her head down at Ziph's feet, and Ziph released another sob before pulling herself out from the crevasse and onto the open terrain. Using her terribly misshapen and soiled shirt, she wiped her eyes before deciding on a direction. Behind her, Lashes watched and readied to move the opposite way. "You're such a smart girl. I'll miss you so much." Ziph sniffled and looked toward the mound her pod landed on, before she turned and pointed in the opposite direction where Lashes needed to move, which was the gap between the planets. Lashes understood and started moving toward the gap but turned back one last time. Ziph waved to her and blew her a kiss like she always did at the end of her performances, something about the familiar action gave Ziph a smidgen of peace.

It's showtime. I need to distract these hunters so much they forget about Lashes. Ziph twirled around and bounced a few times on the ground to determine the gravity level before she jumped as high as she could. In the air, she mapped out her dash toward the only little hill in the endless flat terrain where her drop pod crash landed. A flash of light was visible off to the left of the mound she was aiming for, and that was her signal to run in a wide arch and aim for the right side of the hill of rock. *Make them change directions, and maybe they can't take those big ass trucks into the low gravity area.*

She jumped as high as she could one last time to finalize her journey's path before she started in a sprint across the treacherous landscape, except her sprint was more of a leaping dash. Each time her foot hit the ground she was able to move incredible distances so she neared the mound in a much shorter amount of time than it took when she followed Lashes away from it. Now that she knew how to move in the lower gravity, she felt unstoppable. She easily jumped over the crevasses, and when they turned into smaller cracks, she decided to practice her acrobatics.

Tumbling gracefully, head over heels, she bounced, vaulted, and spun herself all the way to the mound before she sprinted around it and tried to spot the approaching vehicles. The humming of the engines was more of a clicking rumble now, and she could see an outline of boxy vehicles mounted between long trapezoid shaped tracks moving at high speeds.

Oh, fucking Venus! Please bless me on this endeavor. I am pure and untouched. Please Venus! Bitch, you better come through I swear I will make a shrine to you just to burn it! Ziph wasn't sure how she could follow through with such a threat against a god at a time like this. She was a very long way from home with snake booty smell rubbed all over her, trying to save a giant snake she just met from primitive hunters she knew nothing about. She tried to refocus and shake away the image of her igniting her old wooden Venus shrine on the sand on the beaches of Keru, but all she could do was giggle to herself. *I'm about to fucking die, and all I can do is laugh about burning my old Venus shrine. I really need to get it together.*

She rolled her eyes as another image of her dumping pure alcohol all over a knocked over statue of the goddess Venus popped into her mind. She bit her lips together as she imagined herself lighting the fire and the bright flames with her tail sticking straight up as it did when she became excited. *What would burning a statue do anyway. Maybe I'll just slap the bitch in the afterlife. Does she have eyes? I could poke her eyes out. I bet goddesses don't need eyes, though. I need to quit it, right now.* Ziph's breath caught in her throat as the rumble of the vehicles grew loud enough to feel, and she peeked around the corner to find they were so close she could see the windshields.

Oh, gods! I need to move!

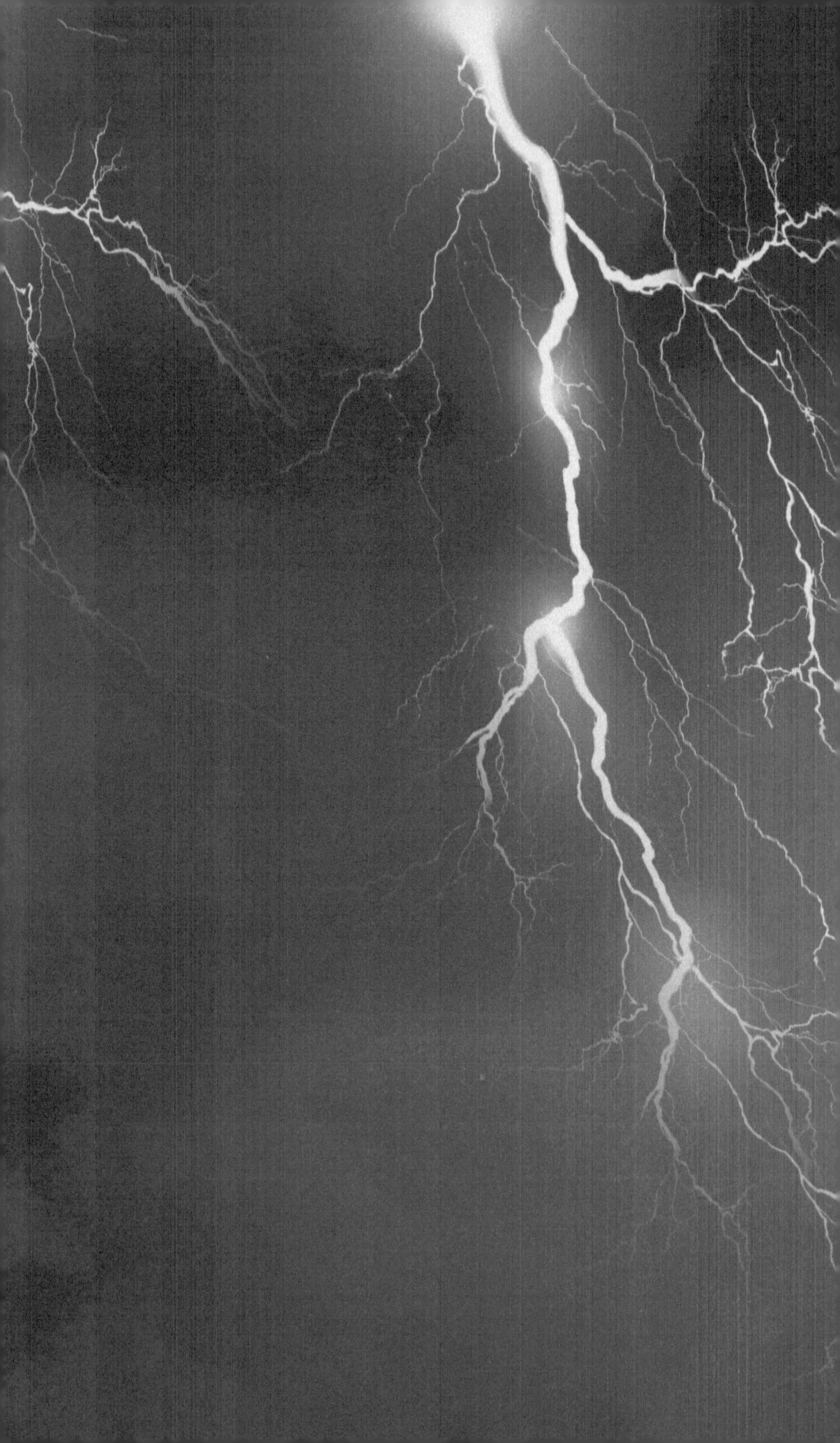

CHAPTER 4
BOUNCING BAIT

Ziph needed a plan, and she needed one quickly. *Think. Think, Ziph! Come on!* A brief wave of silence fell over her, and she stilled. These could be her last moments, and she had to face she was potentially giving her life for a big, sweet snake. She thought long and hard about her life as she watched the vehicles draw nearer. It had been mostly fun and she learned a lot, but her life had been missing so much. She had missed out entirely on love. Ziph thought about Lashes' obvious sweet nature and how her affection was the way she coped on her first day on the planet. *Maybe I did find love after all. It just came in different form than I was expecting.*

Fuck it! If I'm dying today, I'm dying while doing the right thing. Maybe Venus will have some reward for me in the afterlife, stupid fucking bitch. Ziph bolted from her hiding place and aimed for the wide open space, directly between the hunters and the city. It was as far from Lashes as she could lead them, and she ran as quickly as she could. Rubus were champion runners in the galactic center. *Evolving from a squirrel does have its perks.*

She tried to maintain an equal distance from the planet gap to keep the same level of gravity as she ran, but she wasn't sure she would ever be fast enough as she snuck a peek behind her. The tracked vehicles were gaining on her and quickly, and she could hear her heartbeat thumping in her tall, tufted ears as she pushed herself harder. She was in the best shape of her life, and she was brilliant. She knew this well and as she racked her brain for an answer, she imagined herself taking those large, gaping steps as she had run through the lower gravity area.

That's it! Ziph pivoted to the left, and she bolted toward the gap. Over the rumbles of the trucks, she could now hear shouts behind her. They sounded deep which drove her to push even harder. *Of course, it's men.* She was a daughter of the house of Venus, and she bowed to no man.

Invigorated, Ziph began launching herself with every step and when she felt the gravity lessening, she nearly whooped with excitement. Running full force, she threw her arms in front of her as she tucked her fluffy tail around her side, aiming for the ground, and pounced off her hands, sending her into a revolving tumble. Hands to the ground, then feet, she went flying head over heels along the rock and picked up speed. Maintaining a clear head space was important, and she blocked out the strange whooshing sounds closing in behind her. *I know I'm going to be caught. I need to keep my head in the show. I know what I signed up for.*

Knowing her tumbling would need to end soon to check her surroundings and to plan her next vault, she spun and landed perfectly before bouncing backward into the air appreciating the lack of gravity. She regained her balance in-air and landed on her feet, spinning around to find a hulking masked figure with broad shoulders moving toward her instead of the trucks.

Venus, hold my tits, that man has jet packs on his hips and ankles! Gods damn it! Terror streaked through her as she began a leaping run, jumping a long way between each step. He gained on her and she snarled as she saw his tail shift behind him to provide balance, and she yelled, "Cheater!" back at him before frowning and crying out to herself, "Why the fuck do I keep thinking everyone understands me?!" She knew it could take a month for her implanted translator to learn a new language.

Ziph could distinctly hear what she presumed was *the cheater* coming in rapidly behind her, and she braced herself for his impact. When he made contact, she was not prepared for how flexible the being would be as he wrapped himself around her and easily pinned her limbs together. *Gods dammit, if this is a fucking sleezy old snake man, you're getting slapped and losing an eye or two Venus!* They rolled for several yards before coming to a stop.

He held her face down, and she could hear him speaking his language above her. His voice was husky and thick, "Come quick! I've never seen a creature like this before. It's a female, and she has hair on her ears." *Oh wait, I take it back, Pluto's hell, he sounds sexy! This might not be so bad after all. My translator needs to hurry up, I need to know what he's saying. Turn me over dammit, I want to see what you look like!*

He flipped her over, but he wore a solid black mask so she couldn't see his face. She could see he had a florescent yellow tail swaying behind him as he hovered. He had on machine made tactical clothing, thick black reinforced cargo pants with a black utility jacket, and a belt strapped with knives and low-tech mechanical devices. *These people are in their steam engine industrial age.* He had tiny metal cylinders on each hip which she knew were some kind of air jet packs he used to skate on the air. There were tiny jet fans inside of the cylinders, and she was absolutely obsessed. *I want some jet packs for my feet!*

He studied her as she did the same in return, not daring to move. He was steady as he reached up and pulled his mask off. She held in a gasp, but she *knew* her eyes had betrayed her when he narrowed his stare and smirked. *Venus you sneaky fucking bitch! You sent me to a planet with gorgeous snake men. I may not desecrate your shrine after all.* His auburn eyes and bright yellow skin with perfectly groomed milky white, short hair was striking, but his strong jaw and perfect lips had Ziph wanting to wiggle from her pants.

He appeared to lean in to smell her, but when he was close enough she could see herself in his pupil slits, he opened his mouth showing two long fangs sliding from his gums. Ziph sucked in a sharp breath as he pierced her neck with his fangs and injected her with his venom. "Why did you have to go and bite me? I thought we were having a moment there," Ziph whispered to him as she felt her body fall limp. Even her tongue flopped from her mouth as she waited to black out. Only able to stare in one direction after losing the ability to move her eyes, she again wondered when the fuck she would lose consciousness. *Well, this is fucking stupid. What am I supposed to do just fucking lay here like a star fish? Sleep, hello, you can happen any minute, which would be great. I do not want to be awake while I am paralyzed! Why is this even a thing? Also, why can I still feel everything? This is so, so not cool.*

Surely, she would lose consciousness, and feeling right? She felt the cheater man lift her up under her arms and he held her even with his face, appearing to study her. Her head was resting at an odd angle against her shoulder and her legs dangling above the ground. *Oh, wow, this man is at least seven feet tall. I hope his dick matches his height! Oh gods, snake dicks are so fabulous. What if he still has a snake penis this far in evolution?!* She laughed in her own mind as he pushed her tongue back in her mouth and carefully closed her mouth for her before he lifted her head and brought her face-to-face with him.

"What are you? You smell like a serpent, but you look like someone made a fluffy tailed rat into a woman." He frowned at her as crunching boots signaled to her that someone was approaching him from behind. This second man was a deeper vibrant green, and clearly also a snake man. Auburn eyes looked back at his companion, "Have you ever seen a being like this before? Or heard of one? Do you think she is a Kefale experiment?"

"I've heard stories of visitors from other worlds landing here, maybe she is from elsewhere." The second snake man with lemon eyes and black hair, pointed to the sky and shrugged.

Unable to decide, Auburn eyes lifted Ziph into his arms before taking her back to their trucks, and he looked down at her while he spoke, "You might be right. If she's from elsewhere, and cooperates, we will need to hide her in the factory. If she is a problem and an actual animal, we can just return her out here because she is clearly a rodent of some type."

I wish I understood what in Pluto's hell they are talking about! Oh no, no, I'm about to drool. Yep, there it went, out of the corner of my mouth and dribbling down my chin. Most importantly though, why in the FUCK can I still feel every-thing? Her mind went straight back to her studies on snake venom, and she felt a bit of her soul slip away as her fleeing mechanism engaged even though her body was currently out of service. Ziph did her best not to completely crash and burn on the inside as she remembered some snakes can paralyze their victims, but the victim can still feel everything.

This could become really bad, really fast, and Ziph could feel her skin begin to boil with the heat of her inner turmoil. Auburn eyes scrunched his nose at her and kicked at his yellow eyed companion's ankle. "Whit, her temperature is rising quickly. Do you think she's having a bad reaction to my venom?"

Whit slid his eyes to her and frowned, making Ziph even more upset. "Possibly, she is higher than normal for a rodent. We brought the med kit, and I have some ice packs if it keeps rising." Auburn eyes kept his focus on her for a few more steps as they monitored her temperature before Whit snapped, "Dacket," and both men began running for the truck. When they neared the trucks, Whit went around Dacket and popped the back hatch open, and a door on the top rose up as a tailgate lowered.

Whit grabbed the med kit as Dacket laid Ziph out on the tailgate, and her limp body slumped against the cold metal. *Fuck that feels good. It's so hot.* Ziph wasn't sure she could handle any more heat.

Dacket frowned as he studied her. "Her temperature is still rising. What should we do?"

Whit leaned over as he set the first cold pack down by Dacket. "Cut her clothes off, she's overheating. We need to cool her off or she could end up with a searching disease." Dacket pulled a knife from his utility belt and began cutting away her misshapen blue shirt.

Ziph lay there, paralyzed and spinning out of control

on the inside, as Dacket finished cutting away her shirt. She felt the cool air rush against her pierced nipples as he moved to slice off her leggings, and he slid his finger in between her skin and the blade to protect her. Something about it gave her a deep thrill- even in the midst of her panic.

With her pants removed, she felt him put something frigid under her arms and between her thighs before he held her thighs together to hold the ice pack in place. *Venus, if you ever listen to me, please, listen to me now. This poor stupid man has put an ice pack against my pussy, and I have a piercing down there. I might actually die if he doesn't move it, right fucking now.*

Dacket looked down, and he had the ice pack far too close to her intimate area, so he pulled it back a bit before he grabbed another ice pack and set it on her stomach. Her skin pebbled all over as her temperature decreased, and it began to return to normal. Dacket carefully removed the ice packs before turning to Whit, "There is a new carcass wrap in your truck. We can hide her inside of it to pass through the gate checkpoint. They said they're slowing down on inspections, but I don't believe them."

Whit agreed and opened the back of his truck to retrieve the wrap. When he handed Dacket the black treated fabric wrap, he reached over and lifted Ziph to helped him roll her in it. They set her next to the dirty, older wraps which smelled of snake as much as she did, and Dacket hoped they would just assume it was a normal practice day, like it was supposed to have been, and leave them alone. He couldn't afford for the wall guard to give him trouble. He knew every mark against him could increase his chance of being called in for spawning at the palace. It was a fear he shared with many of their people.

Dacket would just continue to be strict as usual and hoped everyone stayed in line.

Stories of what went on behind those walls moved through Valler City like the wind, but Dacket knew many of them were likely true. Rumors circulated of people who were being stolen and never heard from again. *There's nothing I can do about it, and there's no use in worrying constantly. I just need to push it from my mind and hope the day never comes.*

Dacket and Whit finished packing back up their trucks and started their engines to return home. Dacket went first and aimed for Gate Nine as he knew it to be the least chance of a random search. He often paid off a guard at the checkpoint for smoother transitions.

They approached Gate Nine and waited in line behind two other hunter trucks. Neither of the trucks ahead of him had any searches, and he wondered if they had reached a tipping point with the searches at the gates.

He rolled the glass down so he could lean out and see what the holdup was and wished he hadn't. "Dacket Critchlow, coming back after a long practice as well I see?" The rusty orange guard goaded him as usual. The hunters weren't exactly well liked in their society. He wished it was the fellow Doyle, whom he had given a bag of coins for allowing him through without additional searches. Now he was sure to be stopped.

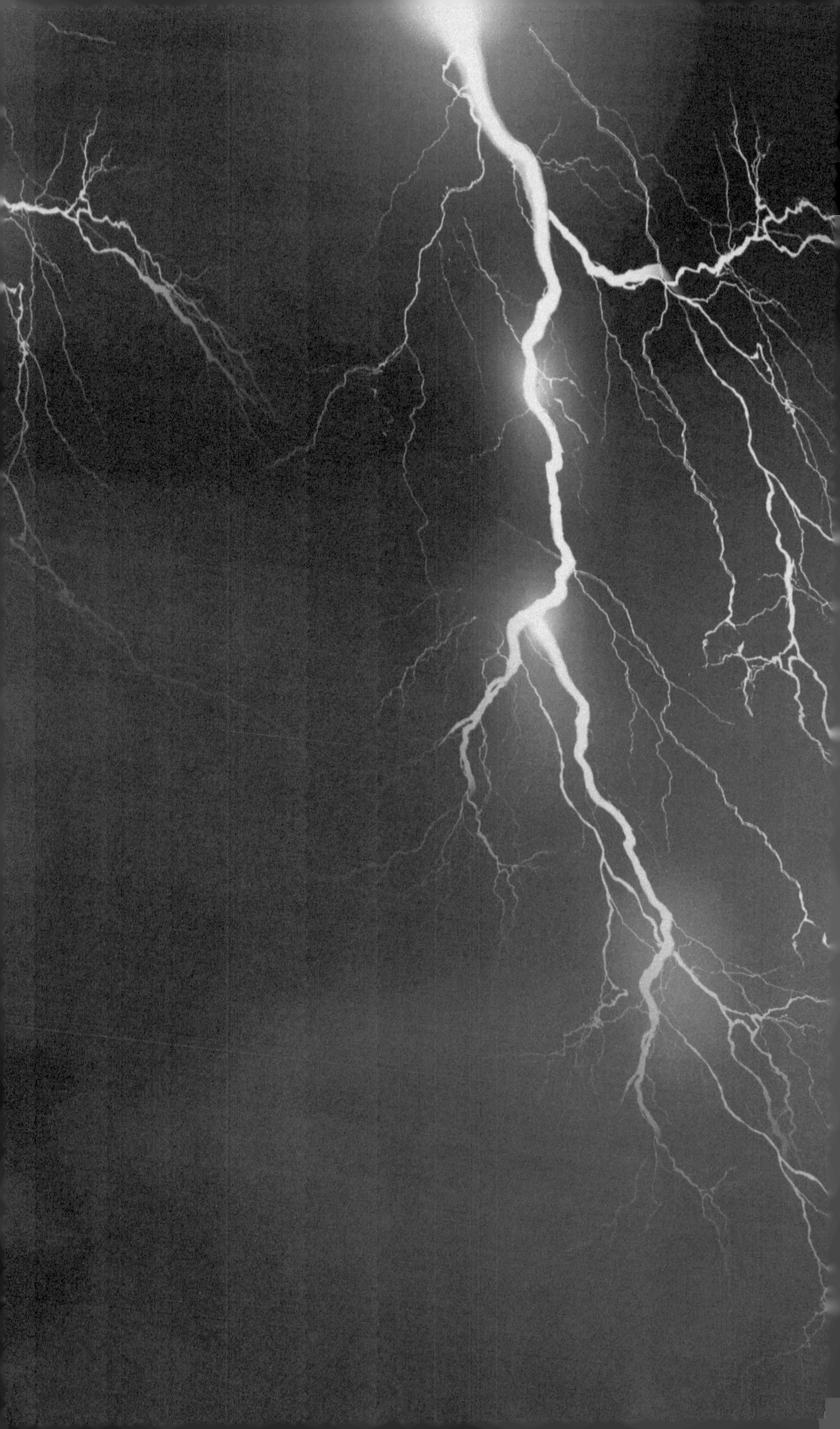

CHAPTER 5
TROUBLE

Dacket checked behind him in the back of his truck where he had the paralyzed female creature hidden in a serpent carcass wrap. *I hope we can convince her to join our hunting team.* She was the most curious thing he had ever seen, and he was fascinated. He turned back around to see the guard pointing at him.

I need a diversion. Knowing Whit might not agree, he lifted his hand and gave the signal to shoot an emergency flare. Whit signaled back a clear no before he threw his hands up. Dacket waited until the guard turned to file the crossing report, and he lifted all the way out of his seat to point to the female he had wrapped up in the back before he again signaled for Whit to shoot a flare. Behind him Whit was in a fit over the request but seemed to be complying. Dacket watched as Whit grabbed his flare gun and pretended to clean it.

When the trucks moved up and Dacket's turn was coming up next, Whit whooped at the top of his lungs before shouting, "Duck! Flare malfunction!" When Whit saw the guards duck, he shot the flare direct at the metal stand causing a blast of sparks to shower the ground. Tiny fires broke out along the dry grasses growing on the bottom edge of the wall and all around the guard stand, leading all the way up to the guards who were pulling their hoses out to spray the area down. The blaze caused a charred sloppy mess when it mixed with the water, and the guards shouted and shook their fists at Whit. "Stupid hunters! We will need to shut down this gate for hours for repairs and to clean this up." The guard wrote down Dacket's hunting code on the side of his truck before waving him through. Whit, on the other hand, had already been signaled by a guard to pull out of line for a search.

Dacket cringed as he passed through the gate, and when he waved back to Whit, he saw Whit was already standing next to his truck arguing with the guard. He entered at Gate Nine which was in the center of Sector Nine, and he lived between Sector One and two. Sector Nine was just on the other side of Sector One, but closer to the direction they needed to travel when they were called out for a hunt, so it just made sense to use Gate Nine.

Valler, like all three of the Elarian cities, was constructed in a circle and much like a spider's web. The royal palace in the center looked out onto specifically the aesthetically appealing Sectors only while maintaining a massive wall blocking the poor and unappealing Sectors. Sectors like one and two were serpent meat processing and the meat markets, and the royals wanted to ignore its existence while benefiting from the heavy taxation on the meat production to feed the lowest paid people. The rodent farms in Three as well as the construction and demolition in Sector Nine, where he was passing through, had nothing but a tall, metal, privacy wall to grace their view instead of the Kefale's majestic capital palace. Some of the rodent food farms in Sector Five were manicured as the royal gardens, while the rich, and rich adjacent, took up all of Sector Six in their mansions. Seven was filled with the almost rich, including the guards, and royal staff who all resided on spacious lots with nice homes.

Last was Eight, and Sector Eight was easily the most unique of the Sectors in all three of the cities on planet, Binara. Eight on the surface was textile production and sales with general markets, but underground was a cave system, which was made when Binara caught the planet Barren when it pulled the surface of Binara causing deep fissures and crevasses in the rock. A network of illegal, underground bars and nightclubs were built in the cracks, which spawned a generous amount of organized crime.

Eight was where Dacket knew he could find some information about Kefale's royal lab experiments, and that's exactly where he planned to be in a few hours when their bright system star slid beyond the horizon. He snarled to himself. He had to remember hunters were not exactly the most beloved of the Elarian people. *We protect the city, yet somehow, we are the lowest of the low in the hierarchy here, I have never understood that.*

Dacket spotted the gate to his home and slowed down before he stopped right in front, but Trent, the lead guard for their home and business, was reading the paper and not exactly doing his job of watching the gate. Rolling down his window, Dacket knocked on the door of his truck creating a loud bang causing Trent to sit up with a start, his bright orange eyes flashing at Dacket before scrambling to open the gate.

"The last offering day someone cheated on their books,

and this paper I bought says the whole family was taken into the palace. I just heard a couple pass by who said the family hasn't been seen since."

Trent's teal skin contrasted with the olive shirt he wore, and Dacket frowned, "I need to visit Eight and ask Vickery some questions, and it looks like you are accompanying me. That shirt is ugly on you. It clashes with your skin. Are you colorblind or something? You always wear odd colors."

"Anybody ever told you you're an asshole? Because you're an asshole. I haven't done laundry this week. It rained every time I was off work last week, and I fell behind." Trent rubbed his hands down his chest while he looked at his shirt. Dacket was right, it didn't match his skin at all, but he wasn't admitting that.

Dacket hoped Trent would be distracted by the insult and ignore him as he tried to slip by with the female. Trent would have far too many questions for him to answer right now. He drove through the gate and down the sloped driveway into the garage under the market to park his truck before he jumped out and ran around to the back to grab the female in the carcass wrap.

When he had her slung over his shoulder, he climbed the creaking stairs through the doors leading to cold market level where customers from all over Valler filled aisles with stacks of serpent meat. Just inside the deep-water air-cooling system which kept the space frigid and covered in frost, his staff was bundled up from head to toe as they worked. He passed by the door and peeked in the window on his way to the stairs to level three where he pushed open the door to his apartment. He came in and cringed at the dirt on his boots. His bathroom was across his living space, and he despised messes. Huffing, he lightly stepped through his living space toward the open bathroom door. *I'll need to scrub my entire apartment after this. This woman smells worse than an actual serpent.* When he reached the bathroom, he gently lay the female in the carcass wrap on the floor so he could remove his boots. He was well aware she could still feel everything around her, and if she had strong feelings, she was likely terrified.

With his boots set at the front door, he returned to the wrap and slowly unrolled her. Once he had it unrolled and she lie nude on her back, he watched her slow breaths and how her chest moved. Sniffing the air, he scrunched his nose. *She smells like she bathed in a serpent's asshole. I cannot let her touch anything in this apartment until she is clean.*

Dacket started to run a bath but pulled the lever to switch it to a shower. He didn't want to scrub the tub after he washed her. *I don't give a damn if it's inappropriate. She can be upset with me all she wants, but she is getting a fucking bath.* Having a whiff of the air in the room again had him nearly gagging and trying to breathe through the fabric of his sleeve as he felt the temperature of the water. It was warm, and he turned around to scoop her up. He lifted her in his arms, and he could see she regained the ability to use her eyes, but that was all.

Dark, warm, and wrapped up comfortably mixed with the engine rumbles made me sleep hard. I think that was the best sleep of my life. WAIT. Is this man about to wash me in his shower? I can fucking feel everything! This cannot be happening. Am I hallucinating? Does his venom have a hallucinogen? Ziph was afraid she was about to be turned on to within an inch of her life if this was real. He lay her down in the warm stream and reached up for a bar of soap and a washing cloth before lathering it in the stream.

I'm not sure it's possible to hallucinate water. This is real.

The warm water blended with the scent of her body odor and the smell wafted by her nose. *Oh gods, I think I was used to the stink. Maybe a bath is not so terrible since I do smell like a snake butt and being paralyzed, I do need help washing my stinky ass. If I weren't paralyzed, I would probably be gagging at how bad this is.* Another strong wave of the scent passed by her nose. *Oh, oh no. It just keeps getting worse as my skin warms up. I would definitely be gagging. I need to be thanking him for this shower the moment we can communicate.*

With his hands and washcloth soapy, he started at her neck and gently scrubbed away the oils on her skin. He paused and removed his jacket and shirt before continuing and Ziph was thanking every god she knew by name she could use her eyes again. *A hot yellow man with thick muscles has me naked in his shower. Why couldn't it be under sexier circumstances? Why did you have to go and bite me? We could be having sexy shower time right now.*

Ziph could feel him slow when he reached her nipples as he carefully cleaned around her piercings. *Venus bless me, he's touching my boobies.* He kept glancing at her with an apologetic eye, but it didn't matter, her heart was slamming against her chest as he moved lower with the cloth and washed her chest and belly before he dipped down between her legs. Ziph knew exactly what was about to happen, and she screamed so loud inside her head she swore a sound escaped her lips.

Dacket gently lifted the cloth from between her legs, but it had become stuck on something, and he sucked in a sharp breath, "Oh fuck, I've snagged it on something. What could you possibly have between your legs that a cloth would be hung on?" He looked at her and met her eyes, giving her a truly sorrowful look. She rolled her eyes, hoping that would give the message, and his brow creased in return.

Did she just roll her eyes? Reluctantly spreading her legs, he leaned down to look and found she had a piercing above her clit which the cloth was snagged on. Biting his lips together, he huffed knowing what he was doing would likely make the female hate him for eternity, but he had to fix this mishap before he could move on.

Aside from not wanting the scent in his apartment, he needed to know if *she* produced the serpent scent herself, or if she had somehow been doused in it, and the only way to know was to clean her up. Plus, if he had to keep smelling it, he was going to vomit.

He parted her legs further, and she could feel him gently removing the cloth from her hood piercing. Ziph was nearly coming out of her skin with delight. This was the first man who had ever touched her down there, and it felt incredible. She just wished he were down there for more than just unhooking the cloth. *This is fucking stupid and extremely unfair.*

Once he had the washcloth free, he finished washing her legs before he turned her over. This time he parted her butt cheeks and checked for a piercing before washing there, and Ziph was coming unglued laughing inside. *This man really just checked my butthole for a barbell or would it be a ring? Oh gods, or would it be called a booty-hole ring, or ass-lip ring? Wait, if the ring had a gemstone, would it be a blingy-hole or a booty-bling? How would that even heal?* She paused for several seconds as she thought it through. *Well, now I've gone too far, and I've grossed myself out.*

After Dacket had the rest of her washed, he turned the water off and brushed her hair away from her face before he began drying her. He leaned in close and began smelling her skin. *She doesn't smell like a serpent at all. Her scent is like sweet cinnamon.* He lifted her up and carried her to his room where he laid her out on his bed on her back.

Dacket couldn't help but look at her curvy body. Elarian people were not built that way. They were hard muscle where she was all soft curves. Her figure made his mouth water, which he tried to ignore as he opened a few of his drawers to find her some clothes. After giving up on his drawers, he moved on to digging in his closet where he found a small enough shirt and some of his undershorts to dress her.

When he was finished, he checked her eyes again and could see her lips beginning to regain movement. Twisting his mouth to the side, he wondered if he had any rope. If she regained control of her body when he was visiting Virgis Vickery under Sector Eight, she might run away, and he would never have any answers. *I need to keep her tied up at least until I know she won't run off and get herself captured by a royal guard on the street.*

Dacket went into his closet again and looked through the small pile of gear he had stored. He lifted a utility belt and some old torn pants before he found a coiled rope. With the rope, he tied her hands together and attached it to the top of the bed, knotting it multiple times until he was sure she couldn't untie it. He cut some of the additional length of rope and tied her feet together as well. As soon as he finished tying her feet, he heard Whit stomping up the stairs.

Whit came inside and took his shoes off before joining Dacket in his room. He was disheveled with no shirt and his jacket open. "They were so angry they made me strip my clothes and stand in the wind naked. You fucking owe me."

Dacket internally cringed and changed the subject. "She doesn't smell like a serpent after I've bathed her. She must have just encountered one at some point and survived. She has piercings all over her body, so I am starting to believe she might be from elsewhere like you said, but I need to be sure. We can't risk harboring a wanted lab experiment if that is what she turns out to be, so I need you to find cover for Trent tonight at the garage gate because he and I are paying Vickery a visit."

"You're ditching me with your paralyzed oversized rodent to party with Trent in Sector Eight?" Whit put his hands on his hips and closed his eyes in annoyance, "I had plans tonight."

Dacket stared blankly at Whit. He knew exactly what those plans entailed. "You mean you were planning to spend six hours manicuring your fingernails and toenails after you finish that book you were reading all while taking a hot bath?"

Whit held his hands out to look at his nails. "Now that you say it, I do need to work on these nails. I chipped one putting my clothes back on at the city gate."

Annoyed, Dacket narrowed his eyes, "Can you not just do that in my bathroom? What is the difference?"

Whit acted like Dacket had committed some heinous crime, and his rapid blink even looked appalled. "Your bathroom looks like a prison cell. Mine is beautiful and peaceful, so there is an enormous difference. You can tie her to my bed if you want me to watch her. Are you planning to keep her here as a pet or something?"

Whit was not just Dacket's best friend and business partner. He was much more than that, and so was Trent. The three had grown up together and shared a wide range of wild experiences, and often those experiences had become sexual. They hadn't cared about much else other than one another for as long as they could remember. "Don't be stupid. The trip to Eight is for information. Did you see the way she can move? I want to recruit her for hunting. I'll come by and move her back here when Trent and I return."

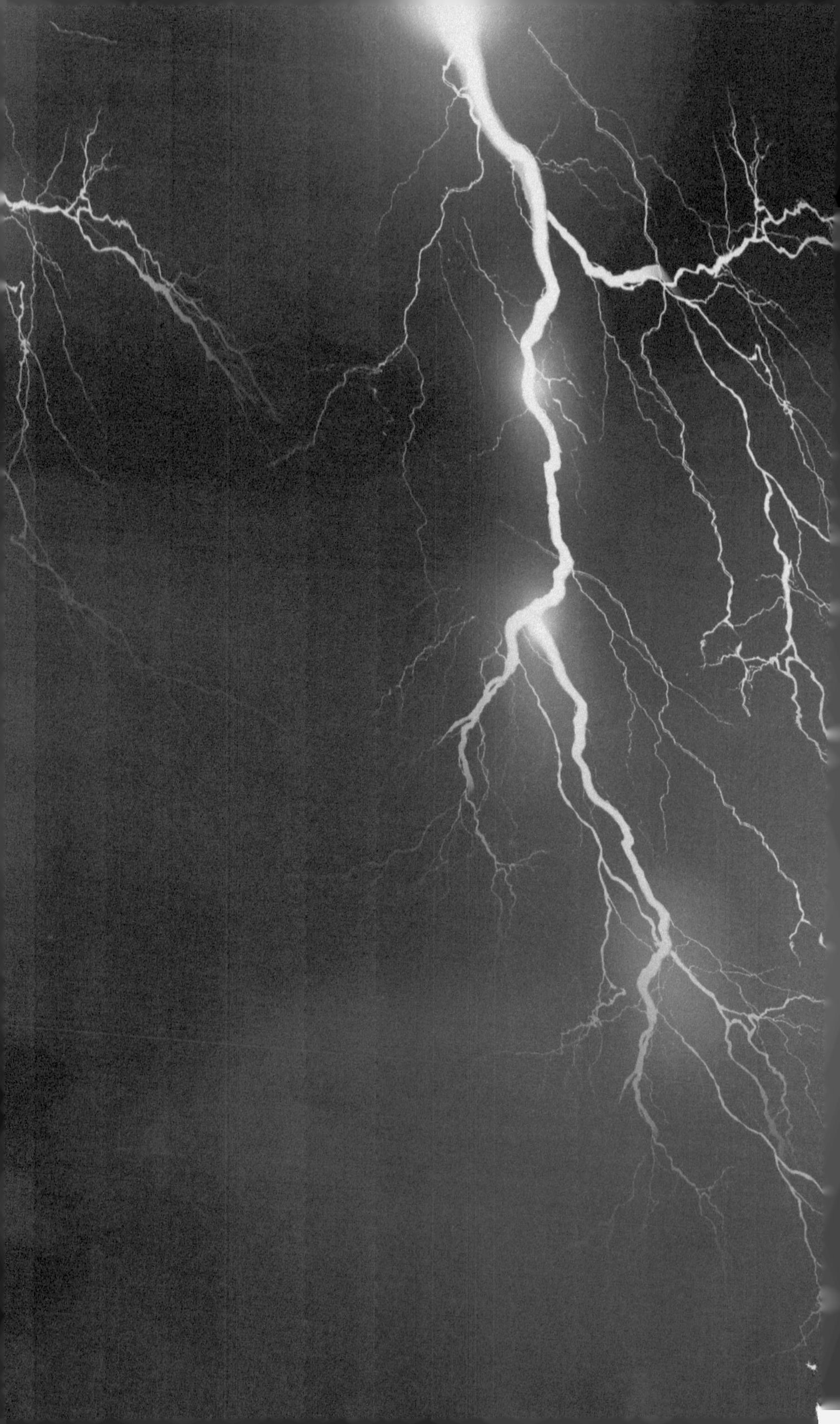

CHAPTER 6

EIGHT UNDERGROUND

After visiting a few stores and buying Trent some new clothes which complimented his color instead of clashing with it, they were ready for the evening. Trent changed in the store into a freshly tailored black suit, and Dacket wore a cream color suit he had in his closet. They needed to be sure to blend in. He might be admitting to Vickery he was a hunter, but he didn't want anyone else to know. They stored their bags in Dacket's truck before climbing down and deciding where the closest entrance was to access the underground club network.

Dacket slid his eyes around the parking area and quickly noticed how much his giant tracked hunter's truck stuck out from everyone else's smaller, personal use six-wheel vehicles. They were so much shorter he could run them over if he wished. That fact gave him immense joy when he was feeling down.

"We should enter through the garment factory off Third Circle and Eighth Street. It's a short walk from here," Trent suggested as Dacket checked in that direction.

"You didn't run into any royal guard last time you used that entrance, did you?" Dacket asked as he surveyed the area for the best path to avoid as many people as they could.

"Why are you always so worried about the guard? Who cares if there are any Kefale Guards there."

I need to be more careful. "We need to move. I'm worried about how our female guest will act, and my venom should be wearing off in the next few hours." Dacket ignored Trent's question about the guard and found the closest sidewalk to Third and Eighth Street. They walked quietly until they approached the back door of the garment factory. It was two plain doors which seemed like nothing but led to a vibrant under-city nightlife which never stopped, day or night.

"What are we really doing down here anyway?" Trent asked as they descended a wide set of stairs to another set of double doors.

Dacket was hoping to avoid this until he had some answers, but he guessed he should let Trent know since he was with him. Hopefully, he would learn the truth about her when they spoke to Vickery. *I need to know if she will be safe with us.* Dacket leaned in close and spoke with a hushed tone, "I found a woman on my way to the sky belt. She is like a person, but I think she's a rodent of some kind. Like, if a rodent was a full-grown person."

Trent halted and slowly turned to Dacket. "You keep saying that, and it's astonishing you thought I would believe any of it. What are we really coming down here for?" Trent questioned as he began moving again.

Dacket frowned at Trent as he walked by and Dacket had to catch up with Trent's quick stride as he reached the next corridor. "It's no joke. I have her tied to Whit's bed, and he's watching her while he does his nails."

Trent stopped again and scowled a moment before curiosity struck and his face melted. He stared at Dacket as he considered it. "You are serious? A female? Well, what do you think about her? You can't just convince me of this and think I wouldn't have questions."

Dacket smiled for the first time in months as they began walking again. "Good point. I think she's from elsewhere. We are meeting Vickery to make sure she's not some kind of sought after experiment a Kefale lab wants back. We all hear the rumors, but only a few people will know what is true. If she is from elsewhere, and she is stuck here, I want to recruit her to be a hunter. You should have seen her moving, it was unlike anything I have ever witnessed. She flipped head over feet to run, and she was nearly as fast as me with my jets when I chased her down."

Trent stopped a third time, and loudly asked, "What? Did you just say she was as fast as you WITH your jets?"

Dacket smirked at Trent and answered, "Yes. Can you imagine what she could do *with* jets? She could help us hunt, and we could rise ahead even further on stock. We could make a hearty profit if we could keep our shelves filled."

Trent thought for a moment. "You *swear* to me you're not lying?"

Dacket turned to fully face him before he answered, "I am not lying. She smelled like she had fallen from a serpent's asshole when I found her."

Trent burst into riotous laughter, and Dacket continued, "Do you believe me now?"

Trent's elated tail swayed behind him as he answered,

"Yes, I believe you. Let's go, I want to meet this flipping elsewhere woman you found. What does she look like?"

Dacket froze. His mind had been replaying bathing her, and he hesitated, causing Trent to narrow his eyes in a knowing glare. "Wait. I know that look. She's gorgeous."

Trent bolted through the next set of doors, and Dacket nearly had to run to keep up, his tail shifting from side to side behind him to keep his balance. Dacket felt his chest tighten. The female he captured was the most gorgeous being he had ever seen. The way her rosy golden hair had bounced behind her when she ran and tumbled, she was *magnificent*. They finally reached the main crevasse walkway and took a left toward the club Visetory. Inside would be the owner, Virgis Vickery.

When they reached the entrance, Dacket rubbed his hands together as he greeted the door attendant. "Is Virgis Vickery here tonight?" The man answered by tipping his head toward Virgis who was sitting like a king at the back of his bustling nightclub. He wore a black suit which complimented his light grey skin tone and his long silver hair cascading over his shoulders.

They made their way through the crowd to the back where he sat and Dacket approached him with caution. "I'm Dacket Critchlow. Do you remember me?"

Virgis nodded his head, his eyes reflected nothing but ice and vitriol. "You're the hunter who made the record serpent kill. You celebrated here. I forget nothing." Dacket hoped this went well, but Virgis glowered, as the Elara had never accepted hunters as equal members of society. According to the people, hunters were barbaric. In the many years since the last serpent reached the city, the people had forgotten the purpose of the hunts was to keep them safe.

"I have one question, I am prepared to pay for the answer if needed." Virgis reluctantly agreed and Dacket went on, "Do the Kefale have any experiments with turning rodents into walking, talking, people like us?"

Virgis deeply frowned at Dacket, "You shame me with such foolish questions. Leave me."

Having his answer, Dacket backed away and turned Trent around for them to leave. Both hurriedly exited the busy club, and Trent reached over to place his hand on Dacket's shoulder as he asked, "What did he say? I couldn't hear with that band playing."

Dacket held back a huff at having to repeat it; it was enough, having to hear it the first time. "He told me to leave. I have my answer."

Trent snarled at the lack of information, but didn't say anything as they made their way back to Dacket's truck and then back home. Dacket parked in his usual place next to Whit's truck and he helped Trent with his bags. "We can just drop the bags off, I want to see this elsewhere woman. Part of me still thinks you're lying, and there will be a giant serpent penis lying on Whit's bed with a wig and lipstick on." Dacket chuckled under his breath as they reached Trent's door and set his things inside his apartment.

When they reached Whit's door, Dacket could hear gentle music playing inside from his record player and when he entered, nothing could have prepared him for what he walked in on. Whit had the female untied and propped up on his bed with curlers in her hair and a mud mask, which Whit loved to force on everyone. All her limbs were spread out, and Whit was lounging beside her filing her fingernails on her left hand. He had clearly already, trimmed, filed, and painted all her other nails, which were a nice warm brown and matched her light golden skin tone.

Whit looked up at Dacket like what he was doing was not absurd. "What did you find out?"

Dacket came over and peered down at her. "She's from elsewhere. Vickery hadn't even heard of such an experiment as turning a rodent into a person. Has she moved much yet?" Whit shook his head as he returned to her nails. "No, she fell asleep for a little while when I took a bath and read, but she's just relaxing right now, or I hope she is anyway. I'm sure it's miserable being paralyzed like this."

"Did you give her a massage too?" Dacket noticed the massage cream Whit always used on him setting next to her on the bed.

Whit gave Dacket a look as if he were dumb. "I'm doing her nails. You always get a massage when you have your nails done. Everyone knows that."

"I even know that, Dacket," Trent added with a smirk.

Dacket turned to him with a scowl, "No one was talking to you."

Trent smiled, he loved crawling under Dacket's skin when he wasn't taking his pants off. "What are we doing with the elsewhere woman?"

Dacket walked over with a damp washcloth and carefully removed the mud mask from her skin, but Ziph had been half asleep with the black haired, green man giving her hand and foot massages. *I knew I heard people talking.* She took a deep breath and noticed she had regained some movement. Once the mud mask was fully removed, she felt Dacket lift her, if that was the name she understood. The one giving her massages and painting her nails was Whit, but she didn't know the teal man's name yet. Her translator was not working with their language, and she was having to sound out and guess at names as they spoke.

She opened her eyes and managed to turn her head so she could see as he carried her into his room. When he lay her on the bed something chimed, and she had to bite her lips together to hold back a moan. Whatever was chiming was causing her metal piercings to hum against her skin. She felt her nipples pebble and wanted to rub her thighs together as the piercing through her hood was enough to send delicious heat flowing through her. It was like all the times she had tried to have an orgasm with a vibrator, but this time it was *working*. Before when using a vibrator, she failed like she had failed when trying everything else. She just couldn't achieve enough stimulation, but this, this was taking her there and fast. The chimes ended just as she was face to face with the magnificent man tying her to his bed. *How in Pluto's hell do I say fuck me in snake?! This is wrong, Venus. WRONG.*

They were alone, and when Dacket was finished tying her to the bed, he lay next to her and she swore he was considering stripping her and giving her a bath, or she hoped that was what his smoldering look meant. Either that, or she was his next meal, but realistically something told her he wanted her for more than just sex. He was a hunter and had seen her tumble. She bet he wanted to recruit her even more than he wanted to fuck her. *I hate the idea of killing those beautiful serpents, but if it saves my skin, I might not have a choice. Maybe I can do something about it one day.*

Ziph knew the fucking her part could be wishful thinking, but *a girl can dream right? I mean I'm already tied to your bed, and I am more than willing. I just need to figure out how to say it in snake.* Ziph took a breath and tried to speak as she hoped the translator would magically start working. "Damn, I wish you would fuck me. Those chimes made my lady parts sing!" Her voice sounded weak and soft, unlike the sentiment behind her words. *Would wagging my tongue at him work? Probably not. He might just think I'm odd. I am odd, but he doesn't need to know that.*

Dacket focused on her and with a curious tilt of his head. He didn't have a clue what she said, but relief washed over him that she was able to move enough to talk and was content instead of screaming in terror. He went to his living room and found a piece of paper and an ink pen before returning to her. Trying to hold his tail still, he drew a picture of a mouse and held it up while he pointed to her.

Ziph stared at the picture and frowned. "I'm not a fucking mouse. My people come from squirrels. Oh, fuck me, he can't understand what I'm saying." She tried to move and show him her tail, but she ended up just snarling. *I have a fluffy tail. Open your eyes, sir.*

Dacket seemed to somehow understand as he searched around his room. Ziph heard him in his living room moving something heavy across the floor before he returned with a large, dusty book. After cleaning it off, he stood in front of her and flipped through it until he found a picture of a chinchilla and pointed to her.

She made a half snarl, half smile and hoped he could interpret it. Dacket seemed to understand as he flipped a few more pages, and his eyes widened as if he had found the answer. When he flipped the book around, he had the page open to a squirrel with tufted ears like her, and she smiled. "Yes! Squirrel! My people evolved from a squirrel!" Dacket gave her a hint of a smile, and she melted inside.

This man is impossibly attractive, I think my fucking underwear are wet. I haven't been this turned on in years.

As Dacket studied the page about squirrels, he made mental notes about food before he reached the part about mating. He stopped reading and slammed the book shut after the first sentence began with, "At specific times of the year, they exude intense pheromones to draw in mates for miles."

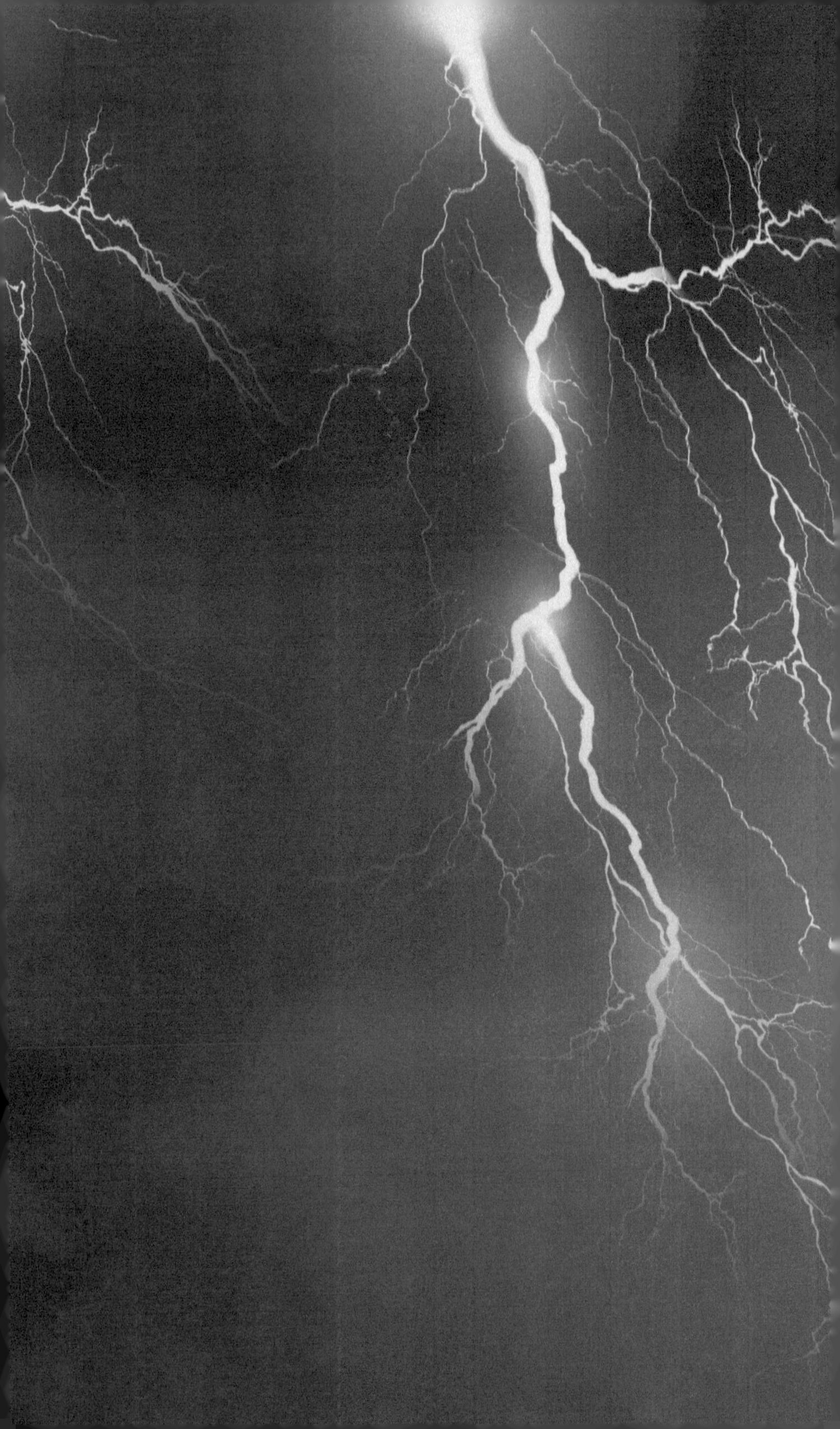

CHAPTER 7

MAKING FRIENDS

Dacket forewent the ropes when she made it clear she felt comfortable and wasn't a risk by acting silly and giving him genuine, kind smiles. Dacket sat up with her while they waited for his venom to wear off, and Ziph was thankful she wasn't alone as she slowly regained her ability to move. The third man she saw, Trent was his name, brought by a basket of berries which now sat on the table next to her beside a now empty water glass.

She had successfully regained her head movement and some of her upper torso, but the rest of her body was still paralyzed. For the last hour, she had been trying to move her fingers by berating them, and she swore she was close. *Come on, move you damn finger!* Ziph screamed in her mind for a moment. *Move, move you stupid finger!*

Ziph finally quieted her mind, and it occurred to her she may need to drink some more water to help flush everything from her system. "How am I supposed to ask for water, and why the hell is this translator taking so long?"

Dacket turned and faced her, still clearly clueless as to what she was saying, but he tried to ask, "Do you need something?" Thinking for a moment, he took the paper he had earlier, and drew a glass of water, fruit, and a toilet on the paper. He held it up and pointed to each one slowly so she could respond.

When he reached the water, she smiled. "Yes, water, I think I need some water." He seemed to agree as he set the paper down and slid from the bed to grab her empty glass and fill it before returning. He gently lifted her head and sat her up before bringing the glass to her lips. Dacket was meticulous not to spill any water.

Ziph guzzled the crisp cool liquid down, and he set the empty glass back on the table before pulling some pillows behind her so she could sit up. Dacket reached over her for his drawing and held it up again pointing to the water. "Do you need more water?"

Ziph heard him say water perfectly, and it snapped her attention to him. "Yes! The translator is picking up words. Can you understand when I say, water?" Dacket's eyes widened, and he tapped the picture of the glass of water again. Ziph nodded before he went and refilled the glass, and she drank another half of a glass and then he *smiled* at her. It was brief, but it was bright and bashful, completely different from what she had expected. He had such a hard exterior, could he really be a soft man on the inside? *Venus, if you toy with me over this sexy man, I will hunt you down in the afterlife. There will be a lot more involved than just my finger in your eye.*

Her entire universe had stopped spinning with that perfect smile, and she was overcome with butterflies in her chest. She smiled back at him, and something in him seemed to shift as he took his time returning to his spot next to her on the bed. After sitting back down and picking up a book he had been reading, Ziph unapologetically stared at him. She noticed his brow coming to points on the outer edges, and she recalled seeing vipers with horn like protrusions coming from their brow area.

Ziph eventually refocused on her mission to move and was finally able to wiggle her fingers. As soon as she had her hand in a fist, she lifted her arm and sighed with relief. Dacket watched her closely as she rubbed her face, and scratched every place she had been itchy, including the furry tips of her ears. Next came her tail which she vigorously scratched and shifted it around into a new position.

This female squirrel woman from elsewhere seems to be far too comfortable for someone I bit, paralyzed, bathed without consent, and then had tied up just a mere day ago. The way she acted toward him, and the situation, truly baffled Dacket. *She's very strange, and yet I think I like it.*

It occurred to Ziph she could finally tell him her name since she could use her arm and hand. Ziph pointed to him, "Dacket," and he nodded before she continued and pointed to herself, "Ziph."

Dacket slowly sounded out, "Zzziifff."

Ziph smiled, and he lifted the corner of his mouth as he spoke softly, "You are infinitely curious, and I don't think I've ever been so enthralled before." Dacket admired the copper gleam in her golden hair spread out behind her, now curled after she had endured Whit, and he couldn't force his eyes away. She was stunning, and he needed air, now. *I cannot become attached. What the fuck am I doing?*

Running out of his front door, Dacket slammed into Trent who was coming from Whit's apartment smelling like Whit's bath oils and massage cream. "Did he trap you in there when I left?" Dacket hoped Trent didn't ask about the fact that he now had him pinned to the wall by Whit's door, entirely by accident.

Dacket's face was inches from Trent's as Trent asked, "Are you trying to come over tonight, or did you honestly just fly from your door and accidentally slam me against the wall."

Dacket, being so unnervingly turned on answered, "Your place, right fucking now." Trent's eyes widened. It had been a while since Dacket had wanted sex from either him or Whit.

"Sure," Trent breathed as he felt Dacket slide his hand up Trent's shirt and grasp his side in desperation.

Trent could already feel his own cock pushing to be released, "Do you want it in the hall, or are we doing this in my room?"

Looking around them, Dacket laughed under his breath as they rushed down the stairs unbuckling their pants and ripping their shirts off. "Where the fuck is this coming from, Dacket?"

"That damn elsewhere woman is making me spin, I had to bathe her to remove the serpent scent, and I know she felt it all. She's regained some of her movement, and she fucking *smiled* at me."

Trent's mouth dropped open at his revelation. "You're joking. She's calm, and *smiling* at you?"

Dacket nodded as Trent pushed his door open, and Dacket decided that was far enough as he shoved Trent against the wall. Trent went weak in Dacket's hands, and Dacket yanked his pants down before dropping to his knees. "Speaking of paralyzing, don't fucking bite me…" Dacket scoffed as he licked along the valley of Trent's hip cutting his words short. He had bit Whit one time on accident when he and Whit were fucking, but it had been years since that happened. It never failed though, Trent always brought it up.

Dacket eased Trent's unsplit quad cock into his mouth but hadn't opened his snakelike jaw. Above him Trent moaned, "Oh, fuck how do you fit it all without unhinging your jaw?" He loved it when Dacket kept his jaw intact, and he felt Dacket place his left hand in the center of his chest before pushing him back against the wall. Dacket took him deep into his throat, and Trent slapped his tail against the wall and before he could split, he erupted in Dacket's mouth. Trent moaned as Dacket sucked him down, and he never quite understood how Dacket managed to make him cum so quickly and without splitting.

Sliding down the wall, Trent collapsed as Dacket leaned back across from him. Trent licked his lips. "Give me a few minutes, and I'll bend you over my couch."

Dacket panted and closed his eyes. He hadn't been railed in far too long. He needed to visit Trent and Whit more often. They were always there for him whether it be in business, hunting, friendship, or sex, and he often neglected the last of those. He ached for an internal release and rubbed his bulge as Trent readied himself for round two.

Staring at Dacket trying to refrain from squirming around had Trent ready faster than usual, and he stood up with his hand out. Dacket took his hand, and Trent led him to the couch before pulling his pants to his ankles and bending him over the back of it. Trent moved his hand under Dacket, rubbing his nipple while he fished for lube in his side table. Once he had his cock lubed up, he eased into Dacket and both groaned with anticipated relief. It had been far too long.

As Trent moved inside of Dacket, he grasped the cushions and nearly ripped the fabric as Trent's cock split in four parts and began rotating inside of him. The little soft spikes moving around so delightfully had him quivering. Dacket felt Trent stroke his hand down the middle of Dacket's stomach aiming to rub his cock in preparation for it to split. Trent leaned over him and moved his hand to begin rubbing in the center of Dacket's rolling, split cock.

Trent always knew exactly what Dacket wanted, and Dacket quickly blasted cum into Trent's hands as Trent tipped over in a second grinding orgasm. Dacket nearly fell over the top of the couch, but knowing it would make a terrible mess, he refrained and tried his best to sit up. He braced the back of the couch to keep himself upright.

Trent slid free from Dacket and went into his kitchen to wash up. "Do you mean to tell me you were *that* turned on just by sitting *next to* the elsewhere woman? Whit and I have had sex like that many times, but never you. You're always quiet about it, and you usually just knock on my door in the middle of the night."

Dacket ignored him intentionally because Trent was right, and he knew it. In their society someone only settled down with a person if you wanted to raise a child or as many as you wanted to apply to care for. The Kefale royals hatched every egg in every city to ensure double headed hatchlings were intercepted for royal placement. All other hatchlings were given out in order of the request for a child. The list was long, but it moved quickly. Single people, couples, or groups could request a child and if they met the requirements, and they could have as many babies as they wanted when their turn came up. He only knew that because his employee Danny's mother worked in the royal hatchery.

Dacket made his way back to his room where the beautiful woman lay in his bed. *After all of that, I know I'm still not sleeping if she is next to me.* Dacket contemplated sleeping on the couch as he decided what to do. He wouldn't dare begin a relationship with anyone new considering the possibility he could die so easily during a hunt, no matter how badly he desired one with her. Hunters do not have relationships. They never have.

Tomorrow, I will set her up with a home next to Trent, and she won't be so close. She can share a home with Danny Winlow, the young woman I hired a few years ago. She is loyal and will keep her mouth shut. He thought about Danny's makeup skills and bet she would even be able to hide Ziph in plain sight. Maybe the two could become friends.

Dacket stood in the doorway of his bedroom, and Ziph was sitting up on her own as she moved her legs and tried to stand up. Her legs wobbled, and Dacket moved to catch her in case she fell.

Ziph smiled at him bashfully. "Thank you." Dacket didn't understand the words, but he did understand her thanks. He helped her take a few steps, and she patted his arm in reassurance she could walk on her own. After a few more unsteady steps, she began walking normally before she started stretching to loosen her tight muscles.

Dacket intently watched as she went through a stretching routine, and by the end of it she looked over to find him hopelessly entranced. *I always heard snake charming was simple, but I had no idea it would be that easy.* Dacket seemed as though he was fighting to stay present as he waved for her to follow him from his apartment.

When they were in the hallway, she pointed to Whit's door excitedly, and he knocked on the door causing her to give a little hop of excitement. When Whit opened the door, Ziph threw her arms around him, "Thank you so much for making me feel safe and cared for. My nails look so pretty, and my skin feels amazing."

Whit grinned at Dacket slyly with narrowed eyes. "I think this means I am her favorite."

Dacket slightly snarled his lip and angled his glare. "Her name is Ziph."

Ziph heard her name and turned to him before Whit repeated, "Ziph is her name? I wonder what that means?" She turned back to look at Whit, wishing her translator would start working.

It was obvious she wanted to communicate and was working toward understanding their language. "She's clearly intelligent, she's been able to communicate some. I am taking her down to Danny to room with."

Whit looked concerned, "Make sure she understands if she leaves, she could be in danger. We don't know how the public will react to her." Dacket agreed and took her over to a window to point down at the busy street. People were walking along the sidewalks, and cars were stuck in traffic below. Dacket pointed to her and then back to the street before running his finger across his own throat. Ziph understood perfectly. She tapped her chest and pointed to the floor and the walls of the hallway before pointing to Whit and then tapping her finger against Dacket's chest.

Knowing they couldn't understand her, she joked, "Don't worry, I am not going anywhere in this snake pit of a city."

CHAPTER 8
DANNY WINLOW

Dacket led Ziph down the stairs and knocked on the first door. Across from them, Trent opened his door as usual to see what was happening in the hallway. He clearly was an unapologetic people watcher.

A woman answered the door Dacket knocked on, and when she saw Ziph, she beamed. She had similar light golden skin color to Ziph, except her hair and eyes were dark brown. As the woman leaned to the side trying to make sense of Ziph's golden fluffy tail, Dacket explained, "Danny, this is Ziph. She is from elsewhere." Dacket waited for Danny to catch up, and when she straightened up to face him looking confused, he continued, "I have no idea how she arrived here, but I caught her when we were hunting. We think she will make a talented hunter, but she doesn't know our language, and she obviously doesn't have any friends here. I was hoping she could stay in your spare room since you live in a double unit. I know you asked for females only, but I wasn't sure if this counted."

Danny grinned and clapped her hands as her tail

nearly hit the wall on either side of her as it swayed back and forth. "YES! She is so pretty. We can do our makeup, and I can camouflage her to look like us so we can go party under Eight!"

Dacket sighed, he should have seen that coming. "Danny, don't take her to the Eight Underground. She's from elsewhere, and you both could be caught too easily."

Danny snarled at him as she reached for Ziph's hand and gleefully pulled her through the doorway. "I just need to shave her ears and make a tail cover for all that fur. Besides, no one really cares about elsewhere people anyway. I heard there is one in Paralled city who has bird wings. Supposedly, he is raising a child with a garment maker, and no one really cares."

Dacket stared at Danny incredulously, "You're shaving her ears?"

Danny laughed at how Dacket sailed over everything else and fixated on her ear tufts. "Yes, look, they are pointy under the hair, and even stick up at almost the same angle ours do. If we shave her ear tufts, and hide her tail, she will look just like an Elarian."

Shaking his head at Danny, Dacket *hated* this idea. "I don't like this at all. Before you do anything come find me. It's not that I don't trust you, I just don't want anything to happen to Ziph."

Danny paused a moment, seeing something in Dacket she hadn't before, a spark of care, and even affection. She softened her stare and agreed, "I will be careful with her, I promise." Dacket reluctantly walked away, and Danny shut her door as he reached the stairs.

Danny twirled to face Ziph, who was nervously tugging at her shirt. "In all the years I've known the name Dacket Critchlow, I have never known him to even notice a woman. You must be something special." Ziph had no idea what she said and just smiled as she shrugged her shoulders causing Danny to laugh. "Come with me, let's see if we can make you look like one of us so we can go out. There is a guy who frequents a club under Eight, and we kissed last time we saw each other."

Leading Ziph into the bathroom connected to Danny's room, she panicked as she realized her makeup and products were spread over the counter. "I didn't even think about having a guest in here! My junk is everywhere!" Danny started to scramble to clean it up, but Ziph reached out to stop her, and Ziph tried to speak as she explained with her hands, "I am messy like this too," and waved her hand over the cluttered counter before she pointed to herself and gave Danny a knowing look. Danny burst into laughter, "Oh, I can already tell we will be good friends. I love you already!"

Ziph laughed with her, before Danny reached up to tap her own ear and she showed Ziph the hair on the tips of her ears and how they were different. Danny moved to her bathroom window and opened it pointing outside before she picked up a shaving razor from the sink area and pretended to shave her own ears. Ziph understood. "Oh, you want to shave my ears so you can take me out there?" She motioned with her hands to explain she understood, tapping her ear tuft, then tapping the razor, before making her fingers walk. *I wonder where she plans to take me.*

Danny grinned at her agreeing and Ziph nodded, angling her head to Danny for her to start. Grabbing her shaving cream and a hair tie, Danny pulled Ziph's hair back and put it up in the tie before she applied a bit of shaving cream on Ziph's ear tuft. Standing over Ziph, Danny carefully shaved her ear and when she stood up next to Danny afterward, she realized Danny had been right. They did have remarkably similar pointed ears with the tuft gone, and Ziph turned for her to finish the other side. *I guess no matter what galaxy, girls stick together. I'm starting to think I could make a good life here as long as the food tastes good. What the fuck am I going to do if it doesn't taste good? Just starve? I don't think so.*

When she was finished, Ziph and Danny turned to look in the mirror, and aside from Ziph's round mammal pupils, they looked eerily similar. Danny was thrilled as she turned to tap on Ziph's tail and Ziph was a little confused and honestly grossed out. "I can deal with shaving my ears, but I don't know about my tail. I would look like a giant rat." When Ziph picked up the razor with a snarl on her face, Danny fell back laughing and waving her hand, that no, they would not be shaving Ziph's tail. Realizing that wasn't what Danny meant, Ziph laughed along with her as they went to her closet. *Thank, fuck, I don't have to shave my tail. It might give me nightmares. It probably would look like a long erect dick emerging from my ass crack.* Ziph bit her lips together trying not to laugh.

After she rummaged around in a bin, Danny pulled out a long stocking and twirled her finger for Ziph to turn around. Ziph eyed her as she took in the stocking, and Danny laughed all over again. "I swear it will look odd at first, but you can wear a dress, and it will cover your tail."

Danny pulled a long dress out to show Ziph, and it all made sense, so Ziph turned and presented her tail to Danny to cover with the stocking. Once it was on, Ziph did her best to lower her tail and keep it there, even practicing swaying it like the people here did. Ziph looked back at her concealed tail. *It looks like a wide rat tail. I still ended up looking like a damn rat. I hope no one sees my tail like this. I guess it doesn't look like a giant penis so that's a win.*

Noticing her nails, Danny tapped them and looked to Ziph expectantly. Ziph tried to explain, "Whit?" Danny understood his name, and Ziph continued, "he painted them for me."

Ziph made a painting gesture over her nails, and Danny asked, "Whit painted your nails?" Ziph understood painted that time and was beyond thankful the translator was beginning to work.

How do the damn translators learn new languages anyway? Ziph thought about it while Danny started on her own makeup. Her mind was blank. She hated when that happened. She knew it had something to do with exposure to the language but couldn't remember anything else about it. She brought herself back to the task of preparing to go somewhere, where, she had no idea, but from the look of the bright pink action happening on Danny's eyelids, they were going out somewhere fun.

Ziph deadpanned Danny and stopped her before she added glitter and pointed to the fabulous eye makeup before hooking her finger at Danny to follow. *If we are going out to the club, she needs to know who she's going with.* When Ziph went into her living room, she had Danny stand by the couch and motioned for her to stay there.

Ziph wanted Danny to know that Ziph was well aware of their plans tonight, and that Danny was bringing along, potentially, the best dancing partner she could ask for. Ziph stood in the long space behind Danny's lounging couch and hiked her skirt before she did a perfect, effortless backflip and then high kicking her leg to her shoulder in a perfect split before holding herself balanced on one foot. That was all it took as

Danny screamed in excitement, leading to Ziph screaming along with her as the two jumped toward one another, and before they knew it, someone knocked on their door.

They fell silent at the knocking, and Danny slowly opened the door to find Trent standing in the hall looking concerned. "Do you have a break in happening? Are you two alright in there?"

Embarrassment creeping up Danny's throat nearly had her unable to speak as she meekly explained, "Dacket told me if I can make Ziph look like an Elarian that I can take her under Eight. She just put it together that we are going out dancing, so I think to show me *how* ready she is, she did a backflip behind my couch. I may have screamed, and then she screamed, which made me scream more."

Trent was open mouthed staring at her, "Ziph did a back flip in your living room? WAIT. You were planning to party without me?" Trent was asking the second question to Ziph, not Danny. His eyes were focused on Ziph like laser-beams.

Danny had never spent time with any of her bosses. They weren't her type anyway; she liked tall and lanky fellows. Besides, she had a rule against dating hunters, as most Elarian people did. "I bet Dacket would be a lot more likely to let Ziph go if you came along." Danny could see the intrigue in Trent's eye as he took in Ziph while she picked through a small trinket collection Danny had in a patchwork frame on her wall.

Ziph gasped as she pulled out a little jar with a tiny lipstick inside before she squealed, "This is so fucking cute, I don't know why I love these tiny things so much! Oh, Venus, bless the girl's girls. I think that's a tiny dildo. This fucking translator needs to start working. We have so much to talk about, and I have known her for five minutes."

Danny knew what Ziph was pointing at and slipped her hand over her mouth. Trent agreed without thought with a twinkle in his eyes as he watched Ziph faun over the trinkets, "I'll meet you in the hallway when you're ready, I'll hear your door open."

Danny shut the door before she pointed to the fading daylight, "We need to hurry!" Grabbing Ziph's hand, she led her into the bathroom where Ziph gave herself some winged liner before she separated some fibers to make herself some lashes. After Danny finished adding the glitter she wanted, Danny dressed first in a short high neck deep brown dress. Once they both were able to squeeze Danny in her dress, they moved on to buttoning up the back of the low-cut long dress on Ziph. It was a cream color and Ziph loved it. She felt sexy but whimsical with the flowing skirt. Danny and Ziph were around the same size, so the dress fit perfectly.

Danny handed Ziph her favorite dusty rose lipstick, a shade Ziph favored in her makeup collection back home, and Ziph held the lipstick to her chest briefly as the memory of her old apartment stirred in her mind. Understanding she was having a moment, Danny put her arm around Ziph and reassured her the only way she could. Ziph could have cried, she felt so seen by Danny. *I may have found a better friend in Danny than I have ever had before.* "This ridiculous situation could not have turned out better. I think I can be happy here, really happy."

Danny tipped her head toward the door and Ziph agreed, mushy emotions could wait. There was dancing to be done, and it had been far too long for Ziph. She danced at work, of course, but she hadn't danced for fun in years.

When the door shut behind Danny and Ziph, it only took moments for Trent to come walking out wearing a black button-down shirt and nice black pants.

Danny's mouth dropped open, but she shut it quickly. Not quickly enough for Ziph to miss it though, and she wondered what it was about. *Why was Danny so surprised Trent looked the way he did? Did she not know Trent was gorgeous before this moment? Honestly, if I thought I could get away with biting him, I would do it.*

That brought her to another thought. *What is with all these beautiful snake people? Are they all this good looking?*

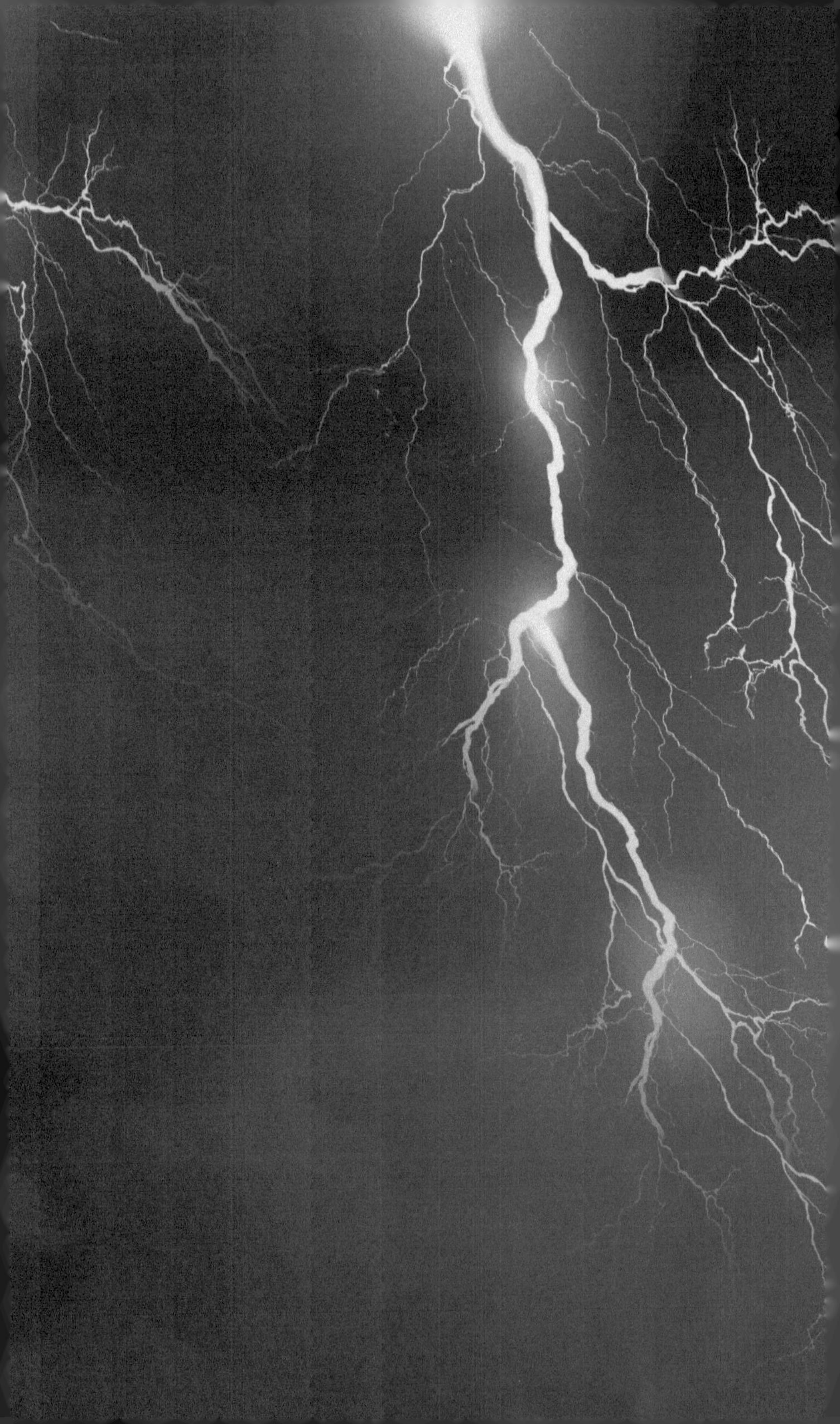

CHAPTER 9
ZIPH-LINES

Ziph followed Trent and Danny up to Dacket's door and knocked. When Dacket opened it, he didn't look anywhere but directly at Ziph, and she locked eyes with him, unable to tear herself away.

"I'll take them to Spatial. That's the big dance club, right?" Trent turned to Danny for confirmation, and she agreed.

Dacket seemed as though he would be sick as he finally relented, "Fine. Do not stay out too late. The guard sent out ready notices to the hunters. There is a curfew on the street now. The palace detected a large pocket of warmth crossing too far from the sky belt earlier today."

"Don't worry I'll have them back early." Trent always worried about Dacket and Whit when they hunted, but when there was a warning from the palace, he knew it could mean a nest of serpents were leaving the sky belt. Many of the hunters wouldn't return from a nest encounter. The last large nest of ten serpents to attack ended the lives of fifteen of the city's best hunters when he was a child. There was a memorial in the hunter's square to remember them by, but only some of their friends and family still frequented the statues. He missed them, but none of them visited the statues after they were built. Their home had been so empty after that day, and it hurt too much to see faces of the people who cared for them in stone. *They weren't technically our parents, but they should've been. They loved us like we were their children.*

Now the two closest people to him in his life were the leading hunters in the city, and he was faced with the fear of losing them regularly. *I know why no one dates hunters. It's obvious; they all die too young. Our people too often deny love when I know damn well, they just love too deeply, and our losses are too often.* Dacket shut his door, and Trent did his best to make the best of the night as he followed Danny leading them down the stairs to the garage. Danny intended to walk like she did everywhere, but Trent went toward his car instead, "We can drive. There is no sense in walking all the way to Eight from here."

Danny didn't really want to walk all that way anyway and gladly hopped in the car as he pulled it up to them. Danny sat in the back and let Ziph sit up front, and Ziph was more than pleased to have somewhere to fit her tail in the V shaped seats. *I'm so glad I landed somewhere where the people have tails.*

The six wheeled car was plain, and by the level of technology, Ziph bet their society was at least thirty or so years away from space exploration. A light rain began as they arrived and parked, and little droplets slid down the windshield as they climbed out. Trent led them down a sidewalk to a single door in an alleyway which led to a long corridor.

After walking through the long, darkened space, Trent opened a door at the end, and it led to a long set of stairs. At the bottom of the stairs was an open entryway to the dark road.

Two clubs down from the entryway was a large neon sign that flashed 'Spatial' in the Elarian language, and Trent led them inside the loud dance club. Elarian of all levels of society mingled in the Eight Underground, and here at Spatial, they all danced without judgement. It was the only place in the city that it didn't really matter who you were, you could be yourself. Danny grabbed Ziph's hand, and they both twirled onto the dance floor, and Trent was nearly running as he followed them.

Trent did his best to stay close enough to watch over them but not get in their way. Ziph saw him standing off to the side. *Oh, I do not think so. You are not standing over there like a sad puppy.*

Trent lit up when Ziph pulled him close to dance with her, but his brief excitement was cut short and replaced with awe when she drew away and began dancing around him like he had never seen before. He was entranced by her spinning with her arms raised and her leg jutting out, then back in, as she twirled around him. She grabbed his hand and pulled him close before twisting them both across the dance floor. Her long legs extending fully as she seemed to dance on air.

Ziph was having the time of her life, the live band, the lights, and now dancing with Trent, it was like a dream come true. The music slowed, and she caught her breath as she listened, and much of the sound in the room was the voices of people chatting at darkened tables. She had been so busy dancing she hadn't noticed how full the room was. She had not even seen Danny for most of the evening.

Trent pulled her against him, and she melted into his warmth as they moved together. He slipped his hands down to her lower back and grasped her waist as they moved. The next song was faster, and she switched between dancing with Trent and around him, following the beat.

After an hour of dancing, Trent was spent and Danny was too, but Ziph was just warming up as she danced by herself next to them. When Ziph gathered her friends were tired, she pointed to the bar and Trent agreed, taking her hand, and leading her over.

Danny followed and nudged Trent, "I don't exactly have any money." Trent chuckled at her. He had no intention of letting anyone else pay. "I was going to pay for everything anyway, but did you not receive your second paycheck this month?"

Danny looked away and admitted, "I may have spent it on makeup."

Trent laughed and waved her off, "Don't worry I will take care of everything tonight. How were you planning to pay for it if I didn't come along?"

Danny smiled awkwardly, unsure if she wanted to admit the truth. "I was going to flirt, and hope someone bought me a drink."

"That's a terrible plan. What do you want, and what should we order for Ziph?" Trent couldn't keep his hands from Ziph as they stood at the bar, and Ziph was not upset about it.

After the intense paralyzed bathing, and then the damn chimes in Dacket's apartment which had her pierced lady parts zinging, Ziph was ready to burst. She wanted to pull Trent to the bathroom and have her way with him. She was sure he wouldn't mind. *What is wrong with me? I wouldn't even let a man near me back home, and here I am wanting to suck Trent's dick in the bathroom. I'm dying to know what his penis looks like.* She couldn't help herself as she backed up to Trent, and slid her tail to the side so she could rub her ass against him. Trent slid his hand around her thigh and up her skirt, but did not touch anything except her inner thigh until she nudged him. He was discreet as he stroked her skin, nearly grazing her sensitive pussy with his thumb as the bartender came over to ask for their order.

"I want a brew, she and Danny there want a fruit mix, and pour the mixes high." Trent knew how Spatial liked to slight on the liquor if you didn't call them on it. The owner was well known for shady practices.

After downing their drinks, they danced a little while longer before several people shuffled out in a hurry. Over the next few minutes people kept exiting quickly, and Trent started to suspect something was happening as he kept an eye on their surroundings.

Ziph was dancing with Danny when she felt a strong arm wrap around her and it hauled her against a hard body. She was quickly spun around to face Dacket, who was dressed the same as when she first met him, in his hunting gear. He seemed distressed, and Trent ran up when he saw him.

"The palace ordered all the hunters out. There is a nest they spotted moving this way from the sky belt. I need all of you home safely before I leave, we need to move. I'm parked in front of the doors on the street where you came in." Dacket was risking a high citation, or even imprisonment, for taking the time to come down and retrieve them.

Trent understood what Dacket was risking, and he grabbed Danny's hand while Dacket took Ziph's, and they all ran full speed for Dacket's truck. When they made it through the long corridor and they were finally climbing in Dacket's tall truck, Ziph was so on fire she could have run all the way back on foot.

"So, does anyone want to explain to me why the big, sexy-dick-I-wanna-lick bossy man came and grabbed us in a rush?" Ziph peered around the truck expecting odd looks of confusion, but instead what she faced was three utterly shocked passengers. "What?" Ziph was confused, or, no. No, no. NO! *Venus, what the entire fuck you dumb ass bitch?! This is when my translator starts working?!* The air in the truck became so thick she swore she could have swam through it.

"I am skipping over what you said, and I'll start with, how did you learn our language that fast?" Dacket was frantically shifting the truck into gear while slamming on the pedal as he was trying to look at her, the road, and ask all at once. *I wonder if I tucked and rolled fast enough if I could make it onto a sidewalk between the parked cars. He's moving too quickly, I don't know if I would make it if I jumped out right now.*

Trapped like a rat in a cage, Ziph was speechless for a moment, and she puckered her lips like a fish trying to figure out how she was going to survive. "Um? I, um, I come from a place with advanced technology, and we have implanted translators which have the capability to learn new languages. Why are we in a rush right now?" *Please for the love of EVERYTHING can we change the subject?*

"The palace issued a warning earlier that we may have a serpent nest moving toward the city. I received the hunter's call out about twenty minutes ago." Dacket was moving far over the speed limit as he drove them through the vacant streets. He had less than ten minutes to make it home, and be crossing out of a city gate, or he would pull up to a shut gate and the guards would write down his truck number and give him a citation. He could not afford a citation. He pressed the pedal harder, and when they arrived at the garage, he skidded to a halt to let them out, but Ziph turned instead of jumping out like the other two.

"I can help. Take me with you." Ziph had her hand on Dacket's forearm, pleading with him to take her along. *I don't care if it's dangerous, I need those ankle jets! Please let me go!*

That's it, if he didn't make it through the gate on time, he could claim he was late because he has a new apprentice. He had a fellow hunter of Ziph's size, Gerara, who had left a clean hunting bag in his truck the last time they practiced together. "Fine. Don't make me regret this. You can dress in the gear in the smaller bag of the two in the back. You have two minutes to be dressed, or the guards will know something is brewing, and we could even be detained."

It's showtime! Ziph dove headfirst over the seat and began digging in the bag. She worked in the showhouse where she had to change whole outfits and hair, in five minutes. She was sliding back in the front seat, and hooking up jets to her hips with thirty seconds to spare, causing Dacket to scoff in disbelief, "How did you dress so quickly?"

"Remember before you caught me how I was tumbling?" Ziph asked as she finished buckling on the last mini-jet pack on her ankle before admiring how well her tail fit in the uniform's tail hole, especially considering a stocking was covering it to make it look like a fleshy tail and not a hairy one. She really needed to remember to keep her tail lowered because it looks like a giant butt penis when she had it up like she was used to.

"Yes, I don't think I could ever forget that." Dacket took a sharp corner, and they held on as the truck slid around, and he slammed on the pedal trying to make it to the gate which they could now see at the end of the road.

"I worked as an acrobat in a horror comedy showhouse. It was like a dance show, but extreme. Sometimes I had bars or flaming hoops I would perform with; it was the perfect job for me. I would always come in over the audience from a zip-line and flipped from it to land on stage. I loved every night I was able to perform." Dacket acted as though he understood, but she could tell he had no idea what in Pluto's hell she was talking about.

What is a ziph-line? Dacket blasted through the gate seconds before it began closing, and he looked back before settling back in his seat. *I need to stop taking risks like this. I cut that far too close.* "Fuck, I didn't think I would make it."

Ziph felt guilty and couldn't help it as she asked, "Why did you come all the way down there for us, if you could have been in trouble for being late?"

Dacket rolled his window down for some much needed air and slowed his truck a bit to level out before he answered. "The underground doesn't announce when the palace sends out alerts, and there was a chance a serpent could have breached the walls and found you three on your way home. I couldn't have lived with myself if I had allowed that to happen."

Ziph understood she had a lot to learn about this new world, but one thing she was discovering was clear. This man Dacket was a kindhearted man on top of being impossibly good looking. As she peered out on the nighttime star lit terrain before them, she wondered exactly how large these serpents actually grew and what she had invited herself into. *I know Lashes was a baby, and I saw how big those bones were. She won't be full grown for years, but maybe I can get a new job by then or even do something about these hunts. Gods. What in Pluto's hell did I just tangle myself in?*

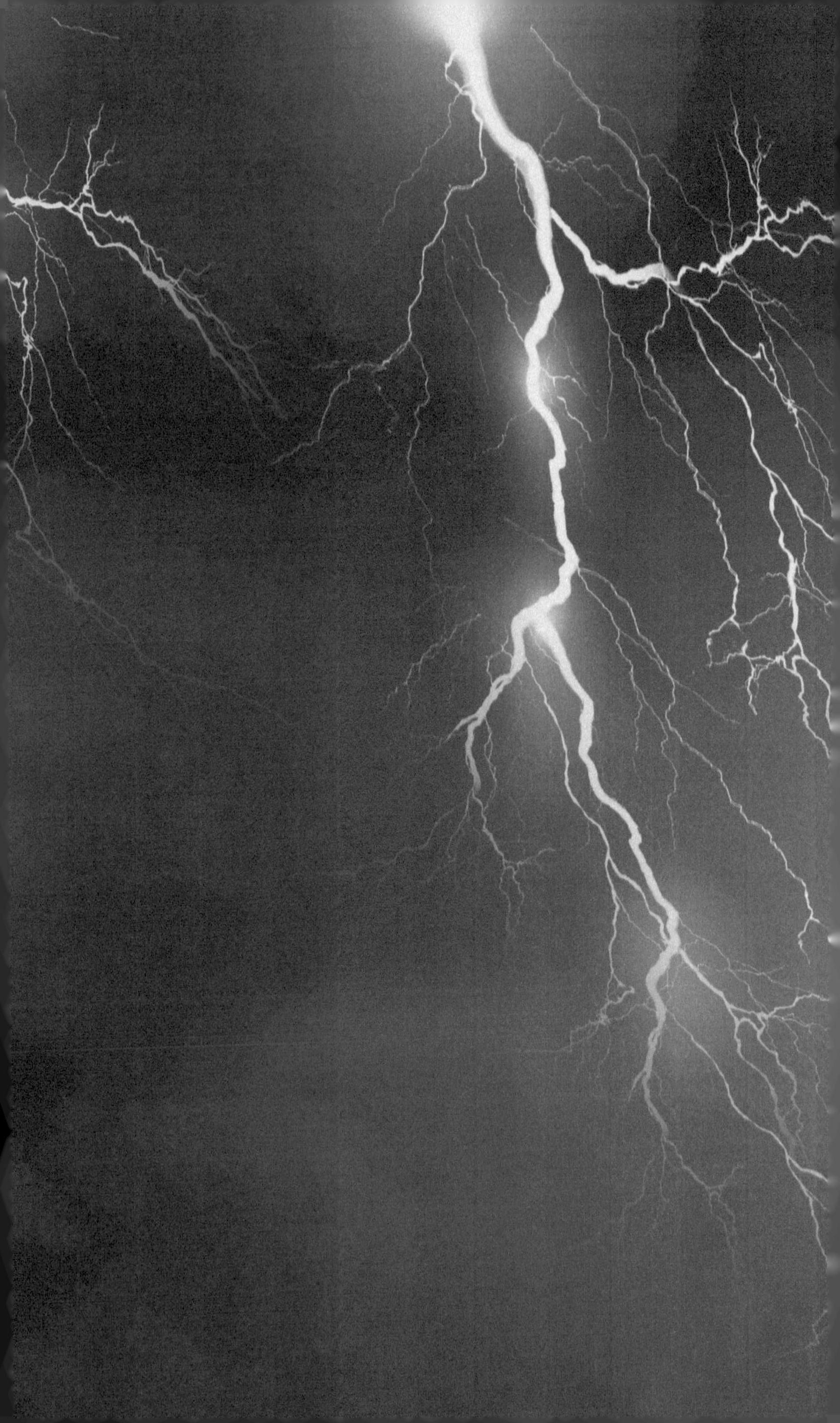

CHAPTER 10
DREAM TEAM

"When we approach the battle ground, you are to remain in the truck. I would never take an apprentice on a nest battle for a first call." Dacket could tell Ziph was not listening as she studied how the ankle jets worked with the boots she wore. He noticed her tail sway back-and-forth when she was deep in thought.

When she flexed her toes downward, the little fan jets shot air downwards causing her knees to bonk the dashboard. "Be careful, you need training before you can use them properly." Dacket's concern was growing by the second, and he was beginning to regret his decision to allow her to accompany him.

Ignoring him entirely, Ziph asked, "When I flex my toes upward, I'm assuming that will send the air jet up so I will travel downwards?"

Now Dacket was certain she would be causing a mountain of problems for him. *I don't think I can get away with purposefully biting her, can I? She would never talk to me again. Or, would she?* He was seriously considering it. "Yes.

Again, you are not accompanying me on this hunt." Ziph ignored him again as she discovered the gloves, attached to her sleeves by a chain with a wire weaved through it, and when she put them on, she discovered they control the jets at her hips. They were to move her forward and backward. Ziph slid the gloves on, and as she closed her hand, her body was shot back into the seat.

Her mind went straight to the sky belt, and her heart thrummed in her chest so vigorously she could hear it in her ears. "This is everything I could have ever wanted."

Has she been completely ignoring me?! Dacket's eyes flared with distress as he tried to remind her, "Ziph, you are not going with me on this hunt. Are you listening?"

Ziph bashfully smiled at him as she fluttered her eyelashes. "Listen, you seem really nice, but there is one thing you should know about me. I don't listen to save my life. I never have, and I never will. I don't know why, but I just physically cannot do it. If you want me to stay behind, you'll have to bite me."

Dacket went slack jawed as he took in her words, and he speechlessly turned back to focus on driving as he came up with a response. *What the fuck did she just say to me?* "Don't tempt me with the easy way out as option one."

"The easy way? Just easy? Is that all? Do I get another fun shower?" Ziph had no idea what had come over her, but she was shamelessly flirting with this man. Yanking at the hem of her shirt from under her jacket, she bit her lip when he turned to look at her, helplessly speechless. "Don't act like you didn't enjoy me being paralyzed and able to feel *everything* when you were cleaning me in your shower."

Overwhelmed, Dacket coughed in his sleeve trying to breathe, and he and his aching cock had never been more thankful to see serpents coming into view. He did enjoy when she was at his mercy, nude and wet, far too much, and his skin was boiling as he tried to maintain his calm exterior. *I think I've recreated that scene in my head, except with her tied up, constantly since it happened. Why the fuck did she choose right now to bring it up?* His life had been simple and straightforward until Ziph burst into it, and now here he was, struggling to simply hold his dick inside from just her playful comments.

With delight etched on her face at the giant serpents battling with the sky hunters ahead of them, Dacket was conflicted and seriously contemplating biting her again just to make sure she didn't try to join him. He briefly squeezed his eyes shut before he began to slow. He knew he was losing the battle to keep Ziph in the truck.

The other hunters had parked in a row just ahead of them, and he was aiming for an open spot next to Whit's truck. "Ziph, I know you think you are capable of joining me, but I cannot explain to you how dangerous this is. You must have training first."

Ziph was pressed all the way forward in the seat with her face almost touching the windshield, and she was hopelessly enthralled by the deadly dance in the sky. She was not listening at all. Dacket pulled to a sharp stop, and she grabbed the handle to climb out. Dacket pulled her back against the seat, and she turned to find him furious with his fangs emerging from his gums. "No! Please, let me go with you! Please! I swear I will be careful!"

Dacket was more distressed than he had ever been before, and he felt as though his heart wanted to beat right from his chest and run away. "You could get us both killed!"

Ziph shook her head, and grasped his arm, pleading

with him not to bite her. "You can bite me and do whatever you want with me later, but right now I need to be a part of this."

This woman is impossible! I would never fucking bite you unless I felt it was necessary to keep you safe! Dacket roughly swallowed and his fangs ached as he processed what had just come from her mouth. *Does she have any idea what she just said to me?* He reluctantly released her, and she grinned so brightly he wanted to scream. *If she dies, how will I live with myself?*

With her mechanical, *whatever weapon this is*, in hand, Ziph was streaking from the truck toward the action so quickly Dacket nearly fell from his truck trying to catch up to her. *How does this woman have so much energy?! And why the fuck is she so drawn to danger?! I feel like I'm going to die! I don't know if my heart can handle this.* He could barely keep up, and he was a foot taller than her, at least. Having enough as he felt the gravity begin to recede, he pressed down with his toes and activated his jets, giving him a slight boost as he ran. His tail was beginning to cramp with how tightly he squeezed it in a coil.

Ziph felt the gravity dropping and activated her jets, sending her soaring ahead of Dacket, and behind her she could hear him yell in a panic, "Ziph! You need to wait!"

Laughing with delight, Ziph just increased her speed. *He has no idea what I can do!* Ziph loved snakes, but these overgrown serpents would eat the people in the city if they weren't killed. She didn't know the specifics of everything, but she just knew she could help them with her polished skill set.

In a terrified panic, Dacket screeched, "You forgot your mask and you don't even know how to use the weapons!"

At that, Ziph cringed internally, and slowed down to

wait for him. *Shit, he has an excellent point. Also, a mask would be immensely helpful with all this wind.*

When he caught up and handed her the mask, he panted and his voice shook as he spoke, "Your recklessness will find you dead here! Listen, please! You need to aim around the neck and just below. Anywhere else will just agitate the serpent and cause it to fixate, if that happens, the entire nest will synchronize their target and only pursue you. There is a button on the side of your spear cylinder. When you're ready, press the button, and the spear will spring from both ends."

Ziph tried to sympathize with him. "I understand you don't know me well, but I promise I can do this. Just trust me." Ziph bolted from him to join the sky hunters who had just met the six serpents in battle. Grasping his jacket at the pain in his chest, Dacket was on the verge of truly losing his wits as stars blossomed in his sight, and he fearfully followed her into the battle.

The gravity was much lower here, and Dacket felt his heart being ripped out of his chest as he watched as Ziph shot herself directly toward one of the largest serpents. Filled to his breaking point with fright, he knew this was no way to go into battle with a serpent. He had to shift his mindset now, or he and other hunters could die because of his mistakes. He knew what he needed to do, and he would do his best to work with her and match her efforts instead of holding her back. No matter how badly his apprehension hammered inside his head, something told him to trust this woman. She would show him her talent.

The six snakes were distracted and lured away from one another by the groups of hunters circling their lifted heads as they swayed high in the sky. One of the smaller serpents struck at a hunter near the ground, and Ziph could hear the hunter's cry muffle as the snake gobbled him down. *Nope. That was all I needed, that won't be me today!*

With a profound threat of looming death, Ziph was in her element as she soared through the sky and aimed for the neck of the closest serpent. Three other hunters circled it, aiming to lead it away and isolate it to overtake it, one of them being Whit. Ziph watched the pattern before she dipped down then shot up between the circling hunters and toward the snake's throat. Ziph knew snake anatomy, she aimed directly at a place she was certain would send her spear into its brain, ending its life instantly. *I don't know how they typically kill the serpents, but I'm not letting this one suffer.*

Dacket watched with a blend of utter amazement and horror as he joined the hunters circling around the snake Ziph was moving in to kill. He knew with the aim she had, if her strike was strong enough, she could make an instant kill. *I have only done such a thing twice in an emergency, but her method of coming in underneath could work well. I spoke too soon about holding her back.*

In disbelief, Dacket saw her slam the spear into the serpent, and she seemed effortless in her actions as she bounced away from its neck and she moved out of the way. The massive beast became still, and the hunters around it all bolted away to the next serpent, but Dacket dipped down to fly beside her for a brief moment as he pulled up his mask. "I recall my words. You are perfection."

Overjoyed, but empty handed, Ziph asked, "What now? Do I retrieve the spear?" Dacket pointed to her hip, and she retrieved a metal cylinder from her belt.

Ziph did as he instructed before and pushed the button causing the ends of the cylinder to slide out and lock into place, creating another solid spear. The moment she heard it lock, they aimed for the nearest serpent slithering its giant body through the low gravity zone. When Ziph and Dacket neared, the circling hunters spread to allow them in.

Ziph decided to back off a bit and watch how the experienced hunters executed the takedown. A pattern emerged as she watched three hunters with similar light green insignia on their collars as the rest of the hunters just continued to circle. They gave one another hand signals, and all three aimed their spears. In sync, the three hunters jammed their spears into the neck of the serpent, causing it to flail a bit before it fell still and limp.

The dead and dying serpents were taking a slow decent to the ground due to the reduced gravity, and Ziph peered around to see all six of them had now been taken down.

She lifted her mask and spotted Whit, who looked at her in wild confusion as he confirmed who she was. Dacket appeared next to her and pointed to the giant serpent she had just slain. "We need to begin stripping the meat. Whit and I will need your assistance. The serpent you killed will stock our meat market for months. The fabric wraps I hid you in are for hauling back the carcass. I'll show you how it works, just follow me."

Whit joined her in the sky as Dacket took off for the serpent Ziph killed, which was just starting to touch the ground after floating down. "What are you doing here? Was that really you who killed that serpent?!" Whit was baffled seeing Ziph in hunting gear and handling her jets like she was a tested professional. It usually took months to learn the jets.

They started after Dacket as Ziph tried to explain quickly, "I told Dacket I wanted to come, so he let me."

Whit seemed even more confused, and slightly distressed, as he asked, "What do you mean he just let you?" Ziph smiled at him as they approached the dead serpent where Dacket was just pulling the spear from its throat. Dacket handed Ziph her spear back, and Whit's mouth dropped open in shock. *Dacket and Ziph are playing games, I know she didn't make this kill. That had to be somebody else.* "You could not have taken that serpent's life. You're not even from here." Racking his brain, Whit did recall Gerara's insignia on the hunter's collar who took out the serpent. Ziph *was* wearing a Grindle uniform. This should've been Dacket's kill, and he just let her have it. None of this was making any fucking sense.

Dacket sliced the skin around the neck before he started peeling it back. "Ziph did make the kill, Whit. You were watching as she did it, and she has Gerara's insignia on her uniform. I didn't believe her at first either, but she proved me wrong. Are you two helping, or not?" Ziph joined him and grabbed hold of the skin on the opposite side of him as Whit drove his spear through the serpent's snout and nailed it into the rock with a mallet. Ziph and Dacket slowly peeled away the skin revealing the sinew and entrails as Whit moved their trucks near the skinned serpent.

Whit unloaded the carcass wraps and spread them out next to the serpent as Dacket began showing Ziph where to slice in order to peel away large slabs of meat. They worked for several hours, and when they finished, they had used up every carcass wrap they owned, barely fitting all the meat.

Ziph had finally tired out which was not normal for her, and she assumed it was an effect left over from Dacket's venom, so she sat in Dacket's truck as he and

Whit loaded the wraps vertically in the beds of the trucks. She watched intently as they finished loading everything and felt a thrill as Dacket climbed back in the truck with her.

After they were well on their way, Dacket finally broke the silence, "You may have been reckless and impulsive, which are deadly in this work, but you did well. More than well, you performed exceptionally, and I apologize for doubting you."

Giddy with his praise, Ziph gave him her brightest smile. "We did make a good team, didn't we?"

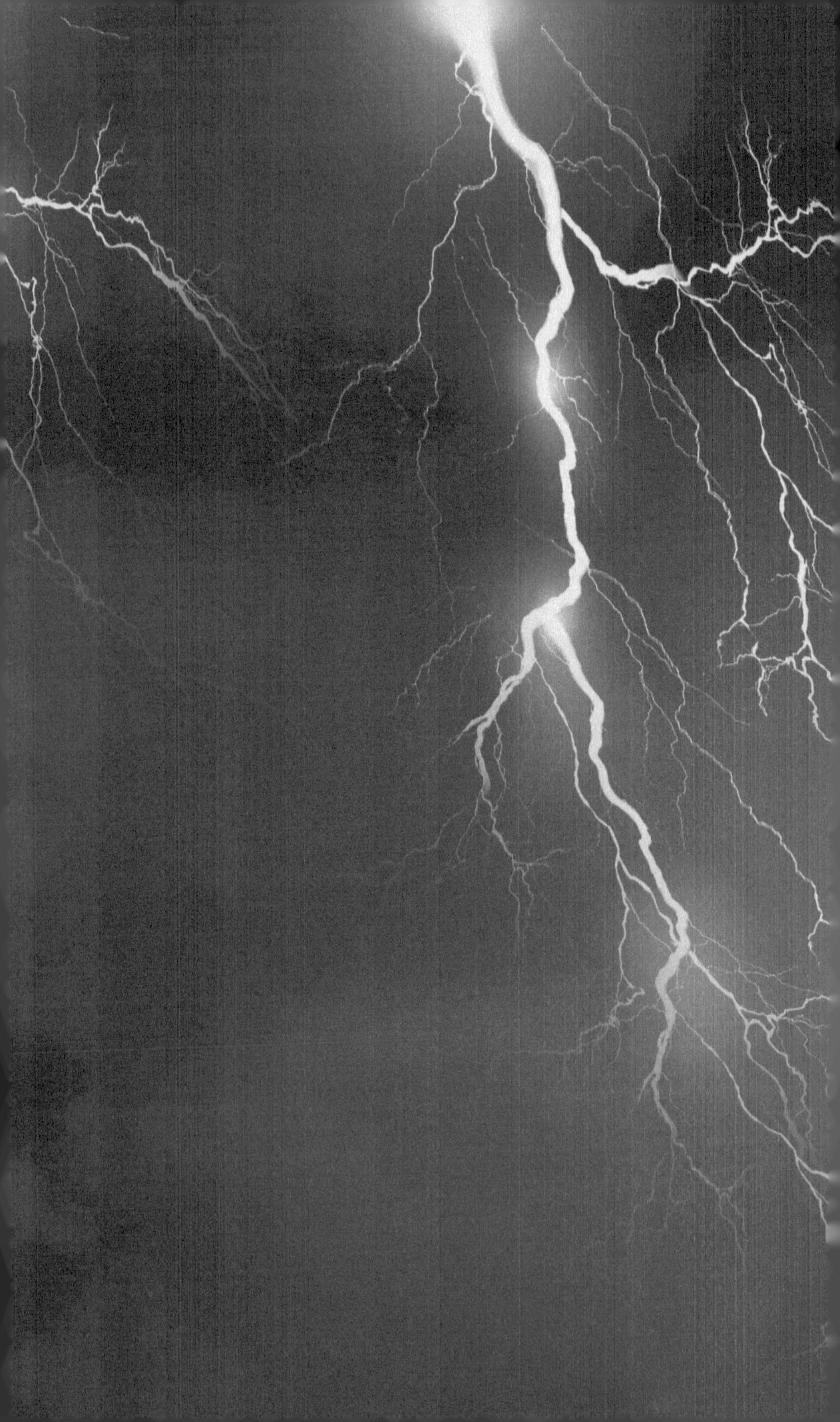

CHAPTER 11
MEAT

Ziph woke to Danny gently rubbing her shoulder. She sat up and blinked at Danny who was giggling. "What?" Danny peeled Ziph's hair from her cheek and took her hand to lead her into the bathroom connected to her new room. Ziph had fallen asleep still dressed in the reinforced hunting uniform.

When Ziph saw herself in the mirror, she yelped. She had slept on her arm, and she had the imprint of her sleeve depressed into her skin. "Oh, fuck I hate when this happens!" Ziph ran some water and splashed it on her face before huffing while Danny giggled and started for Ziph's doorway.

"Whit came by. We need to be downstairs for meat processing in an hour. I set some clothes for you on the bed." Danny explained as she leaned back on Ziph's doorframe. Ziph knew her face would still show sleeping lines for at least another hour and hoped they faded before she had to accompany Danny to the factory.

Ziph stripped everything off and groaned as she noticed dried serpent blood was all over her and her uniform, and she had stained the cream sheets on the bed. "Shit. Danny? I need to do some washing. How do you wash clothes here?"

Danny popped her head back in the room as Ziph stripped her uniform off. "We scrub them against rough stones with bar soap then dry them on lines. It's all on the rooftops."

Ziph sighed, she knew that was a possibility with the level of development their society was in. She pulled on the factory uniform Danny set out, and the black pants and matching long sleeve shirt looked like something from a movie set in a pre-space faring societies, it was rather boxy with strong seams but otherwise comfortable. Ziph tied on the rubbery apron as she asked, "Since we have a little time, can you tell me about this planet and your people?"

Ziph came out of her room, and Danny was lounging on the couch as she answered, "We need to be there early, but yes, we can talk for a little while. The gravity on north Binara is too high for anything to withstand, but with planet Barren hovering over the southern pole, and creating the sky belt where there is no gravity, there is a narrow ring of land around the southern pole where gravity is just right, and that land is the only place on the planet where we are able to survive. We have three walled cities, Adallin, Paralled, and we live in Valler. Each one functions the same to keep us safe from the serpents who grow uncontrollably large in the sky belt."

Ziph, who had sat down next to Danny while she spoke, was enthralled, and needed to know more. "Who is in charge here?"

Danny snarled as she carefully chose her words, "They're called the Kefale Royalty. All eggs are delivered to the palace for blessings from the Kefale priest as they develop, but my mother worked in the palace hatchery, and I know the truth. The practice is also so the Kefale can intercept any double headed offspring right away, and usher them into a Kefale family. All the other hatched offspring are divided up to awaiting families who have applied and qualify for children. Often it can be hard for Elarian men to fertilize eggs due to some hormonal issues when we evolved and because birthrates stay low, the Kefale also have a royal breeding program where you are called into spawning duty if you are added to the list, but the list is mostly criminals and delusional loyal people who have volunteered, saying it's a calling. Other than the egg transfer interaction with their chamber priests, we don't hear from or see them at all. None of the staff ever sees them either, only the priests. They went fully reclusive thousands of years ago, and things have been this way for as long as anyone can remember."

Ziph was horrified and bursting with curiosity at the same time. "You do realize how odd this all sounds looking in from the outside right?"

Her question made its mark as Danny snickered a bit before she answered, "Many of us hate the Kefale, but many of the rich are dedicated and receive too many lavish benefits for us to overthrow them. Plus, they have all the technology keeping us safe, which we know by passive threat, they would destroy if we challenged them. The people who hate them are all far too ingrained in their routines of comfort or fear of punishment to want to change anything. I know there are resistance groups, but they stay hidden."

A clock chimed once in the factory, and Ziph froze in place as her piercings all zinged to the sound vibrations. Danny went to look out her living room window facing down into the factory below, "That was our warning bell that morning shift begins in half an hour."

Ziph wondered how the translator was figuring time so easily. "You must have a similar time scale as one used where I am from. My translator even understands your time units."

Danny seemed intrigued. "You come from a place where you travel space too?"

Ziph didn't want to think of home too much, to keep her emotions under control, so she just stuck to facts. "Yes, but we have a complicated history in the galactic center. The world I come from is harsh and run by the rich, but I grew up with a lot of privilege, so I have a good idea of what life is like on both sides. I honestly had a lot more fun when I was poor and working at the showhouse than I ever did when I was around the Arkwright family on my father's side. The showhouse was a production with a daring dance show and horror comedy acts. I was part of the daring dance show where I used to paint my face and do stunts like flip through burning hoops in fun costumes."

Danny's eyes lit up with understanding. "That makes sense why Dacket took you hunting. I still can't believe you had the chance to go. Are they making you a hunter?"

Ziph had no idea what Dacket had planned for her. "I don't know, I think I stress him out too much, but I made the first kill last night. It's the serpent's meat we are processing today."

Danny, who was still standing at the window, threw her hands out and yelled, "WHAT?" and Ziph smiled awkwardly as she shrugged as she answered, "I studied biology back home, so I knew where to aim the spear to take it out in one quick blow."

Danny stood with her arms out and mouth hanging open, "You're telling me the same woman who called Dacket a 'big-sexy-dick-I-wanna-lick bossy man' went out and killed a serpent with no serpent hunter's training?"

Ziph sat up a little straighter at Danny's praise, and she added, "It was the largest one too."

Danny threw her hands up and walked to the door. "You're about to have every hunter in this Sector wanting to simultaneously kill and fuck you. I bet unless it's hunting, Dacket never lets you leave the house again." Danny laughed, and Ziph followed her into the hallway where Trent was coming out of his door to start his gate shift.

Seeing Trent, Danny blurted, "Ziph killed the biggest serpent in last night's hunt."

Trent stood shocked and couldn't hide it as he stared at Ziph. "You killed the biggest serpent? Is that why I heard Dacket leaving earlier to alert the standby shift at the next factory they will be needed. I could hear them through my door when he and Whit were talking about the kill, I can't believe that was you they were talking about."

Ziph grinned with pride as it registered that she had already made a name for herself. *I hate that I have to kill the big, beautiful snakes, but I think I'm going to be really good at this job.*

When they reached the bottom of the stairs, Danny led them from the hallway connecting the stairs to the garage level, through the back of the meat market, and into the processing factory just on the other side. The meat market and factory shared a freezer, and Ziph marveled at the use of geothermal technology to freeze and heat the buildings. The setup was visible along the wall of the factory, and she could see the frozen lines flowing into the freezer, while the hot water lines spread out to the apartments above.

The factory was nothing more than long stainless-steel butchering tables which stretched the length of the enormous space. Ziph could tell the factory backed up to the great wall around the city, but the windows along the sides and roof revealed nothing other than tall metal buildings around them. She bet all the windows were to let in solar light and heat. Although they were warm blooded, they still evolved from snakes, and she bet a few of their old tendencies still carried over. *For a factory, especially a meat factory, this space is very aesthetically pleasing.*

A few big men in uniforms matching Ziph came in from the freezer with the wrapped slabs of meat she, Dacket, and Whit had sliced from the snake carcass the night before. She bet the wildlife from the sky belt would scavenge what was left as she contemplated what those giant serpents were eating out there. She would need to ask about that later, for now, she had a giant piece of meat she needed to focus on cutting up with Danny. She watched as Danny made long cuts to make a specific size of rectangular brick of meat. Ziph followed her lead and made the same cuts.

"Perfect. When we finish this table, there is a bell at the end we can ring. It signals the market workers, and they will come out and collect the bricks for wrapping and stocking." Danny returned to her work, and Ziph followed suit. The two spent several hours dicing through one full table as others trickled in and began butchering along with them. She used her disassociation superpowers, and the time seemed to pass by in a snap. *I wonder if I look as stupid as I feel when I zone out.*

The mid-day bell rang, and Ziph closed her eyes as she waited for the chiming to stop. Her lady parts were singing in soprano now that she was in the same room as the bell, and she wanted to slide her hands over her nipples and cross her legs, but she attempted to ignore it. Feeling the sensation of someone staring at her, she slowly scanned the room but didn't notice anyone. As her eyes roamed the windows, she noticed a dark figure looming in the top spread of windows. She could feel Danny come up behind her to look where she was. "That's Dacket. He sometimes watches from up there. That bell means your shift is over. Since you're an apprentice hunter, you only have one factory shift." Ziph was still staring up at Dacket through the windows as a cloud moved and allowed the daylight to shine in his windows, illuminating his neon yellow skin.

He seemed to be looking right at her, and Ziph quickly turned back to Danny and handed over her heavy knife. "I'll see you upstairs in a few hours then. I need to do some washing while you're working. Want to go dancing under Eight again?"

Danny lit up with excitement, "Of course, I always want to dance under Eight. Tonight, I think we should try a place that sounds like your old job, like a showhouse."

Ziph was so thrilled she could hardly form words correctly. "YES! I would love that. Do they wear different makeup, like exaggerated around the eyes and a big wide smile?"

Danny bit her lip and smiled as she nodded. "That sounds exactly like the makeup the performers wear, I cannot wait to take you. It's called Dare. They have amazing drinks too."

Ziph waved to Danny as she made her way through the back of the meat market and into the garage. She waved to Trent who was perched on a stool, which was too small, while reading a newspaper before she began climbing the stairs.

When she reached her room, she changed into some lounge clothes Danny gave her, a loose crop and some sweatpants, before she collected her hunting gear and bedsheets in a heap. She continued up the stairs and opened the roof access door after passing Dacket and Whit's level. *I wonder what Dacket is doing in there. I bet Whit is in his apartment practicing some self-care, something I really needed to work on. Maybe I could talk to Whit about having a self-care day, except this time, not paralyzed.* She laughed to herself, thinking about how sweet Whit had been to her while she couldn't move. She was also remembering all the naughty looks he was giving her, and she couldn't help wanting so much more. She wanted to see all those delicious looks from him again.

Just as she began scrubbing her bedsheets, Whit joined her on the rooftop with a basket of his laundry. "Well, hello. How was your beauty sleep after you stole the entire show last night? By the way, I apologize that I could not accept it was you who made that kill because you looked like a professional. It was magical watching you slide right up the center and make the kill in one shot."

Whit sat right next to her, and she ate up the attention. "Danny is taking me to Dare tonight. Do you want to go?"

Whit thought for a moment, before he agreed, "That does sound fun. Sure, you and Danny come over after her shift, and we can do our makeup at my place."

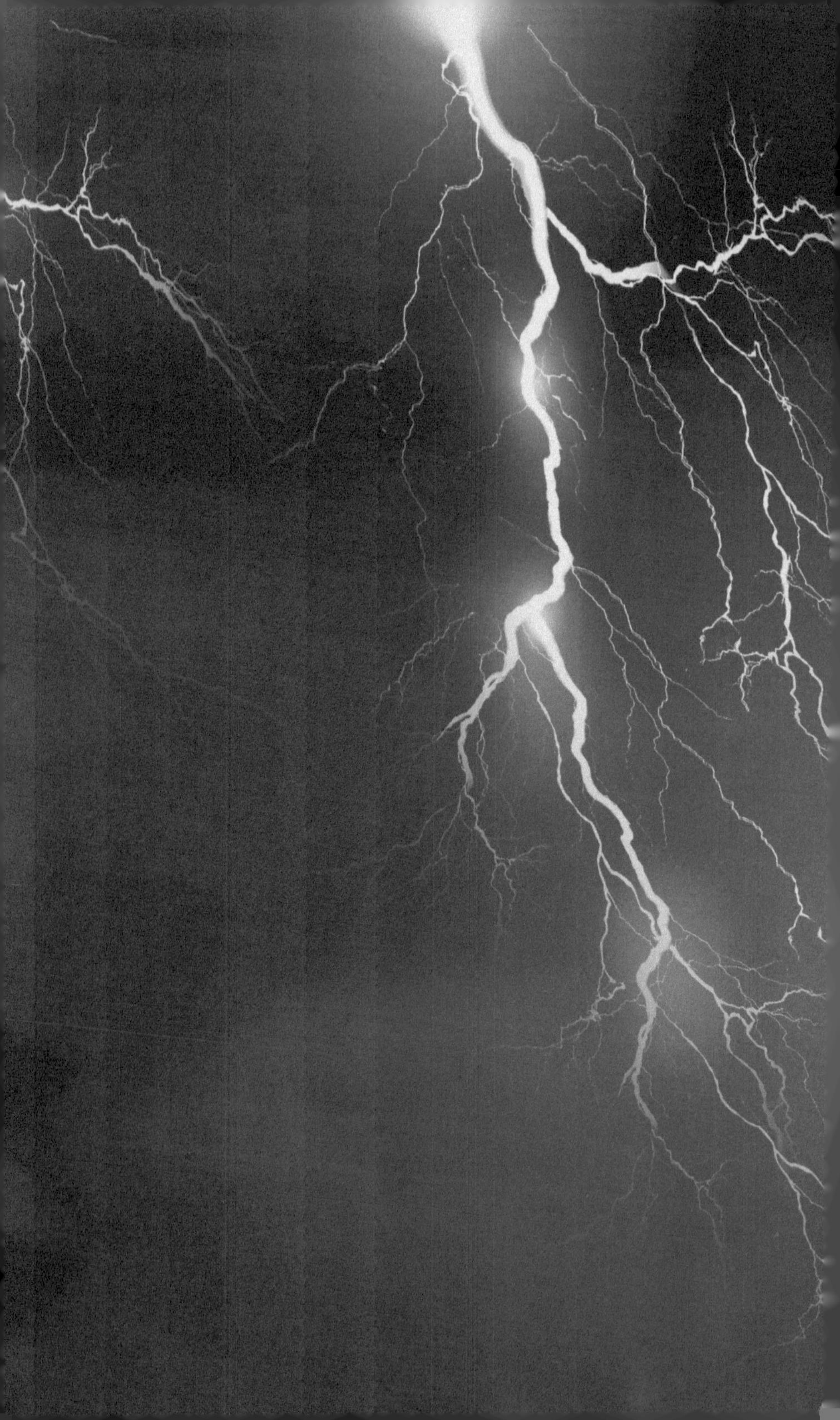

CHAPTER 12
DARE

Whit, Danny, and Ziph sat in a line on the floor in front of a giant mirror in Whit's apartment with makeup spread out in front of them. The popular look for Dare was a dark stripe of makeup, any color, all the way across the face at eye level. Danny and Ziph chose a matte brown dark enough to look black while Whit chose a matte black.

Ziph picked a soft pink for her lips while Danny had a deep red. She was astonished Whit was able to select a color for a blush, it was a warm brown, and it looked rosy on his forest green cheeks. Whit was still deciding as he held up a black and a grey tone.

Danny and Ziph both answered in unison, "Black." Whit pursed his lips and whipped his tail behind him. "That was easy." Whit applied his lipstick like a professional, and Ziph loved watching him. When they were finished Whit led them into his closest, "I'm more into masculine clothing now, but I have plenty of old dresses on the back rack from when I was younger. I never even wore most of them, and they don't come close to fitting me now, so have at it."

As they looked through the dresses, Ziph and Danny were overcome by the beautiful fabrics and varied styles. With her tail flitting back-and-forth at the tip, Ziph noticed something about Whit's closest, everything seemed to be for the same season. "Do you not have seasons here?"

Whit and Danny looked to one another strangely before Whit seemed to understand, "Whatever word you used before 'here' doesn't translate."

Understanding fell over Ziph. "Where I am from the planets often have a wobble which causes seasons to occur, or changes in weather patterns, which are consistent over months and years."

Whit and Danny finally understood, and Whit explained, "We don't have 'seasons' as you call it. We don't really have time or energy within our society for much science, so I couldn't tell you why. Except for Gerara, but she's into some weird shit."

Ziph wondered if the planet Barren was once a moon to Binara, and if they didn't have seasons because when Barren was caught and suspended in place under the southern pole, it shifted and stabilized Binara's spin to be perfectly vertical on its axis. *That's so cool. I wonder if it's true.*

They picked out lightweight black sleeveless dresses. Danny wore a shorter skirt while Ziph wore a long one to conceal her tail. Whit wore a black long sleeve shirt with sharp and boxy cut black pants.

As they went down the stairs, they passed by Dacket, and he had his hands filled with bags. When he reached Ziph, she felt like he stole a piece of her soul the way his auburn eyes bore into her. Every time she was near him, it left her breathless, and her skin heated to the point of needing a cold shower. She knew it was super fucked up, but she kind of wanted him to bite her again or maybe she really wanted him to bite her again, but without the venom. *I just wish he didn't have venom, so when he did bite me, we would still be able to have sex afterward, and that would be the entire point. Maybe he could just tie me up. That's basically the same thing, right? Maybe Dacket will be my first. That's one thing I am keeping perfectly concealed. I don't want any of these men knowing I've never done the deed.* She didn't know what the social expectations were here, but she had her own and that was enough. *I saved it for a stupid reason. Now I regret it, and I don't want to explain it. I should've known better than to fall for religious bullshit. How do you stop centering a religion in your life when it was all you ever knew before? I need to stop praying to gods who either don't exist or don't care. Bunch of fucking assholes convincing people to save themselves and not pursue relationships, and for what? Some mythical reward for real life sacrifice? Who the fuck knows what comes after we die anyway?*

Everyone back home had been led to believe she had sex, and was over it, choosing to stay celibate. She really didn't want to explain the pledge to Venus, and the reality was, she was too awkward and uncomfortable to do anything with anyone. She had never even been able to figure out how to pleasure herself enough for an orgasm either, which had technically been against the stupid rules, but she tried anyway. She had spent hours trying, to no favorable results. If she couldn't figure it out for herself, the last thing she wanted was some man down there fiddling around.

That was also how she ended up with piercings because she had seen an advertisement suggesting they helped with stimulation. *So much for that.* She stumbled a bit and realized that she needed to snap out of her thoughts and pay attention to where she was walking.

They climbed into Whit's truck, and Ziph noticed right away that Whit had a bit of dust in his truck and some smudges on the glass while Dacket's was glossy and spotless. Whit's apartment had seemed much more lived in to. Maybe Dacket was just an exceptionally clean person. *Why does he also seem like he's hiding something? He's so secretive and quiet when I'm not stressing him out to the end of his rope. Ugh, rope. Can the man just tie me up and fuck me already? I would gladly take any of them.*

When they arrived at the parking lot, Whit came to a stop before pointing across the street. "There is a palace guard. I wonder what they're plotting over here?"

Danny leaned over the seat and scowled, "Honestly, right now, all I care about is attempting to see the guy I kissed." Whit chuckled a bit as he opened his door and climbed out, and Danny and Ziph did the same.

Whit led them through the maze of hallways and doors leading to the underground, and when they reached the darkened underground road, Dare was right in front of them. The band was playing on a lit-up stage in the back while a balcony filled with people surrounded a lower pit. In the pit was a show much like the one she performed in back on Emendo at the showhouse. Whit led them to a little cove where they could see while sitting at a table. He leaned over to Ziph, who was hopelessly entranced by the flipping and twirling dance happening on stage. "I see you are thoroughly enjoying this."

His voice pulled her back into reality, and Ziph turned to grin at him. "This was my former career. I loved it more than I can put into words. To be able to see it in a different form on a world in a completely different galaxy is honestly making me so happy I could burst." She scooted closer to Whit and she remembered how he treated her when she was paralyzed, and she felt he was one of the safest men she had ever met. She felt the same way about Dacket and Trent. He slid his arm around her and pulled her close as a younger man came to take their order, "What will it be?"

Whit ordered, "I'll have the house brew while the ladies want the top shelf mixed drink. I know you always have a delightful one."

Danny beamed as she spotted the man she had previously kissed, "I will be back."

She disappeared into the crowd and a few minutes passed before the waiter came back with the drinks. Danny spun toward the table, grabbed her drink, and disappeared back into the crowd. Whit leaned over to Ziph as he reached for his drink. "She must have found her make-out partner."

Ziph laughed as she tried her drink. It was a mix of fruit juices, and she couldn't taste anything but sweet peach and cherry. "This is deceptively strong isn't it." Ziph could already feel herself warming inside from the drink.

Whit leaned his brew back to drink some before setting it back down. *He is so damn beautiful, I love when men wear makeup.* Whit noticed her looking at him, and he returned the stare, leaning over to brush her hair from her shoulder. She felt so warm inside, for more than one reason, and she didn't want to look away from him.

He wordlessly stroked the back of his hand against her jaw before he reached around her waist and tugged her into his lap by her hips. Ziph leaned into him, and he gently moved her hair around her shoulder before she felt him brush his fingers down her neck. He moved closer to smell her hair and then moved to her neck, brushing his nose against her skin. She could feel his heated breath at her neck, and she couldn't help it as she ground into his lap. His lips finally touched her skin, and she leaned her head to the side to allow him more access. *Please give me something, I just want to know what it's like.*

Whit kissed up her neck to right under her ear, and whispered, "You're not too experienced are you, Golden Girl?" Ziph slowly turned to look at him. She couldn't bring herself to admit it, but her face must've betrayed her as usual. "It's alright. We can't do much anyway." He leaned forward, to ghost his lips against her skin and continued, "Too bad Dacket's venom lasts so long. I imagined so much more when I was painting your pretty fingernails and toenails. Maybe one day we can recreate that moment with rope and have a lot more fun when we do."

Bitch, if you don't breathe, you're going to die. Ziph felt as though Whit had stolen her thoughts as she melted at his proposal of her fantasy. *Air, I need air. Breathe right now.*

Ziph knew he could sense it somehow because she felt him smile against her neck before he twisted her around to straddle him, "That does sound fun to you Golden Girl, I can see the center of your chest beginning to warm." Whit pulled her in to kiss her, and when their mouths met, he was gentle and slow. Ziph felt him reach around her plentiful ass and squeeze it before pressing her into his lap. She pressed her pussy against him, and when she noticed him tense under her, she felt him split open and there was movement happening inside.

She froze, and Whit grinned as he pressed her onto what were clearly four devious moving parts under her.

Two of them were moving under her pussy while the other two were wriggling toward the back. Ziph gasped, and Whit pulled her face close to his. "When we are ready, including you, we have a nice surprise for you."

Ziph could have fallen from his lap at the realization. *This man has a four-armed penis and that is probably standard for his people. Venus, I swear I will be the best damn girl ever, I just want one of those four prong wiggling dicks in me at least once. Wait, who is we? I know he said we. WHEN we are ready? What does that mean?!*

Grabbing her face and caressing her lips with his, Whit held her by the back of her neck while he slid his tongue past her teeth, pushing it against her tongue. He kissed her until the end of the song, and he didn't move for more, no matter how much Ziph wanted it. Something told her she would be forced to wait a lot longer than she wanted before these men did anything more with her than kiss. No matter what Whit said, something told her they were waiting on Dacket.

He reached around her and drank down the rest of his brew before he squeezed her hips. "Danny is coming, and I see how tired you are. I assume you're ready to go home?"

"I am tired. You're right, we should probably get some rest." Ziph slid off Whit's lap, and he wrapped his tail around her ankle as Danny came up, a picture of beaming happiness. "He had to leave, but I have a name now, Doyle. He frequently visits here, so we will have to come back soon!"

Ziph was excited for her as she slid in the alcove. "Are you ready? We had a long night, and then we had long day, and now that I've had a drink, I feel really tired." Danny agreed, and they all moved out of the alcove. Whit tossed some coins on the table for their drinks before they walked back to the truck.

I can't believe I had my first kiss, and it was a bad-ass hot hunter who wears makeup. That wasn't a goal of mine, but it should have been. The ride back was uneventful, and when Ziph made it back to her room, she discovered she had forgotten her drying laundry on the roof. *I'm really glad I have a good personality and a nice smile because I am awful at this life thing.* She came out and Danny had already closed her door for the night.

She left the apartment and went up the stairs for the roof access door. When she pushed the door open, the last thing she expected was Dacket standing there, admiring the stars with his hands in his pockets. He was the most handsome thing she'd ever seen. These men made her melt every time.

The door closed behind her, and when the door clicked, he turned around, and as he saw her, he pulled his hands from his pockets. "What brings you to the roof this time of night?"

"I forgot my laundry." She pointed to the sheets and hunting uniform gently moving in the breeze. Holding his eyes on her, Dacket went quiet long enough for her to count her breaths, four.

"Did you have fun tonight?"

With her tail flitting at the tip, Ziph moved toward the laundry and began collecting it. "Yes. It was a lot like where I performed back home."

When she turned, he was standing much closer. "We start your training tomorrow morning. Make sure you get some rest tonight."

Dacket seemed to taste the scent of the air around her as he leaned in and brushed her hair away from her neck where Whit left black kisses on her skin. "You and Whit had fun I see." Dacket gently stroked a finger down her neck over the kiss marks, giving her a shiver that slithered down her spine. He slowly backed away and opened the roof access door. Without another word, he disappeared downstairs and left Ziph wanting to fall over on the roof top and stay there forever. *What in the fuck just happened*

? Does he want me too? I can't fucking tell whether he really does or not, and now I must somehow sleep?! Venus, this better be heading somewhere good, bitch, because if it's not, I will curse you for the rest of time.

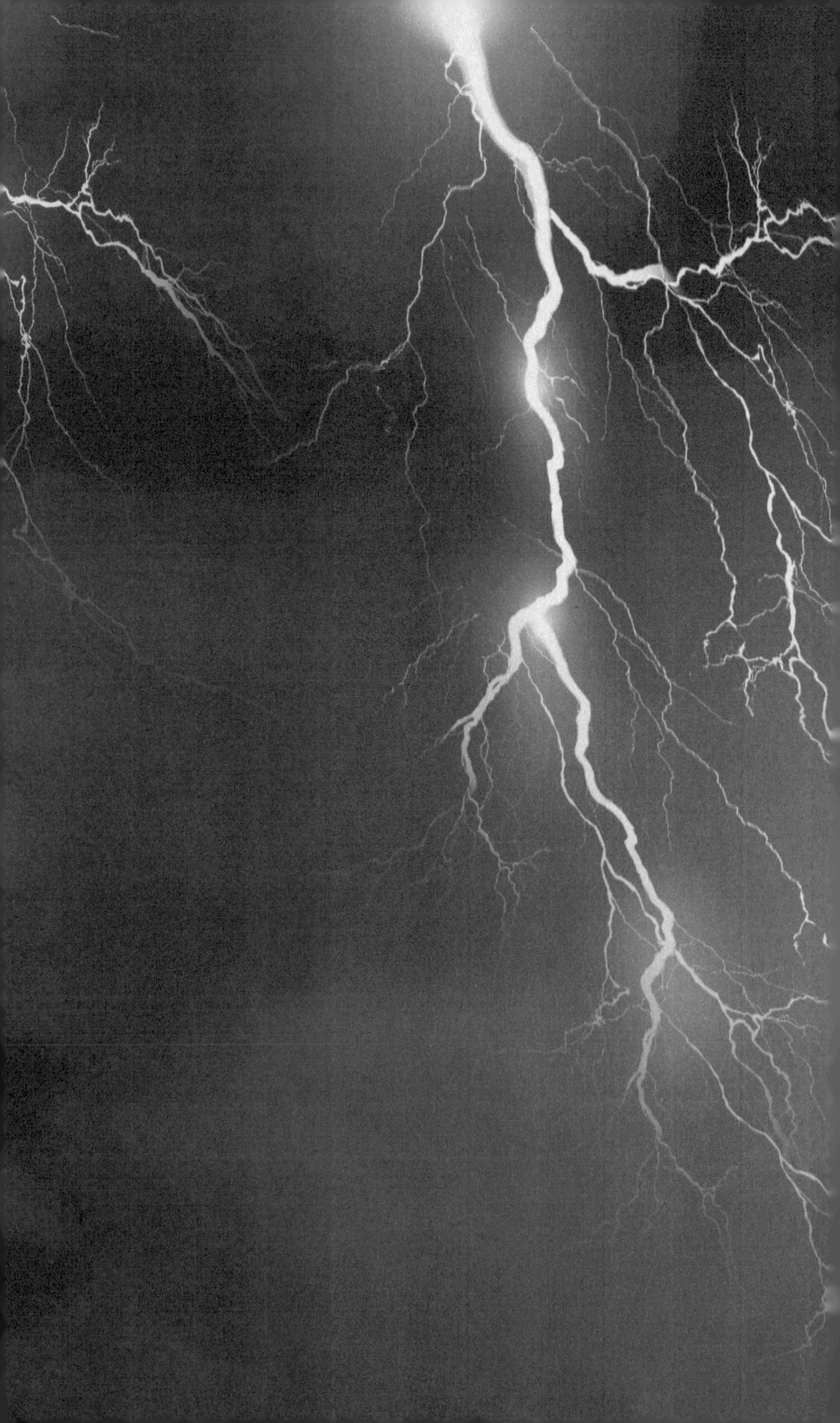

CHAPTER 13
TRAINING

Ziph somehow fell asleep after she put her bed back together, and she stood outside her apartment door early like Danny suggested. When Dacket came down the stairs in his hunting uniform, strapped with weapons, Ziph filled with heat all over again, and she wanted to strip it off and suck whatever was happening downstairs.

His tail coiled at the tip and uncoiled, and he seemed pleased she was ready early, "Were you able to sleep?"

Cringing inside, Ziph nodded, and asked, "What kind of training are we doing today?" *I need to change the subject.*

"We are sky dancing to learn formation. It's just you and I this time, but next time Whit said he wants to join. We want to rehearse your kill method so we can implement it. The Kefale released an update saying the serpent numbers are high this year. The zero-gravity environment allows them to keep growing to the point where they need to seek out larger prey. We know these upcoming months will be brutal, and we need to be prepared." Dacket led her to the garage where his truck was parked, and they climbed in.

Ziph was oozing with pride as she sat down in the passenger seat of Dacket's truck. It always smelled so fresh, and today she could tell he had deep cleaned it again. *I probably annoy the hell out of this man, and I feel like that's a good thing. It definitely feels right.*

They took off for the gate Dacket always used, Nine. This time when they passed through there was no one paying attention, and Dacket sighed with annoyance. He hated when they didn't take down his truck number because he could be questioned about it when he came back.

As they traveled at a steady pace, Ziph did her best to stay quiet, but she was busting at the seams. She honestly wanted to chat Dacket's ear off, but was holding back because she knew exactly how hard it could be dealing with someone who talks too much. *I've been ditched more times than I can count because of my big mouth. The last thing I want to do is take it too far and make these new people not want to be around me anymore.* She pushed away the memories of her friends, *or I guess they were never really my friends.*

Dacket could tell something was happening as Ziph wiggled in her seat as the tip of her tail whorled around. "Are you alright?"

Shit I knew I was moving too much. "Yes, I just have a lot of energy sometimes, and it's hard to keep it contained." Ziph tried to make it as short and to the point as she could.

Dacket's truck was on tracked wheels so he could release the wheel, and the truck would stay steady. He rested his hands on his thighs, before he asked, "Why are you trying to contain it?" Dacket was sincerely confused.

Ziph had a long history of being the obnoxious one of

her friend group, and they made sure she knew it. She was well aware it was due to her impulsivity and talkativeness. She couldn't blame them; she knew she was a lot. "I tend to be too much to handle sometimes." Ziph hadn't realized how much it would hurt to admit that. *I can't help the way I am. Why can't I just be calm like everyone else?*

Dacket slowed to a stop, and waited for her to look at him, and he seemed genuinely upset for her. "What is it you want to say?"

Holy mother Venus help me. What do I say, because I'm about to blurt out how much I want to sit on his dick. "Err, I, um, well, I guess, you are really quiet, and I feel like I am disrupting your peace." *I went from dick sitting to blurting out a deep self-revelation. Really? I should've said the dick thing.* He stared at her as he tried to find a way to respond. Ziph felt terrible, "I'm alright. I don't need to talk all the time anyway. I should learn to be quieter like you."

Dacket cringed inside. He was quiet because he was a hunter, and he didn't have the heart to grow too close to anyone. He wasn't sure how Whit coped with just the hunter part of it, but Dacket also couldn't bear the idea of leaving someone behind who he was in love with if he were killed in a hunt. He loved Whit and Trent, and they were his best friends, but he knew they would go on and live happy lives if he ever died hunting. He lived a lonely and empty existence, and he needed it to stay that way. "I don't think anyone should be more like me."

He pressed the accelerator, and they were moving again, but she could tell Dacket was still stuck. Ziph felt like he was holding back, but she didn't dare ask. No matter how bad she wanted to talk, she held back her chatter, and by the time they arrived, Ziph felt like crawling in a hole and dying. All her thrill about hunting practice had faded watching Dacket slide deeper into himself beside her. *What burden is he carrying which is so heavy he doesn't feel like he can share it?*

Ziph felt them roll over a crevasse, and the truck dipped before it lifted a little further than it did when the gravity was stronger. She wished the lessening gravity made emotions lighter too. It did not matter what the gravity was, for she still felt like she was carrying a load of bricks as she climbed out and took in the incredible sights. The planet Barren came so close to the planet Binara. They seemed to touch until standing as close as she was, where she could see the two planetary surfaces were still many miles apart.

She wanted to swim through the greenery flowing in the winds. It looked like the giant kelp swaying in the seas of Keru. She knew it was as tall as the giant trees on her home world Vidar, and swimming through it would result in her being eaten by a serpent, but she could dream. *Who knows, it might be worth it even if I did get eaten.* Remembering the hunter who was eaten recently, she quickly changed her mind. *So, maybe that is a terrible idea.*

When Dacket had the gear he was collecting from the back, he came around the truck and stood in front of Ziph and reached out to hand her one of two round devices. She took it from him, and she couldn't help but notice how sorrowful he still seemed, so she whispered, "Are you alright?"

He wasn't, but he lied, "I am." He paused before he said anything more. He wasn't sure how much deflecting Ziph would accept. "Are you ready to practice? These devices will send random jets of air from various sides causing it to shoot off in different directions. When we approach the sky belt, we will throw them in the air one at a time. They allow us to imitate the occasional erratic movements of the serpents so we can become faster with our reactions. I want to practice your method of a single hunter kill, so I think today we should aim to just circle and then capture the device."

Ziph nodded and followed him as he began the long walk to the lower gravity belt. Every time she started walking faster to catch up, he would move even faster, and he was almost running by the time Ziph felt the gravity reduce enough to take long strides. Something inside told her to reach out to him, that he was holding so much back, and she just needed to pry a bit to lift away the hard surface.

Ziph wasn't chasing anyone, or anything though, so if this man didn't want her to pursue him, she wouldn't. She already had her hopes on Trent and Whit anyway, either one would be wonderful men to be with, or just have fun with. She was young, and it didn't really matter.

Dacket was becoming harder to keep up with as he moved into the lower gravity area, and when he finally lifted off, Ziph almost felt like he was trying to ditch her, or maybe he was having an emotional moment, and she needed to back off and leave him alone for a bit.

Ziph slowed some, and when she felt herself lift from the ground entirely, she activated her jets and reluctantly followed him into the sky. He finally reached a height where she remembered the head of the serpent reaching before she watched as he turned to speak to her, but she was still making her way to him. *He didn't even realize he was moving that fast. I wish I knew what has him so rattled.*

His tail, which had been excitedly whipping back-and-forth to keep him balanced, drooped, and he paused what he planned to say until she neared. His voice seemed distant as he asked, "Are you ready? Toss yours first." Ziph nodded and tossed her device in the air in front of them.

They circled it several times before Dacket swung in underneath to grab the device. He whistled when he snatched it from the air. "That was much easier than I expected. Do you want to run it again?"

Ziph was still feeling odd from their discussion in the truck, but she agreed anyway. They ran through the routine many times over the course of the day before Dacket leveled out by Ziph and tossed the device toward his truck. It would take a while, but it would eventually make it there like Ziph's, which was sitting next to his truck.

"Usually with an apprenticeship I would have you run sky dance drills, but since you use the jets better than most of the experienced hunters, I feel that we can skip that part," Dacket explained, but Ziph was already thinking about something completely different.

"Why don't you ever go with any of us when we party under Eight?" Ziph watched his inner lights fade away like she had flipped the switch. *Fuck, I should've just kept my big mouth shut.*

It took Dacket a few seconds to respond, "It's not for me." Ziph hated his cryptic responses, but there was nothing she could say. He was technically her boss now, and she wasn't sure what was appropriate on this world, but on hers that was a smashing no. *I hope that's not a thing here.*

He stared at her for some time before he tipped his head to the horizon where the system star would be setting in a few hours. "We should return home, it will be dark soon." Ziph agreed, and they skated along the air until they could walk back to the truck. This time Dacket didn't seem eager to run away from her, or whatever he was running from.

When they put away the training devices, they climbed in the truck, but before Dacket started it, he asked, "Can I ask you something?"

Ziph turned to give him her attention. "Why did you smell like you rubbed a serpent's asshole juice all over you when I found you?"

Ziph burst into laughter. She knew the translator had made a mistake, but she couldn't help it. "I'm assuming you intended to say anal gland scent, but it translated as asshole juice." Dacket tried to hide a smile but failed miserably as Ziph resumed laughing. "Sometimes the translators do some strange things."

Venus, his smile alone could kill a sweet old lady, why the fuck are you dangling this gorgeous man in my face? Venus, I think I hate you more than I have ever hated anything in my life. His smile faded, but he didn't seem near as closed off as he was when they arrived. The drive was slow, and Ziph couldn't help but wiggle in her seat. Long travels were not her thing, at all.

Long before they reached the gate, she had pulled her legs into the seat and crossed them three times, and now she had them spread and was stretching the best she could.

"Are you alright? Do I need to stop?" Dacket seemed genuinely concerned, and Ziph tried not to giggle. "I'm sorry, I'll hold still."

Dacket seemed perplexed, "Are you sure?" Ziph bit her

lips in her mouth and nodded as she slid her hands under her thighs.

It took her about two minutes to start moving again, and Dacket had to ask, "You seem very agitated with the seat. Are you uncomfortable?"

Ziph stared at him and wondered if she should try to explain or try to sit still. *Fuck it, if I show him who I am, and he ditches me like everyone else, so be it.* "I have some impulsivity and hyperactivity issues. I'm sorry if I'm bothering you," Ziph admitted quietly.

They were only around halfway home when Dacket stopped the truck and climbed out before coming to her side and opening the door to help her out. Ziph was confused, "What are we doing?"

Dacket simply held his hand out. "You said you have hyperactivity, so let's walk, and then you can rest." Ziph was speechless, no one had ever suggested something like taking a walk. Everyone always just expected her to gain control of it, even though it always felt so impossible. When she found the showhouse and started exercising more, she was able to rest easier.

Dacket seemed like he wanted to talk about something, but he stayed silent as they walked toward the bright setting star. The flat rocky terrain seemed to stretch forever, and she could hear a faint rumble from a storm in the distance. When Ziph felt like she had expended the energy she reached out to tap Dacket on the arm. "I think I'll be able to sit still now."

He turned to her and frowned as his tail coiled behind him. "This wasn't so you would sit still. This was so you would want to." Ziph had never felt so revealed and acknowledged, unfortunately for Dacket, that meant her flood gates just burst open.

"Thank you." Ziph held her breath trying not to cry, and thankfully for her, Dacket turned and started back to the truck, and as he walked, he stayed in front of her. Tears flowed down her cheeks, silently dripping from her chin, and for once they were happy tears.

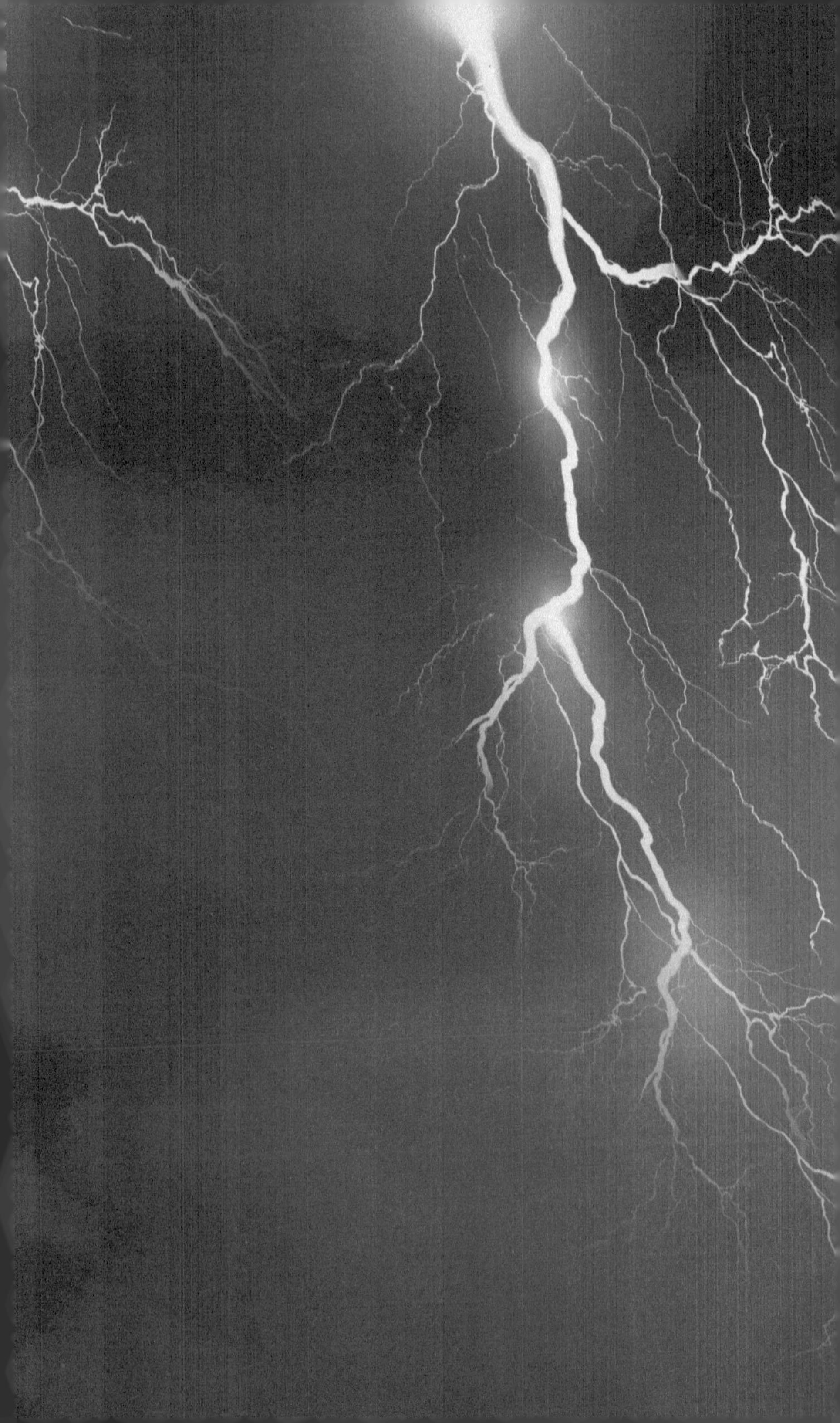

CHAPTER 14
HORMONES

Groaning as she heard, and felt, the bell ring from the meat factory, Ziph curled up in bed and grasped her breasts in her hands. *If I could just get ONE of these snake men to figure out how to make me orgasm. Venus, do you hear me bitch? I can't take this torture anymore! Oh, fuck, I think my cheek is leaking.*

Ziph's eyes popped open, and she flew out of her bed with her tail straight up behind her. "Venus, fucking help me, my hormone blocker is wearing off!" *I forgot all about it! No wonder I've been wanting to screw these snake men so hard!* Rubus females produced a strong sexual hormone and pheromone during their mating phase when they weren't in hibernation. Unfortunately for Ziph, with her condition of no hibernation cycle, she was doomed to be trapped in a perpetual mating cycle. She had always taken care of the issue with an implanted hormone blocker. It needed to be replaced once a year, but there was likely no such thing on this planet.

Her heart wrenched in a ball in her chest as she tried to take in a breath. She was about to project some of the most potent mating pheromones in the galaxy. They bottle the stuff after extracting it from Rubus in heat because it was a strong aphrodisiac no matter what species you were. It came from little ducts in her cheeks, and she could taste it secreting into her mouth, and she knew if she spit it out the, scent would magnify, and if she swallowed it, she would just concentrate her own misery. She gagged as she swallowed it down because that was her only choice. *Now what the fuck am I going to do?!*

Her mind went straight to the one person she knew had iron restraint Dacket. Heaving in breaths and holding them for a few seconds trying to halt her panic was making her dizzy as she rushed to wash. She dressed in some simple black leggings and a cream distressed T shirt Danny gave her. It was too early for shift change, but she popped her head out into the hallway first before she ran up the stairs, skipping three steps at a time. When she made it to Dacket's door, she was sweating and could already smell the hormones returning in her sweat. The heavier pheromones would begin any moment. She could tell the taste was becoming more concentrated, it was sickly sweet, and she gagged once again trying to force it down her throat. She softly knocked on Dacket's door, and she could hear his steps coming from his bedroom as he crossed the floor.

There was a pause before he opened his door, and Ziph whispered, "Oh, no," as she took in the profound yearning in his eyes the moment he opened it. His pupils expanding from slits to saucers instantly, Dacket's eyes glistened as he licked his lips, "Can I help you?"

"Can I come inside?" Ziph wasn't so sure Dacket would even be able to hold himself back as he opened his door and leaned in to smell her as she passed by to sit on his couch.

With a mesmerized and slightly distressed expression, Dacket shut his door and followed her to the couch before he sat on the little table in front of her and leaned forward. "Why do you smell like heaven?"

Ziph gulped and tried to keep her mouth as closed as possible, only speaking through a sliver of space between her lips. "I produce a pheromone during my mating cycle, but I'm stuck in a mating cycle all the time, so now that my hormone blocker is wearing off, everyone in two blocks will probably want to hunt me down and fuck me."

Not moving away from her, Dacket bit his lip before he nodded. "I have someone I can call on, but I can't guarantee anything."

Ziph tried to smile but failed and felt awkward, so as usual she blurted out the truth, "I came to you because, I guess, if I have to endure being used for my body until I die, it might as well be someone kind and someone who I actually like." She scowled at herself, yet continued after she wished she hadn't said that. "We don't have very long, and if I don't find a way to block it, it will be so intense I'll probably need to stay in the caves out by the sky belt."

Desperately trying to restrain himself, Dacket reached up and put his hand against her face. "I won't let anything like that happen. If you are unwilling, no one would ever put their hands on you if I can stop it. None of us here would allow that to happen. We would kill for much less. I want you to lock my door when I leave, I will wake Whit and tell him what's happening. I know of a hunter who secretly dabbles in biochemistry. She could have something to help."

Ziph nodded, tears forming in her eyes as Dacket

rubbed his thumb against her cheek. The bell rang in the factory and Ziph squeezed her eyes shut and slapped her hands over her breasts. She struggled through the sound before she looked back at Dacket who had intently watched everything. A rush of hormones had Ziph giving up trying to hold her mouth shut, and she panted with need. Dacket took a long deep breath and closed his eyes, his tail coiled up and he shook his head. "I need to go, quickly." Ziph agreed in her mind, but her body was screaming as she reached out and grabbed Dacket's hand while he tried to rise to his feet.

He held her hand tightly as he stared down at her, and something told her she was not going to like what he had to say. "I know what I am experiencing now is the power of your pheromones, but make no mistake, you are just as intoxicating without them. The only difference is now my inhibitions have been pulled away like a curtain and nothing is concealing the truth. None of that matters though, I can't be with you or anyone else. That's not for people like me." Dacket didn't explain further as he kissed her hand and disappeared through his doorway. She slowly approached and latched his door, locking it. *What did he mean by I can't be with you, or anyone else?* Was Dacket part of some celibacy pact or was this part of what he had been hiding?

Ziph heard the bell starting again for shift change in the factory, and being in Dacket's apartment brought her much closer to the bell. When it rang this time, she groaned and ended up in a pile on the floor. Her piercings vibrated so perfectly she swore if they continued, she might be able to have an actual orgasm.

What bullshit to be born with a never-ending mating cycle, but never able to orgasm. Honestly, Venus, I'm starting to think you're quite the smelly cunt. Ziph could hear Dacket's muffled speech from where she lay on the ground by the door, so she scooted across the floor and put her ear by the crack so she could hear what he was saying to Whit. "... cannot resist her. Soon no one near our building will be able to. I read about the animal she comes from. The pheromones stretch for miles to call in a mating chase. I told her to keep my door locked while I call on Gerara Grindle, so do not let anyone near that door."

Ziph could feel the pheromone nodules which had finished reforming in her mouth, and she grimaced, the process was moving exceedingly fast. She had no idea she could transform into her breeding state so rapidly. This had never happened to her before. Every single year she was on time for her appointment with the endocrinologist on Vidar who had kept seeing her digitally, even though she had no money to pay him.

She frowned remembering how bad it was replacing her own implant with no pain medication, which had cost too much extra, and she lied to her doctor saying she had been able to buy it. She just didn't want him to pity her, she hated that. She rubbed her tongue along the tiny implant inside her cheek next to the secretion nodule, remembering when she had to cut a hole to pull the old one out and insert the new one. It had taken a lot of alcohol and hours of self-assurance that she could in fact perform surgery on herself, but she managed to replace it herself without passing out.

She could hear Whit slide down the door outside. He knocked softly before he spoke gently, "Can you hear me in there? You are projecting those pheromones so intensely that I am hallucinating you dancing nude for me in the hallway. Would we be able to bottle this lovely sex drug you produce?" Whit was grasping his splitting bulge so hard it was causing pain, but he felt so bad for Ziph that guilt was keeping him from trying to relieve himself.

Ziph sat up and leaned against the door. "They do bottle it where I'm from, but I wish I could be rid of it forever. I know it's not me everyone wants. It's a lie when it happens, everyone just wants my body, or I guess the pheromone. Whatever, it's not me they want."

As he shifted positions on the floor, Whit corrected, "Oh Ziph, you don't think near highly enough of yourself. You're the most beautiful woman I have ever seen, but you are also talented. When I am seeing you dancing nude, it's not erotic. It's a picture of heavenly grace. You're like a dream, my Golden Girl. I don't always fancy women, but you are a shining star I could never ignore. Even now, with the twisted desperation, I imagine the way I would make you cry for me, tears of joy and passion."

It took Ziph sitting on her hands to keep her from unlocking the door. "How am I supposed to keep this fucking door shut with you talking like that?"

Whit groaned and rubbed his hands down his face. "Don't unlock the door for anyone except Gerara Grindle. Not me and certainly not Trent. Poor Trent is probably downstairs rutting a hole in his pillow right now, confused out of his mind."

Ziph burst into laughter and hoped Danny wasn't feeling it too. Shaking her head, she knew everyone was probably feeling it as she could taste the pheromone leaking into her mouth. She knew with every breath the dispersion would increase the range that much more.

Ziph could hear someone coming up the stairs before Whit addressed them, "If you felt like giving your pillow a good fuck, you should know, it's Ziph's fault. She's in

Dacket's apartment right now with the door locked because she has entered a mating cycle."

Trent stared at Whit with his mouth dropped open, "I couldn't even put my pants on without sticking my penis in the icebox to wedge it back inside me first." Trent became quiet before he admitted, "I was actually coming up for a fuck."

Whit nearly wheezed at the offer as he crawled toward Trent trying to make his way to his feet. "Take your fucking clothes off." Trent wasted no time ripping his shirt off and tossing it on the stairs as he nearly ran for Whit. By the time he reached Whit, they were both nude, and Trent eased him to the stone floor of the hallway. It was unlike any passionate experience they could have imagined. Every touch felt electric as their hands roamed one another. On the other side of the door, Ziph could hear everything, and she was lying on the ground with her hands up her own shirt squeezing her aching breasts.

With their sweet sounds of desperation, Ziph shifted around and put her eye to the crack with her hand above her on the door. She could see Whit on the ground with Trent feverishly kissing Whit down his chest. She could have cried she wanted that kind of affection so badly her heart threatened to burst. Ziph could feel her glands become enlarged as she grew more desperate for touch.

Watching them have sex would make her even worse and tears sprouted in her eyes as she whispered, "What do I have to do to have that kind of pleasure? Why am I never allowed to feel loving touch like that, Venus? You stupid lying bitch. I should have stopped following you years ago. Saving myself for eternal blessings was such a mistake."

Whit and Trent slowed, trying not to make it obvious

they heard every word of Ziph's confession. They had exceptional hearing and knew the words had not been meant for them. Trent peered up at Whit before he sat back on his heels, and Whit nodded to him in understanding. They stood up to dress, reluctantly shoving their wriggling, angry cocks back into their pants.

Ziph was so far entranced into her own cycle she didn't even notice Whit and Trent had dressed and were now sitting on the other side of the door from her. Each stewing in sorrow over what they discovered about her, but not wanting her to know they heard every word she said. Whit and Trent were both heartbroken for her, she had experienced some profound religious trauma, and she had missed out on a pivotal part of her life. Whit tapped on the door softly, "Ziph, I need to ask you something personal. Are you alright with that?"

Ziph sniffled trying to hold in her boiling emotions. "Yes, anything."

Whit clasped his hands together before he gently asked, "Was I the first person you ever kissed?" The pain in Ziph's chest kept her silence extended as she tried to find a way to lie, but she was just so terrible at it. "Fine. Yes, I don't know why that matters. How did you know anyway? Was I that bad?" Ziph was mortified and wanted to run somewhere and hide.

Dropping his face into his hands, Whit sighed, "No beautiful Golden Girl, you are not a bad kisser. I think about your lips often. They brought me joy and so much more."

Ziph gasped with Whit's sentiment and had no words of her own. *I can't keep torturing everyone. I have to stop this airflow somehow.* She saw a blanket over the back of the couch and scrambled over to grab it so she could shove it under the door. She knew the pheromone molecules were much too small and would still move through the fabric, but it would block the airflow. "I hope this gives you some relief until Dacket returns." She could hear Whit and Trent breathing deeply as they each did their best to remain calm.

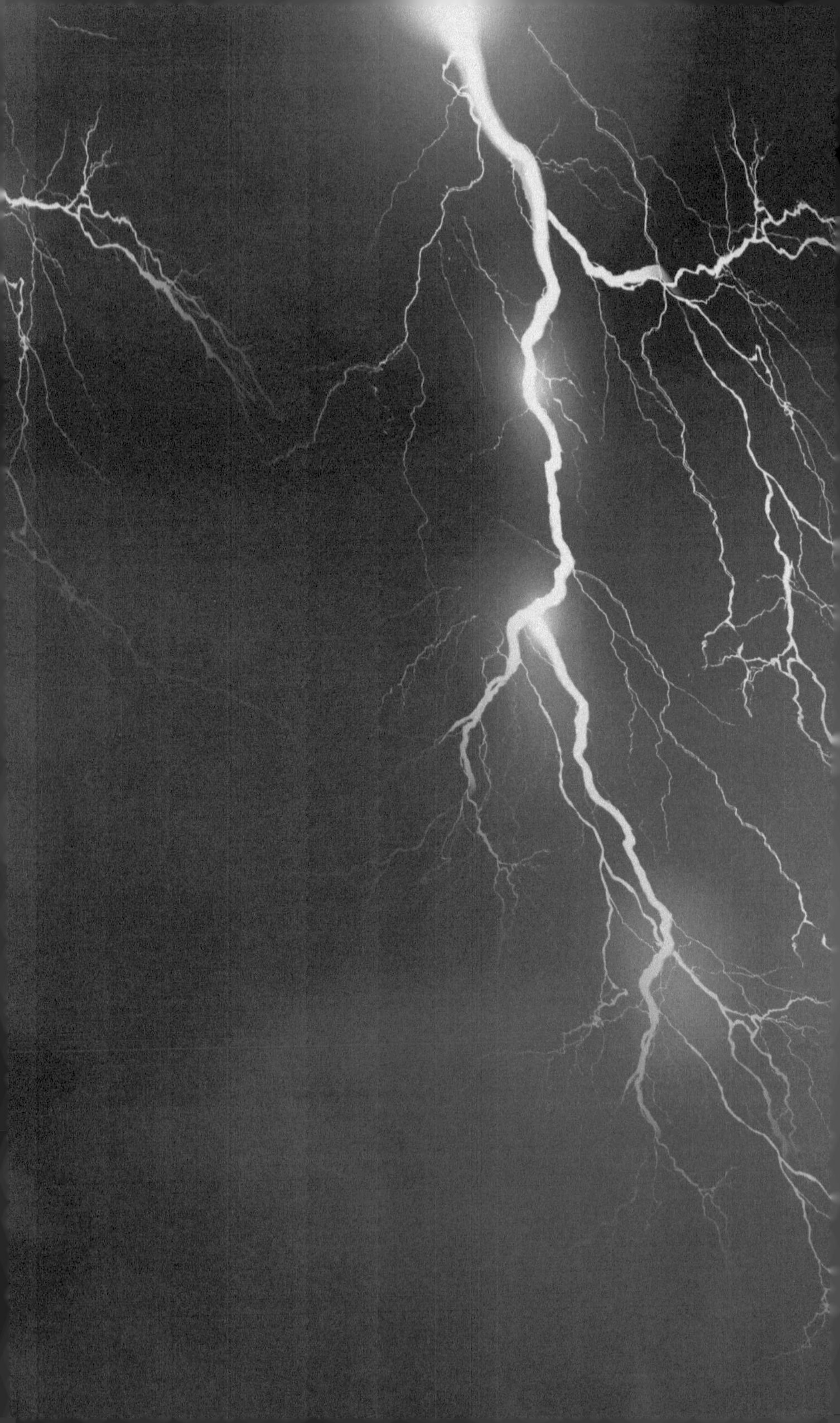

CHAPTER 15
GERARA GRINDLE

After briskly jogging three blocks before he could force his cock back into its hiding place, Dacket finally stood put back together in front of the obscure home of Gerara Grindle. She was a hunter by birth order, but a biology and chemistry enthusiast by the hand of true love. Plants of all kinds grew around her door. Some with mouths that shut over bugs and others that made skin itch for days. He learned the hard way not to touch anything at Gerara Grindle's home.

The giant metal door swung open and revealed a vibrant yellow woman with white hair and long microscope goggles over her eyes, causing them to look far too enormous to make out clearly. "This is the home of Gerara Grindle. What business do you have here?"

Dacket cleared his throat and reached over to lift her goggles, revealing her bright auburn eyes, mirrors to his own. "It's me. I need help."

Gerara stared at Dacket for a moment and nodded before waving her hand for him to come inside. "What brings you back here after I so egregiously poisoned you with my door plants?"

Dacket snarled at the memory. "I didn't know such plants existed, and I may have panicked when I found the rash had spread to my ass. Is that all right with you?"

She laughed and put her hand on her hip. "So, Dacket Critchlow, the top hunter of all time with the new flashy apprentice with an odd tail, what brings you here?" Her familiar demeanor always threw Dacket off, and he long suspected them of being from the same batch of eggs. Of course, he suppressed his own light personality, but he had to. If he allowed himself to be authentic, he would love too deeply, and when it was time to say goodbye, it would be too hard for everyone involved. *I wish the nightmares would stop. I can't take it anymore.* He looked up and tried to refocus on the conversation at hand.

"This will sound outrageous, but I need you to trust me. I found an elsewhere woman who evolved from squirrels in the sky belt. I may have brought her home, and she is the new apprentice. We have a problem though. She has a mating cycle which has begun, and she has no way to stop her mating pheromones from spreading. She says they could spread for miles which would be a disaster." Dacket watched Gerara's light expression melt into a grimace, and her eyes widened to a point he didn't think was possible.

"You what, and what happened? Wait. Take me now." Gerara ran for her treatment bags before opening her front door and throwing her arm out for Dacket to lead her. Dacket took off at a brisk pace and Gerara followed closely behind, her long white hair loose and flowing behind her.

When they reached Dacket's door, Whit and Trent were huddled with their knees smashed into their chests by the door and both slumped with relief to see Gerara. Whit stared at Dacket solemnly as he and Trent nearly fell over one another trying to enter Whit's apartment. "Um, good luck with all of that. We will be in here for a while." Dacket frowned at Whit as he maintained eye contact while he slowly shut his door.

Dacket shook his head as he turned to knock on his own door, inside he could hear the water running. *Oh fuck, she's in the bathroom.* Thoughts of her nude, touching her own body nearly made him moan aloud. He leaned his forehead against the door as he pulled his key from his pocket, "Gerara, I don't think I can resist her. If I cannot control myself, I will need you to bite me. I know your venom is the same as mine."

Gerara reared back as she resisted the magnified urge to rub her thighs together. "I feel it just as much. You will need to help me more than you want. Where did all your unmatched willpower go? Do you want me to slap it back into you?"

Dacket sneered at her and huffed as he turned the key in his lock. Once inside, he locked the door behind them and made his way to his bathroom, where the door was open.

Frozen in place, Dacket's eyes fluttered shut as he saw Ziph laid out on his bathroom floor with her wet towel crumped next to her. She had her hands covering her face but pulled them away when Gerara dropped her bag on the ground at the sight of Ziph nude. "Oh no, I didn't hear you come in. I got really hot, so I had to take my clothes off. I was waiting for the water to warm to rewet my cloth for my eyes." Realizing that didn't make much sense, Ziph sat up and quickly turned the sink water off before grabbing a towel from the rack next to her. She wrapped herself and met the two speechless Elara with identical coloration in the hallway. With the two hunters in street clothing and side-by-side, their resemblance was uncanny. Ziph struggled to stop staring. "Are you here to help me?"

The desperation in her tone made their toes curl. After wrenching Dacket's arm in a brief death grip, wordlessly signaling her distress to him, Gerara picked up her bag, and they all moved to the couch. Dacket sat next to Ziph and wrung his hands trying to keep them off her, and when that didn't work, he sat on them.

"I am assuming your glands are in your mouth?" Gerara watched Ziph nod and put her fingers in her mouth and pull back her cheeks to reveal two small nodules inside. "I am assuming draining them is not an option, and removal is out of the question because it could interfere with your natural hormones. I have a glue salve that dries in seconds, and we could encapsulate them temporarily." She dove both of her arms into her tall bag and retrieved a small tube. Gerara used a paper fan she folded up and dried Ziph's inner cheek before depositing some of the salve onto Ziph's two glands. Gerara waved her fan again to dry the glue and nodded for Ziph to let go when the glue was cured.

"Are they staying in place well?" Ziph nodded and lay back against the cushion as she sighed with relief. *At least one of my problems has been taken care of.* "Yes, they feel secure. How often do you think I will need to seal them? Are there any other options for hormone blocking? Even with the sealed glands, I will still feel the effects of my mating cycle."

Gerara looked at her with eyes filled with sorrow, and Ziph already knew the answer. "We don't have technology for something like that in the hunting district, and I am not sure anything of the sort even exists on the planet." Ziph tried to hide her devastation, but Dacket could see right through it. She could feel his eyes burrowing into her, and all she wanted was to run away and hide from everyone. She was so turned on she thought her lady bits would plot her murder if she didn't convince Dacket to touch them at once, which he made clear was out of the question. All that did was make her want him even more. *Venus, I loathe you so much. Did your stupid ass send me here to just be teased forever?*

Trying to be helpful Gerara suggested, "You may want to find a willing partner, and find some relief the natural way." Ziph could hear Dacket's breathing stop abruptly and she tried to plan an escape route from the room. Sensing Ziph's panic, Gerara grabbed her bag and shoved the glue salve into Ziph's hand. "I'll be on my way now. I'll see you two in the sky belt, or whenever you run out of salve." Gerara all but ran from the apartment and Dacket locked the door behind her before turning to face Ziph. He learned against the door and took several deep breaths, noticing the thinning of her pheromones in the air.

Ziph continued to sink into despair, and into the couch cushions, as she tried to hold back a sob. To desire sex so deeply it nonstop ripped at your heart strings for satisfaction was nearly torture with a partner, but without one it was murder. Dacket sat next to her on the couch and tried to comfort her, but she reared back and braced herself to keep from falling from the cushion. "I need to run, but I don't have anywhere to run to. I'm overwhelmed, and I need so much, but I don't even really know any of you. I am so scared I can't see straight. I don't think I can live like this."

Dacket wasn't sure what else to do, so he offered her

what he could. "You don't need to work in the factory or hunt. I will find a way to make a sealed apartment for you, and I swear I will do whatever I can to help you through this."

I'll do whatever I can? Except the one thing I need. Ziph's vision blurred with fury as she finally lost her cool, "See that's the entire problem. You won't do whatever you can to help me. There is one thing you made clear you won't do, and that's what I need, so please help me back to my apartment."

Guilt wrapped claws around his throat, and Dacket knew she was right, but he also knew the building was far too filled with her pheromones for her to leave his apartment. "You can stay in my spare room. The door is down from my room. You have your own bathroom." Ziph surged from her place at the couch and bolted to his back room where she was so thankful to see an empty room that she had to hold back her tears.

Inside was a nice and tidy basic bedroom with a plush navy bed. She dropped her towel and slid in the covers, finding them soft and inviting. She curled up in a ball and did her best to hold it together, but when her thoughts moved to her mother, she couldn't stop the flood of emotion which burst from her. Her tears flowed like rivers as she thought about how she would never be able to talk to her again. She couldn't call her and tell her about the new hormone nightmare, three gorgeous men she worked with, or about how she was stuck on this world with no way to come back home.

Desire distracted her once again, and the heat in her lower belly was enough to make her feel feverish. She slid her hand between her thighs and wanted to scream. She knew it was pointless to try to pleasure herself and her tears flowed, further soaking her pillow.

She could hear Dacket quietly approach her door, and she desperately wanted to open it and invite him in, but she knew better. He would say no, and right now, she had to know why. So, anger it was because that was the only thing she could trust.

Ziph raced to the door and swung it open, finding Dacket stunned on the other side, and she demanded, "Why can't you be with me? Why do you say you can't?"

Dacket's lips parted as he searched her eyes. "I'm sorry. I'm just not meant to have what others have. I know you want more than I can give you, and that's not fair to you."

Ziph slammed the door in his face and locked it. "Then stop coming to my door, I am dying in here, and you're not fucking helping anything. All you're doing is being a fucking tease." Ziph stormed into the bathroom and splashed herself with cold water. Realizing she may never sleep again, she made her way back to the door where she noticed Dacket's shadow still hovered where he leaned against the door outside her room, so she quietly asked, "Can you at least find me a sleeping pill so I can get some rest?"

"Of course, I have a sedative which will work for you."

Ziph wasn't asking why Dacket said it in that way, but when he returned it was obvious. Ziph opened the door, and he stood before her with a small liquid vile with a measure and the little shape of a mouse on the side of the cup. "You sedate live mice before you eat them don't you."

She slowly took the tiny cup from him, and he awkwardly smiled at her as he explained almost in a whisper, "They scratch up our throats if we don't. It's that or bash them first. I usually bash them because the sedative sometimes makes me tired after I eat." Ziph's lips peeled back in a grimace as she slowly shut the door. She stared at the lock on the door. She didn't lock it because if there was a chance he wanted to change his mind, she was not stopping him with a locked door.

She downed the small cup of liquid finding it sickly sweet. She climbed into bed and as darkness fell outside, the room became eerie with shadows and creaking sounds sending her mind into a tailspin. The sedative was certainly working for her body, but her mind reeled with thoughts and possibilities. It took several more hours of staring at the ceiling before she finally drifted off, only to be woken up with the vibrations of the morning factory bell. The sound seemed like it was so much longer this time, and she grasped her breasts trying to make her piercings stop vibrating. The one through her hood was the worst, and when it didn't stop for several seconds more, Ziph climbed from the bed to see what was happening.

"Oh Venus, you stupid, awful goddess! I think if my lady parts are turned on any more without relief, they might kill me in my sleep!" Ziph tried to be quiet but nearly yelled her words as she wrapped the towel around her and she burst into the living room.

Dacket stood at the opened doors on the back of the factory clock, it was made into the wall outside of his apartment, and she guessed it had to have maintenance somehow. Trying not to scream with pleasure, Ziph waddled over to Dacket and tapped his shoulder. He turned to look at her, and she begged, "Please, if you don't make that sound stop, I might actually die."

Dacket held up something which looked like a tuning fork. It was making all the sound and vibrations and he wrapped his hand around it to muffle it. "I'm sorry. Does it cause you pain?"

Ziph wanted to throat punch the dumbass man, but instead opened her eyes as wide as they would go. "It makes my piercings zing like they're tiny vibrators, and I already think my tingly lady parts are plotting my death, so let's not give them more reason to carry out the assassination." Ziph imagined her vagina and uterus crawling out and strangling her to death, but she couldn't help feeling like her pussy parts realistically had every reason to.

Seeming confused, Dacket awkwardly asked, "I don't mean to be rude, but can you not take care of your personal needs?"

Ziph snarled and bared her teeth at him as she tried to hold back a scream. "You mean fucking *masturbate*? Don't you think I would have done that if I could?!" Ziph stalked back to the spare room and shut the door a little too aggressively, shaking half the apartment.

In the living room, Dacket went to the entryway, and she could hear the door open, "I'll fetch you some clean clothing from your apartment."

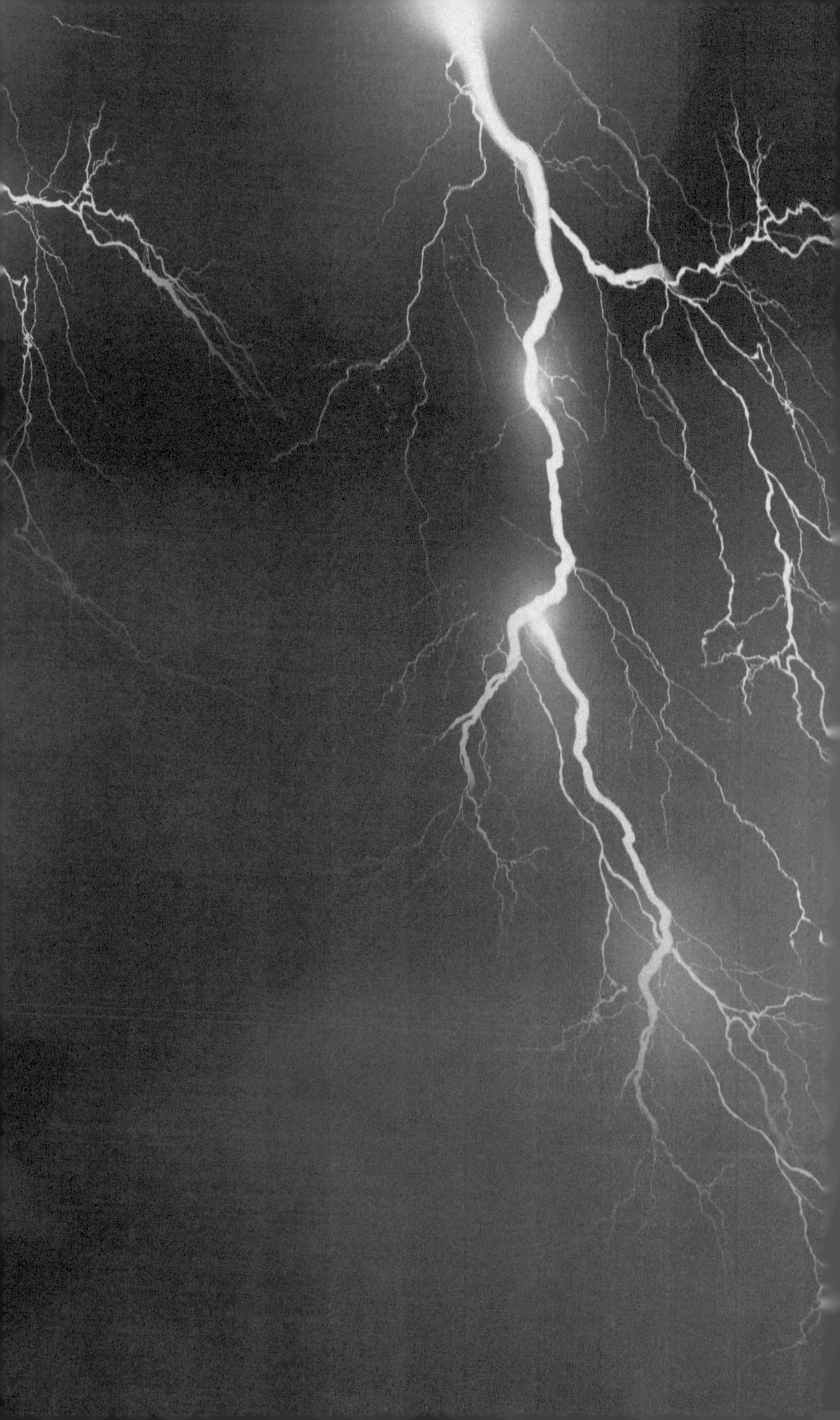

CHAPTER 16

NEW ROOMMATE

Danny squinted her eyes as she focused on the sealed nodules in Ziph's mouth, "You were right to come up for Dacket's help. He has willpower like no one I've ever met. Me, on the other hand, I have zero restraint, so when your pheromones began, I would have tried everything I could to fuck you. No question, and I'm not even attracted to women!" Ziph couldn't help laughing and tapping her toes on the cold stone floor. "So, what happens when the glue falls away at night?" Danny couldn't help but ask.

Ziph stared at Danny while she tried to find an answer, but Danny had nothing to offer except a forced smile and a hardly reassuring pat on the knee. "I guess Dacket is my new permanent roommate then. I have to room with the hottest and most unavailable man I've ever met. This should be great fun."

Danny snarled as she patted Ziph's leg again, "Good luck."

Ziph closed her eyes and took a deep breath trying to not blab away her whole life. "I can't finish when I try myself, and I've never been with anyone. I was a Venus pledge, and since I've said it aloud, I am now thoroughly disgusted with myself for falling for that damn cult. Everyone said it was, and I should have listened."

Danny couldn't hide her surprise at Ziph, "That makes me really sad for you. Not in a pity way, but in a sense that you deserved to experience that part of life, and it's sad you haven't because a cult tricked you into avoiding it. Sex is wonderful, and having the pheromones and hormone drive you have, it must be really hard. I'm sorry I joked about all of this. I didn't realize you were struggling with so much. If it means anything, if I liked girls, I would be more than willing to help you out."

Ziph set aside everything they were discussing for a moment to appreciate how much Danny cared about her. All she could do in response was hug her friend until she could form her words. "I had some shitty friends back home. Thank you for being genuine and caring."

Danny stood up and straightened her work uniform. "Let me know when you want to try and go out again. Maybe when you've tested that glue a little longer? Hopefully, you can move back down here if it's reliable enough." Ziph nodded and giggled under her breath thinking about a dance club turning into an orgy because of her as she followed Danny to the door and closed it behind her. *Now what the hell am I supposed to do? Just sit up in Dacket's apartment on house arrest? This entire situation is stupid, and I hate everything.*

Where in Pluto's hell was Dacket anyway, he had been gone since she woke up. He had set a pile of clothes on her nightstand after he hadn't returned until she was asleep the night before. She woke up to empty apartment. *He was probably so annoyed by me and my bullshit that he couldn't handle it anymore. Typical for him to run away like everybody else.*

Her ears perked up a few minutes later when she heard his boots coming down the hallway toward his door. Ziph rushed back into her room, so she didn't seem so obvious that she was miserable. She wasn't sure why that was important in that moment, but she felt so awkward and out of place she could have screamed.

She could see him in the entryway. He had been doing some kind of workout in the sky belt she guessed. *I wish I could have gone with him. This is such a fucking nightmare. Literally.* She balked at her stupid joke and sucked in a breath as she realized she had made a sound and looked up to see Dacket staring right at her with his striking auburn eyes. *Why does he have to look at me like that?* He had been sweating, and his white undershirt clung to his thickly muscled body, showing off much more than Ziph could handle at the moment. She clenched her thighs and resisted the urge to rub them together as she hoped he did anything except come and talk to her.

He appeared in her doorway after she backed away, and she could have died. "How are you doing?"

Ziph glared at him, she never really planned to reveal her true feelings, but they seemed to slip by her filter too often. "I am wishing you could have invited me to work out since that's about the only relief I've ever had." She hadn't really experienced her full cycle, but she had felt some of the urges even with her blocker in place. She had always turned to exercise in those moments.

"I came back early to see if you had woken up. I didn't want to wake you this morning after what you went through last night."

Ziph held a blank expression as she corrected, "You

mean what I'll be enduring the rest of my fucking life? My kind doesn't have an ending age to our cycle."

Dacket looked away from her and quietly replied, "Do you want to suit up, and come with Whit and I for an afternoon sky run? We make a full run at least twice a week after morning drills. We have a weight room with a mechanical track for running. It's an old conveyer belt Whit and I converted into a gear powered running machine."

Ziph perked up at that suggestion. "We called those runners at home. I would love to see the weight room before we go for a run. I just need a few minutes to dress." She turned around and when she realized she didn't have her uniform, she whirled back. Dacket was biting his lips together as she admitted, "I will need my hunting uniform. Dacket handed her a bag, and it had her uniform inside. *Thank Venus. Wait, you know what? Fuck that bitch. I need to stop saying that. She doesn't deserve any kind of thanks.*

"Do you worship any gods here?" Ziph asked before she shut her door.

Dacket appeared to slump his shoulders a bit, and he didn't meet her eyes as he explained, "The Kefale Royals are our gods. They demand sacrifice, ultimate loyalty, and control all of life for the Elara. They leave no room for other mythical deities." Something about that made Ziph feel uneasy. There was more under the surface of his words. She shut her door and dressed before checking her mouth in the mirror to ensure her glue was in place. She put the tube in her pocket and pulled her hair back in a high pony before she slid on her boots.

She opened the door to her room, and Dacket was sitting on his couch, facing her. He looked up at her, and she sincerely wondered if she should ask him what in his head went so damn wrong every time they brought up the Kefale Royals. He quickly perked up as she met him at the door, and he slid his hunting jacket back on. Before he opened the door, he handed her a mask as he faced her, "This is the same mask you used before with a strap, but we will need to call Gerara Grindle back to install your magnetic mask clips onto your skull. It sounds worse than it is, and you will have plenty of pain medication for it."

Ziph had been poked on her whole life with her cycle condition and the bend and her tail she was born with. "I'm not a newbie to medical procedures. That's no problem. Are there any other modifications you suggest?" Her tail flitted behind her, and she lowered it, remembering Elarian didn't have raised tails.

"No, but we probably need to figure out a better cover for your tail soon. I'm sure Whit can make you a cover that looks like ours which you could slip on. To be honest with you, I'm not even sure that's going to be necessary. Trent has been asking around and nobody seems to care even a bit about anyone from elsewhere." Dacket closed the door behind them, and they descended the stairs for the equipment gym. Ziph was not surprised to find all self-made equipment. Although, it was all clearly well thought out and would be highly effective. She went right over to the runner and Dacket nodded she could try it. "Just start running. It glides under you with every step, and it will keep up with your pace with the gears underneath."

Intrigued, Ziph began running and felt the slip with each step, giving her a thrill. This was an effective design, and after a quick warm up, she decided to top out her speed. She pounded the track, and the gears created a rhythm as they ticked under her. A few minutes at top speed had her delighted, and she slowed to a stop before climbing off. *This could actually help me feel better. I need to do this more often.* "That was helpful. I will probably be down here all the time." She finally looked over at Dacket who seemed utterly flabbergasted. "Are you alright?"

He just stared at her in disbelief as he slowly admitted, "I've never seen anyone run like that before. You can move like the winds of a funnel cloud. Let's join Whit for that afternoon sky run, and you can show us all how much faster you are." Ziph didn't detect one ounce of sarcasm in his words. He was serious as he held the gym door open for her to follow him back out into the garage so they could meet Whit in the sky belt.

Climbing in the truck, Ziph felt lightyears better now that she had such a vigorous run. They were on their way for another run, and she could have exploded with excitement. "The run was helpful, but now I am entirely too pumped for another one, and I might move around a lot in my seat."

Ziph watched Dacket begin to frown as he kept his eyes on the road, "You're perfect the way you are. You should stop excusing your nature as bothersome. I hate everyone, and I enjoy your company." Ziph tried not to laugh because she knew he was being serious, and she bottled herself up causing her cheeks to burn.

"Why do you look as though you're close to combustion?" Dacket could easily see the heat growing on her face. He, like all Elara, had heat sensory organs in their faces, and could create heat maps in their minds.

"Because what you said was a lot sweeter than I think you realize." She could feel herself curl up inside as she tried to avoid his gaze. Shifting to look out the window, Ziph wiggled her toes and fingers to help keep herself seated. It didn't last long, and she was moving around the seat within minutes, crossing her legs and then uncrossing them before putting one underneath her. The journey was never quick, and she had time to move in every seated position possible.

Today he seemed to be driving on the faster side, and she was so very thankful as the thick heat began to stir low in her belly. Ziph closed her eyes. *I cannot grind my fucking pussy on this seat in this truck. I cannot grind my fucking pussy on this seat in this truck. Chanting is not fucking working I'm absolutely about to grind my pussy on this seat, gods help me.*

Ziph sat with her back straight and squeezed her eyes shut before she dared to look over at Dacket. His neon yellow skin seemed stretched to its limits across his knuckles as he gripped the wheel with both hands. *Well, that's enough of looking at that,* she turned back to look out the window and took long slow breaths trying to calm her raging desires as she sat next to the off-limits man whom she was wildly attracted to. *Maybe I can drive back with Whit, and I can give him head on the way home.* That though nearly had her in tears, *maybe he would even let me sit on it. Oh gods, I want that wiggly penis inside of me so bad.* She would have moaned if she had been alone, and if she didn't find some kind of dick to put inside of her soon, she would crash like the drop ship which brought her here.

When she could see Whit's truck in the distance, she had to resist the urge to leap out and run for him. She knew better though, she would need to behave until it was time to head back home. *Behaving is stupid. I want to be a dirty little Ziph and get some dick!*

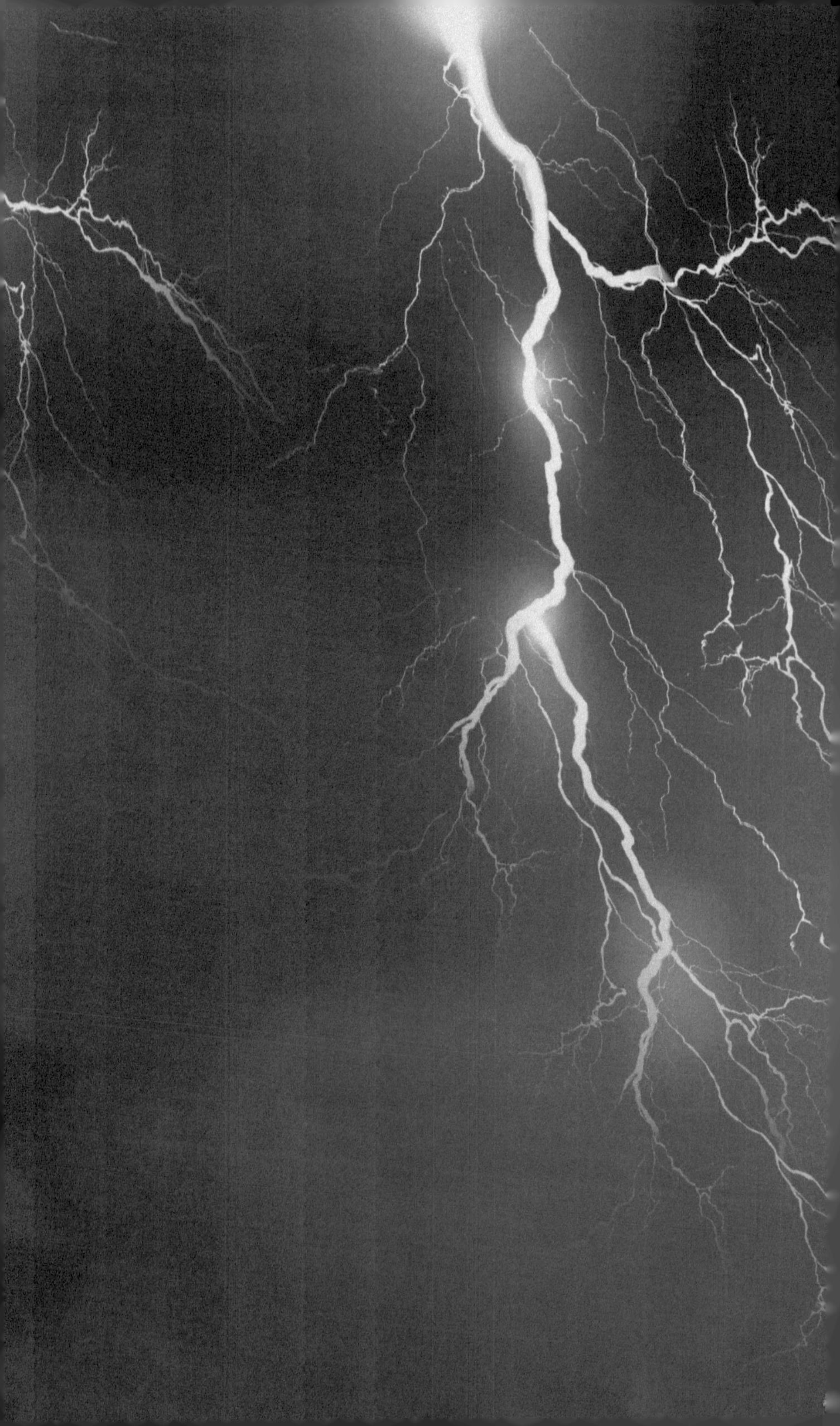

CHAPTER 17
KILLING DACKET

Ziph nearly fell from Dacket's tall truck after they arrived, and she bailed out so quickly she forgot her air jets and mask. Realizing she forgot them after she began running toward the awaiting group of hunters, she slowed to a stop and turned to find Dacket who had everything outstretched in his hands. "I'm sorry."

With his tail curled in a knot behind him, Dacket frowned at her as he handed over her things. "Stop apologizing. There is nothing wrong with you, you just function quicker than I do. We can find a bag for your uniform, mask, and jets, and we can even attach thin rope to the mask and jets so you can't separate them from the uniform." Ziph stood before the man she had undressed with her mind about a hundred times since she woke up, and she had to refrain from falling to her knees to suck his dick after what he just said to her. *I've never wanted to suck a man's dick so bad in my whole life. Why does he keep acting like Mr. Wonderful when he is so painfully unavailable?!* What could she even respond to that? No one had ever made her feel so revealed and raw in such a caring way.

"Thank you," she whispered as she knelt to attach her ankle jets. When she looked down, she noticed her under-shirt was sagging under her jacket, and she tucked it in her pants. *I need to stop pulling on all my damn shirts.*

He stood by her while she attached the remaining jets and her mask so he could hold his hand out and help her up. When she was ready, they jogged for the group together, and as she did, her mind spun with imagery of her, Dacket, Whit, and Trent all having sex in the gym, then in Whit's room, then Dacket's. One thing was certain, if someone didn't fuck her soon, she would combust. She didn't even care about a stupid orgasm anymore. Her hormones demanded she be railed, and she couldn't shake the idea of her offering herself for each of them to fuck as they want. Her drive demanded for her to be fucked from behind with her ass in the air, and the entire urge was absurd, but nonetheless overwhelming and demanding. *Damn, I really need to run this out of my system.*

They reached the group of hunters who often gathered for a run or to practice drills, and Ziph noticed Gerara Grindle was standing among the hunters. *She even stands like Dacket. I bet they are siblings.* Her white hair was pulled back in two braids down her back made Ziph wonder if her high ponytail would be enough and reached back to braid it down. Whit saw her and came over with a band to tie it off for her. He tapped her on the ass afterward, and she nearly backed her ass up into him and rubbed him with it. *I am too horny for anything, how the fuck am I supposed to live this way? My mother went through this every six months back home, and she never seemed to complain.* The memory of her mother frequenting one of the many brothels in the Venus District came crashing into her head, and she real-ized her mother wasn't just going to have a brew and chat with her friends at the bar. *No wonder mom was so against the Venus pledge. I miss her so much.* Ziph stored away the interesting memory and promised herself she would allow time to grieve her mom later when she was alone, and she prepared herself as they all lined up.

Dacket tapped her arm and lifted his mask. "We follow a path marked with orange air buoys for one rotation to warm up, and eight rotations at high speed before we slow and follow it for four more to cool down." Ziph nodded as they each lifted off the ground with their jets and began their sky run.

The first lap, Ziph was dancing inside trying to hold herself back but managed to halfway focus on form, which felt more like ice-skating than running. She could easily work with that. As they gained speed as a group, Ziph was thrilled, but when they topped out at a speed much lower than Ziph wanted, she could have screamed in her mask. She would have, but she didn't know if it was soundproof, and she didn't want anyone to hear.

Towards the end of the higher speed sky run, Dacket lifted his mask and was loud enough she could hear him through the whipping winds, "You don't need to hold back. Go ahead." Ziph could not have been happier, and she blasted it off at twice the speed she had been before as she drilled the leg movements into her mind and muscles. The free sky run was exhilarating. *This is the kind of sport that was made for me. Too bad there are no brothels in Valler. Maybe I can survive this eternal horniness if I can come here and run like this all the time.*

She went around the group twice at top speeds before she finally slowed and joined their cool down. She felt like she had exercised enough for a bit of lasting relief, and that meant the world to her.

When they all landed on the higher gravity ground and began taking off their masks, a man with muddy orange skin and golden eyes approached them aggressively causing Dacket and Whit to quickly move between the man and Ziph. "Who do you think you are bringing some youngling hyped on something brewed up in the Eight Underground out here to train with us?" He was staring directly at Dacket, who maintained his cool.

Before anyone could say anything, Ziph lifted her tail, and untied the base so the protective cover would fall off as she shook it. Danny had already explained elsewhere people had landed there before, and no one had really made any kind of deal about it. Her fluffy tail flitted back and forth behind her as she explained, "I'm not from here. Dacket took pity on me and has allowed me to stay with them if I hunt. I am just lucky, and my species is fast. That's all. No one is trying to offend anyone today."

Dacket slowly turned and stared at Ziph with fury in his eyes before he turned back to the man. "Vante, she's not trying to show off. She needs to burn more energy than we do. Leave her alone willfully, or I will make you." Vante frowned and showed his teeth to Dacket before he stalked back to his truck along with the rest of his group. Gerara waved at Ziph with a kind grin before following her team back to their trucks.

"Don't worry about him. He's always hated us because our factory outputs more than his, but we make more kills, so he has no room to complain. He should come to practice more if he wants higher output." Dacket explained as they went back to their trucks. Ziph stood in between the trucks and sighed, wondering if it would be rude to Dacket if she asked to drive back with Whit. She felt better, but she still wanted some dick if she could have it. There was something about walking across the hall and having sex with Whit while Dacket was in the next apartment which made her skin crawl. She assumed that's why he and Trent had not tried yet, but if only she could have Whit by himself, she knew she could convince him to help her somehow.

Dacket started up his truck, and has she grabbed the handle to open the door to tell him she was riding with Whit, Whit's truck made a strange sound. It clearly wasn't starting, so Ziph sat down and kept her mouth shut as Dacket moved in front of Whit's truck to tow it. Whit hooked them together and climbed in the back behind Ziph. *Great there goes my plans for fun time in the truck on the way back.*

Whit shut the door and slowly turned to look at Ziph as he sniffed the air. "You mean I have to ride all the way back home with you, and your sex beacon is on?" Ziph froze as she tried to register if she still felt the glue over the nodules in her cheeks. Her tongue slowly slid over to feel for them, and she blinked repeatedly trying to remember if she brought the glue.

"The glue fell off while you were running, didn't it." Whit seemed delighted as he licked his lips, all while Dacket seemed as though he was hyperventilating and not breathing all at once. Ziph nodded at Whit, and she was not sure what to say as her face soured with anxiety.

Whit laughed like a maniacal villain in the back before he moved close and brought his lips against Ziph's ear, "Why don't you crawl in the back with me." Ziph had never moved so fast, but her heart broke as she saw Dacket's face drop while she crawled over the seat. *I need to remember this is his choice, and I have needs. I don't want to hurt Dacket, but I can't say no to relief.*

Her heartbreak was soon soothed by the roaming

hands of Whit as he helped her out of her jacket. His hands were under her shirt, and he held her generous hips in his grasp while he ground her against his lap. Whit leaned forward and kissed her, raising his hands to her face and deepening his lust.

From the front they could hear Dacket groan with desperation as he rested his head against the driver seat window. "Please don't have sex in my backseat. You are fucking killing me up here."

Whit paused and his excitement faded. He brushed his lips against Ziph's before he replied, "It's always been your choice, Dacket."

Whit met Ziph's eyes, and they slowed, both understanding they couldn't do much more than kiss. It may have been his choice, but they were not cruel. So that's exactly what they did. Whit slid his hands under her shirt and gently rubbed her nipples while he explored her mouth with his own. Ziph noticed Dacket was driving at much higher speeds than he did when they were on their way, and although it gave her pause considering he was towing a whole other truck behind his, she couldn't help the draw back into Whit's attention as he played with her nipple piercings.

She wanted his mouth on them so badly they ached, and she could have cried when he lifted her shirt and did just that. His warm lips over her flesh was something she never wanted to forget, and it was everything she ever wanted. His split tongue flitted and twirled over her nipples, causing her eyes to close and her head to fall back. She had never felt something so incredible, but she knew it wasn't fair to be doing all of this in the back seat while Dacket was directly behind her. She knew he was just trying to protect his heart, and she felt like she was being incredibly insensitive by allowing herself to give in so close to him. *But it is his fucking choice!*

Whit must have sensed her shifting and pulled her shirt back down. He took her face in his hands and kissed her again. He pulled her close, and his hot breath at her ear gave her a shiver. "I am not rushing anything, but we can see about some relief for you." She nodded, and he gently rubbed his hand over her lower belly before grabbing her hips and shifting her around, so she was cradled in his lap. He spread her legs just enough so he could gently rub her clit over her pants without making it obvious to Dacket. Whit's other hand slithered in under her shirt and he carefully explored her chest while she rested against his shoulder. Dacket slowed a bit, and Ziph did her best to hold still as Whit continued roaming her chest while he began tapping his finger against her clit. The rhythm he kept was everything she needed, and her body melted into Whit's. *It's not enough to get me off, but gods this is helping so much I could cry.*

She was nowhere near an orgasm, but after the long drive back of Whit quietly playing with her nipples and her pussy had Ziph calmer than she ever had been in her life. Almost too exhausted to climb the stairs when they returned, Ziph hugged Whit before she reluctantly followed Dacket into the apartment to try to sleep.

Dacket seemed spent and anxious as he went straight to his room and shut the door. Ziph heard the water start seconds later and she waddled into the kitchen where she found a new basket of fruit and several types of granolas. Her stomach growled, and she knew she needed to eat soon so she decided not to let the fruit rot like one of the last baskets. It didn't take more than thirty minutes for Ziph to finish everything in the basket and head to her room. She was positive that was supposed to be a week worth of food, but Dacket just didn't understand how her metabolism worked. She knew he said the baskets were cheap and he would need to buy her more. As she went back to her room, she passed Dacket's door, and she swore she could hear him groaning.

Fuck! Stop listening at his door like a creep, and let the poor man masturbate in peace. At least someone here is getting off. Ziph went into her room and stripped off her clothes before bathing.

She stood naked waiting for the water to warm as she tried to reason with herself that banging on Whit's door was a bad idea. *It is a bad idea, right? Oh fuck, I need to glue these damn nodules before this apartment building turns into an orgy. Why the fuck didn't I look for my glue in the truck?! What is wrong with me?!* She frowned at herself as she reached for the glue she swore she brought in her hunting clothes, and discovered it wasn't there. She rolled her eyes and cleaned herself quickly before she knocked on Dacket's door to tell him she lost the glue.

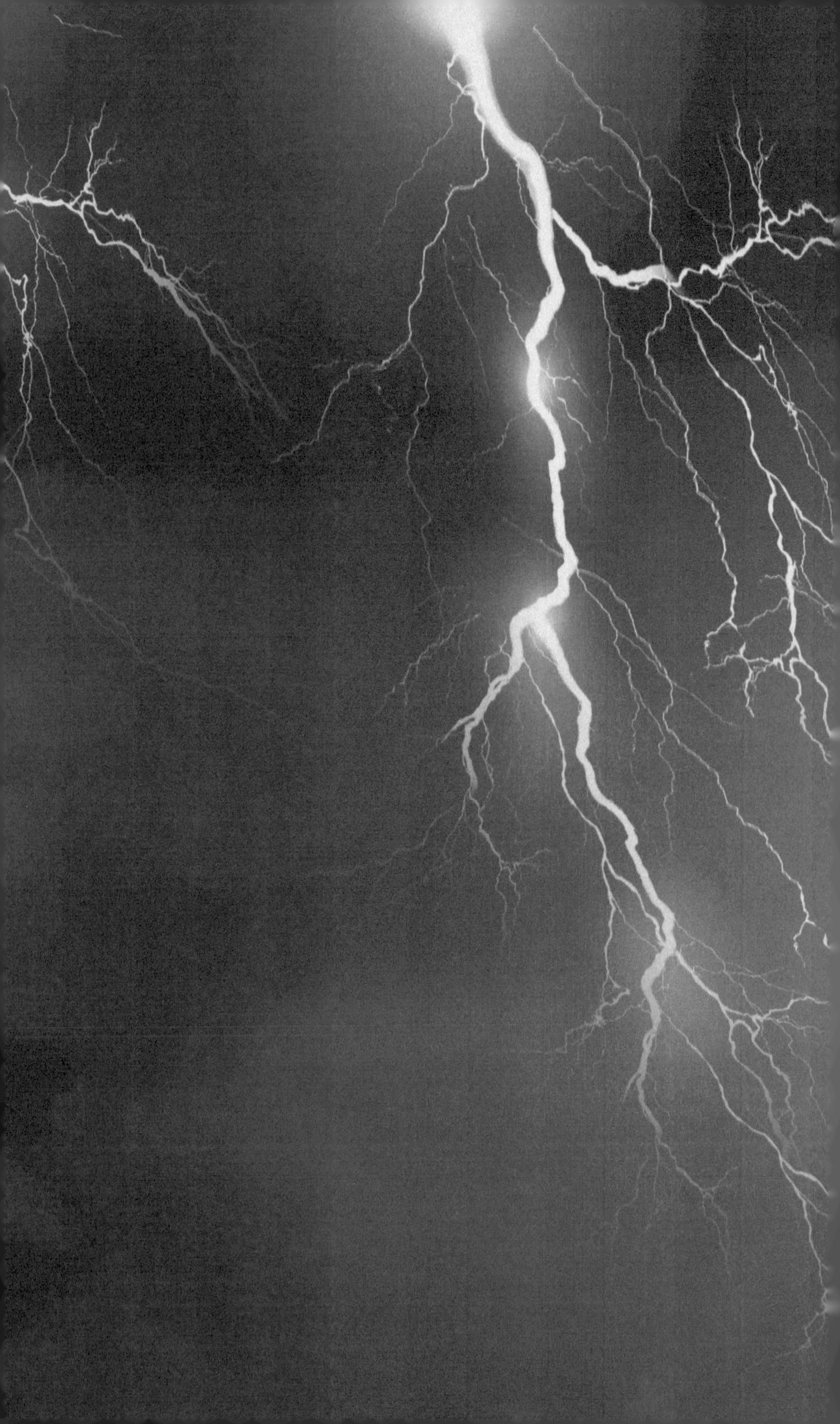

CHAPTER 18
GLUE

Ziph stood at Dacket's door in her towel with her golden hair cascading down her shoulders. She had just knocked, and she could hear him approaching the door. It swung open, and she stared at him with distress in her eyes. "I lost my glue."

Wearing his underclothes with his pale short hair still wet and droplets sliding down his forehead, Dacket gave her a sad smile. He was trying to be reassuring, but it just made Ziph feel guilty. "Gerara told me today she has more ready, and I can come by for it anytime. I can go now."

Ziph nodded and started to apologize, but he stopped himself before he shut the door and interrupted her, "Don't say it." Ziph bit her lips together as he shut his bedroom door, and she forced a smile as she ran back to her room to climb in bed. She could hear him dressing, and when he came out, he darkened her open doorway. "I'm leaving. You should probably stuff something under the front door." Ziph slid out of the bed and followed him. He looked at her hands and asked, "What are you stuffing under the door?"

Ziph stared at him blankly, "My towel."

Dacket looked down at the towel she had wrapped round her and seemed as though he was in pain as he nodded before he hurried to exit the apartment. Ziph, re-energized for a short time after she stuffed her towel under the door, jumped around Dacket's apartment in the nude for a little while before she climbed in bed. She felt something fall over her she hadn't felt in a long while. Calm, she was calm, and she could have sobbed she was so relieved she was finally at peace for the moment. She stared at the ceiling for a time before she felt herself slide off into dreamland.

When Dacket returned, he didn't sense her pheromones until he reached his door and as he turned the key, he took a deep breath preparing for what he would face on the other side. Inside, her pheromones were so thick he coughed, and he tried to shield his breathing from them, but realized the pheromones were infinitely too small for fabric to help filter them.

He locked the door and replaced her towel underneath the door seal, and as he did, he realized if he wanted any sleep, he would need to wake her. *Fuck, she's probably naked.* He pleaded that she had clothes on at the very least as he approached her doorway.

Not only did she not have any clothes on, but she was also asleep and spread out on top of her bed. *This woman is going to kill me.* Dacket tried to swallow away the gravel feeling in his throat, and he had to walk away from her doorway as he tried to catch his breath. *All I want is to rush in her room, and bury my face in between her legs. Fuck I would do anything to just taste her once.* He slid his hand in his pocket where he stored the tubes of glue and pulled one out. Dacket held it up in front of his face and shook his head. His desires ran so thick he contemplated tossing out the glue, carrying her down to his truck, and fucking her in the sky belt for a week straight. After the first fantasy, his mind went on a tailspin.

He quickly fabricated another wild, and highly impossible future, where he, Whit, and Trent, all took Ziph to the sky belt with her pheromones set free, and they all fucked her under the stars like deranged animals. *I still need to wake her before I do something I regret.*

Dacket was aching for her and his painful cock pressed against his flesh trying to escape from his slit. It was begging to be set free so he could bury himself deep into the gorgeous golden woman he knew was just around the corner, nude and ready for him.

Unable to break himself from the trance, Dacket took small steps back toward Ziph's room. Her scent was too much, and his mind created ten thousand ways he wanted to make her cum, all of which included her at his mercy and writhing under him. He couldn't help himself as he crawled over her nude form and breathed deeply at her breasts, desperate to sense how she tastes. With her skin so close, he could feel her heat on his face as he watched her chest move up and down from an inch away. Her eyes twitched with a dream and Dacket moved up to watch her wiggling irises under her eyelids. *This woman is perfection.* Her fluffy tail was spread beside her, and her hip was up at a slight angle, showing off her curvy figure. Dacket moved down her body and breathed in at her pussy, taking in her scent like it was sustenance.

Ziph groaned, and Dacket realized what he was doing at the same moment, causing him to rear back and climb off her before he twirled around and faced the wall blinking and considered slapping himself in the face. *What the fuck are you doing, Dacket? She was peacefully asleep, and you hovered over her like a creep seeking to assault her.* Dacket felt truly disgusted.

Turning back, he saw she was still asleep, and he closed his eyes as he reached over to lay his hand on her shoulder. He could hear her suck in a sharp breath, and he reached in his pocket for the glue. He held it up with his eyes still shut, and he could hear her climb under the covers. Ziph took the glue from him and set it on the side table. "Thank you. I'm covered up now. I almost apologized again, but I stopped myself."

Dacket opened his eyes and looked at her with a longing that made her toes curl. "Good. You don't apologize to anyone, for anything."

Ziph watched the hottest man, who just said the hottest thing to her, walk from her room and shut the door before she whispered to herself, "Why can't you just fuck me since you've buttered me up with your words about six times now. Fuck, I miss butter so much. If I ever get to have butter again, I'm going to eat it every day for the rest of my life." Ziph slammed herself back onto the bed and pulled a pillow over her face to scream in it. She tried to muffle the scream, but she was positive Dacket could still hear it. There was no way she could hold back as she let it all out. *I just want this snake man to lick butter off my breasts and fuck me silly. Is that too much to ask?*

Grabbing the glue, she went to the bathroom to glue her nodules shut and give Dacket a break. He seemed even more sexually frustrated than she was when he handed her the glue, and she was hard to beat. She opened her mouth and dried the insides of her cheeks before applying the glue like Gerara did.

As she allowed the glue to cure and dry, she leaned

over the sink, and her saliva dripped down her chin and into the drain below. *Nasty little spit river.* Ziph giggled to herself and almost released the hooked finger in her stretched-out cheek, so she tried to refrain from any more stupid jokes. *I know what else is a nasty little river. I lasted five entire seconds. I really need to stop it.*

She sighed as she tested the glue, finding it dry. She released her cheeks and smacked her dry mouth a few times before glaring at the faucet and deciding she didn't want to drink tap water. Her hair was almost dry, so she dressed in some night clothes she found in a drawer and went to the kitchen. Dacket was in his room with the door closed, and she noticed he had moved the empty fruit basket near the apartment door. She opened a few cabinets before she found cups and filled one at his sink.

She walked over to the wall of windows in his living room overlooking the factory and admired how unique and industrial this building was. It felt comfortable in a way she couldn't describe, and she really felt she fit in well here. She missed her mother desperately, but she forced herself to be positive and was determined to figure everything out so her life here could be a good one.

She smiled to herself. Although things were tense and she was as needy for sex as ever, she felt safe and cared for. She was lucky and understood how bad her situation could have ended, and she needed to remember that. She yawned and went back to bed, tossing away her night clothes before she climbed in to sleep. She was so exhausted she fell asleep in seconds.

Light blasted against her eyelids, and she felt it was a cruel assault as she turned away from it. "Since when does my apartment have a sunny window?" she grumbled into the pillow, thinking she was back on Emendo in her one room apartment.

Shooting up, Ziph remembered everything and groaned as she slammed her face back down into her pillow. Her skin felt chilled, and she looked down, finding herself fully uncovered and her ass stuck up in the air. Her tail was hovering over her head. Her door had been pulled shut, and she flattened against the bed in relief that she hadn't shined Dacket with all her lady parts in the air. Or did she?

Oh, oh fuck, is that why the door is shut now? I don't think I shut it last night. I never used to sleep with the door shut. Ziph dressed in some gym clothes and came out to Dacket looking like he hadn't slept in weeks. The man appeared as though he had fallen down a flight of stairs.

"I should probably move back down to my apartment with Danny. You don't look like you've slept well." Ziph didn't want to tell him he looked like shit, but he almost looked sick. Dacket perked up and shook his head as he set his laser focus on her. "That would not be a good idea. I'm not sure anyone else could keep their hands off you." Dacket's breath caught remembering a few minutes before when his face was so close to her ass in the air all he could breathe was her pussy scented air. He wanted to taste her so badly he nearly shivered.

Ziph stared at him, he was not telling her everything, and she wished he would open up. "You at least need a break, so I'm going to the gym for a workout." Ziph went around the couch, and Dacket stayed as still as a statue as she shut the door behind her.

When she walked through the gym door from the garage, and Trent was lifting weights next to Whit, both were covered in sweat soaked through their shirts. They eyed Ziph like she was a whole meal as she went to use the runner. Her pheromones still lingered in the air, and she felt terrible for making everyone sex fiends for a second time.

Damn squirrels and their great mating chase. She felt the urges so strong it made her want to puke. All she wanted was to run away just to be railed ass up by whomever arrived first. *What a bullshit urge to have. Why couldn't I have a useful urge?* Her tail flitted behind her as she aimed for the runner, she needed to burn these hormones off before she climbed Whit and Trent at the same time. All these Elarian men were too good to be true, she knew there had to be a catch somewhere. *Stalking ex, secret love child, or maybe they're really assassins. Who am I kidding, none of that would stop me. They could probably be serial killers, and I wouldn't care.*

She began her run and noticed in her periphery Whit and Trent were hardly concentrating on their own workouts. Both of them were lifting weights while watching her run. As time passed, she periodically checked, and every time they were seemingly entranced by her. She felt like it was all a lie though, and she couldn't help but think they wouldn't like her this much if she didn't have the pheromones. She knew that wasn't true, but it was impossible to keep the thought from her head.

She finished her blazing run with a cooldown, and when she climbed down from the track, Whit and Trent approached her. Trent handed her a glass of water and asked, "Whit and I made plans for Under Eight tonight to visit Dare. Would you like to join us?"

Before Ziph could answer the lights flickered, and Whit sighed, "The wind turbines on the wall must be under maintenance."

Ziph wondered how they had power for lights. "Yes, I would love to come. I need to release energy however I can."

Trent smiled and offered, "We do have that old sky run machine you made Whit. Why don't we assemble it for her?"

Whit agreed, "That's perfect. She could practice while she expels energy. Help me take the parts from the storage closet." Trent followed Whit to a closet nearby, and they pulled some equipment out of the way to make room. Next to the runner, they drug out several metal parts and began assembling them. When they were finished, she realized what she was looking at was similar to what they called a ski machine where she was from. *I fucking love skiing. I wonder if they have snow covered mountains here. These people need to be introduced to skiing.*

Ziph was thrilled as she watched them finish assembling it. "This looks like I will be at the gym a lot."

CHAPTER 19
A WALK AND A SNACK

Ziph faced her mirror and was satisfied with her makeup as she reached for her glue and slid some in her bra. She was wearing a low-cut maxi dress with a high leg slit, and she had her tail out. She wasn't hiding it if she didn't need to because Danny told her the rumors about an elsewhere woman had been lackluster at best. She was in no danger, and she loved her tail, it was a golden color, and the fur was so long it draped down making it resemble a droopy feather. The way her fur moved when she ran or danced made her love it even more. The fur never tangled, and it was always shiny and healthy.

The black dress contrasted with the beige of her skin, rosy golden hair, and tail. She had a deep brown smokey eye with added lashes and a cherry red lipstick on to complete her look. She guessed makeup was just colorful rocks and dirt refined into powders, and this planet had an abundance of rocks. *Thank the gods this world has good makeup. Wait, I forgot, never mind, fuck the gods, I'm not saying that any more.*

She paused before leaving her room. She knew Dacket was seated on his couch with a new jet design he was working on spread all around him. *Deep breath Ziph, he's just the finest man I've ever seen, and he says the hottest things I have ever heard. Fuck me, please, what the fuck are you waiting for?* As soon as the thought was spoken in her mind, she felt guilty all over again. *I really just need to leave that man alone before we both get our hearts broken. Maybe I can convince Whit to help me find someone to date.* Turning the handle, she willed herself to pass by him on her way out. She needed to meet Whit and Trent at Trent's apartment soon or she would make them wait. *I used to be late all the time, and I'm not doing it anymore. I'm going to be on time, dammit.*

Dacket froze when she came in, and Ziph was unprepared for how hard it would be to walk by him. By the time she reached the door, he had gone from focused on his work to distraught. Ziph opened the door of the apartment and closed it behind her quickly, before pressing her back into the door. Whit was in the hallway and asked, "Are you alright?"

Ziph came up to him, and they linked arms before heading down the stairs. "I am all right considering, but I think Dacket is struggling with something more than just my pheromones."

Whit stopped them on the stairs as he halfway explained, "Why do you think I haven't invited you to my bed? Do you really believe I am the type of man who waits patiently? Not a chance. I've wanted you in depraved ways since day one, but I know Dacket too well to take you for myself like I want. He would skin me like a serpent. Trent feels the same way I do, and Dacket would skin him too. But to answer your inquiry, he is very secretive, and I am not happy about it." Whit continued their descent, and Ziph wasn't sure what to say. She just thought they were being respectful.

"So, you really don't know what's happening with him either and that means no to everything? Good to know." Ziph was infinitely discouraged by that piece of information as they met Trent at his door.

Danny was just walking in with bags from a nearby store and wearily approached her door. "You have fun. I am sleeping tonight. Your damn pheromones have had me up at all hours."

Ziph frowned and started to apologize, but she wasn't in control of her pheromones and had no real reason to apologize. Remembering what Dacket was explaining, she changed her words around to fit better. "I hope you can rest tonight. I'll be out tonight, so I'm sure you will." Danny smiled and shut the door behind her. *Fine, he was right. That did feel a lot better than apologizing.*

Trent and Whit escorted Ziph to the truck, and they all sat quietly as they traveled and parked. Trent and Whit linked arms on either side of Ziph, and they guided her to the club down the maze of hallways and staircases. When they arrived, the live music had a catchy beat while the acrobatics performed below. People were dancing on the balcony, and Ziph couldn't wait to join them. She nearly dragged Whit and Trent up the stairs. *I needed this night out so bad.*

Danny had been right about the rumors, hardly anyone even looked in her direction with her bushy tail on display. She could have yelped for joy but held back as Whit moved ahead and found them a round booth.

Just as Ziph sat down, she saw a man who looked far too similar to Dacket, and all the excitement she held inside died away. Trent noticed and looked to where her eyes were focused before he signaled to Whit they would be leaving. They led her out and she didn't understand at first, but when she felt the cool air outside the club, it all made sense. *I'm too emotional to be out dancing tonight. This open air is exactly what I needed.*

Trent moved ahead and spoke more to Whit than Ziph, "Why don't we all take a walk through the fruit tree gardens on the edge of Sector Five and Six, she needs the exercise." Ziph couldn't help but laugh as she recalled people walking their pets on the streets of Emendo. *Fruit trees accessible to the public? What in the commune is going on here?* "Do you mean your city has fruit trees available to everyone?" As soon as she asked, she felt a wave of stupidity rush over her, and she leaned her head back to pinch the bridge of her nose. "Never mind." Trent couldn't help but laugh, and Whit followed. She followed up with another question, "Speaking of eating, I haven't seen anyone eat anything since I've been here. Are you hiding something? It's not terribly gross, is it?"

Whit cleared his throat and tried not to chuckle before he answered, "I will be happy to show you when we go home."

Trent burst with a half scoff, half laugh, "You're showing her? I am not missing this." Ziph was beginning to think watching them eat would not be a pleasant experience. Remembering how snakes ate, she wondered if it was anything like that. *If they can unhook their jaw, I will become obsessed. I already know it.*

They walked for several blocks before they arrived at the gardens, and Ziph was delighted to walk through such a beautiful place. She approached a tree and plucked a bright rosy, red apple before devouring it. "Your food tastes untainted by pollution and human interference." Ziph was thankful for one thing, to be away from humans.

"What's a human?" Whit asked as he watched her eat the apple, core of the apple, stem, and all. "They're a type of being I read this ancient creature made from chimpanzees. They ended up being rather mean and exploitive in nature, and the human's killed their gentle makers. They almost destroyed my galaxy with a virus made to warp evolution into making more humans develop instead of whatever being should have developed for the planet's environment. They probably prevented at least a hundred independent species from developing. It's an evil I'm not sure anyone has any idea how to rectify. Humans are who kidnapped me at a lab and sent me here. They seem to corrupt anything and everything, they touch. I hope I never have to see another one." Ziph cringed thinking of how she had been stuffed into the pod and transported to Binara.

I don't miss home, but I do miss my mother. She wanted to hug her mother desperately, so badly she would even settle for a conversation. "Can you tell me about your families?"

Trent went silent, and Whit tried to explain, "Hunters, well, we don't usually live that long. We are raised by other hunters, but it's not really a parent child situation like it is for other Sectors. We avoid building close relationships with anyone." Ziph felt a rush of understanding, followed by extreme guilt, and she sat down on a nearby bench. His last statement stabbed in her in the gut and twisted. *How could hunter's lives be unfair on every level, even with parenting?*

Ziph sat in silence as she stared up between the trees to the bright stars above, the beautiful stripe of stars so clear, unlike her feelings. She wished she could have understood sooner, before she had hopelessly fallen for these three men. *I'm bound to lose them all, or my own life. What is the fucking point of love when they could die so easily, and it would all be gone all in an instant? Fuck this, I want see Whit eat a live rat. Please be a live rat. I really need to see something fucked up.*

"I want to go home and see you eat something. Maybe it will help me stop my spiraling thoughts," Ziph spoke just above a whisper as she turned to Whit. He gave her a sad smile and nodded before they all rose from the bench and made their way back to the truck. A quiet ride back to the garage followed, and Ziph didn't pull herself out of her mournful feelings until they reached Whit's kitchen.

Ziph could hear a faint scratching sound coming from his pantry, and she wondered if she was about to see him eat a live rat. *Oh gods, he's really going to eat a live rat!* That was exactly what was about to happen as Whit pulled a small cage with two plump rats onto the countertop. "Are you sure you want to watch?"

Ziph nodded to him, hoping they didn't think she was weird for staring at them while they ate. "Yes, and I already knew your people did this. I just hadn't accepted it as reality yet. Let's see it." *I know I'm going to get obsessed with this because I know this is going to be fucked up. Why do I love fucked up things so much? I hope they don't think I'm weird. Fine, maybe I am weird, but I don't really want that broadcast, or do I?*

Whit smirked at Ziph as he reached in and took the tail of the large rat before grabbing the other one and handing it over to Trent. They each unhinged their jaw before they slammed the rats against the counter and slowly lowered them into their gaping open mouths. They swallowed the rats down, and she could see the lump moving down their throats as their muscles constricted around the animal and pushed it toward their stomachs.

Ziph was wide eyed and hopelessly entranced by them swallowing the rats whole. She gulped audibly as they brought their eyes back to her. *That was gross, and really disturbing, but it was also one of the coolest things I've ever seen, and now I'm obsessed.* She was speechless, for once. Finally giving up that she would feel any better, Ziph imagined her bed and fought a yawn. *I need to accept that I will just have to work out for the rest of my life.* "I think that's enough for tonight. I'm ready for bed."

Whit and Trent guided her to the door, and she was painfully aware of how Trent stayed behind in Whit's room. She was jealous, but knew why they were more than apprehensive to add another sexual relationship to their group. *I'm sure they think I can't handle it, and I'll end up with too many feelings. As chaotic as I am, I'm sure they think I'm bursting with emotion ready to dump it all on them. I wish they understood how wrong they are. Anything is better than this.* When she slid the key in Dacket's door, she felt her heart jump in her chest as she opened the door to him asleep on his couch. His jet plans were still all around him and his shirt was off, hanging on the side of the couch.

She couldn't help it; she stopped and watched him sleep. He was perfect, so were Whit, and Trent. She wanted them all, but Dacket was too afraid she would fall for them too hard and the end would be too much. *The end is already too much to even think about and they've hardly laid a hand on me. Maybe they're right. I think I need a fucking drink. I wonder if Dacket has any liquor in his kitchen.* Ziph quietly opened a few cabinets and found a bottle of liquor with some dust on the top.

She sat on the kitchen floor in her dress with her legs

crossed and unscrewed the top before sniffing the liquor. It was terrible, and she grimaced, but it was all she had, so she tipped it back and guzzled some before sticking her tongue out fighting a gag. *This is probably ninety percent alcohol. I need to be careful. The last thing I want is to be running through the streets of the city, naked and blackout drunk.* After her little pep-talk, Ziph was not careful at all as she tipped up the bottle again and drank down more of the searing liquid like it was water. She rested the bottle in her lap and began absently yanking on the place the dress bunched at her middle when she sat.

Only I would land in a place with beautiful men I can't have, men who I will certainly have to grieve dearly one day. Ziph was devastated for them and for herself. *Why can't my happiness exist? Why can't it ever be me, or the people I care about? I'm the best at blocking out feelings. I avoided all relationships my entire life to this point. I could totally handle a no attachment relationship.*

The liquor became thick in her veins as she lay back on the kitchen floor. *This situation is bullshit. Do they really not think I can handle sex without having my feelings involved? Fuck this. I will show Dacket. I can have sex and not feel a damn thing.*

Ziph was too drunk to be walking around, so she set the bottle down and pulled her dress up before she crawled across the floor on her hands and knees over to Dacket's couch. She peered over the side of the couch at him still asleep in the same place before she moved next to him. She watched him breathe for a moment before she swiftly stood and swung her leg up and over him, and she eased herself down onto his lap.

The moment she made contact with him, his eyes flew

open, but he didn't move as she rested her hands on his flat, thickly muscled stomach. "Ziph, what are you doing?"

Ziph slurred as she answered, "I, I can fuck you with no feelings. You don't have to even like me. I promise I won't want anything else. I can do it, I swear."

Dacket moved his hands to her waist and closed his eyes briefly before he looked at her longingly and quietly admitted, "You might be able to turn it all off, but I can't."

Ziph froze. She knew she had done something terrible, and she shook her head, "I am, um, I, I am so sorry." She couldn't escape any faster as she half crawled, and half ran to her bedroom before locking the door behind her.

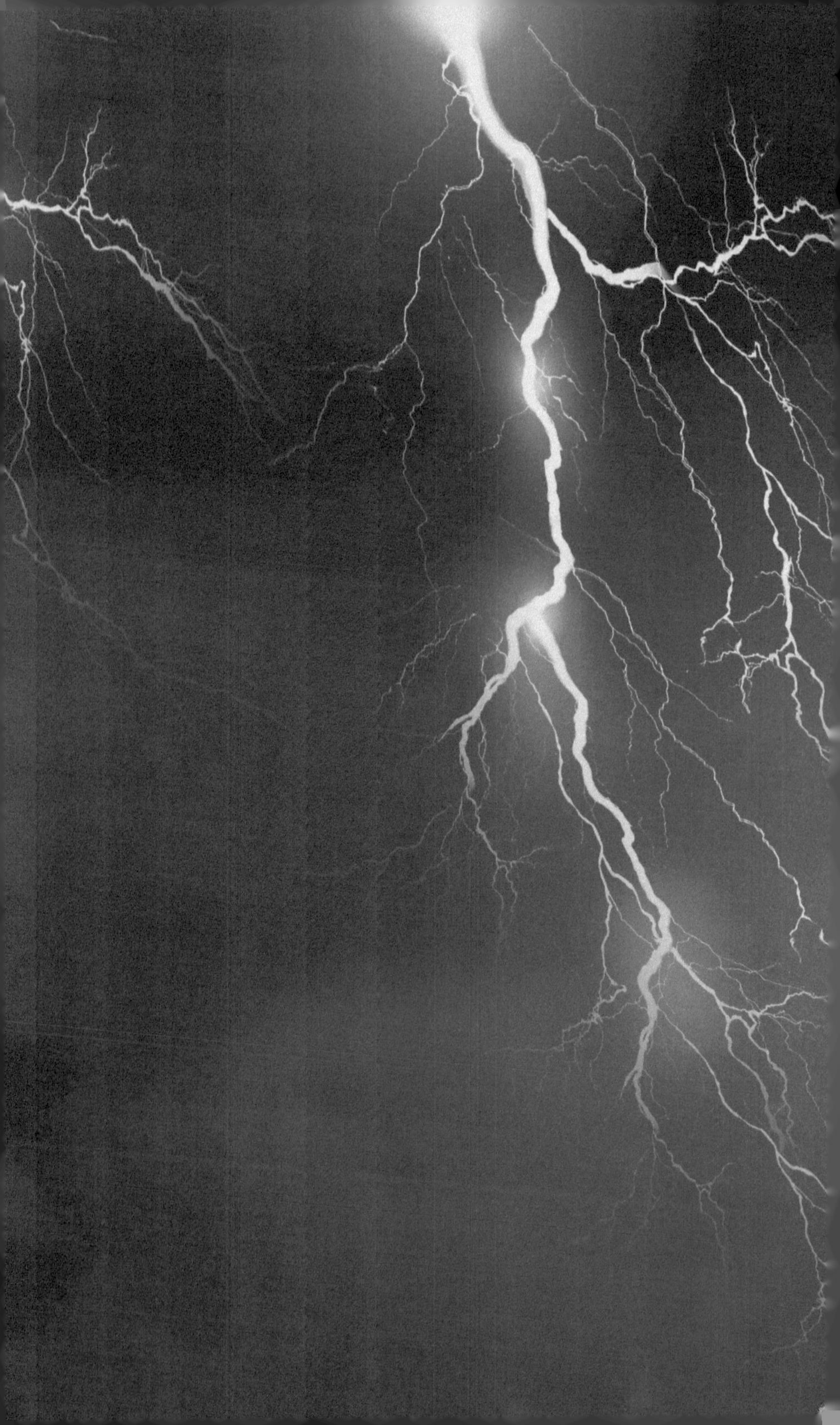

CHAPTER 20
VANTE

It was still dark, and Ziph sat straight up with her throat so dry she felt like she was becoming desiccated from the inside out. Rushing to her bathroom, she stuck her head under the sink and sucked up as much water as she could. Staring at herself in the mirror, she rubbed at the smeared makeup under her eyes. She had forgotten to take it off the night before. She had left her night clothes from the night before on her counter, so she changed into them and told herself she could bathe and wash the sheets in the morning. The bed was calling to her.

She started to crawl back into bed when she heard a sound, *is that in the apartment or in the factory?* Ziph was too curious to let it go, so she slid on her boots and made her way into the apartment. Dacket was in his room with the door shut. His papers were all picked up, and everything seemed in order. She went to the windows and saw a shadow moving down in the factory. Again, curiosity overrode logic, and she had to know what was lurking down there. *Could an animal be in the factory? Do they have animals here?*

Ziph slipped downstairs quietly, and as she was passing Dacket's truck in the garage to check on the factory, she saw a truck she didn't recognize parked outside across the street. *That feels out of place, I should grab a knife from Dacket's truck. Shit. Could this be a break-in?* Ziph did just that and when she had the long knife in her hand, she felt much better about going inside.

Tiptoeing into the store, she passed the register and the freezer before she slowly opened the processing factory door. Another shadow moved where she had seen it before. It was the area she knew held the connections for their lighting system. That would knock out power to the whole building, and in that moment, she knew exactly what this was. *Someone is robbing them, but not today, bitch. I don't have time to run upstairs and warn anyone, I guess they'll just have to rush out here when they see what's happening.* Ziph smirked remembering a time she kicked those two big men's ass in the alleyway who tried to rob her in Pluto's district on a Emendo. She dropped low and snuck around the table. As she peeked around the side, she saw three Elarian just beginning to cut wires.

Ziph grabbed a tiny pebble she spotted under the leg of the table and tossed it at the closest man. He slapped the back of his neck where it struck and the man next to him hissed at him. *Damn, I need something bigger to throw at them.* She looked up at the table and there was a small stone brick, *well, I guess that works.* She picked it up and felt the weight before she stood up and whistled at them, causing the three men to turn to look at her.

She had already thrown the brick, and it was soaring at the face of the center man. It struck before he could react and he yelped in pain as the other two pounced on Ziph, but she saw them coming and did a backflip onto the table behind her before running along the tabletops. The sounds of her boots hitting the metal tables and the legs scraping the stone floors underneath were ear piercing, and she knew she wouldn't be in this fight alone for long.

Ziph could hear doors slamming in the apartments behind her as she whirled to find one of the men had gained on her and was far too close for comfort. She knew how to run, but she loved a good fight, and she held the knife up, preparing for the approaching man. He laughed as he charged her, and she screamed as he tackled her. She slashed his arm before he batted the knife, and it fell away, causing her to grunt. She adjusted her eyes to the dark and shadowed area they landed in, she could see the man's position. He was still kneeling in front of her, and she took the opportunity to attack.

Ziph slammed her elbows down onto his shoulders as she wrapped her legs around his torso before slamming her fist in his nose causing his head to flop to the side. She tried to push away, but his strong hand grabbed her by the throat and began squeezing. She didn't know what else to do, and she saw one of his nipples through his shirt, so she went for it. He squealed as she twisted his nipple between her strong fingers, and he roared while he violently compressed her throat in response.

She could hear boots pounding all around her, but the stars in her eyes told her they might not make it to her in time. *I did good though, I made up for everything I did wrong. It's alright, I did everything I could. I made the best of what I had, and I finally did a good thing.* She felt him crush something in her throat, causing her terrible pain, just as the stars merged into darkness.

The dark seemed to stretch forever, it was so peaceful, and she felt like she was somewhere safe. A light formed and she smiled, it was bright and happy, was this the afterlife? It smelled sweet and seemed so lovely, the breeze was gentle, and the light was welcoming.

In an instant she was back to reality and wishing she wasn't conscious, her throat ached, and she felt a hand stroking her face. "She's breathing. Ziph, can you hear me?"

Dacket sounded so full of fear, she tried to answer and it came out scratchy, "I'm alright. People broke in and I caught them." She opened her eyes and Dacket, Whit, and Trent, all surrounded her. The concern on their faces squeezed her heart.

Dacket had his hand on her upper chest and the other cradling her neck. "Can you move?" Ziph moved her neck from side to side, but she was certain something had torn, and it felt like it might be a tendon.

"My neck and chest hurt but I can move. Can you help me up?" They all moved and Dacket helped ease her upright. She looked over to see the three intruders had been brutally slaughtered, their bodies twisted and dismembered. Vante was among the three, and she was positive he had been the one who tried to kill her. Whit and Trent were covered in blood while Dacket was clean. Did that mean Dacket ran to her while the other two killed the intruders? Her guilt over trying to seduce him was so much worse now, and she wanted to die of shame.

She could feel her face burn, and Dacket stepped in front of her. "Your skin is heating, are you alright?"

He was genuinely concerned which made it even harder to speak. She whispered, "Can I please be embarrassed in peace?"

Dacket had no idea what she meant. "Please explain. How could you be embarrassed? You stopped three hunters from potentially killing several of us in our sleep. They had begun to cut the lights, a typical move for hunters to take out an entire rival hunting group. If we search their homes, I'm sure we would find the floor plans to our building. Next time, please just wake one of us first. Don't risk your life."

Ziph swore she saw Dacket reach for her hand, but he shifted to guide her upstairs. When they made it to the apartment, Ziph was having strong feelings about being alone as she eased on the couch. Dacket started off to the kitchen, but Ziph asked, "Can you sit with me?" He whirled around and went straight back to the couch, sitting right next to her, but not saying a word. His tail wrapped around his leg, and he buried the tip under the couch cushion. The system star was just rising, and Ziph was thankful for the natural light pouring into the windows. She wasn't sure she could handle the darkness yet. She had been far too close to the end and had even glimpsed the other side. "I think I almost died."

Dacket's voice cracked as he softly replied, "I know." Ziph looked over at him and he was staring at the wall, boring holes into the bookshelf in front of them.

"I saw the other side. It was everything I've ever wanted the afterlife to be. It was peaceful, and it was so warm, I wanted to follow the light and jump through."

Dacket finally turned to face her, and she realized she may have said the wrong thing. He looked devastated and could hardly look her in the eye for more than a brief moment when he asked, "I need a drink, do you want one?"

"Was that what you went to the kitchen for when we came up here?" Ziph asked, and he nodded solemnly. "Oh, um, yeah, a drink sounds great. Maybe you should just bring the bottle in here." Ziph heard him as he grabbed the bottle from the floor where she had left it the night before, and he grabbed two cups from the cabinet before coming back to the couch. He set the glasses down next to him and started to pour a glass before he noticed Ziph's lipstick around the rim, and he shrugged before tipping it up himself.

He hissed and frowned as he handed the bottle to Ziph. "I don't usually drink. This is for mixing and it's rough. I wish I had something else."

Tipping it back Ziph noticed her chest was sore and she rubbed her sternum gently as she set the bottle down. "I had to force you to breathe, that's why your chest is sore." Ziph tried to smile at him, but she wasn't sure in that moment if she was more traumatized, or if he was. It was cruel that this soft hearted man had been thrust into such a harsh hunter's life. Now that she knew the truth, she would do her best to try not to seduce him, accidentally or otherwise.

"I know you said not to apologize for anything, but I have something I need to say I'm sorry for."

Dacket tried to remain still but shook his head briefly. "You have had a tough time since you were dropped on this world. You have nothing to apologize for." In another lifetime this would be Ziph's dream man, how had she found him just for him to be too far out of reach for her to ever have? This was all a cruel joke.

Just above a whisper, Ziph apologized anyway, "I'm sorry I've acted like such an immature brat. I paraded myself around you like you had a choice in any of this, and you never did. I pried into your business, and I have been treating you like I am owed information about your life when you've been nothing but wonderful to me. I feel like a piece of shit. Maybe I should have crossed over. Maybe I could have seen my grandparents again, and you wouldn't have to deal with me anymore."

Dacket frowned and searched the room with his eyes before he finally looked back at Ziph. "Please don't say that. When I saw Vante with his hands around your neck, and your body was limp, the factory, and even myself, Whit, or Trent didn't matter. I accepted our deaths years ago. Nothing mattered except reaching you, but when you weren't breathing, I had never really felt anything as disturbing as the realization you were dead, and my entire reality came to a halt. I wasn't sure what I was doing, but I knew I needed to help you breathe. I pressed on your chest and made you breathe until you began on your own. I heard the screams of the hunters as Whit and Trent killed them, but nothing could have taken my attention from you. They joined me once they were all dead, and that's when you woke up. I don't ever want to endure that again."

Ziph rested her hand on his and he didn't move. She pulled her legs up and wrapped her arms around them as she asked, "Can you pass me the bottle?" Dacket took a reluctant swig of the liquor before he passed it to Ziph. She tipped it back and drank down a few big gulps before handing it back.

Dacket stood and returned the bottle and cups to the kitchen before helping Ziph to her bed, "We have a hunting practice scheduled today. You should rest. Trent is on duty today so you will be safe here."

Ziph agreed and let him help her into bed, she knew she was bathing before she fell asleep, but she wasn't resisting him. She had put this man through enough.

He closed her door, and she heard him dress in his

room before he left the apartment, locking the door on the way out. The liquor had just started to kick in when she realized she hadn't noticed, or felt, the bells chime in a while. Just as her mind moved on from the thought, she heard the bells start up, but they were at a frequency which didn't vibrate her piercings, and she took a desperately needed sigh of relief. Dacket had adjusted the chimes.

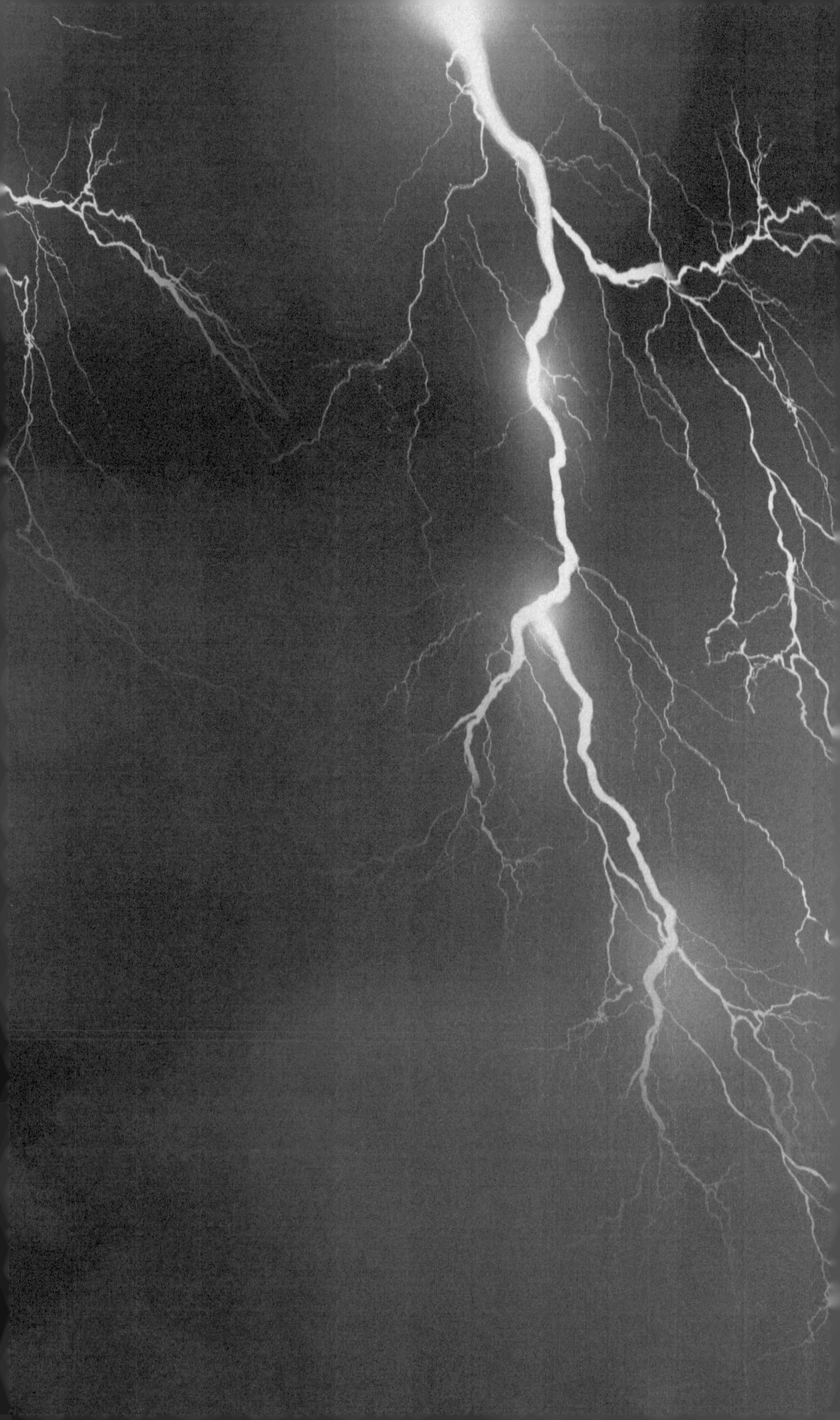

CHAPTER 21

RUSTED WIRES

A crack of thunder rumbled through the metal walls, causing Ziph to sit straight up in bed. It was the middle of the night, and a storm beat on the windows followed by more rumbles of thunder. Her hand was at her neck, rubbing her sore skin gently, trying to push the memory of being strangled to death from her mind like as if it was even a possibility. She knew better, just like she knew the stretch of nightmares she had after she fell asleep would take some time to work through. *How the fuck am I going to work through this trauma? There are no fucking therapists here.* Her head ached as she tried to remember her therapy sessions and what she would have to do to desensitize herself.

Ziph climbed from bed to search for her communicator to call her mother, but when her feet hit the floor, she remembered her mother wasn't just a call away. She could never speak to her again. Sliding down the bed to the floor, Ziph curled in a ball and pulled her knees to her chest, hugging them tightly. *I miss my grandparents, and I miss my mom. I just wish I had someone to talk to.*

Lightning streaked across the sky, and thunder blasted through the metal walls of the building. She wasn't sure she could handle this life. On the surface for her it seemed like she had it made, but reality was so much worse. Three gorgeous men, all wanting to be with her, all working and hunting together. Men she could spend hours in deep conversation with, and they were the type of good-hearted people who didn't even exist on Emendo. There was a catch though. She couldn't actually have any of them because they were too fucking scared to fall in love and be faced with losing it.

Not one thing in my life has panned out. What have I done to deserve this? She recalled what creature her species came from, how they innocently bury their treasured nuts and seeds, only to forget where they buried them. They were always saving seeds they would never eat, working so hard for nothing. *A lifetime of hard work has never amounted to anything for me. How am I supposed to keep going?*

Tears gathered in her eyes, she had been too strong for too long, and now it was time to let it out. She felt the rush of emotion overtake her as she melted onto the cold, stone floor. Her heart ached for her mother; she just wanted to call her. If she could just hear her voice one last time, she knew she would be all right again, and she could continue here. Her mother always said the right thing, no matter how much it hurt her to do it. Ziph knew she would tell her to be strong and brave, to not fall for trickery. She would advise her to be wary of anything too good to be true. *Sorry, Mom, I already fell for that one. I've already broken one of your rules. You would be so disappointed.*

More tears spilled over onto the floor as her thoughts became whirlwinds of terror, her mind tormenting her with the possible loss of Dacket, Whit, and Trent after she grieved for her mother. Flashes of what could happen, what she could lose, blasted in her mind as bile churned inside of her gut.

Stars began spinning in her vision as she recalled the alcohol, and the tears she swallowed were aggravating her stomach, so she crawled for the toilet knowing what was coming next. After dry heaving nothing for a few minutes, Ziph gave up and tried to sip some water from the sink. She wet her face more than anything, but her mouth no longer had the taste of bile. Staring at her own reflection, puffy eyes and rosy red face mocked her, further driving her into her own despair. *I don't even know if I want to exist anymore. What is the point? To serve others your entire life and never have a bit of joy. I wish Dacket had just let me die. I could be hugging my grandparents right now.*

Thunder crashed again, and she remembered Danny was just downstairs. She knew her friend wouldn't mind a middle of the night visit considering her alternative of spinning endlessly. Continuing to lay balled up on the cold bathroom floor wasn't an option. It would give her no closure, and she needed to be able to function. She knew serpents were coming, and she needed to be ready, or she would end up dead. *Maybe I should just let a serpent eat me.* Her mind swung right back to facing Dacket, Whit, and Trent's deaths and she scrambled from her bathroom for clothes. Something inside of her screamed to run and never return.

She put on her comfortable hunting underclothes before she slipped out of her room with her boots in hand and closed the apartment door behind her. She carefully locked it without making a sound and tip toed down the stairs to the apartment she shared with Danny for a few days.

She had not been here long enough to be having this level of a breakdown, was this part of her hormones? This was a nightmare, and she couldn't wait to talk to Danny. She unlocked the door and went inside where she found Danny's bedroom door shut. She softly knocked on Danny's door in case she had company.

She could hear her moving around, and when Danny opened her door, she threw her arms around Ziph, "What's wrong? You look so sad, have you been crying?" Ziph couldn't answer as tears over flowed and she squeezed her friend. She knew Danny would be the perfect person to talk to, and she had not been wrong.

"I miss my mother. I just wish I could talk to her somehow," Ziph could hardly speak but managed to let it all out between her crying.

Danny led her to the couch, and they sat together. "I wish there was something I could do, but I don't think I've ever even heard of communication by anything other than letter. Is it like through the lights or something?" Danny looked clueless, but Ziph smiled a bit.

"Yeah, digital signals are kind of like light, I guess. I'm sure there was tech in the pod I arrived in, but I smashed the console when I realized they sent me one way and weren't bringing me back. I didn't want them to have any information about the planet I landed on. I don't regret smashing it, but I just wish there were a way I could have used the technology to make calls to say goodbye at the very least. I'm not sure I would even know how to do something like that though, all I ever studied was biology."

Danny scowled in thought and wrapped her arm around Ziph. "I mean, would it hurt to cross some wires, or push some buttons to see if you can get a signal to push through? Maybe someone will hear it?"

Ziph knew there was a chance Danny was right, and now she fully regretted coming down here and not falling asleep. *Fuck, I'm about to do something so stupid.* She was impulsive and she needed to try to fix the pod communication signal, right that moment. "Danny, I need to…"

Danny cut her off, "I know. Don't ask me how I know this, but Whit hides a key in his tracks. It's next to a small red mark on the side. Dacket never let anyone drive his truck, but Whit lets people drive his truck all the time."

Ziph's eyes filled with tears again. "Thank you. I need to do something, or I might explode."

Danny smiled at her in reassurance. "You do realize this is a horrible idea, and we will both be in a lump of trouble?"

Ziph reached out for Danny's hand and through a sob agreed, "I know. The best friends you have will understand your wrongs just as much as your rights. I think that's called unconditional love. I'll be careful. Where I'm going isn't too close to the sky belt to run into anything I can't handle."

Danny walked Ziph to her front door and locked it behind her. In the hallway, Ziph held her boots to her chest, and tip toed down to the garage before squinting in the dark for the red mark on Whit's tracks. *How the fuck do you even drive these things? I didn't even know how to drive back home. I guess I'll find out now.* Ziph popped the key from the track before she checked the guard station. It was a younger person. They looked new and unsure of themselves, *perfect.* Ziph went back to Whit's truck and on the way, grabbed her spare bag of hunting clothes Dacket kept because she always forgot something. *I need to attach every-thing together like he suggested, that really was a great idea.*

She fired up Whit's truck, thankful his was the quiet one of the two trucks, and she pulled out to the gate. She waved at the young man, and he opened the gate without delay, *well, here we go off to try and call my mother. I know there's not a chance in hell this will work but I'm trying it anyway. I need to know.*

Tears trickled down her face as rain beat the wind-shield. She was just thankful she had the hang of driving in seconds after watching somebody do something one time. Nothing ever took her too long to figure out, and that was precisely why she was even trying this. The buildings all around looked like patchwork, they were so cramped in places that buildings were clearly built right on top of one another. She refocused on the road as nausea raged in her belly, but she swallowed it back as she traveled in the direction she knew. Approaching the gate, she saw no one manning it, so she drove right through as Whit or Dacket would.

When she was on the other side, she took a deep sigh of relief. There was nothing to stop her now, and she stepped on the pedal as the truck took off. Ziph was briefly entranced as she realized the truck was mostly well-oiled gears and magnets as she peered through the glass instruments at the driver's seat. *This truck design is genius.* When she pressed the accelerator, it created a chain reaction of gears turning, progressively faster and larger in a maze before it reached the wheels. It looked complicated beyond what she could comprehend as she tried to understand how a small press of a pedal could transfer so much energy. She finally found a small elec-trical meter in the corner of the dash, but the charge read

90%, and she watched as it didn't move over a long stretch.

She was glad she had something to take her mind from her current objective because she was afraid she would change it. She couldn't stop now. She had to try and talk to her mother, at least one last time. Lightning struck the truck, and she watched the meter rush up to 100%. *Now that is interesting. These trucks collect lightning for energy.*

Ahead, she could finally see the small hill her pod landed on. It was hard to miss in the mostly flat terrain. The rain continued to rush over the windshield, but the glass was repelling it well enough she understood why they didn't use anything to wipe it away. *I wish I could wash away thoughts and feelings so easily.*

She pulled up to the hill and changed into her hunting clothes. She sighed wishing she had a hair tie to pull her hair back as she climbed out. *Whit would've handed me one if he were here.* The sounds of the storm raged around her as she made the short trek up the hill, and toward the pod where she was now beyond determined to create a way to speak to her mother. *I'll stay out here as long as it takes for me to wire this piece of shit into a communicator.*

Rain began soaking her undershirt, which was hanging under her jacket from her yanking on it. When she spotted the pod surrounded by rock, it seemed intact and just the way she left it. She finally felt a ping of hope as she approached and lifted the glass lid to climb inside. She crawled in, and before she began, she closed her eyes and centered herself, just taking deep breaths for a moment to gather her thoughts. She had made it, she was in the pod, and she could do this.

She pushed her mask up and used it to hold her hair back, she was glad for the elastic which held in its place because it was keeping her wet hair off her neck. She leaned down to find everything far too dark and waited for the lightning above to light the sky and hopefully the inside of the pod.

When the sky delivered what she needed, she peered down on a broken mess of completely rusted wires. It was as if the pod had decayed and rotted over the short time she had been on Binara, but that couldn't have been possible. The cities here were made of metal. How could metal components rust and rot away like this? *Something feels off, this can't be right.*

She crawled down to look under the instruments, and as the lightning shone brightly into the pod, her heart broke into a million pieces. There was a hard block of salt screwed to the back of the panel, and condensation from the glass lid dripped onto the block. *They designed this pod to rust the components.*

This was intentional so the electronics would rot away quickly, and there would be no hope of communicating with home. She leaned back and screamed at the top of her lungs in anger and sorrow, as a fresh cascade of tears burst from her eyes.

CHAPTER 22

RAIN

Ziph growled and hissed as she kicked at the mounted components, sending them crashing into the nose of the pod. "Fuck you! Fuck all of you! How could you fucking send me into a living nightmare with no way out! I just wanted to talk to my mother one last fucking time! Is that too much to ask?!" she screeched as she tried to reason with herself, but reason had no place here. The only thing she could feel was vitriol and violence scorching the inside of her veins as she thought about the people who did this to her, including her former beloved goddess, Venus.

She swung open the fogged lid to the pod and slid down the side headfirst onto the wet ground. Crumpled on the ground, she sobbed and curled into a ball as the downpour soaked through her clothes. The seams were terrible at keeping out the rain, but she couldn't force herself to care. It wasn't all that cold, and even if it were, she wasn't sure she would do a thing about it then either.

Tears continued to flow from her eyes, streaming endlessly. *I just wanted to talk to my mom.* Her tears fell harder than the rain, and all she could do was hug her knees closer to her chest. It didn't take long before the rain lightened, but the thunder still rumbled through the air like a growling giant hovering over her.

She heard steps behind her, and she knew who was there without looking up. Ziph didn't need to. She could tell by the sound of their boots on the stone because she had memorized the way their boots sounded echoing through the apartment building. Dacket, Whit, and Trent approached as she lay limp in misery, but she didn't have the slightest will to sit up. *They came for me.*

Dacket gently placed his hand on her shoulder, and she felt him scoop her up before he pulled her into his lap. Trent and Whit sat down next to them, and Dacket didn't say a word as he held her. She sobbed all over again, and he tried to wipe the tears from her face, but the lingering rain made it impossible.

She tried to sit up so she could explain. "I was just trying to talk to my mother. I thought if found my pod I could somehow find a way to communicate with her. It was all rusted…"

Dacket stopped her words when he moved her around to straddle him so their faces were even, and he gently placed his hands on either side of her face, "I shouldn't have pushed you away. I should have known better. I was wrong. Regret is much worse than grief could ever be."

He leaned in and kissed her, and she shed even more tears, but these were finally cool tears of relief. He was so warm and tasted just like she imagined, metal and smoke. The way he kissed her filled her with need as he deepened the kiss. His forked tongue explored her mouth as his hands stroked her face. She could feel his bulge moving below her ass, and she hoped she would finally experience what she had been waiting for.

The rain began to lighten, and Dacket lifted Ziph as he stood, shifting her so her legs draped over his arm. Whit went ahead of them and climbed in the truck, and when Dacket set her inside the front passenger seat, she understood why Whit had rushed ahead.

All the seats were reclined and spread out into a makeshift bed, and she guessed it made sense if they were ever caught out in a storm to have somewhere to sleep. When they were all inside, Ziph felt Whit pull her back against his chest as he leaned against the back window. Next to him, Trent began pulling her wet jacket off while Dacket started unbuckling her pants, and her breaths became quick, but she tried not to expect anything, she couldn't handle any more unmet expectations.

When she was down to her wet underclothes, Trent and Whit helped her out of her shirt while Dacket collected her wet items and spread them on the dashboard. He turned back and slid her underpants off as she lifted for him.

She wasn't sure what to do as Dacket climbed over her nude body and began kissing her again. She felt Whit's hands moving against her skin toward her breasts as Trent took her hand and kissed her palm. *Please tell me this is really happening right now, if I wake up, and this is not real...* Dacket kissed her thoroughly before he moved down her neck and gently kissed along the bruising there. He was exceptionally gentle as he moved to her breasts, which Whit was massaging. Whit moved to rubbing her thighs as Dacket took her breasts in his hands and flicked his tongue over both of her nipples, shifting back and forth a few times before kissing down the swell of her belly.

Ziph was overwhelmed with pleasure as Whit kissed

down her neck, and Trent began licking and sucking her nipples. Dacket slid his face between her thighs, and she could feel his hot breath at her pussy, making her whimper for more.

Dacket clearly heard the sound she made as he descended on her, giving a low growl as he tasted her. Ziph writhed with pleasure as he ran his forked tongue along the center of her pussy. He gave her everything she could ever want, but Ziph knew no matter how much stimulation she had, she would not be able to finish. "I can't cum. I've tried for years, and it's never happened, so we can just have sex. I just don't want you to keep wasting your time."

Lifting his head, Dacket glowered at her, "That's not happening. We will try until you find your climax of plea-sure. You have never been, and will never be a waste of time, and you are so much more than a want. You are a need." Ziph's heart soared as she felt Whit shift her to the side, giving him access to kiss her. "Maybe you just need some additional mental and body stimulation. If average stimuli isn't enough for you, there are three of us, and it's nothing we haven't desired." Ziph could feel herself closer than ever with what he said, and the way he leaned in to slide his lips along her jaw had her melting.

They were all so different, and they were incredible on their own, but these three men could coordinate like she had never imagined during sex. Whit had his hand up stroking her face and kissing her sweetly, keeping her thor-oughly enthralled and distracted, while Trent gave her chest all his attention, and Dacket almost seemed to be gently pressing around in her pussy with his fingers. *He is definitely poking around in there. What in Pluto's hell is he looking for?!*

"Dacket, what?" was all she could say before she realized he was locating her illusive clit which only teased her to the edge every time, never allowing her to reach a climax. When he had her clit between his fingers, she let out a high-pitched whimper as she felt him gently bite down on her sensitive flesh with his blunt front teeth. He pressed around her pussy just right, and he trapped her clit in his mouth. When he rubbed his tongue along the sensitive skin, Ziph came undone and thrust her hips up and away from the overwhelming pleasure.

Dacket, Whit, and Trent, all moved her in unison, as they had all discovered the secret at once. Whit and Trent were on either side, holding her arms down while they toyed with her nipples. Dacket spread her legs and Whit and Trent pinned her legs under their own. Dacket resumed his search for her deep clit and when he found it, she bucked and fought them, no matter how much she wanted it. "It's too much, I can't do it!"

Whit leaned in and whispered against her ear, "Let it all go, Golden Girl. Let Dacket do his thing sweetheart. That man has a tongue of dreams."

Ziph felt him bite down slightly harder on her clit this time, and she reared back against Whit and Trent eyeing them wildly. They didn't budge and held her steady as Dacket began flitting his tongue over her clit he had trapped in his teeth.

Ziph went ballistic as they held her down and kissed her neck, and Whit breathed against her ear, "You're doing good. Just take a deep breath and try to calm yourself. You're safe with us sweet Golden Girl, and we will do whatever we need to make sure you cum. That's it, just take a slow breath, you can do it. Breathe through it, that's so good."

Ziph felt something else building, "Oh, oh gods, it's coming!" As soon as she said the words, she screamed with delight and pulsating pleasure as Dacket pushed his forked tongue against her clit and then sucked on it in a rhythm.

Taking in all the air she could, Ziph felt the one thing she had waited so long for, pleasure so thick and sweet it was like a river of molten sugar flowed from her lower belly. Her soul was a waterfall of love and life, she had never dreamed it could be so wonderful. She hummed as it struck deep, sending her whirling inside and gasping for air.

Whit was listening to her breathe as it struck her and stroked her face while he kissed along her jaw. "That's it, sweet Golden Girl. Ride it out until it's too much." She did as he guided, and she let it flow until Dacket moved a bit, and she burst with far too much pleasure, sending her into a screeching mess.

Dacket smiled, hovering over her as he licked his lips and pulled off his jacket. "Now that you've had your first orgasm, it's time for your second." Whit and Trent moved her down as Dacket crawled between her legs and unbuckled his pants. Dacket leaned down to kiss her, and she felt Trent crawling around her to reach Whit, who was undressing as fast as he could.

Trent came behind Whit with his cock already lubed, and entered him quickly, and a lovely sound erupted from Whit as Dacket stole back her attention with his cock pressing in at her pussy. Taking his time, Dacket rubbed his tip in her wetness before he began to slide inside. He moved slow and careful as he eased his way in, the sting of her stretching was nothing compared to how incredible he felt filling her.

Dacket fully seated himself inside of her, and she gasped as his tip touched a place inside making her want to groan with delight. Moving in her with a slow pace to start, she felt his cock expand, but she wasn't sure she could handle being filled much more. *It feels like he's going to rip me in half, I don't know if I can take any more.*

That's when it broke into four parts, each one with moving nodules on the inside edge. Ziph reached up and grasped Dacket's shoulders and dug her fingernails into his flesh, "What do you mean it comes apart *inside of me*?! *Where has this been all my life?!*" The men all laughed under their breath as they continued their thrusting, and Whit began moaning as he tipped over, sending Trent into a heavy orgasm, and the two rocked as one and their bodies melted.

The view of the two men she cared about, locked together in such pleasure had boiled inside as Dacket lifted her hips for better access. He pressed in just right, and Ziph let out a breathy "Whoo!" As she tipped over again, this time the feeling was deeper and stronger, but much more mellow. It was like swimming in warm saltwater, floating and feeling enveloped.

Ziph squeezed Dacket's shoulders again as her orgasm crested, the way he was watching her as she broke apart caused him to cum along with her. He spilled over into her as he groaned, "You're fucking perfect, every inch of you." Dacket lay his hand against her face as he leaned down and their lips locked together. She could feel the love this man held back, how he hid that part of himself.

Ziph wasn't sure what she saw in his eyes as he looked at her, but it wasn't all good. He still hid something from her, and from everyone else too, and she wasn't sure he would ever reveal it. *What dark secrets are you hiding?* She hoped it was something they could help him with, or that he would at the least eventually tell them what was so wrong. Now wasn't the time for that, Ziph had no reason to pry in this moment. *I can't think of that while he's still buried inside of me.*

Once they cleaned up and settled, they all four lay together, nude and limbs entwined as the rain slowed to a mist and a thick fog developed outside. The inside of the truck was warm, and they fell into a deep sleep, Ziph only woke in brief waves of half consciousness with rumbles of thunder. Waking only to feel the warmth wrapped around her, making her feel secure and safe. Giving her a place to rest deeply enough for whimsical, delightful dreams of running along the wooden bridges back home, toward her grandparent's treehouse and their beautiful smiling faces. *Home, I am home.*

She knew how lucky she was to have had a family, so many where she lived on Emendo, had no one. Ziph understood now, the men around her had already chosen her as their family, but she was too self-absorbed to see it before. Now she knew with no doubts she was cared for, and she had found herself a new home.

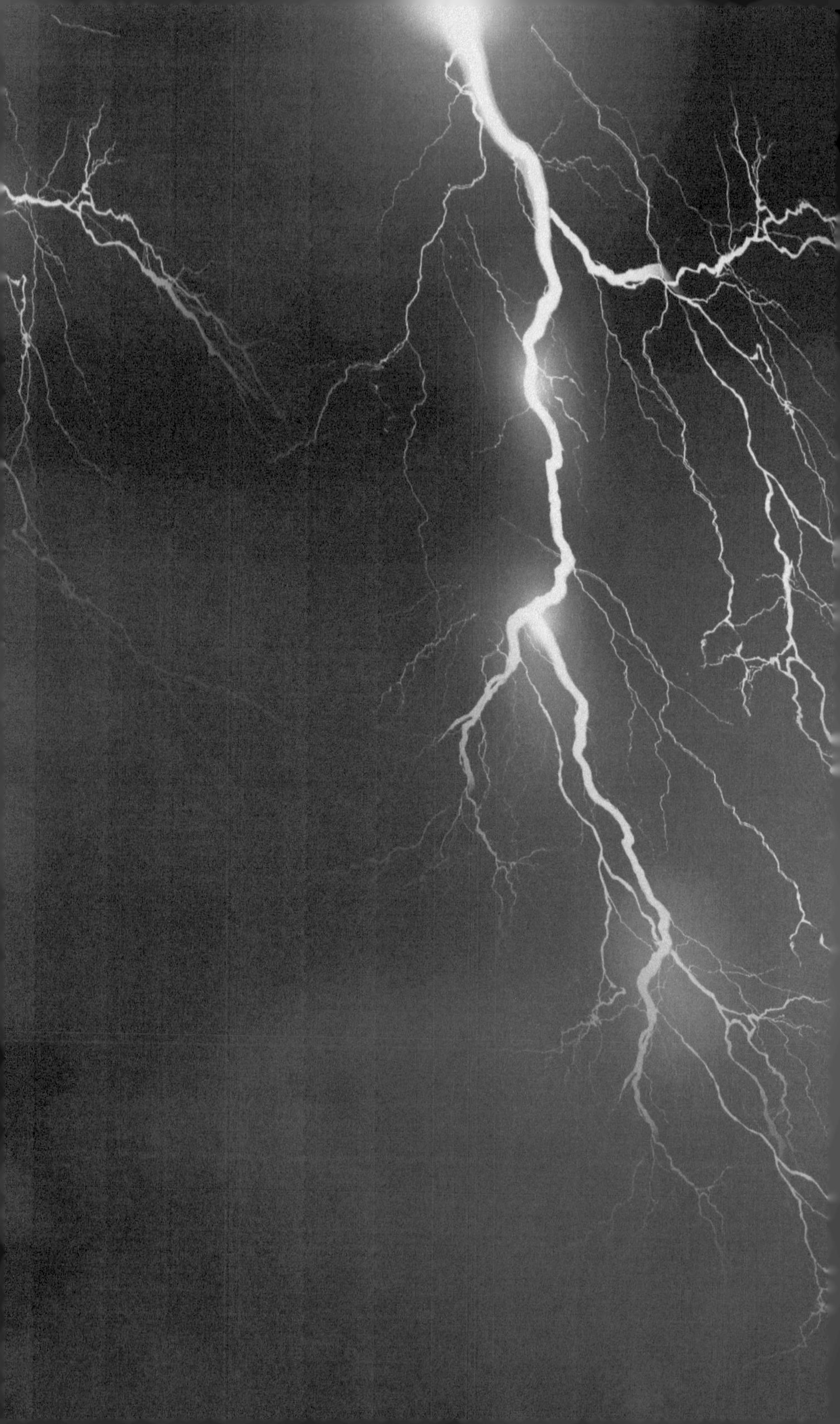

CHAPTER 23

VENUS CAN SUCK IT

After two weeks straight of nothing but thunderstorms and deep cleaning the factory, freezer, and market store, everyone wanted a few days off. Every night they had all been so exhausted they went to bed without even speaking to one another. After a break in, there was no telling what could have happened or what was contaminated, so their entire stock had to be disposed of. Thankfully, they had already sold the majority of meat they had in stock.

They had earned so much from Ziph's recent kill that Dacket assured everyone there would be no need to worry as they had enough coin locked away in the vault to last them many cycles, and this serpent hunt would follow the rains as usual, giving them a chance to fully restock.

The sounds of rain droplets falling against the windows began to lull her back to sleep. It was early in the morning and the system star had just begun to rise, sending streams of light through the clouds. Nightmares of angry hands around her neck had been waking her at night. The memories of what she went through tormented her and she had to fight the disturbing thoughts during quiet moments. A familiar voice pulled her from the dark cycle of thoughts. She could hear Dacket speaking to Trent in the entryway, but she ignored it until she could hear Dacket running.

Oh fuck, it's a serpent alarm. The new notification light must be working in the guard station. Ziph stood up and her skin prickled in the chilly air sending a shiver through her. She hated clothes at night, so when Dacket swung her door open, he stood for a moment taking in her nude body. "The light came on in the guard station." With the confirmation, Ziph moved quickly to dress and Dacket went to his room to do the same. She made sure to grab her face mask and jets this time as she met Dacket in the entryway.

He seemed more nervous than usual, and she felt guilty all over again, she knew this man had a heart of gold he hid behind his quiet, stone-like exterior. "You don't need to worry about me out there. I will be all right."

Dacket glared at her as he opened the door. "You don't know that."

Whit was ready and waiting by his door. They descended the stairs in a rush and were on their way in less than a minute. Ziph rode with Dacket, and as they passed through Gate Nine, he checked around them. "The other teams need to hurry. I don't want to be the first to arrive." Ziph didn't ask why as she felt him slow his truck to allow the remaining hunters to catch up. It was pretty obvious that the last thing they wanted was to be first on the scene of a hunt if they didn't need to be or if it wasn't their turn.

After a few minutes of slower speeds, they saw a truck pull up beside them and slow to match their speed. "That's Gerara. She lives alone but hunts with a team she lives next to. Roll your window down and check behind her in our blind spot."

Ziph rolled the window down with the crank and smiled to herself for knowing what such a thing was. *I am so glad I paid attention in my primitive cultures class. I would feel so stupid navigating this basic technology if I hadn't.* Seeing the additional truck beside Gerara, Ziph pulled her wind-blown head back in the truck and rolled it shut. "Yes, there is a truck behind her with two or more occupants." She reached up to start braiding her hair as Dacket slammed on the accelerator, and the other trucks followed.

"Why do you seem to know how everything works here? I would think someone from elsewhere, especially with higher technology like you had before would struggle to understand how a mechanical door window crank works. I would assume anything difficult for a youngling would be a challenge for someone encountering it for the first time."

Ziph whipped her head in his direction. *Damn, that was intuitive.* "You must have read my mind. I was just thinking about the primitive cultures class I took back home." The moment it left her lips, she widened her eyes and slowly faced Dacket, whose mouth was dropped open.

He shut it quickly and turned back to drive before he admitted quietly, "I asked for that."

Ziph was frozen in time, and she wasn't sure how she could ever breathe again. The urge to run from her slipup was overwhelming. *I just called my perfect, gorgeous boyfriend a primitive being. Should I just jump out? I think if I aimed right, I could miss the other truck and then just run. Who knows where, maybe I'll just let the serpent eat me. At this point, I don't even know if that would work because the serpent would probably get secondhand embarrassment as it digested me. I would end up embarrassment induced snake barf, and I'm not sure I want such an end for my dead body.*

"Your facial temperature has risen. Are you feeling alright?" Dacket asked genuinely concerned.

Ziph could hardly look over but made herself anyway, "My body pumps blood to my face and my skin heats up as a result. It happens when I become embarrassed or panic." Dacket smiled a bit before he turned back to driving. *Why the fuck did he just smile?* "Are you glad I'm embarrassed?"

Dacket laughed a bit as he explained, "Was that why you overheated when I bit you?"

Ziph rolled her eyes. She had a panic trigger, which wasn't something she really wanted to talk about. "I was panicking, especially when you put that ice pack against my damn hood piercing. It was the same one you caught your cloth on." Ziph felt her skin heat up again, and Dacket gave her a perfect smile. *I would give anything to see that smile over and over again.*

"Why do you have those anyway? We don't have that sort of thing, or not that I know of," Dacket asked. It was more than he had spoken to her in weeks, and she was relieved he was at least talking.

"I thought they would help me have an orgasm along with toys. It didn't work, and I had spent food money to get them." Ziph paused for a moment, before she remembered she needed to thank him. "You changed the bell tone. Thank you for that."

"If anything like that ever happens, please tell me. We have all lived in the same rooms we live in now since we were children, and we all know the building well. I assure you if you're uncomfortable at home, we will do what we can to rectify it."

Ziph wasn't sure how much more Dacket wanted to discuss right now, but she did have one more thing she needed to speak to him about. "I know what you're going to say, but I did something terrible to you, and I feel like I need to say I'm sorry again. I didn't think about your feelings. I just considered my own. I should never have sat on you on the couch. It was so insensitive."

Dacket went silent for a while, and Ziph thought she may have said the wrong thing until he finally replied, "You might be a whirlwind, but you're a soft person inside. This harsh world is unforgiving, and I thought in a way I could keep you bottled up and safe from the pain of it all, but it's not fair to cage a wild bird. You deserve to be happy." Ziph wasn't sure exactly what he meant, but what he said was beautiful. She didn't know what to say, so she said nothing as they finished the last stretch of the journey.

She could already see the giant serpent lifting its head as it moved toward them and the city of people behind them. The beast so hungry it was willing to crush its own organs and lungs in the increasing gravity to eat the people of the city. *I wish there were a better solution. They deserve so much better.* Ziph was obsessed with solving how they grow so big, and she broke the silence with her question, "How do they grow so large but withstand the higher gravity of the city areas?"

Dacket thankfully believed he knew the answer. "When they're growing, they travel down between the cities to feed on the wildlife that exists there. It's mostly giant rodents. When I first found you, I believed you might be an escaped Kefale experiment. I thought somehow they turned one of the giant rodents into a woman."

Ziph smirked, "Nope, just a giant rodent woman from another galaxy." Dacket laughed and Ziph shifted her gaze to take it in. She knew this man rarely found joy, and she needed to remember this moment. His laugh made her feel warm and cozy in the rugged truck, and she watched his shoulders relax as they neared their stopping point.

They pulled to a stop at the same time as Gerara, but before they climbed out, Ziph crawled over and kissed Dacket on his cheek. "You should let yourself laugh more." He grabbed her face, and their lips met with passion before he opened his door, and she followed him out.

He looked down at her pants and pointed at her waist. "We need to remember to permanently attach your jets." Ziph ran to the other side of his truck to grab the jets and her mask as Whit parked by them and jumped out. Ziph attached her jets and slid her mask on as the hunters gathered in front of the trucks. They could see more trucks coming in the distance, but the serpent was coming too close, and they needed to move.

There was only one large serpent, and as soon as they had enough hunters, they began running toward the zero-gravity zone. Ziph was exhilarated as the gravity reduced enough for her to begin skating on the air, and the hum of the little jets added to her thrill. The heavier hunters followed suit soon after, and Ziph's favorite part was skating through the air toward the giant slithering beast. *I can't lie to myself. I feel like a superhero.* When they elevated enough to circle just under the serpent's head, led by Whit they made their move. As always, the serpent seemed to become entranced by the circling hunters and it slowed as its eyes began to glass over.

Now came for the part Ziph hated. The kill. She could see Gerara's white hair approaching under the circling hunters, and her heart went wild as she watched her mimic the move Ziph came up with. *Gerara is such a bad ass. Her movements are so smooth.*

In seconds, Gerara drove a spear directly through its head and had the serpent floating to the ground. The kill was clean, and Ziph watched Gerara try to refrain from celebrating too much to avoid pissing off the other hunter groups as they all made their way back toward the trucks. As they skated on the air, Gerara came up to Ziph and lifted her mask, "Your move was as golden as you are. Thank you for leveling us all up when we hunt. This method is infinitely safer for everyone, and the serpent experiences less pain."

Several other hunter groups in ear shot nodded agreement, and Ziph smiled to herself as they finally reached the part where they began the walking part of the journey back to the trucks. She was thrilled for Gerara, but mostly because she hated skinning the serpents. That part made her sick, and she could do without that ever again, although she knew it would happen again and likely very soon.

When they reached the trucks after the long walk, Ziph felt better than she had ever in her life. *I know it was the orgasm. I've felt fantastic since. I guess I just needed to have sex, and I didn't need the mating cycle suppressing hormone blocker after all.* She sat down in the truck to rest, and Whit walked up so she left her door open. He tossed his mask in the back of his truck before he turned back to her. "After your procedure tomorrow with Gerara, I want you to spend your time in recovery at my apartment. Dacket and Trent don't know the first thing about recovery care, and we need to redo your nails anyway."

Ziph looked down at her chipped nails, and the corners of her mouth tipped down at the sight. "They do look rough. I would love that. Thank you." Whit leaned in and kissed the side of her mouth before he climbed in his truck. *I never realized how having my nails done made me feel so much better.* Her skin heated remembering all the naughty looks he gave to her the last time he had her in his care. He was right. His caring hands were unmatched, and she felt a warm shiver, remembering the way he massaged her feet when she was paralyzed.

She snapped from her thoughts as Dacket climbed in the truck and sat down next to her. The way home was long and quiet, but Ziph reveled in how calm and content Dacket seemed. It was a stark difference from how he had acted before, and it in turn made her much calmer. She hardly felt the urge to move around in her seat, and she didn't even want to talk. Maybe that was a lie. She always wanted to talk, but she didn't have it gnawing at her like usual. It was a nice change, and she wondered if her problem all her life was being exasperated by her sexual and romantic frustrations.

Stupid fucking Venus cult. Venus, you can suck on ass-balls, you dumb bitch. Wait, I think those are called hemorrhoids. Whatever, she can suck on all of it.

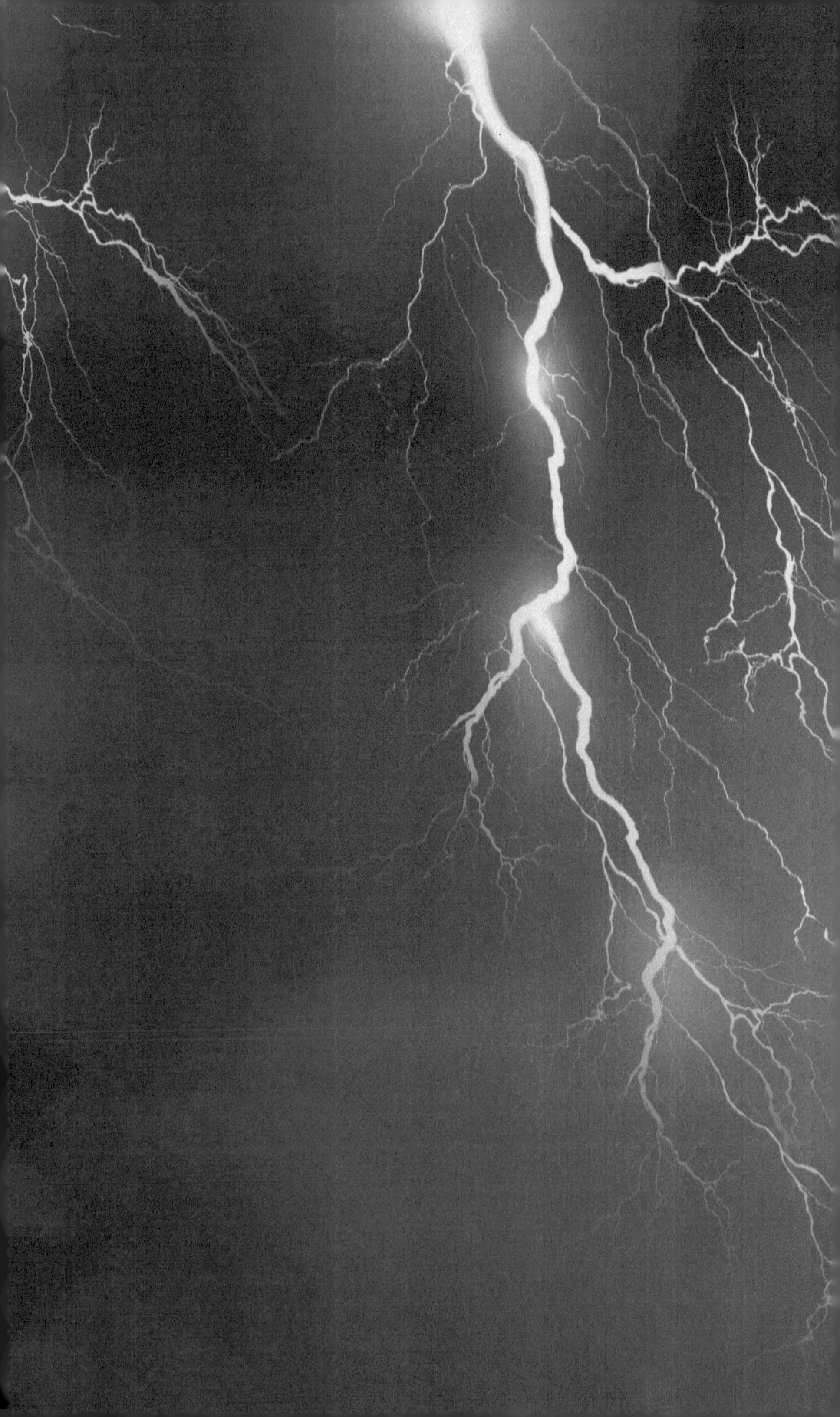

CHAPTER 24
DACKET CRITCHLOW

Their boots were heavy on their feet as they trudged up the stairs. Halfway up Dacket took his jacket off and untucked his undershirt before he folded his jacket and flopped it over his shoulder. *I wish I was that jacket. I wonder if he would carry me if I asked.* Ziph's lusty desires were taking hold again, and she rolled her eyes at herself as she checked inside her cheeks to make sure the glue was still in place.

As soon as Dacket opened the door, her stomach whined like she had a dying rabbit trapped inside of her. Her gorging cycle was normal for her species. She would be furiously hungry for the next few months and easily gain twenty or more pounds in her butt and legs. He smirked at her and led her to the kitchen after she slapped a hand over her stomach while it cried out in hunger once again. *Listen, I understand you're hungry, but I'm going to need you to shut the fuck up because you are EMBARRASSING me right now.*

"I'll need to eat and work out a lot more for a few months, and I might need to use the ski machine or runner in the middle of the night." She came around the corner to the kitchen and spotted what he was leading her toward. There was a tall wicker basket filled with various fabric bags with labels showing apples, a type of citrus, a box with blackberries and raspberry painted on the top, along with a few bags of grains and nuts. There was also a large rodent on the front with some writing in their language, and she knew it was rodent food, but she wasn't giving that a second thought. She was too damn hungry to care where the food came from. "Oh, is that carrots in the bottom?" She reached in for them and pulled one out before chomping down on it. She devoured it as she pulled out the rest of the food and set it on the kitchen table. "I never ate like this at home. I only had enough to keep myself from losing too much weight. Do you have a bowl?"

He reached in his cabinet and handed one over to her. Something odd occurred to her and like usual, it came free flowing from her mouth. "Why would your kind have bowls?"

Dacket gave her a curious look before he answered, "We sometimes like to make our children cooked stews after intensive play times to help rehydrate, and our younglings require cooked food until they're adults. They often eat meat stews and roasted and blended meats."

Ziph had her cheeks full of walnuts as she absently asked, "Do you think if the wrong hunter had found me, they would have just eaten me?"

With his tail curling at the tip, Dacket looked over at her disturbed. "I hope not. That feels too much like cannibalism."

Ziph swallowed some before she added, "I mean, I do have a juicy fat ass. I'm sure I taste good."

Dacket couldn't help laughing as he agreed, "You do taste good."

Ziph's eyes filled with shock as she realized what she said had set her up for that, and now her face was becoming heated again. She swallowed the rest of the food in her mouth before she answered, "Am I supposed to say thank you to that comment?" Dacket chuckled at her and didn't say a word as she resumed stuffing her face but maintained her eye contact with him. She paused after gulping down several bites. "I already saw Whit and Trent eat. If you have some rats hidden somewhere I don't mind if you join me." Dacket stood stoic and he stared at her as he shook his head slightly and he went to his icebox to retrieve a cold slab of meat. He set it next to where she was eating at the table, and he grabbed some utensils and napkins for both of them before he sat down. Ziph smiled at him as he handed over a two prong fork and razor sharp knife. She patted the napkin on her face, and it came back covered in fruit juice, causing her to scoff at herself. She noticed him holding back a smile again as he cut his serpent meat and took small bites.

"I'm not eating a rat in front of you."

Ziph smiled sweetly, "Why, because I'm an overgrown fluffy tailed rat?"

Dacket seemed as though he was searching for a way to run away when she burst into laughter, "I'm joking."

Dacket was confused as he replied, "You are not an overgrown rat, and now that I'm thinking about it, I'm not sure it would make a difference even if you were."

Ziph couldn't hold back a smile as she finished stuffing her face, and once she finished, she cleaned up her substantial mess of peelings, inedible seeds, and hard stems. Dacket did the same with his own plate and followed her until he went into his room. Ziph was a little sad he didn't invite her in, or follow her to her room, but she wasn't pushing anything. She knew how hard this was for everyone involved, and she wasn't trying to rush anything either. *If all I receive from this is sexual relief then I will be grateful.*

Once clean, she watched the system star turn the sky orange from her cozy spot in her bed. She loved that she could see the sky from the windows in her room. The bed behind her dipped, and her heart melted as she felt Dacket crawl in behind her. He smelled like a fresh rain. Her feelings swirled through her like a cyclone, always shifting from deep affection to the terror of loss back to deep affection, and it was too obvious why Dacket had resisted all of this. He had already been through it for years with Whit and Trent, and he had to face the potential loss of both of the men he loved. *I can't spin out of control right now. I need to calm the fuck down and enjoy the time I have with this man.*

He wrapped his arms around her, and she wiggled closer, moving her ass up against his hard body. She could feel him relax, which was wonderful on its own, but as his hand moved up her belly to her breasts, she was thrilled and fire spread throughout her. She felt him kiss her behind her ear and down her throat before he placed his hand around her neck and turned her to face him. "There is something irresistible about you, and it's not your pheromones. It's as if you have a magnet inside of you, and I cannot pull away." He kissed her and after that little speech, she was so turned on she could feel the flame spreading through her lower belly like wildfire.

When he moved down to her breasts, he licked one of her nipples before he sat up and kissed her cheek near her ear before he whispered, "I have an idea." Her flesh chilled as he slid off the bed and Ziph thoroughly enjoyed the perfect view of his naked ass as he went into the next room.

When he returned, and she saw what he had in his hand, she had the urge to jump off the bed and hide underneath. "What do you think you're doing with that?" Dacket smiled as he struck the tuning fork, and Ziph came unglued as her piercings hummed along with it. The tingling in her nipples and hood amplified with his proximity, and she yelped as her hands pressed against her breasts couldn't stop the vibrations. "You cannot be serious!"

Dacket grinned with enthusiasm as he struck the tuning fork, again and she moaned as she leaned back against the bed. "I have been thinking about this since you told me what the bells were doing to you. How could I resist?"

Dacket struck the fork again, and she held her hands over her hood piercing as she admitted, "Oh gods, I can feel it deep with you striking it that close."

Hearing that, Dacket wedged the fork, in the drawer of the table next to her bed before he tossed the covers back and moved her ass to the edge of the bed. He stood beside the bed and moved her legs so her calves rested against his chest, and she was mystified at what he was doing, *I think this man is about to make me cum with a tuning fork.*

Oh gods, I was right. He used his knuckles to pinch her hidden clit before he struck the tuning fork again. Ziph shivered and rolled her hips as she sucked in a sharp breath, and she clamped her feet on either side of Dacket's head, causing him to give her one of those smiles she was so desperate for. She knew it wouldn't take her long this time, and when he tapped the fork once again, she whimpered as she began to succumb to the pleasure and release poured from her.

With the eruption of pleasure evident on her face, she cried out in a singsong yelp as Dacket reached down tapped her hood piercing with the tuning fork, sending her clit below into a frenzied orgasm. With her powerful legs thrashing, Ziph smacked Dacket's shoulders with her feet and flipped herself backward and off the opposite side of the bed, while Dacket hit the ground where he stood. At first, she was afraid she may have injured him, but he began laughing, and when she crawled over the bed to look, he was still trying to climb from the ground, a picture of pure joy.

He pounced on her and leaned down to kiss her, diving his tongue in her mouth and tasting every inch. She felt his hands roam her body, squeezing her softest parts seeming to love them the most. "I'm glad you like the squishy parts. I'll gain at least twenty more in the next few months before I'll slowly lose it when my hunger fades again."

Dacket stopped briefly to kiss her and as he did, he grabbed the widest part of her hips before he answered, "I can't wait. This is fucking gorgeous, and if you are adding more, I'll take all I can get." He slid into her, and she gasped as he filled her so tightly. She was not sore anymore, and it felt incredible, something Dacket noticed, and he grinned as he bit his lip before he had her pinned on her back with her legs against his chest, holding them down. She felt his cock split in four parts and begin to swirl inside of her, hitting just the right place. Her heart slammed as she felt herself near the edge again. He must have been watching her because his four-part cock fluttered at the tip all at once and Dacket groaned as he came in her. She twitched and wiggled as her second orgasm settled in.

"You make me cum too quickly," he whispered as he rubbed her legs and held them to his chest.

She flopped against the bed as Dacket slid from her, and he stood over her nude form catching his breath. "Don't move." Ziph had no problem with that as she lay out feeling like satisfied goo spread over the top of the bed. *I feel like I have no bones.* She heard him start the sink in his bathroom. He came back and picked her up into his arms, and she could distinctly feel the substantial wet spot in the bed as he lifted her.

"I sprayed you and the entire side of your bed with cum. We can do laundry tomorrow, and you can sleep in my bed tonight." Dacket offered as he went in his bathroom with her and set her on her feet. "Were you planning to stay with me in my bed before you made a mess of it?"

Dacket turned to her, "Honestly? I planned to fuck you, and then I hadn't really thought any further than that. I've never shared a bed with anyone, but I don't mind trying with you."

Ziph smiled as she leaned against the counter. The warm wet cloth he used to clean her felt like magic. Her heart swelled as he tossed away the cloth and rubbed her back. *These arms around me feel like forever, but I can't become too attached to these men. I've been given too many warnings not to listen.* "What are you thinking about, you're becoming warm in your chest." Dacket asked as he looked down at her concerned.

She met his gaze and knew she didn't want it to come out of her mouth, but she could rarely control it. "I don't understand how I can keep myself from becoming too attached to you. I see why you kept trying to push me away." Dacket stopped rubbing her back and seemed haunted as he held her close.

He kissed the top of her head and replied softly over her hair, "We don't have a choice."

He brushed her hair away from her shoulder and rubbed her neck, changing the subject as he asked, "What's your full name? Or are you just Ziph?" Dacket gave her a small smile as he watched her.

She rubbed her ass against him as she answered, "Tarephine Ziphalie Arkwright is my full name. I hate my first name, Ziphalie is too uncommon, and I was scolded too much to be called my full name, so it's been Ziph since I was a child. Do your people have last names?"

Dacket nodded as he wrapped his arms around her. "My full name is Dacket Critchlow, Whit is Whitlock Tansey, and Trent is Trentel Tyman. Some of our people have middle names but not many. We inherit last names and are given first names by the hunters who raised us. This has been a Critchlow owned factory for over seventy generations. Our society hasn't changed at all in that time."

CHAPTER 25
MAGNETIC

Ziph chomped on a bowl of warm, softened oats and fruit while she replayed Dacket waking her by kissing her neck. She squeezed her thighs together. It wasn't time for that right now. *Cool it down there, I haven't even finished breakfast.* It was too late. She began to feel the heat gathering low in her belly and her heart rate picked up. *Not even the imagery of chopping meat in the factory is touching this. Why the fuck did my hormone blocker have to wear out so fast?* She remembered thinking about how she didn't need the blocker anymore and wanted to kick herself. Even her time chopping meat in the factory had been interrupted by Dacket, looking down on her from his apartment above. Again, she felt it like a whisper, his warm breath and hot lips on her skin giving her a thrill down her spine as she took another bite.

It was perfectly clear why Whit and Trent cared for Dacket so deeply. What seemed like a cold, quiet man at first has turned out to be the exact opposite, and now she wasn't sure how she could possibly keep herself from falling in love with him. *I'm fucking stupid to pretend that I haven't already. A fucking half-eaten walnut could love that man.*

Maybe I should imagine snake guts instead of the meat? Her oats became sand in her mouth as she recalled why she needed to keep hold of reality. *Those damn deadly serpents. Well, that worked a little too well. How could gravity alone be causing them to grow so large so quickly?* It took years for a snake back in the galactic center to grow to maturity, and that was true even on worlds where snakes grew enormous. Not as large as here though, and it didn't seem like they were taking long to grow. Ziph's biology knowledge knocked on the inside of her skull like a wood pecking bird as it only made sense that the Kefale, or some other force, had to be behind it. She had a sick feeling about the Kefale. *I really think something fucked up is happening on this planet.*

"Dacket? Do you ever wonder about the serpents and how strange it is that they grow so big, so fast? I understand the gravity piece of the puzzle, but the timing doesn't make sense at all. It should take a long time for them to grow to the massive size, right?" Ziph stared at her oats hoping they would miraculously become appetizing again as she could hear Dacket approaching behind her from the next room.

"I have thought about that for years, and it has never made sense to me. Our people can take twenty years to mature." He sat next to her and continued, "The Critchlow couple who raised me were very interested in science. The only reason I knew anything about you in the beginning was because they left me a book about the animals here. There is no formal school or education here, but we pass down knowledge to the next generation as our personal duty. At one time there were towers which touched the clouds where the Elara held public university lectures, but that was long before the Kefale took power. This building was built from the advanced alloy they created, but we don't have the technology anymore to re-create it, so we take meticulous care of our buildings and reuse everything we can. I believe, as a society, we would be much further developed if the Kefale had not enacted such harsh and unwavering control."

Ziph felt ill as she explained, "That sounds a lot like the First Human's in the galaxy I'm from. Why is everyone so subservient here? Why haven't the people toppled the Kefale for holding back progress? Something seems rotten with this. It sounds like what happened to a species of people in the galactic center, but here it's your own people."

Dacket sighed as he explained, "They keep us in line with threats of imprisonment in the palace. No one knows what happens there and no one has ever escaped." Ziph could tell he wanted to say more, but she wasn't prying if it was something sensitive. She had already done enough to this kind man.

Dacket looked at the ticking clock and back at Ziph. "We need to have you at Gerara's soon. We will take the truck since you will be under sedation." Ziph just needed to finish up the rest of her morning routine and she would be ready, so she stowed her bowl in the ice box for later.

When she met Dacket in the entryway after getting ready, he seemed relaxed and content compared to how he had seemed since she first met him. *If I can even call that meeting him.* Even his tail was swaying freely instead of balled up in a knot. The ride was short, and before she knew it, she was reclined in Gerara's procedure chair, which she could tell Gerara welded together herself. The chair looked like it had been precision manufactured, just like all her other equipment. Aside from her medical equipment, Gerara's home was an eclectic mix of science and geology with specimen jars and rocks galore. After a sharp poke, Dacket pulled a chair up next to her as Gerara angled a bright light which now shone in her eyes. *I want to be friends with her, but I'm kind of scared.*

"Well, here we go. Don't worry you won't feel or remember a thing." Ziph stared up at Gerara as a warm cozy feeling spread in her chest and her eyes began to droop. Dormant giggles which refused to escape before began bubbling up.

Gerara watched Ziph closely, and when Ziph's eyes were fully dilated and rolling around from the sedative, she explained, "She can't feel anything, but I don't want to sedate her too much because I don't know how much her species can handle. I'll need you to hold her arms down in case she tries to grab at my hands while I'm working."

Dacket stared at Gerara like she had suggested he performed the procedure instead. "You must be joking."

Gerara studied Dacket through her long magnifying goggles, making her eyes seem enormous through the lenses. "I'm not joking. You need to hold her down. All I have is a head strap."

Dacket frowned as he leaned over Ziph and reluctantly held her arms down. "If she is in any pain, I will do much worse to you."

Gerara smiled knowingly at Dacket. "I would expect nothing less from the ruthless hunter Dacket Critchlow. Now be quiet so I can start."

Dacket had been a teen when he had the procedure, and because he was an Elarian, they put him out completely. He wasn't positive, but he thought they had to drill into the facial bones. If Gerara began drilling into Ziph's face, he might not make it through the procedure. She had said nothing about him having to be involved.

When Gerara pulled out a drill and a scalpel, Dacket could feel stars growing in his vision. "What the fuck do you think you're doing with that drill?!"

Gerara stared at him again with her oversized eyes shining through the lenses on her goggles and replied, "I told you she is numb, and she cannot feel anything. Will you need sedation as well? I could just use your body-weight to hold her down, and we can call Whit to pick you both up. She needs a mask which won't fall off, Dacket, stop whining, and let me work." Dacket knew he would have nightmares about this as Gerara sliced into Ziph's hairline and picked up the drill with the magnetic screw she needed to install. She paused and looked over at Dacket, who was clearly not well. "Stop watching, you dumb ass."

"Fuck you, just do your job." Dacket felt nauseous as he watched her cut a hole in Ziph's facial skin to slip the screw inside and began drilling it down onto her skull. Ziph wasn't helping in the slightest, even with her head strapped down she was crossing her eyes and wagging her tongue at Dacket, who was desperate to hold back his raging panic.

After the second screw was installed, Dacket began profusely sweating as he watched her drill in the third screw on the side of Ziph's face. "Will you calm yourself? We battle giant serpents, and you look like you might lose your last meal over a mild procedure."

Dacket glowered at Gerara and argued, "You are drilling into her skull. You call this mild?"

Gerara snarled as she replied, "She cannot feel anything, what is your problem?"

Ziph echoed with a slurred and painfully slow, "Yeah, what's the problem, Mr. Sexy Snaky man?" before she resumed making faces at him, and this time she pulled her lips back and laughed with a hiss as Gerara continued. When the drill started buzzing, Ziph's eyes flared with excitement before she would resume her faces, and Dacket could feel the bile rising in his throat.

Gerara just managed to slide her trashcan over before Dacket hurled in it. After a second round of vomit, Dacket asked, "Are you almost finished? I should have had Whit bring her." Gerara handed him a few damp hand towels, and Dacket groaned as he cleaned his face while Gerara began sewing up Ziph's last incision.

When she was finished, she leaned down and lifted her goggles up to stare at Dacket. "Since when has Dacket Critchlow ever given a shit about anything other than himself and his two best-friends?"

He glared at her with murder in his eyes as she unbuckled the strap over Ziph's head. "If you speak about this I will..." Gerara interrupted him, "I will not reveal your secret softy side, and your woman here made me a fortune, so you don't owe me anything."

Ziph shot her most beautiful grin at Dacket, and whispered, "Did you hear that? I'm your woman! Ha! I think that means I win."

Dacket took a deep breath to center himself before he lifted her from the chair, and Gerara went ahead of them to her front door, opening it for them. "She needs rest and give her a painkiller once every four to six hours. No hunts for a week, and she needs to use the strap on mask for another two weeks. After two weeks she should be fine to start using the magnetic mask."

Ziph jumped in with her random thoughts as she watched them speaking, "Having a translator is so odd, your mouths don't match the words I hear at all." They both stared at her confused and blinked a few times before Dacket carried her to his truck.

Ziph nuzzled herself into his rock-hard chest before she pulled his collar down and licked his neck causing Dacket to suck in a sharp breath. He kissed her forehead before he set her in the passenger seat of his truck, and she could have died from happiness, she loved that entirely too much.

Her mind was jumbled with strange thoughts, and her heart raged with new feelings as Dacket climbed in next to her and drove them home. Ziph stared at him as she drooled down her chin the entire way back, and he held back a grin, but he couldn't deny how much he enjoyed the attention from her. *I've never been this happy before, and I've simultaneously never felt more afraid.*

Ziph moved next to him as he turned the truck off, and she crawled in his lap before he could open the door. "You're so perfect. I hate that you're so sad all the time. Why won't you tell anyone why you're sad?"

Dacket wasn't sure what to say, so he lied, "I think that's just the way I am."

Ziph hated that answer, and she leaned against him to wrap her arms around his neck. "I'm sorry. I won't ask anymore. I think you're perfect the way you are. If that means you're sad, then you can be sad all you want." Ziph leaned up and kissed him, and she swore he looked pained as he returned her affection.

He carried her up the stairs and when they reached Whit's door, Dacket knocked on it. Whit opened it wearing a towel wrapped at his waist, his cut muscled body on full display, which Ziph openly stared at. Dacket passed her over to Whit and kissed the top of her head before he closed Whit's door.

Whit had prepared his bedroom for them, and he set her on his bed, which was covered in various sized and shaped pillows. "How long will it take for me to recover?" Ziph asked as she noticed from where she was sitting there were several baskets of food he had lined up in his kitchen. Her mind felt like it was beginning to clear as Whit came over to her with a glass of water and a rough looking home pressed pill.

"It's an opiate painkiller. You need to take this before your head starts aching. If we keep you on it for a week and keep you resting, you won't feel a thing."

Ziph swallowed the pill and drank all the water before she replied, "Thank you. Thank you for taking care of me."

Whit patted her thigh as he explained, "Golden Girl, I have a whole week planned for us. I have books to read to you, puzzles to work on, and I even dug out my painting supplies."

Still a little groggy from the sedative, Ziph blurted out, "Where have you been all my life?" Whit smiled at her sweetly and went into the kitchen to prepare her something to eat. She noticed when he smiled, he had makeup on. She loved it when he wore make up. She noticed many men wore make up here as well as wore feminine clothing while exuding masculine or neutral energy. *The rules of society are so different here, and I love it. It's like living in the Venus District, except without all the toxic religious bullshit.*

"Do you want your pears sliced or whole? Should I warm this for you, or do you eat pear and pecans cold?

There is also a sweet honey here, I'll bring you some to try."

She could hear him filling her plate and she replied, "Pear's kind of melt when you heat them. They're good that way, but I would love some at room temperature and sliced." *A gorgeous, muscly man is bringing me honey drizzled pears and walnuts? Is this heaven? Venus, I still hate you, but maybe a little less now.* When Whit came in and handed her the plate he had prepared, which was absurdly aesthetically pleasing, she was sure she had landed on the best planet in the universe.

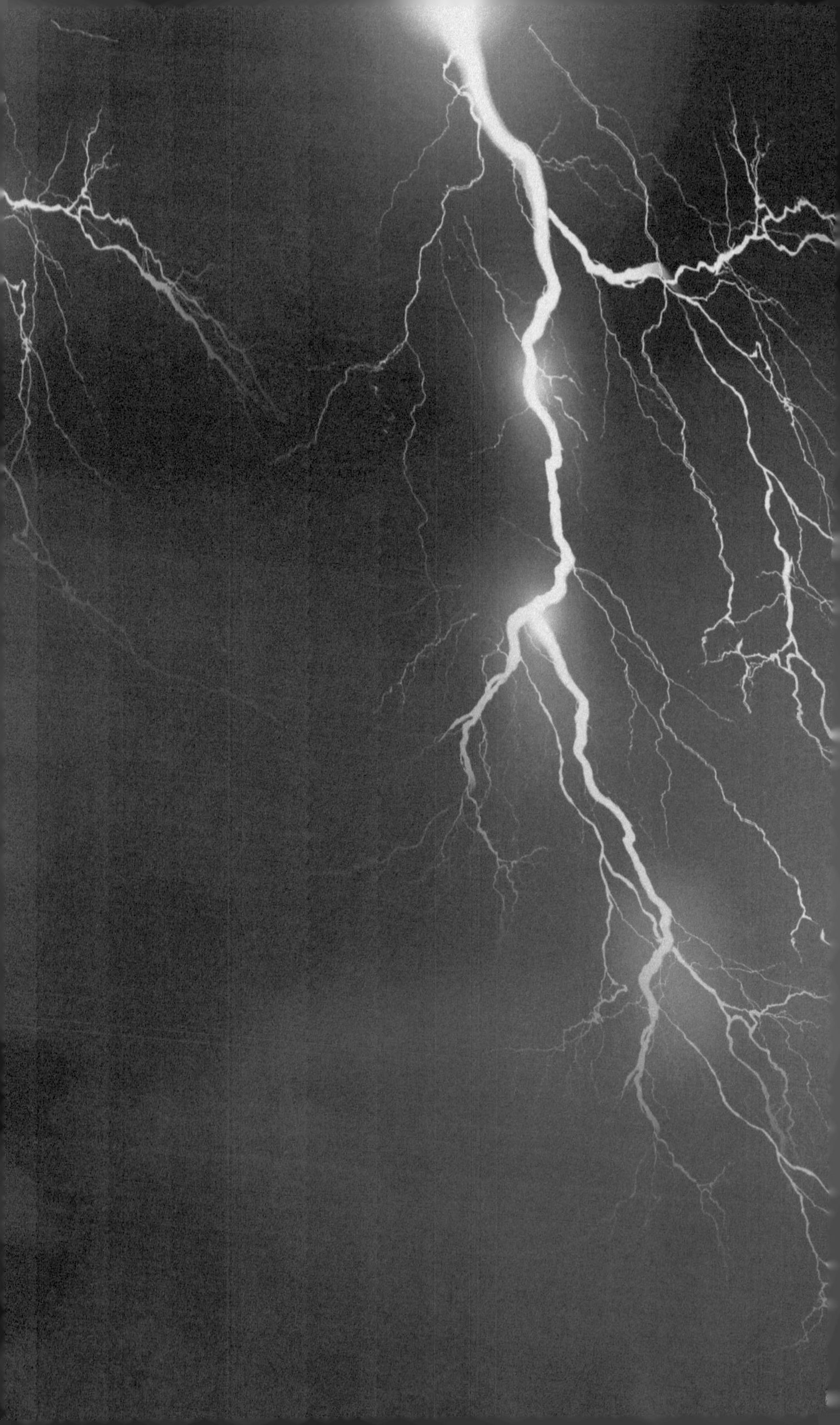

Ziph lay awake when she felt Whit softly stroke his fingertips down her spine. She stretched and turned over to face him. He held her against him the last two nights, waking her periodically for her pain medicine. "How are you feeling?" Whit asked, searching her eyes for any sign of discomfort as she answered, "I feel great. It doesn't even hurt when I move my head. I usually heal quickly from procedures. I used to have a bend in my tail, so I had to have surgeries as a kid to fix it. I had to have some surgical revisions when I was in school on Keru, which healed in a few days, so I bet I will feel normal by tomorrow. I probably won't even need the pain meds anymore by then."

Whit smirked as he licked his lips. "So, what you're saying is, you're ready to start considering some actual fun?" Whit moved the covers back and licked her nipple before he added, "We still have a little work to do with you before we can play the way I like. Since you're recovering, we will have to move extra slow, but that will just prolong my own fun."

Ziph stared at him, confused out of her mind. "I have no idea what the fuck you're talking about."

Whit gave her a wide grin before he answered, "I suspect this might be more fun than I even anticipated. I'll remove your stitches tomorrow, and then you can finish after I know you're healed, but I don't see why we can't start our fun now. Well, my fun."

Ziph had no idea what he meant as he gently kissed one nipple and rubbed a finger around her piercing on the other. He thoroughly enjoyed massaging and tasting her breasts before he slid from his bed and went into his bathroom. He emerged with something small and metal in his hand, and as he came closer, she recognized the little toy. It was a small egg shaped device with a flared base and the tip was glistening with lube. *Oh, fuck he's edging me until tomorrow. Gods damn it, I should have known that was what he meant.*

Whit pulled the covers back and ran his tongue down her side making her squirm before he rolled her over. Curious about how the plug would feel, she lifted her hips and flopped her tail forward. Whit grabbed either side of her hips and licked around the rim of her asshole until she was trembling before he slipped the plug into her. He was gentle and had thoroughly warmed her up beforehand, so it fit well and went in painlessly. He massaged her ass before he moved down and toyed with her hood piercing. Finding her clit with his fingers, she held back a whine when she felt him rub her far too softly, knowing this was part of his game.

"Whit, please, just a little more," Ziph begged, desperately wanting his mouth on her.

"Remember, we will finish this when you have your stitches out tomorrow morning. Until then, we will spend the day preparing your body for me." Whit gave her a pinch, just where she wanted it, and she whimpered when she felt him pull away. "You seemed quite enthusiastic when I suggested role playing with you at my mercy. Are you changing your mind?" Ziph's mind began spinning. Whit was planning to tie her up and fuck her? Her mind went blank, but her face said it all. Whit laughed, "Did you not see the rope chair in my living room? What do you think that's for?" Ziph rolled over and stared at him briefly before she slid from his bed and walked into his living room. She stared in the corner and realized the rope chair she had passed by several times was a sex chair with additional rope to restrain the occupant. *I really don't think I could be more naïve.*

Whit came up behind her and wrapped his arms around her before he leaned over her shoulder to lick the edge of her ear. "I'm planning on having a delightful time with you, Golden Girl, and I promise you'll be begging for more." Ziph recalled when Trent stayed in Whit's room. She couldn't help but imagine Trent tied down and begging Whit to make him cum. When her mind turned to Dacket in that position, she had the urge to ask Whit if he could make that happen sooner than later. "You're becoming awfully warm, Golden Girl. Are you thinking of naughty things too?" *Are you fucking serious?*

He shifted his arms and reached down between her legs to rub her, not enough for an orgasm, but enough to feel good, and she leaned into him. "I want it now," Ziph begged, but he kissed her neck softly over her healing bruises, and whispered in her ear, "You are nowhere near ready." To prove his point, he leaned down and kissed the back of her right shoulder, sending her into a shiver. "Now we're getting closer."

Ziph felt him trace down her spine and when he reached the center, he leaned down and kissed her there. The gentle kiss made her belly flutter, and she pulled in a harsh breath as she trembled. She was more than wet between her thighs, and she needed him to give her what she wanted, but instead he turned her around and twirled his fingers around her nipples. After a few strokes, he kissed her lips before he leaned over and kissed her side, followed by him nipping at her skin in the same place he gripped her waist.

She leaned her head back and whimpered as she begged, "Please, what do I need to do to have what I want?"

Whit fell to his knees and briefly licked the crease of her thigh before he looked up at her and gave her a devilish grin. "I'm tasting and toying with every inch of you before you will ever feel a rope against your skin. I know what that mind of yours needs, and my style of sex will always fulfill it." Whit straightened up and held her waist as he licked and kissed her nipples. Her stomach growled, and he tapped her belly button with his finger, "What an odd thing to have, a small hole in your belly."

Ziph stared at him with her lip snarled. "I think it's odd your kind doesn't have one. I guess a snake born from an egg might not. Some species born from eggs do, but I guess that's not always the case."

Whit clearly understood as his brows raised. "You have live birth. Of course, that would make sense." He kissed her above her navel before he stood up and swooped her into his arms, "I don't think you're supposed to be out of bed yet."

He took her back to his room and lay her in the bed before he pulled out a jar from his nightstand. He slathered his hands with it before starting at Ziph's shoulders, rubbing the cream into her skin as he massaged her body. He thoroughly rubbed it into her breast and nipples before he moved down her stomach and lower belly. He spread her legs and covered his hands in cream before he rubbed it between her thighs, making sure to twirl his fingers around her hood and toy with her clit, causing her hips to tilt. He rubbed it down her legs but came back to her pussy and rubbed his finger down the middle. She clenched her fists and rolled her wrists making Whit bite his lip. "See, you're almost there. How does the plug feel?"

Ziph wiggled around and had to admit she liked it. "It feels good, but I want so much more. When can I have more?"

Whit smiled at her and shook his head no. "Let's find you something to eat. I suspect your stomach will keep yelling at you if you don't feed it."

Whit went to make her some fruit and honey, and Ziph devoured it. When she was finished Whit made her turn over so he could apply cream to her backside. "I almost forgot to tell you when you were asleep, Dacket went for a serpent hunt. He lagged behind when moving out since it was after dark, and he stayed back to stay safe since I am on leave to care for you. Other than that, I have no news."

Ziph smiled into the pillow as she asked, "Have you been telling everyone to stay away?"

Whit went silent for a few moments before he admitted, "You have spent a lot of time with Dacket, and it is my turn. Trent has made it clear he wants to take you out after you feel better if you're alright with that."

Ziph couldn't help but ask, "Is this sort of sexual arrangement typical for hunters or Elarian?"

Whit quickly responded, "You mean groups of people who care for one another and share beds? Of course. It happens just as much as pairs, especially with hunters." Ziph wondered if she should even discuss the galactic center she was from and how fluid sexuality and gender were both accepted and clearly outlined, but here it seems they don't even have a construct for the labels because of true normalcy.

"Why?" Whit asked, and she internally cringed now that she had to explain it.

"In my galaxy, gender, poly relationships, and sexuality were quite common, but it was still defined under a construct. Here, I bet you don't have a word for gay."

Ziph turned to look at Whit who asked, "What do these words poly and gay mean?" Ziph smiled and shook her head. *There's no way I am introducing this construct.* "I'm not explaining it. You're too perfect without the risk of tainting any of what makes you so wonderful." She knew back home Whit would be considered to have more fluid gender, but here he was just Whit, and she loved that more than she could explain.

This was where she left behind her old way of thinking. She made a decision then to ignore all her programed labels and constructs. *This is my home now, and these are my people.* She did want to know one thing however, "How old are you, Dacket, and Trent?"

Whit answered easily, "We are all thirty-five. How old are you Golden Girl?"

Whit finished massaging her calves as she answered, "I'm not sure how the translator figures out how to convert the time, but I am twenty-five. Do your kind usually live to be a hundred and fifty?"

Whit responded honestly, no matter how much it stung for Ziph to hear. "Elarian live to be one hundred and fifty, but hunters usually don't make it past sixty. Average for us is actually fifty in the last few years."

Ziph tried to hide her heartbreak, but she couldn't hold it back. Her voice came out scratchy and raw as she cried and with all the medications in her system, she couldn't resist as she demanded, "I can't accept that. I won't accept any of that. We need to change things."

Ziph turned to look at Whit before pulling him over her. He seemed as heavy hearted as she was as she kissed him. "I refuse to watch our wonderful future turn sour every time because of this untimely death sentence hunters have. I will not watch the men I, hm, care about end up serpent food. There must be something we can do to make this safer." She knew Whit had caught her slip up. She had almost admitted she loved them. The thought was already entrenched in her psyche when the feeling had made its home in her heart, and it was just a matter of time before she blurted it out. *I think I just earned sex early. Please let my reward be sex.* Whit, with his face hovering just inches from hers, could see him change his mind before her eyes. *Please break the rules, and have sex with me.*

Whit carried her into his living room and guided her onto the rope contraption she had honestly believed was just a chair. *I need to be honest with myself. I might be a little bit stupid.*

Before he began, he leaned in close to her face and meticulously checked her healing wounds before he continued. "I need you to scrunch your face. If it doesn't hurt at all, we can continue."

She scrunched her face as he asked, and she did not even feel a twinge. "Nothing, I'm ready."

He blinked at her a few times before he asked, "Are you lying?" Ziph gave him a sweet smile and shook her head no. He carefully removed her clothes and guided her into the position he wanted before he began tying her limbs. When she was seated with her back arched, her arms secured above her, and her legs spread and tied down, Whit seemed satisfied as she was far more accessible to him.

He slid a ball in her mouth with a strap and stroked her cheek as he descended on her breasts, kissing and sucking them, twirling his tongue over the tips causing her pussy to drip with need. He moved down her stomach, licking a line down the center before nipping at her lower belly making her skin tighten.

When he spread her pussy and pinched her clit between his fingers, she moaned around the ball in her mouth, and he kneaded the flesh into a ball like Dacket had done. Whit leaned in and sucked on the sensitive clit he forced to the surface, and Ziph screamed around the ball as she came with a crash. Heat poured from her core as Whit continued to flick and suck until she was jolting away from him.

He gently bit down on her, and she let out a high pitch screech as he slowly released her, and he lowered the chair so he could line up with her pussy. Whit took her breasts in his hands and rubbed his thumbs over her nipples, playing with her piercings as he slowly pushed inside of her.

Ziph came undone as his cock split in four, and they began squirming and flitting inside of her, hitting just the right places with their fluttering tips. Drool poured from her mouth around the ball, and Whit dragged his finger through it before he used it to lube her nipple before he carefully pinched it.

He thrust once more, and she leaned her head back and clenched her core as Whit took her over the edge again, and when her inner walls pulsed, he followed her and came with a deep breathy rumble as cum spilled from their joining and dripped onto the floor.

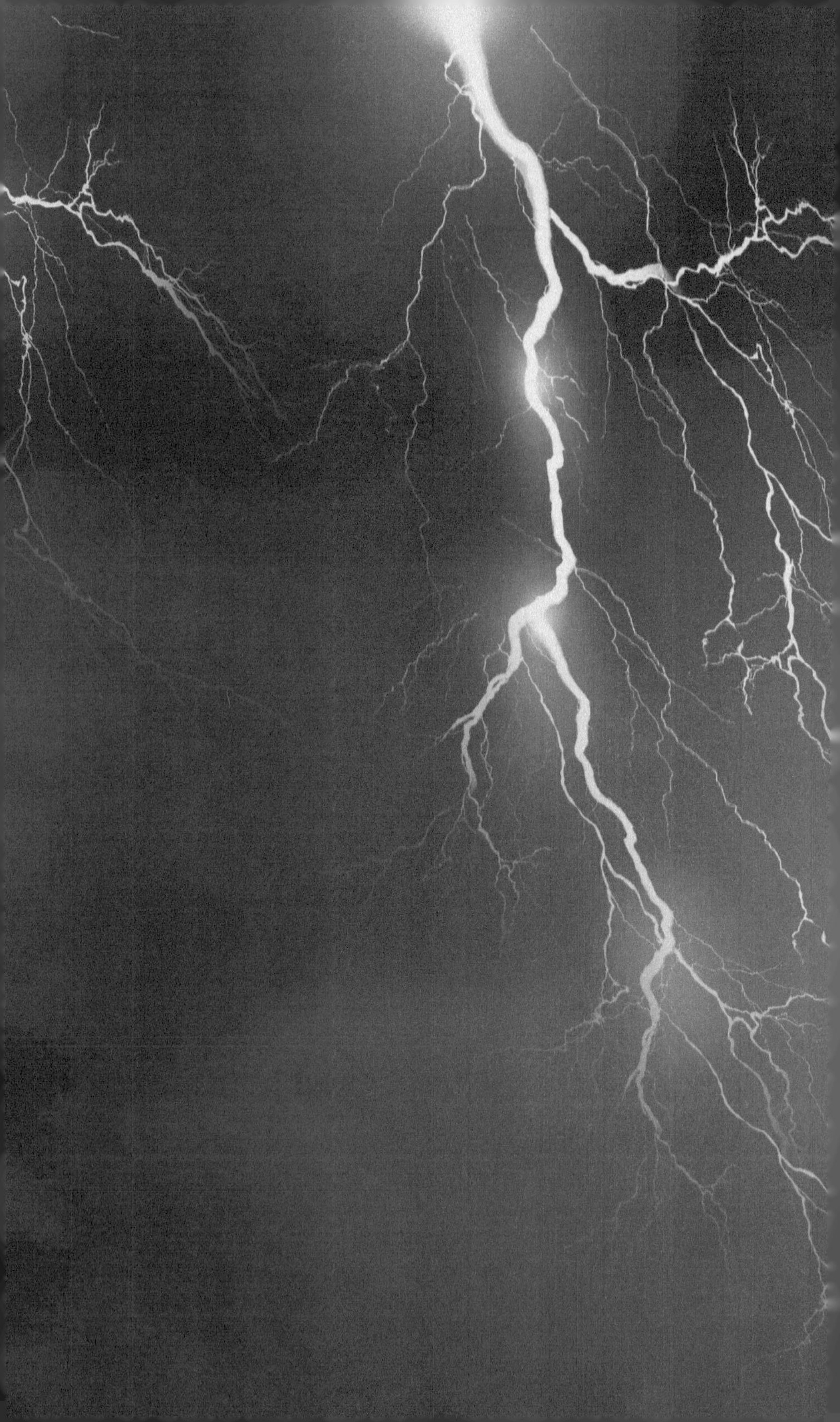

CHAPTER 27

OFFERING DAY

After an eerily quiet, dragging week passed with the palace remaining silent about any serpents, it was now time for Offering Day. Ziph still had no idea what that meant, they had all been so busy cleaning and performing maintenance on their hunting gear and recharging their jets that she hadn't felt it was right to interrupt and ask.

Dacket had sent Danny to a clothing store in Sector Eight, and she was now standing in Dacket's entryway with his and Ziph's clothing for the event. Her arms were outstretched with two hanging garment bags. Dacket took his suit and Ziph's dress he picked out, and Danny winked at Ziph before she shut the door to make her other deliveries. Ziph, impatient as always, couldn't hold back her question anymore. "Is Offering Day like paying taxes?" Ziph, avoiding eye contact because she had asked him about fifteen questions already, looked over at the kitchen table, which she was genuinely surprised could hold the two large bags of silver coins. Ziph peered down at the nice dress she was about to slip on before she looked around the room. *Snap a fuck stick! He's not even in here!* Ziph rolled her eyes at herself.

Hearing her question, Dacket answered from his room, "It's taxation and a ceremony to show allegiance to our royalty. We are encouraged to bring gifts along with our taxes. The people learned, the better the gift, the less likely you are to have an audit. Gerara has a side business preparing the gifts, so we need to stop by her house before we join the line. The line takes hours, so be prepared to stand in the heat or rain, whatever we may have today."

When did industrial civilizations develop weather prediction? Didn't it happen fairly early? She huffed, she was always seeking answers she may never find. *Oh shit, I need to get dressed.* Ziph also noticed the dress had a large enough skirt to hide her tail, and she sighed to herself before she went to her room and changed. She guessed just because the society had accepted her, it didn't mean the palace would. It was a navy-blue strapless gown with a full, flowing skirt, and when she slid it on, she was shocked at how comfortable it was. *This dress must have cost a fortune. It felt custom made, how in Pluto's hell did Dacket pull this off?*

It took a few minutes for her to do her makeup, which was just lashes and some of her favorite dusty pink lipstick since she recalled the standing in line part. The last thing she was doing was applying layers of makeup on her face which could slide off in the heat or rain. *It's not the time for testing make up durability.* She found some comfortable shoes since her feet weren't visible under her dress, and she briskly walked into the living room with her eyes downcast, making sure she didn't accidentally step on her skirts.

Ziph came up to Dacket and saw his feet first, nice,

polished boots and a dark grey suit. She lifted her eyes and when she saw his face, she could have died right there. *He has no reason to be that pretty.*

He stared at her like he wanted to take a bite of her, and she wished he would, but they didn't have time. He opened the door after Whit knocked, and he entered without a word. Whit and Dacket grabbed the bags of silver before Ziph closed the door behind everyone. Whit wore a jet-black suit, and she loved how the lapel angle was high and sharp on the suits. Both men had collared white shirts under their suits, but neither had a tie, and Ziph wondered if ties weren't a thing here.

Trent met them in the hallway, and Danny opened her door just to wave at Ziph and shut it back. Trent wore a light grey suit, and he spun around Ziph and wrapped his arm around her waist. "You look beautiful."

She bashfully smiled at him, quietly complementing, "Thank you." *I can't think of what to say! They are so damn hot, and I'm such a goof I can't even compliment him back?*

Trent made it clear he wanted to spend time with her as he gave her his entire focus while they descended the stairs. He opened the back door of Dacket's truck and helped Ziph inside by holding his hand out for her to use as support. As usual the truck was spotless, and she wondered how Dacket kept it so clean with all the dust they track in from hunting, but her thoughts on the truck didn't last long as Trent put his arm around her and tugged her close to him. His body was hard as a rock, and she wished away her naughty thoughts. This day was far too busy for her pussy to be screaming at her for a fuck.

Trent was by far the bulkiest build of the three men, and she already had a plan for their eventual sex. *Fuck me thrice, so much for avoiding dirty thoughts. Wait. Fuck me thrice? That sounds like way too much fun. Damn, here I go again!* The way her heart stammered in fear and excitement as her mind re-constructed her ideas, had Trent noticing her internal heat elevating and leaned in closer. Her skin simmered as he moved her hair and whispered close to her ear, "What thoughts have you bothered?" His tone made her toes curl as she bit her lip. He noticed and smirked at her before leaning back in the seat. *Why does it seem like they can read my mind? Am I that obvious?* She placed her hand on her chest, feeling the warmth. *How am I supposed to control that?!*

They reached Gerara's house and squeezed in a parking place on the street before they all climbed out. Trent lifted Ziph from the seat and stood her on the pavement so she didn't step on the hem of her dress. "Thank you." *Bitch, you really can't think of anything other than thank you to say? Or I could just save this energy for sexy time. That is exactly what's happening.*

Gerara brought out a wagon with a large metal basket filled with the best serpent meat available under a layer of ice, and she added some of her most popular inventions to the wagon, including a set of her magnifying goggles. Ziph watched as Dacket and Whit slid the silver bags onto the wagon, and they pushed it towards Trent and Ziph. Dacket and Whit walked ahead and as they moved onto a main street into the heart of the city, and she could see everyone else had similar wagons covered in goods along with bags of coins.

An uneasy silence fell over everyone as they walked, and not just the group of hunters she was with, everyone on the street refrained from speaking. Ziph felt unease spread and take hold like roots as they neared the palace. The ominous wall around the back side to keep the royals from having to look at the unfavorably deemed Sectors cast a deep chilling shadow onto the street. When they moved into the bright daylight and emerged from the shadow, Ziph felt a rush of fear. *I thought the light would improve my mood, not worsen it.*

The unsettling palace was a patchwork of bright light metallic tall cylindrical towers, all with windows only on the highest levels. The flawlessness of the grounds surrounding the palace seemed far too picturesque, the way the bushes were meticulously trimmed and met the edges of the winding sidewalks. This was not art. This was a message. This garden displayed the level of uniform perfection only the threat of death, or worse, can foster. To make herself move forward through her fear, she pretended she was in an eerie amusement park, and someone covered in faux blood with a plastic K'hornibus blade would jump out and startle her into screaming.

But this wasn't Emendo, and she became sick to her stomach the closer the moved in line to the little desk and collection area set up at the mouth of a small bridge. There was no protection from the elements, just a table and uncomfortable looking metal chairs for the palace representatives to sit. A mostly cosmetic looking moat wrapped all the way around the palace from what she could see, and she wondered if they raised creatures to be feared in the water. She noticed the moat angled directly into the palace, and there was no other entrance other than by water, and her nauseated stomach twisted in her gut. Why would they need that sort of odd entrance? *What are these Kefale so afraid of?*

The closer they came to the table, the more Dacket became agitated and nervous. Trying to be reassuring, Trent held her against his firm body as they walked. He must have known this experience would not end a positive one. They all must have known, for they had been stewing and grumbling all week, and she now guessed this was why.

A skiff came from the center of the palace interior moat and came aground behind a path to the table of palace representatives. At first Ziph just thought the little boat was for collecting the mounting pile of taxes and gifts behind the table, but when the three guards began marching toward them, Ziph could feel the collective panic develop around her. Shifting on his feet, Dacket was distressed with his tail in a knot, as the guards neared, and Whit reached out to take his arm and steady him.

The guards marched directly by Dacket, brushing his shoulder, and grabbed the arms of a grey toned man behind him. The man's blue eyes shone with terror as the leading guardsman read off a small paper, "You have been honored by the Kefale Royals, and they find your service to the palace a true gift. We congratulate you as you have been selected for spawning. Please come with us to begin your new life of luxury and relaxation." The man's eyes were filled with terror, and he stumbled, so they began dragging him away, not waiting for him to regain his balance.

A beige woman next to him followed and she grew louder as they pulled the man away, "You can't! No! You lie! There is no luxury! We know the truth you Kefale scum! We know you use us for our bodies! We know the truth! They use our o…" Her words were silenced as the lead guard pulled a gun from his belt and shot the woman in the head. The woman hit the ground with a sickening thud, and the people behind her froze in time, too afraid to move. The silence from the crowd, despite her blood dripping from their nice clothes and skin, was something Ziph struggled to process. *Where are the screams?* Her own shouts had been strangled in her throat, far too shocked to break free. Ziph watched in horror as the guard holstered his gun like he had just shot a paper target, not a living and breathing being with thoughts and desires.

Ziph, motionless with dread, saw the man fall limp in the guard's hands as they dragged him to the skiff, and the four men disappeared into the dark entryway of the palace. Ziph shifted her gaze to Dacket, and he seemed truly shaken to his core. Now Trent and Whit had their arms around Dacket, and both were comforting him.

No one said a word as the scene played out, and Ziph was ready to run back to her pod, and find a way to rewire it. They needed *the fuck* out of here. *We can just use wires from the electric grid in the factory. It will be fine, I can just squeeze Dacket in the nose, Whit can squish under the controls, and I can sit in Trent's lap. I bet we can even fit Danny in with us.*

Whatever was happening in that palace was *wrong*, and Ziph knew it. This entire situation smelled foul and as they approached the offering table, she thought Dacket would be sick. His usual vibrant yellow complexion was dull and pale. Whit pulled the wagon up, and the man at the table looked at him as he provided him their information, "Critchlow Market, Sector 2, taxes in full with gifts." He tipped his head to the side and a woman, seeming to be a dedicated palace representative, took the wagon and added it to their growing pile.

Just as everyone else had done when dismissed, Dacket took off like a rocket away from the offering table. They followed him, and he didn't stop until they were back at his truck. He scrambled inside, and everyone else followed almost as quickly. They slammed their doors shut as if to keep out the soiled air. Dacket took a few slow breaths before he started his truck, and he drove them the short way back to their home.

When they parked, Dacket climbed out and went upstairs without waiting on anyone. Ziph, was too curious to keep her mouth shut, "Is he alright? Is there something I don't know?"

Whit stared at her as he answered, "There is something none of us know. I'm not sure he will ever admit it. He is this way with any of the royal guards we are forced to submit to. No one blames anyone for not fighting back. They drag you into the palace, and you're never seen again, or they shoot you on the spot. Dacket will need a few days, but he will be fine." Fear bubbled inside of Ziph as she took in the reality they all faced. No wonder they were so careful not to break any laws or rules. Maybe that was what Dacket was so afraid of, someone from the palace taking him or one of us.

She wasn't sure but she wasn't shaking this any time soon. Trent kissed her forehead before he asked, "Will you stay with me tonight?"

Ziph was exhausted, but she couldn't have agreed faster as she joked, "Can you carry me?" He swooped her into his arms and headed to his room with her as she laughed, "I was honestly kidding, but I will never say no to being carried." She knew she was not a lithe lady, yet Trent carried her like she was a feather as he brought her into his apartment.

"Are you hungry? Whit dropped off some of your food earlier."

Ziph wasn't all that hungry. "Can we just go to sleep? I

know it's early, but I'm exhausted, and I may have a favor to ask you, and that favor requires some rested energy."

Trent grinned and asked as he twirled his finger in the tuft of hair growing back on the top of her pointed ear, "Anything beautiful, what do you need?"

Fighting unease, Ziph used some of her typical blurt-it-out energy as she explained, "I'm having some issues with what happened during the break in. I've been through enough therapy in college to know how effective exposure in a safe environment is. So, I guess what I'm asking is, will you help me face the attack trauma, but we can have a much better time?"

"Are you asking me to physically attack you, and then fuck you?" Trent asked and seemed perturbed, so Ziph went on, "Yes, I need you to come after me, and I need you to *gently* strangle me while you fuck me."

Trent eyed her slyly as he lifted her into his arms and carried her to his bed. "You want me to *what*?"

CHAPTER 28

THUNDER

A crack of thunder rattled the building waking Ziph abruptly. She and Trent had been asleep for a few hours. She blinked a few times before she realized her face was stuck to his chest. She peeled her face away and rubbed it as she slid off him and onto the bed. He had pulled her on top of him, and she had fallen asleep there. A clear rounded indention dimpled her cheek, and she rubbed it with her pointer finger. *Is that a fucking nipple imprint?*

Another rumble of thunder and Trent's eyes opened before he blinked a few times and grabbed Ziph and hauled her back on his chest. Trent brushed her hair away and kissed the back of her neck before trailing kisses down her shoulder.

She was just warming to the idea of midnight sex with Trent when there was a loud, forceful knock. Trent groaned and slapped her ass as he pushed her off him. "You have a hunt. You better run."

Oh, fuck that's exactly what that knock was. Damn, sex will need to wait. Ziph ran to the door nude knowing it was

Dacket. The corner of his mouth tipped up as he took in her naked form and handed over her hunting under-clothes, uniform, and gear. She quickly dressed in the doorway, and they hurried off to Dacket's truck. Whit was already waiting for them at the garage guard station in his truck, and they took off quickly toward city Gate Nine.

When they passed through the gate and had some ground behind them, Ziph moved over in the truck and leaned her head on Dacket's shoulder. He readjusted and put his arm around her and pulled her closer as rain beat down on the truck.

She couldn't help but ask, "Are you alright?" With her ear so close to his chest, she heard his heartbeat quicken with her question, and that was answer enough as he remained silent. She crossed her arm to stop his hand rubbing her side and held it. He intertwined his fingers with hers and she squeezed his hand. He just kissed her head, and kept driving through the rain.

I wish he would just tell us what was wrong, I know we could help. When he finally spoke, it wasn't to answer her question. "We need to be prepared. There are two serpents, and they're both larger than you've seen yet. They're moving quickly toward the city."

Ziph had more questions, and she hoped he felt like answering, "Do all the cities on Binara have this serpent problem?" Dacket narrowed his eyes to see if he could see the serpents ahead, but even with his heat detection vision, in the darkness and rain, it was nearly impossible. "Yes, all three of our cities battle serpents."

As usual, Ziph asked another question, "And the Kefale rule all three?"

Curious, Dacket turned and studied her intently. "What do you imply?"

Trying to not make it sound so much like the farfetched conspiracy she believed it could be, she explained, "We already talked about it a bit, but I think the Kefale are doing something to the serpents. I think, like I said before with my biology background, I can confidently say these serpents are growing far too large, too fast, even for zero gravity. I think they're using the serpents to further control the population with confinement."

Dacket seemed to agree as his brow formed a deep crease. "You're probably right, but there's nothing we can do. The royal's control everything."

The truck began smoothing out, and that was their signal to park. It was time to run. The gravity spread wasn't even, and she noticed the sharp decrease in gravitational pull fell sharply as they neared the sky belt. Ziph was prepared this time with her mask and jets, and she, Dacket, and Whit took off running toward two warm spots Dacket and Whit could see in the distance.

She needed to speak to them about waterproof hunting gear as the rain dripped down her back and soaked her underclothes. As she ran though, she soon understood why they likely hadn't made them waterproof as the rain was keeping her cool. She also realized if the Elara people could see heat, a serpent would be able to as well, and being cooled down would make them more difficult to see.

Maybe she would just run and quit with all the ideas, she needed to focus. She had a deadly job ahead of her. Dacket barreled into her, and they both hit the ground as Whit slammed down by them right as lightning struck just ahead of them, lighting up the sky and showing the two massive serpents. Ziph hadn't seen them yet, and she gasped at their size. They were easily twice as large as the last serpent they'd killed.

Dacket lifted his mask, his snakelike eyes wide and blinking rapidly, "Are you alright?"

Ziph nodded and lifted her own mask to answer, infinitely thankful for the magnetic connections holding it on, "Yes, I'm ready." He tried to smile as he helped her up and they both replaced their masks as Gerara and her team caught up to them.

They all ran and merged into a larger group, and Ziph began feeling extreme unease as she couldn't see the serpents at all unless the sky lit up with streaks of lightning. *We are fucking flying, lightning rods out here!* As they began skating through the air, she lifted her mask and yelled to Dacket, "I can't see heat. I'll have to follow you!"

Dacket lifted his mask and answered, "I'm taking this kill. Follow Whit." Whit, next to her, nodded as she looked over at him and moved behind him in line. When a bright streak of lightning filled the sky, something told Ziph this would be a different type of kill as she could see another large group of hunters create a similar formation in their group of individual teams.

As they began the ascent toward the serpents' heads, Ziph tailed Whit and she knew Gerara was behind her, followed by the rest of Gerara's team. With Dacket at the lead, they formed a spaced line and began circling the massive serpents' head, sending it into the trance like state they needed to make the kill without additional risk to their lives.

Nothing could have prepared Ziph for how this kill would be performed as she watched Dacket stop in front of the serpent's mouth and toss one of their practice jets down its throat. The serpent opened its mouth wide and shook its tongue outside of its mouth. The light pink interior of the serpent's mouth was stark against the dark of the night. Her heart knocked inside her chest as she watched Dacket fly inside the serpents' gaping mouth.

She would have gone after him if she weren't *sure* he knew what he was doing, but she couldn't explain that to her heart which was screaming at her to go after him. The serpent went still, and Dacket slipped from its mouth just as it began its slow descent to the ground. *Dacket is fearless against a serpent, but frozen at the sight of a royal. I fucking hate not knowing what's wrong. Does he just have a deep fear of the guards and the Royals, or did something happen to him?*

Ziph turned to see the other team had made their own kill, and their serpent was also in a sluggish free fall to the ground. Ziph was less than thrilled about this next part, but she drudged through the job of skinning and flaying of the serpent meat as she daydreamed of Trent's bed. She knew it was a small fortune for them, but after the offering day she just wanted some rest. Plus, she and Trent had some intense sex planned, and she didn't want to be worn out for it. She saw the look in Trent's eye. She knew he would do whatever she needed, and he would probably like it, whether he admitted it or not.

Whit dragged a wrap over, and she helped Dacket flop a giant chunk of meat onto it before Whit rolled it and dragged it back to his truck. It took a few hours, but when they were finished, there was enough meat to share some with Gerara and her team. There would be no way Dacket and Whit could have stuffed any more wraps of meat into their truck. By the time they climbed into the truck, Ziph was ready to take a nap and leaned over in the seat to do just that. She could handle endless cardio, but when it came to heavy lifting, she wore out quickly.

"You can go to bed. We will haul the meat into the freezer." Dacket brushed her hair from her face and kissed her forehead. He would need to stop being so perfect if he didn't want her falling in love. She cringed knowing she was already in deep with Dacket, Whit and Trent. It was far too late for that.

He helped her down and led her to Trent's door, but before he opened it for her, he pinned her against the wall and kissed her. "Sleep well," was all he whispered over her lips before he opened Trent's door behind her back and disappeared down the stairs to the garage.

She shut the door and stripped in the living room, dropping her clothes in a pile on the stone floor and peeling off her underclothes before slapping them onto the pile of her grotesque hunting clothes. She gagged as she sniffed her body and nearly ran as she slipped in Trent's bathroom to wash. The door to the bathroom creaked slightly as she pushed it open. *Don't wake Trent, you stinky bitch!*

The lights flickered as thunder crashed, and she could hear the wind picking up outside the bathroom window. Trent's room faced toward the buildings next door, and not into the factory like Dacket's, so she could see the rain turn into sheets.

The lights flashed off, and it went dark in the bathroom, but she was already in the stream. Trying to be quiet, she scolded the lights with her fists in the air, "How the fuck am I supposed to get out and not smack my ass on the floor?" She could hear Trent chuckling from the other room, she must have woken him. He opened the bathroom door with a candle lit and set it on the counter before he tipped his head to the side at her naked in his shower.

He tossed away his night shorts and joined her, and she panicked realizing she hadn't washed yet. "What are you doing?!" She was frantically searching for the soap, and she didn't want to say that, but there it was, heading for her lips, and she couldn't hold it back. "I need to wash my stinky ass before you smell me! Don't breathe in yet! The steam is wafting my stinky everywhere! Oh gods! Just don't breathe in yet!" By the time she was finished, she was shrieking, and Trent's laughter filled the bathroom as he grabbed her and hauled her to him.

"I don't give a fuck. I'll lick it off." Ziph thought she might die as Trent pushed her against the cold tile wall and licked her from her shoulder down to her hip. He didn't stop as he lifted her leg and ran his tongue from her ass crack to her hood piercing where he swirled his tongue and growled at her pussy. "Fucking delicious." He continued by slipping his tongue inside of her, and she squirmed as he tasted her inside and out.

"I am more than good with you liking to eat funk, but this steamy bathroom smells like serpent guts and sex, and I cannot fucking breathe. Gross, oh gods, it's in the steam. I think I can taste it."

He reached between her legs to knead her flesh and gently nipped at her inner thigh before relenting. "We can wash, but we are going straight to bed, and you are mine all day tomorrow." Ziph bit her lip and her core clenched as she anticipated the next day.

He reached over and handed her the soap bar before he leaned down and closed his mouth over her nipple, sucking it and flicking it with his tongue. "I thought we were waiting until tomorrow."

"You're waiting for your orgasm, but I'm not waiting for shit." He smiled when her eyes widened, "I said we were going to bed. I didn't say how much sleep we would have." She slathered her body and finished bathing as he watched her closely in the candlelight. "You have serpent blood in your tail fur." Trent held it over so she could see, and she rolled her eyes. "Where is your soap for hair?" Trent reached over her in the dark and took a bottle and squeezed some soap into his hands before he twirled his finger for her to allow him to wash her.

Ziph turned and let him wash her tail. He seemed to be enjoying himself, especially when he reached the base where he kept sliding his finger between her ass cheeks. She loved every second and leaned onto the cold wall as he played with her tail and ass. When he grabbed the lube and slipped his finger in her ass, she knew she was in for a long night.

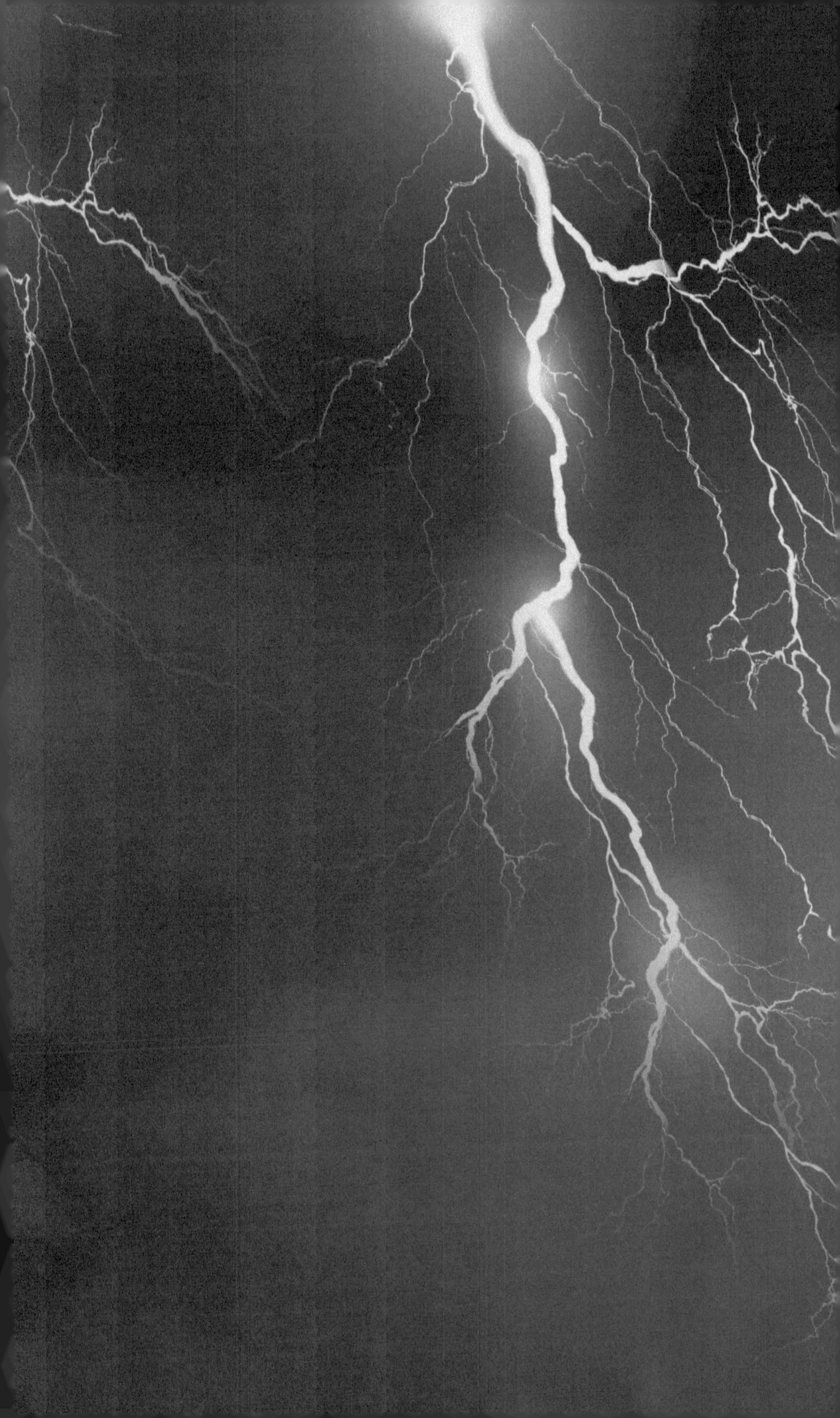

CHAPTER 29
RED VAPOR

Daylight shone in Ziph's eyes, she had been sitting up in Trent's bed for, well, who knows how long staring at the birds flitting around a tall tree across the street. They were bright orange with a long dark red tail that stretched down into a round tuft. They were diving through the air for bugs swarming around a small container of flowers hidden on a second story balcony. The little show had put her in a lovely state of disassociation. The moments her mind felt at peace were like floating on a cloud, of pure nothingness and she reveled in every second.

It was a long, stormy night and she had slept on top of Trent, it wasn't as if she had a choice. Every time she tried to slide off, he pulled her right back into the middle of his chest, before he wrapped his arms around her, and played with her nipples until he fell back asleep.

As she recalled her dreams, which were her flying through the bright sky and drifting along endless rivers of light, she felt free and light as a feather. Something startled her a bit when she remembered a different dream she had, and she blinked away her sleepy eyes as she thought hard trying to dig it up. *The dream was, uncomfortable, even scary?*

A flash of the dream sailed through her mind. It was just Trent, and Whit. They were in Dacket's room without her and Dacket, reading from an envelope in his desk and they seemed devastated. *What the fuck does that mean?* Fear had just begun to settle in when she heard Trent groan and stretch behind her, and she relaxed herself, knowing what was coming next.

He grabbed her waist and pulled her to him, curling around her as he crossed his arms over her chest and massaged her breasts. "So fucking soft. I just want to smother you." He growled as he rolled over on her, making her scream and laugh as he squished her into the mattress. With her pinned under him, he reached down to her hips and kneaded them as he licked the edge of her ear. "I love how soft you are," Trent gently whispered into her ear before he kissed her under her chin. He crawled down and nipped at the skin at her side before he bit down on her ass and sunk his fangs into her flesh. She shot half up and stared at him in horror but relaxed when he licked the wound and smirked, "My venom doesn't do a damn thing, but Whit still fucking hates when I bite him. If you bite him before he ties you up for sex, it doesn't matter who does it, he will scream and then cum in his pants. Dacket accidentally bit him one time when we were seventeen, and it paralyzed him for two days. They won't admit it, but I know they were fucking when it happened."

Ziph fell back against the bed laughing before he turned her hips to lick her wound again and slapped her ass. "No wonder he took such diligent care of me after Dacket bit me. That might also be why he has a bondage obsession with a ball gag."

Trent slipped his forked tongue between her ass cheeks making her arch and clench before he leaned over and rested his arms on her hip. "That's exactly why." Ziph smiled when her thoughts turned to how long they had all been together, and Trent narrowed his eyes at her.

"What are you grinning about?"

The more she learned, the more Ziph understood much clearer why they had been so apprehensive to add her to their relationship. "You've been together for over Eighteen years, that's almost as long as I've been alive."

Trent corrected her as he rose up with a hand outstretched for her, "Twenty years, to be exact. Listen, Dacket, Whit, and I have been with women a few times, but we haven't sought anything other than one another since they began hunting full time. That's a conversation for another time though. Right now, I want to talk to you about taking you somewhere nice tonight."

Unable to control her thoughts, Ziph replayed Dacket making his kill the night before, *inside the fucking serpent's mouth.* The thought of losing Dacket or Whit made her nauseous. *Why the fuck did he go inside the serpent's mouth? Is there really not a better way to do that? Wait. Did Trent say something about taking me somewhere? Why am I bouncing around so much? Is my brain short circuiting? I need to change the subject. I wonder why he works at the gate.*

"Why did you not become a hunter?" He handed her a dress she knew he had borrowed from Danny. "I went along once as an apprentice for Whit to see if I wanted to do it, and I'm not ashamed to say that I still have nightmares. It is not for me. I need solid ground. If that means being a simple guard for the factory then I am happy to sit in the guard station and people watch all day while I lift weights." *He openly admits he people watches. What a cute thing to say. I love the social rules here, they're so untainted and fresh. Back home, people watching was just an old lady activity for anyone rich enough to afford a window.*

Ziph took in the beautiful long black dress she had just slipped on with straps crossed between her breasts, and a slit that went all the way up to her hip with straps holding the top of the slit together. She slipped on some comfortable black flats and wondered if she needed to change them to something nicer. "Where are we going?" He handed her a woven basket which had all her makeup carefully organized, and clearly Dacket had meticulously cleaned all of it before he brought it down. The mirror tops on the lipsticks had been polished to a sparkling shine and she could see herself in them.

"It's a new club under Eight. I hear it has a different, darker style of music."

Dramatic night makeup would work, and Ziph began digging in the basket, spreading it over his bathroom counter. It took her an hour, but when she was finished, she came out and Trent was speechless. She had winged her eyeliner, applied lashes, and added gold to the inner corners of her eyes. She tied it together with black lipstick, which Trent was staring at.

His gaze roamed from her mouth to her feet and back up to her eyes before he smirked. "We should leave before I rip that dress off." Ziph smiled as he reached for her hand, and it dwarfed hers.

He led her from the apartment and down to the garage, but Trent stopped halfway to the trucks and spun on his heals. "Would you rather walk since you didn't have your run today?" Trent knew it was a long way, but Ziph became restless when she didn't do some type of exercise.

The way she lit up, he knew he offered the right thing.

"I'm glad I went with the comfortable shoes." She beamed as he linked his arm in hers, and he led her out onto the sidewalk to begin the long walk to Sector Eight.

As they passed block after block, Ziph noticed something peculiar. In all her studies on the progression and development of civilizations, every single world at one time had some form of street vendors. People who created art, creative goods, or fun delicious treats for passersby to enjoy was a consistent societal practice, which one of her professors had her dive into for a project. The reason street vendors were found in every civilization was due to the profound economic and cultural contributions they provided. They often signify strong, tight knit communities.

The streets in Valler were empty save a few people walking, and Ziph felt unease wriggle up her spine as she tried to wrap her head around why there were no vendors in this city. "Do you have open markets for people who make and sell goods?"

Trent narrowed his eyes at her, "Can you explain. What do you mean markets where people sell goods?"

Ziph couldn't take another step and her gut twisted in a knot as she tried to find a way to put into words what she was thinking and feeling. "You don't have any street markets where people can create art and sell it?"

Concern grew on Trent's face, and he frowned, "No, people here paint and create things, but we are not permitted to sell anything without the consent of the Kefale palace." Ziph swallowed trying to rid her throat of the lump forming. "Why do you ask?" Trent's worry was becoming intense, and Ziph wasn't sure how to explain what her heart was screaming.

"Trent, your people are being controlled to a degree

that is considered totalitarianism. I'm concerned if I explain it all right now someone could hear, and we can't let that happen." Trent stared at her, and he nodded briefly before they resumed their journey. Block after block, plain metal building after building with no difference to anything. No color, no art, no expression, and *no control over their own lives.* All the clues confirming this revelation was coming together in her mind as they quietly made their way to Sector Eight. *They have been living this way for thousands of years. They have been living this way for so long that they don't even know anything is wrong.*

Ziph could see Sector Eight ahead, and scowled when even there she couldn't find any sign of individuality, how had she not been aware of this before? *I guess now I'm having regular sex my mind has had time to finally think about something else.*

When they reached Sector Eight Trent led them to a door behind a large bush and opened it for her. She had never been this way, and as he opened the door, Trent explained, "We can't use the other routes to the underground anymore. The palace blocked them off. The guards make just enough from bribe money to allow them to stay open, but when the palace becomes aware of one of the entrances, they send construction teams to seal the entry with concrete."

Ziph cringed with each revelation and fear settled deeper inside, and she was far too aware the Elarian people had been unknowingly programmed into submission. The ruling power was thorough in their control, and because of that, there had never been a rebellion. These circumstances felt all too familiar, except here the rulers had perfected the craft and balance, unlike the First Human's back home. *Home, I miss my mother.*

The bloody red lights of the club Red Vapor shone from the wide, arched door flooding the ground in the dark corridor as Ziph gripped Trent's arm as they crossed into the swanky nightclub. Slow beats and strumming stringed instruments with deep melodies flowed from a light pink woman on a stage in the corner. The band behind her seemed to loom in the darkness, and Ziph noticed a blip of light from under the curtain before Trent led her to a table with a large crescent shaped seat and a tall back cushion along the back wall. They had a curtain around the back to provide additional privacy, and Ziph was pleased when they sat down because she could still see the stage.

There it was again. The light under the curtain next to the stage, but this time she noticed someone lurking in the dark. She followed the darkened form as they appeared near the exit. They went out the opposite way she and Trent had come. Before the song had changed, Ziph had come up with ten different scenarios from the kitchen staff running for an ingredient all the way to a secret society meeting. *It's definitely a secret society meeting.*

A server with lime green skin and solid black eyes came up to take their order, standing quietly. Trent thought for a moment before ordering, "We want two house specials." They came back setting two drinks down before disappearing again. Ziph couldn't see the bar and wondered if there was one in the open at all. Trent paused his own survey of the room to pick up his drink and take a sip. "I can't tell what this tastes like, but it's good."

Ziph studied the drink and found it curious; it was a tomato sauce, pepper, and liquor combo, but extra heavy on the liquor. "I thought you couldn't eat anything except meat?"

Trent grimaced as he answered, "We can't, but we like

flavor with alcohol, so we blend vegetables occasionally for drinks. It gives most of us some digestive discomfort."

Ziph felt curiosity override her, and her lips puckered before he asked, "Does a blended meat cocktail sound good to you?"

Ziph's mouth snarled to one side and Trent smiled at her before he took her face in his hands and kissed her. "You're cute when you're grossed out." He pulled away and she admired how well her lipstick stayed put. *I need to say thank you to Danny.*

When she met his eyes, he seemed confused. "I was checking to see if I had transferred any lipstick."

She expected a response, but Trent frowned as his eyes focused behind her on two people entering the club. They watched the two women move along the shadows before Ziph saw the little blip of light under the curtain again.

Trent slowly turned his head as he looked around the room, his mouth slightly parted as if he was too deep in thought to notice. He turned to her and leaned against her shoulder to whisper in her ear, "I scented the air. The two women who came in just now are members of a resistance group. I remember the scent of one of them. She ran past me when I was a child before six royal guards blew by me shoving me to the ground. I learned later there was a symbol they would wear, an X with a circle under it, and I just saw she had it drawn on her arm in ink.

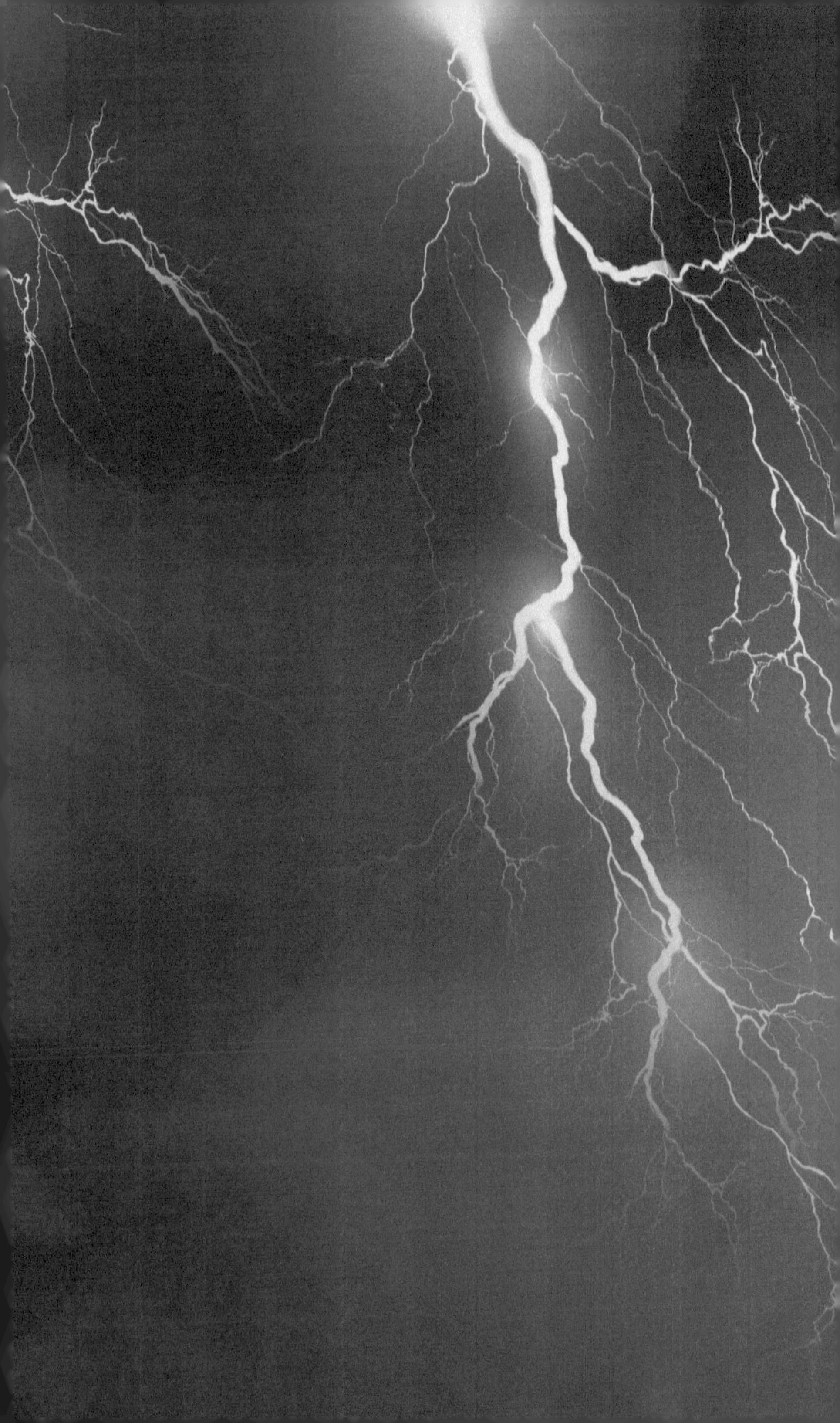

CHAPTER 30

TWO AND EIGHT

After a few hours of music, and no additional suspicious activity, Trent led Ziph home on his arm. The walk was slow and quiet, but filled with sweet moments of affection from Trent. *This man is about to fuck me against this wall in the street if he doesn't quit that.*

When they reached the stairs, Trent swooped her into his arms before he softly asked, "You need to give me a word or a signal, so I'll know you want me to stop."

Ziph rested her head on his shoulder as she answered, "Bumble bees."

He nodded and licked the edge of her ear before nuzzling his nose to the tip. "I like the fur growing on your ears. Will you shave them again or allow them grow back fully?" Ziph reached up and felt the fur growing back. She had never shaved them before, so the answer was easy, "I only shaved them to hide at first, but since no one seems to care, I'll let them grow back."

Trent was more than pleased as he opened his apartment door and carried her inside. *I could get used to having this woman in my arms.* He brought them into his room and set her down on his bed.

Ziph felt him tip her chin up so he could kiss her, and when he did, he whispered against her lips, "Take your dress off." He stroked a finger down her neck and a thrill built low in her belly. She knew this man would ravage her, and that was exactly what she craved. She was also desperate to stop the flashes of her assault in her mind, and all she wanted was to smother the intrusive memory with the feeling of loving hands around her and Trent buried inside her.

"You can be as loud as you want in my apartment. The walls have additional insulation." Trent smirked, and Ziph had a good idea why as she watched him strip. The idea was so delicious her breath fluttered as Trent backed up and pointed to the door of his room. "Take that damn dress off and run Golden Girl." *That is not really what I meant, but fuck me, this is all I want now.* Her squirrel mating chase urges were causing her pussy to drench with need.

Ziph shimmied off the dress in seconds before she bolted from Trent's room. His apartment was more than large enough for a chase. Ziph sailed over his couch and felt him behind her as she pounded her feet through his kitchen and into his weight room before coming back around to his hallway. She could've easily outrun him, but that was not the point. She looked behind her and knew at her pace she only had one more round before he would catch her, so she needed to make this one count. She jumped headfirst over his couch and bounced into a somersault before running back through his weight room and around the corner. She didn't dare turn around. She knew he had to be right behind her.

When he caught her, she had just reached his couch,

and he jumped at her, wrapping his arms around her waist and taking them both down onto the couch. He twisted around so he landed on his back, and Ziph thrashed in his arms as he jumped back up.

Trent twisted them both around and pushed her against the couch before reaching up and gently wrapping his hand around her throat. Ziph's breath caught, and Trent moved carefully as he hovered her, straddling her against the cushions.

His teal hand was warm against her neck, and she reached up to hold onto his arm as he leaned down and licked her bottom lip before nipping at it. When he slid his tongue in her mouth, she felt his hand roam her body before he slid it up to her breast and gently pinched her nipple.

Ziph locked onto his bright tangerine eyes. His pupil's widened as he continued to lose himself in her. He kissed her jaw before moving down to her breast to suck and flick her nipple with his forked tongue.

He held her down with his hand still firmly around her neck as he lifted her leg and folded her body to reach her pussy with his mouth. Running his tongue through her thoroughly a few times first to taste all of her, he gently reached down with his finger and thumb to find her buried clit. When he pinched the most pleasurable place on her body and rolled her clit up between his fingers for him to take into his mouth, she moaned with relief and held as still as she could. Her body was desperate for him to take her further, and she felt searing heat spread through her as he began sucking and nipping at her clit.

He gently increased pressure on her neck as he growled with her flesh between his teeth, and Ziph released a soft, singing whimper as she felt herself come undone with pleasure. Euphoria rolled through her in euphoric waves as Trent lightened up on her throat. He licked her clean before he allowed her leg down and moved to line himself up with her pussy.

Ziph felt his tip and moved her hips up to angle herself for him, causing Trent to snap as he huffed. He swung her up and impaled her onto his cock, stretching her and filling her up so perfectly she was frozen in time. All she could do was breathe and stare at his big, beautiful tangerine eyes.

"Fuck, how can I last at all with you looking at me like that." Ziph felt him separate into four parts inside of her, and she threw her head back to cry out as she dug her nails into Trent's shoulders.

The way the four parts all rolled with the tips fluttering deep inside of her, Ziph shifted her hips with each thrust to wedge him deeper. Trent growled as he gripped her hips, grinding her down onto his cock. He grabbed her by the neck and pulled her forward to sink his fangs into her shoulder causing Ziph to scream in panic and pleasure as she fell apart and clenched her pussy around his cock.

Trent exploded cum into her as he bit down, tasting her blood dripping from the wound. When they finally settled, Trent's fangs retracted, and Ziph fell over onto him, slick with sweat, panting against his chest.

She wrapped her arms around him and nuzzled her face in the crook of his neck, making no attempt to pull herself off his cock. "That's happening again."

Trent licked his lips and sincerely asked, "Which part?"

Ziph sat up and shot him an incredulous stare. "All of it, are you serious?"

Trent laughed as he lifted them up and carefully slid her off him before setting her down. His cum was running down her inner thigh, and he chuckled, "Let's clean you up." Trent guided her into his bathroom where he wet a cloth and knelt to clean her.

Watching him between her legs with the cloth gently wiping away his mess was making her want him all over again. "Do you have any idea how hot it is watching you clean me on your knees?"

Trent gave her a maniacal smile, sending a chill down her spine. He tossed away the rag and scooped her into his arms before taking them to his bed to jump in the center while still holding her. She screamed with delight as they landed on the bed, and Trent flipped her around to lay against him.

With him touching her as much as possible, Ziph snuggled against his big chest and her heart swelled as she felt an inner calm she missed so dearly. The way she had felt so settled before her assault here, she wasn't sure before if she could regain the sense of peace she originally had, but now she knew it was still there. It would take much more than just a round of loving, rough sex, but with time and talking about it in a safe space, she knew she would be able to cope.

Her eyes focused on Trent's muscular chest, his teal skin a striking color, and his dark blue nipple seemed to call to her to lick. *I wonder if he would fuck me again if I bit him back?*

Ziph couldn't resist trying as she leaned up and licked his nipple before nipping at the tip.

"Are you asking for round two?"

Ziph grinned at him, "What if I am?"

The thrill on Trent's face faded as he thought for a moment. "Can we invite Whit?" We have been talking about both of us taking you at once since we met you."

Ziph knew she shouldn't be surprised with the attention they had been giving her ass, but she was, and Trent immediately responded to her expression, "If you're not ready for something like…"

Ziph reared back and cut him off with her finger wagging at him, "No, no, are you going upstairs after him, or am I?"

With no hesitation and no answer, Trent tossed her off his chest and swiped his pants from the floor before running toward his door as he slipped the pants on. Ziph heard the door not quite shut all the way and bounce against the door frame as he ran for Whit's room. Seconds later, they were both barreling down the stairs, with a quickness they didn't usually have unless it was time to hunt. Their feet were *pounding* the stairs.

Ziph couldn't hold back a giggle as the two men tried to act like they hadn't just shaken the entire apartment building trying to reach Trent's apartment in record time when they strolled in. Trent was nude by the time he came back into the bedroom and Whit was stepping out of his pants as he aimed for the bed.

Trent grabbed Ziph and started to wedge her between him and Whit, but Whit kissed Ziph's shoulder and lay his chin on the top of her head while he explained, "She's not ready for anything in her ass, fitting my plug in her was like squeezing it in you the first time, it barely fit. She's almost ready, but not quite. I meant, I wanted to fuck you, while you fuck her."

Trent seemed just as excited, or maybe more, "Oh, of course you did." Ziph laughed as she leaned in to kiss the silly look from Trent's face. He deepened the kiss as Whit moved around Trent.

Trent spread her out under him at the edge of the bed

and lined himself up as Whit did the same to him from behind. Whit poured lube onto his hand and tossed the tube onto his clothes on the floor before slathering it over his cock and waiting for Trent to sink into Ziph.

Trent pushed his cock inside her as he pulled her closer to the end of the bed for Whit to have better access to him. Whit slid into Trent while he held his waist, and Trent couldn't help groaning and rolling his hips from being filled from both sides. Whit let him milk him before he began moving, he knew how quickly Trent would cum and he wanted to ensure Ziph had her fill first.

Ziph could feel the pressure of both men as she angled herself to take Trent as deep as she could. Her body complied allowing him to fully seat himself inside. He broke apart and Ziph whimpered with the delicious feeling of him rolling inside of her. Whit groaned from behind as he held back as much as possible, and Trent knew Whit was buying him time, so he moved quickly. Trent started slow but gained speed and soon the sound of slapping skin filled the room as Ziph was pounded by both men at once.

The way she pressed into the mattress and her back slowly moved across the bed, had her shattering like glass in an opera before she even reached the middle. "Oh, fuck I'm cumming!" Ziph breathed, and that was all Whit could stand as he split in four and began slamming himself into Trent, which in turn caused Ziph to cry out with her overflowing pleasure.

Trent blasted into Ziph as Whit did the same to him from behind, giving Trent the satisfaction of his own cum as well as the relief inside his ass at his pleasure center. He and Whit slumped over, and Trent rolled them so they didn't crush Ziph. Neither of them could hold their own weight. They took several long moments to rest and catch their breath.

Finally rising, Trent looked giant above Ziph. She could hear Whit clean himself up and find a towel to wet for her as Trent crawled into the bed next to her. Whit took the damp towel and cleaned her before tossing it in Trent's dirty clothes bin.

She watched him reach for his pants, but the idea of him leaving and not sleeping with them seemed inconceivable. "Will you stay?" Whit paused and thought for a moment before he turned to face her. He didn't say a word as he dropped his pants back on the floor and crawled in the bed.

CHAPTER 31
BEHEMOTH

There was a knock at the door and Ziph was the only one awake enough to answer so she pulled on Trent's shirt and shuffled to the door. When she opened it and saw Dacket with her hunting clothes in his hands, she yelled out, "Whit, it's Dacket. There's a serpent." She could hear Whit fall from bed and run for the door before he blew by them for his apartment to change.

"The light just came on, we have time," Dacket reminded him, and they could hear Whit slow down as he reached his door.

Ziph changed in Trent's hallway and followed Dacket to the truck in the garage. Right before they pulled out, they could see Whit opening his truck door and climbing inside.

Trying to get ahead, Ziph attached her jets to her ankles and hips before fishing her mask from her bag and setting it next to her in the seat. After rubbing the sleep from her eyes, she slapped a hand over her mouth realizing she hadn't brushed her teeth after the long night she had. *What the whole fuck and a half, you cannot tell me I have to breathe my own funk breath in this mask while trying to kill a giant monster snake.*

Dacket gave her a knowing grin from the corner of his mouth and pointed to the dash where there was a cup of water and her toothbrush setting on a napkin with toothpaste already on the bristles. *Bless these thoughtful men and their wiggly dicks.* Ziph snatched them from the dashboard and furiously brushed her teeth before hanging her head from the truck window to rinse. She drank the rest of the water and set the cup down long before pulling her head inside and rolling her window up. The cool wind was refreshing against her skin. She was so glad it was clear and bright for this hunt, hunting at night was awful, and it was worse when it rained at the same time.

As she braided her hair back, she began thinking about the planet and had to ask, "How far north on Binara have your people been able to travel?"

He leaned back in his seat and looked over at her. "The gravity levels north of the latitude line of the Elarian cities are too high, and anyone who ventures there ends up with cardiac problems. The top half of the planet is an ocean. We think there are algae blooms which create our oxygen since the floating grasslands in the sky belt couldn't possibly provide enough."

Ziph was having a hard time understanding the lines placement without a map. "The latitude lines, can you explain their width differently? Maybe in terms of average travel time in your truck? That class was a long time ago."

Dacket nodded before he explained, "If we drive at an average speed, it takes us thirty minutes south to reach the latitude line we need to stop our trucks for hunting the sky belt, and thirty minutes to the north would take us to the latitude line where we would need to stop because of gravity becoming too great. You can walk a little way further, but not far before your heart has trouble keeping up. The only reason we have complex life here is because of Barren giving us a single ring of livable gravity."

That makes a lot more sense. I'm so glad I asked. Ziph looked up at Barren with more questions, "Don't you think Barren would have the right gravity all over to support life?"

Dacket seems intrigued as he joined her in looking up at the planet. "I've never thought about that, but we know that's where the younger serpents spend most of their time hunting for prey. There are many species of smaller animals which migrated there and hide among the grass-lands. If there is breathable air all over Barren, I am sure plants and animals span the surface. If my people weren't so held back by our rulers, I bet we could have built safer cities there." Dacket stared up at Barren, and his gaze turned dreamy as Ziph watched him develop the idea in his mind. She couldn't help herself as she moved across the bench seat, and he reached out to put his arm around her to pull her close. The protective coziness of this man was unmatched, and Ziph could have fallen asleep on his shoulder if he had not been leaning over to kiss her head every few minutes.

When they parked, they could see the serpent rise, reaching its face to the sky. Ziph could hear Dacket audibly gasp from where she was standing on the other side of his truck. The serpent was considerably larger than the last one they killed, and Ziph could tell the hunters were concerned as they pulled up next to her and Dacket. The absurdly giant serpent was still far enough away that they had time to spare, and they seemed to soak up those extra minutes after seeing the size of their target.

Dacket was visibly rattled as he approached Ziph. "It's Gerara's turn to take the kill if she wants it, and we never take another hunter's turn."

Ziph stared at him wearily and asked, "What about the kill I took?"

Dacket paused remembering her first time, "You're lucky that was my kill. I would have said something if I had known your plan was to take the kill on your first hunt."

Gerara walked up as she attached her hip jets. "My turn seems to be unfortunate, but I'm still taking it." Dacket nodded to her, concern for Gerara written all over his face but he forced his words to tell a different story.

"You've made your share of mouth strikes, and I won't make a backup outer strike unless you signal."

Gerara held her mask up to her face and it connected with her magnetic implants with a light pop against her skin. Gerara took off for the unreasonably large serpent from what Ziph could tell as she put on her own mask. *Maybe unreasonably large is not enough, I think its honestly more of absurdly fucking giant.*

Ziph's gut twisted as she watched the enormity of the serpent grow as the distance decreased between them. *Gerara is seriously planning to fly in its mouth and kill it? Why don't they have a larger weapon for a serpent this size? Have they ever seen one this large?* As they neared the beast, Ziph's mind reeled. *We need bigger weapons, that thing could swallow a bus!*

Skating on the air, Ziph brought herself even with Dacket and tipped her mask up, "Don't you have some kind of explosives we can toss in that monster's mouth?!"

Dacket shook his head as he lifted his mask, "You're an apprentice. You don't need to do this!" Ziph snarled at

Dacket. She had no intention of leaving them to battle this behemoth without her. She knew what kind of skills she possessed, and her mother didn't raise her to back down, especially not when the people she cared about were at risk. *The only thing I'm afraid of is not knowing when I'm talking too much. They don't need to know that though. Dammit, please don't blurt that out later.* She watched the way Gerara skated toward the serpent, determination in every movement. *I can't say I would do any different.*

As they ascended, the serpent rose to meet them and Gerara began circling the head with her team first while Ziph, Dacket, and Whit trailed behind in the formation. After circling multiple rounds, they finally caused the serpent to slow, and Gerara tossed three of her practice jets into its mouth, eliciting a deep hiss from the monster, and the air vibrated around them. Gerara waited until the serpent opened its mouth all the way before she bolted inside with her spear, but unlike before, the serpent continued moving its head, and Ziph had a stone form in her gut.

Gerara's team began signaling to Dacket and Whit. *What the fuck are they trying to plan?! Did that fucking giant snake just eat Gerara!* Ziph knew she needed to act fast or Gerara would suffocate to death, so she recalled snake anatomy and made her move. *Dacket can be mad at me all he wants. I'm not allowing her die, not like this.* She would not allow anyone else to be thrust in harm's way, so she skated up and slammed the blunt end of her spear against the nose of the serpent.

The beasts mouth snapped open, and Ziph gripped her spear with every bit of strength she possessed as she flew inside the giant's pale pink mouth. She could hear Dacket screaming something, but she didn't have time to waste.

Gerara needed to be cut from this snake's gut before she suffocated.

With her target aimed, Ziph waited until darkness enveloped her to plant her feet on the monster's rough tongue and slam the end of the spear directly into its brain. In less than a second, she felt the flesh under her feet still, and she knew she had made the kill. Ziph pushed herself away from the throat of the beast and crawled through a gap in its gums before she leveraged the jaw to push herself through its closed lips.

Once she was free and could breathe, she pulled her mask off as Dacket came rushing over and grasped her shoulders in a bruising hold. "What were you thinking?!" Ziph ignored him and grabbed a long knife from his belt. She utilized the serpent saliva to slip from his hold to rush down against the side of the serpent, slicing the knife along its scales as she went. Blood seeped into the air from the open wound as everything slowly moved to the ground, and it seemed as though the blood was moving through a viscous goo. Ziph sliced into the esophagus and hooked her arm inside before pointing the knife outward, and using her jets, she slid down the long organ as she searched for Gerara. *Why the fuck is no one helping me pull her free?!*

Dacket soon joined her, and they both dug for Gerara through what the enormous snake had been eating. Partially digested Elarian people began sliding from the opened stomach, all of them wearing palace style garments, and the hunters gathered around as Ziph finally found Gerara.

Ziph yanked Gerara up from the blood, digestive juices, and acid eaten corpses spread over the ground before ripping away her mask. After clearing her airway,

Ziph flipped her around where she had Gerara in a backward hug position, and Ziph began squeezing her forearms around Gerara's chest in a rhythm. Without gravity, she could not do normal chest compressions. There was likely stomach acid in her lungs, and it must be cleared before she could take a full breath. "Come on, breathe!" Gerara's team of three surrounded Ziph with their masks off and their expressions brimming with dread.

Gerara groaned and coughed as Dacket came close to Ziph, helping her guide Gerara to dry ground nearby. Everyone surrounded Ziph and Gerara as Ziph held Gerara close. "Are you hurting anywhere? What can we do?"

Gerara looked up at Ziph and smiled before she coughed up blood and spoke with the sound of sandpaper in her throat, "As a young girl growing up in the meat Sector, I wanted to be the best hunter Valler had ever seen. I finally had my chance, and not only did I fail, but now I'm dying for taking it." Gerara coughed up more blood before continuing, "And the worst part is, I lost my greatest kill to an overgrown fluffy tailed rodent." Gerara smiled up at Ziph as the light slipped from her eyes, and Ziph sobbed while her team reached out to lay their hands on their lost team leader.

I didn't reach her in time. How could I have failed her so profoundly? I'm so sorry. I wanted us to be friends. I wonder if she knew she was Dacket's sister?

Dacket was crouched behind Ziph and reached over her to help Gerara's team take her body to their truck, and they wrapped her before sliding her into the back. Dacket returned and sat down next to Ziph. He took her hand into his, "We are forbidden from cutting into the belly of the serpents. I know you could not have known that, and this kill is far enough in the sky belt that the palace won't be able to see anything."

Gerara's team came back, and Whit pointed to the multiple Elarian bodies with ragged palace clothes and no way to tell which city they came from. Some with no clothing left had what appeared to be autopsies performed before they had been fed to the serpent.

"Why the fuck are there so many bodies inside this serpent? Is this why we are forbidden from cutting into the belly of this monster?" Whit went over to inspect further and shook his head as he pointed at four suspicious bodies slumped in a pile. "These people here all have distended bellies like they were all stuffed with something." Turning to face the rest of Gerara's team with Dacket and Ziph standing close to him, Whit twisted his mouth as he stared at the closest body.

Dacket pointed to the bodies next to Whit. "We're already this deep. We might as well see what these people were force fed." Whit nodded and knelt by the closest body before slicing open the person's gut.

Whit reached inside and pulled out a long cylinder-shaped soft object, almost like a waterlogged sausage. A wrapper was around the center and Whit peeled it off. Whit's face paled as he read the computer printed label aloud, "Serpent growth hormone Kefale Palace Lab batch 76-2048."

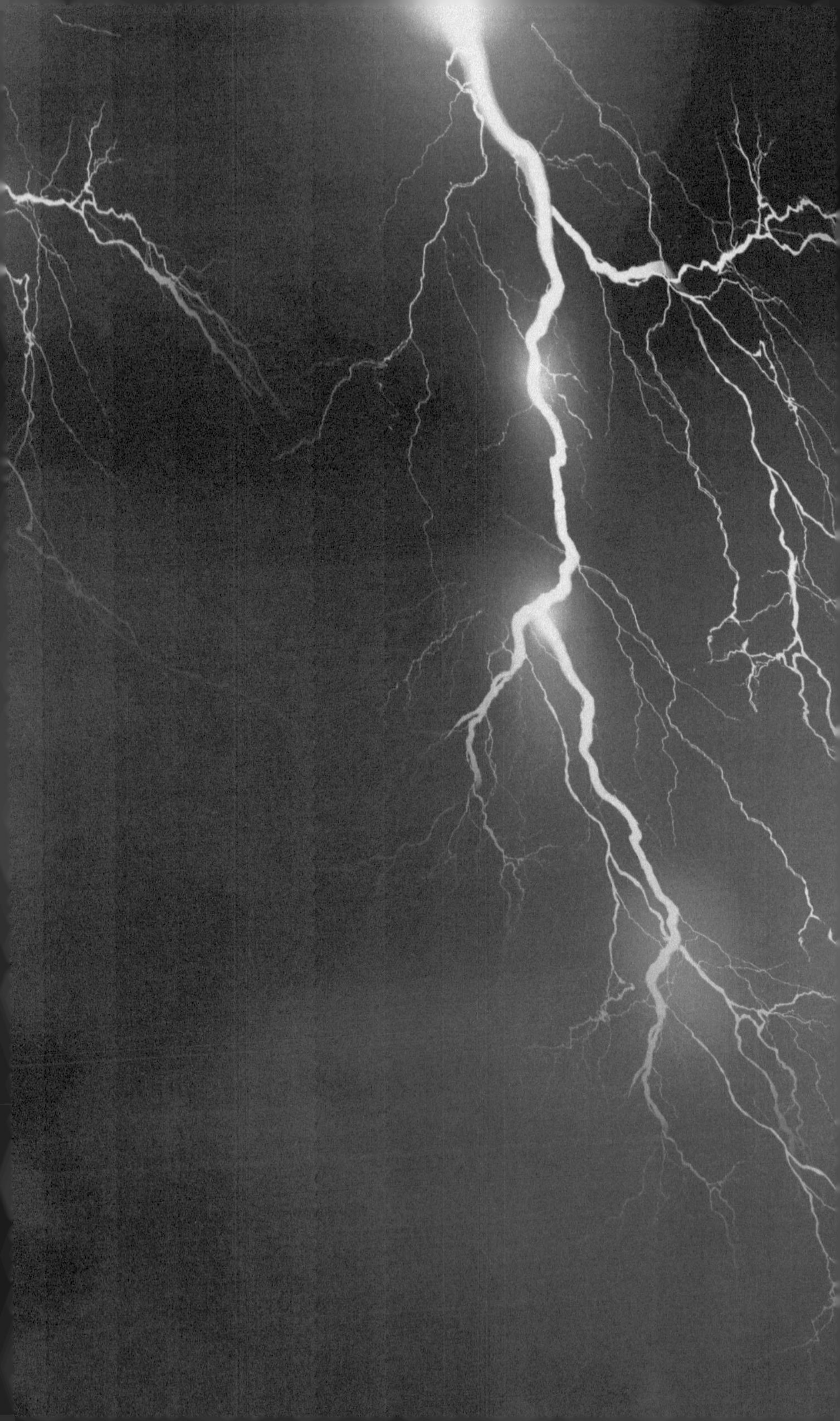

CHAPTER 32
ROOFTOP FOOT RUBS

After Gerara's team split the meat up evenly with them, they all agreed to keep their discovery about the serpent's stomach contents a secret. Ziph was grateful for the acknowledgment, but something told her the actions she took with Gerara had earned her a solid place within the two main hunting houses. Even with logic telling her the facts, she was still eaten with guilt for failing to save Gerara. *If I would've just moved a little bit faster.*

Behind them they could see the line of trucks turning around and heading back home. The next serpent would belong to one of them, and Ziph assured herself she would back off from taking too hard of a lead. Disrupting the balance of power with the hunters in the meat processing Sector was on the top of her list of things to avoid at all costs.

Dacket came up to Ziph and put his arm around her to stop her before she climbed in the truck. "What you did was stupid, but it was inspiring in a way I am not sure I have the words to convey. Hunters aren't given a peaceful death like you gave to Gerara, and you risked your life for it." Dacket held her to him as he fought back his emotions.

Ziph spoke softly as she asked, "Gerara, she was your sister, wasn't she?"

Dacket squeezed Ziph and pressed his forehead against hers, not saying a word as he finally allowed his tears to flow. There was no need for him to confirm because she knew the truth. Dacket and Gerara had looked too similar, and Ziph even noticed similarity in their mannerisms. They both always twisted their mouth to the left when they began to smile and they both had the same type of intuitiveness with design.

"After we unload everything, we should clean up, and maybe we can sit on the roof while we have a meal." Ziph offered and Dacket brought his lips to hers for a drawn out kiss before he opened her door and helped her inside.

On their journey back to the city, Ziph couldn't help but daydream about living on Barren. It looked as though the vegetation was spreading around where the planet's atmospheres mixed, and Ziph dreamed of a time when the planet could be covered in greenery. "Does Barren not have water? Is that why it has taken so long for things to grow there?"

Dacket looked over at Ziph who was turned backward and hanging over the backseat while she stared at the hovering planet. "As far as I know, no. Barren did not have water to begin with. Our storm systems pass down through the sky belt and rain falls onto the north end of Barren. We have seen more storms pass further down into Barren in recent years."

Ziph twisted back around to face him and asked, "Do you get tired of all my questions?" Dacket shook his head and tried to smile, but she knew he was hurting too much to fake it. She moved closer and rested her head on his shoulder for the rest of the drive, holding his arm while he gipped her thigh.

Dacket parked, and Ziph followed him upstairs to his apartment, but she guessed she could call it their apartment. This was home now, and she was beginning to love it. After they were clean and changed, Ziph met Dacket in the kitchen where he was mid swallow with a rat tail still between his fingers.

He forced it down, and Ziph handed him the glass of water she had been drinking. He stared at her as he took it and drank the rest. "I bet Elarian people give good head."

Dacket's eyes flew open, and he burst into laughter as he set the glass next to the sink. "Pick out what food you want to take to the roof. I have some laundry I need to bring."

She picked out several pieces of fruit as well as some carrots and met Dacket in the living room where he was holding both of their laundry in a hamper. *Is this man really about to do my laundry?* She followed him up to the rooftop and she noticed a new table and soft lounging chairs.

Dacket's rooftop was tall enough that when she stood, she could see over the top to the north where the cracked rocky land seemed to spread endlessly. "You're always searching for more. Will you ever be at peace?"

Ziph turned to Dacket and gave him a sweet smile, "I don't think I'm meant for peace." She was being honest, but Dacket didn't seem to like that answer at all.

He dropped the laundry he was scrubbing with a slap onto the stone rooftop before he leaned her back and kissed her, "What brings you peace?"

She thought for a moment and couldn't hold it back as she blurted, "You." She was sure that was not an answer he was looking for, but it was the truth. *I really need to stop being so damn impulsive. What kind of fucking answer is that anyway? Why couldn't I just say painting, or maybe dancing, or even running?*

Dacket swooped her up and sat them both down in one of the new plush outdoor chairs before he stared at her, narrowing his eyes. "I need to remember you were not raised to be a hunter. You're you, someone completely unique. I should not have assumed one way or the other. If you need peace from me, then that's what you'll have."

Ziph nuzzled herself into his chest, and she could hear his heart beating in a perfect rhythm. It was strong, and she felt herself nearly lull into a trance with the beat. *Dacket thinks I want peace from him, but he doesn't understand he is my peace.*

The way he rubbed her lower back while she lay against him was enough to make her fall asleep, but she had other, far more important plans to allow that to happen, plans she had been thinking about since the truck ride home from their hunt.

She was sucking Dacket's dick until he finished, and she was making it happen even if she had to wrangle with his four-piece penis inside her mouth. She could fit *plenty* in her mouth, she had evolved from a squirrel after all. Ziph moved to straddle him and began grinding on his lap. "Out here? It's daylight." With his hands on her hips, pressing her down onto him, Dacket searched around, but there were no obvious windows or other people on any near rooftops.

"I'll be quick, I promise." He tilted his head in confusion, but when she swung her leg over and crawled between his legs.

He understood with a quiet, "Oh," as Ziph pulled his

sleep pants down to free his cock, which was already protruding all the way from his slit.

"I want to know what you taste like," Ziph whispered before she descended her mouth onto him. He sharply inhaled as she took him as deep as she could, and Ziph wrapped her lips tight around his cock as she felt the pieces begin to separate in the back of her mouth. The four parts burst apart and rolled, and she could feel the small soft nodules rubbing against her tongue as his tips began fluttering. She did what she could to keep him all inside her mouth as she pumped his cock with her lips and hand, and her mouth felt so full it seemed as if her cheeks would burst.

She looked up at Dacket just as he opened his eyes and looked down at her, and when he saw her, he slapped a hand over his mouth. Ziph scowled as she felt his body shake. *Is this fucker really laughing at me while I'm sucking him off?!*

Not more than a moment went by before his cum blasted into her mouth, the taste was thick and salty, and she swallowed it down while Dacket slipped himself from her mouth. His body still shook with laughter. "What is so funny, you asshole?!"

He sat with his hand plastered to his mouth and Ziph regretted asking when he moved his hand and puffed out his cheeks as he desperately held back his grin. Ziph's mouth gaped as he burst into raucous laughter, "I'm sorry, I'm so sorry." He could hardly speak as she began giggling too, imagining how ridiculous she probably looked with his penis wiggling around inside her puffed cheeks. *I really should've thought about that. No more daylight blowjobs, those are for darkness only. At least he feels better now, that was the goal, right?*

When Dacket calmed, he pulled his pants up and patted Ziph on the shoulder before he tugged her into his lap. "I am not sure I have ever laughed like that." He brushed her hair from her face and kissed her forehead. "Let me finish this laundry, and we can go inside." Ziph let him up and watched as he scrubbed and wrung the clothes before he hung the laundry on the drying line. He had been so rigid and tight when she met him, and now his movements seemed as if he was gliding effortlessly.

When he came back, he knelt before her and lifted her foot to rub it. "It's your turn, but it's not happening out here." He kissed her ankle before setting it down and reaching out for her. Dacket pulled her to him and held her to his chest before he reached for her hand and led her down to their apartment.

Dacket locked his front door and guided Ziph to the center of his living room where he didn't wait and pulled her clothes off, and they landed in a pile by the couch. He took her face in his hands and kissed her with sensual, heated focus before he slid his arm around her and walked them to his room without breaking the kiss. His tongue delved inside her mouth and his sweet attention stole her breath.

No wonder he hides so much, he is all heart under his hard exterior. The way his eyes were set on her, she felt like he could see right through to her soul and everything which made her Ziph. She felt her soul was bare, much more stripped than simply nude. He saw everything she ever wanted someone to notice while his lips found every place she wanted to be touched. She crawled onto his bed, and he followed her, shedding his clothes as he moved.

"I didn't know it could be like this," Dacket admitted as he hovered over her, studying every detail of her face.

She knew this was his ongoing apology, he didn't need to explain.

"I wasted years of my life withholding my virginity for a religious blessing pledge. The House of Venus promised it was the only way I would be blessed enough for a wealthy man to find me worthy, and I was convinced because I was hungry."

Dacket kissed her again, slowly, before he responded, "Holding myself back from you was a mistake I will spend the rest of my time correcting." He moved down and took her nipple into his mouth before kissing across her chest and doing the same to the other side. He wrapped his tail around her calf, and she felt him rub the inside of her ankle with the tip.

Dacket was meticulous as he parted her pussy and found her elusive clit with his fingers before he leaned in and pinched it between his teeth. Ziph arched off the bed and moaned as he began assaulting her with his forked tongue, and her hips rocked with his perfect rhythm. Heat poured from deep in her belly as he ravished her, the way she wanted it the most, his strong hands gripped her thick hips and held her up for better access.

Ziph wrapped her legs around his head and squeezed when she felt him reach that perfect point, just for him to growl causing her to cry out with delight as she exploded with pleasure. Her core clenched trying to break free, but Dacket couldn't get enough and held her pussy to his face until she screamed for him.

Ziph's breath was uneven as Dacket yanked her hips to the end of this bed. His bed covers were now in a wad on the floor underneath them. His rock-hard cock pushed at her pussy, and Ziph whimpered with joy as she felt him slide inside and fill her. By the second thrust, he was spreading apart, and her breaths quickened all over again as his quad cock waved inside of her. She cried out as he held her hips and ground against her, her legs wrapped around his hard body like a vise. Dacket burst inside of her with a groan while Ziph curled as her own pleasure crested.

Still buried inside of her, Dacket leaned in and kissed her forehead, cradling her head with his hands. He slid from her and cleaned her up with a wet cloth before he crawled in beside her and wrapped her in his strong arms. *This man feels like he was made for me. If this is my reward, then maybe it was worth it after all.*

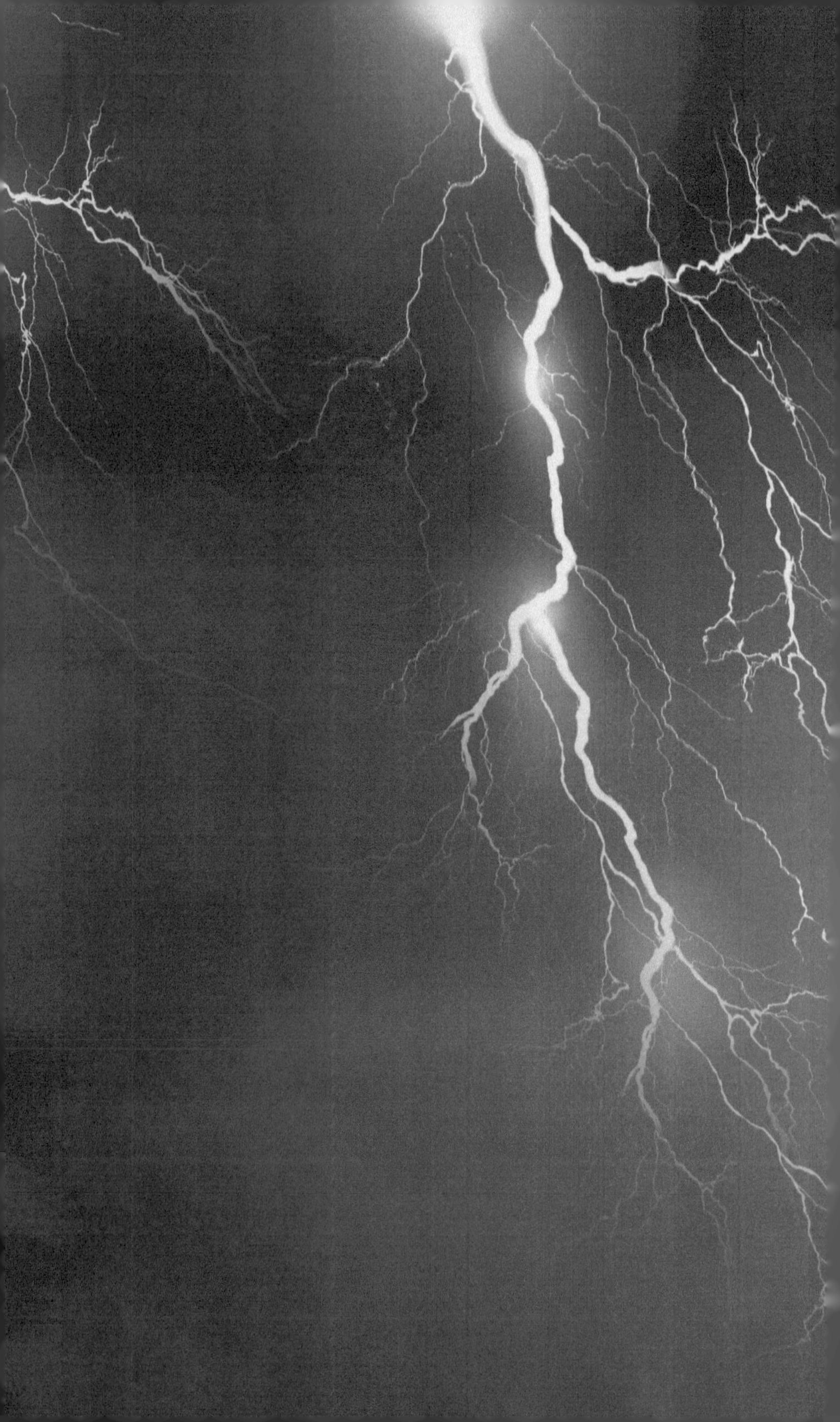

CHAPTER 33
CRACKS

Ziph was falling in love with the storms, they were so pure and refreshing. A flash of lightning streaked through the darkness of the night, striking the metal rod on the collection towers along the city wall and causing the lights to flicker as the current moved by their building. The current rushed into a nearby conversion hub where it was changed into usable electricity then sent into the electric grid. Ziph watched until the hub lights shone and noticed the far too modern electrical connections into the hub seemed suspicious. When the sky lit up again with a wall strike causing the hub lights to glow, she confirmed it.

It was something about the smoothness of the materials compared to the rings and contraptions all over the other electric connections. *Something feels off here, but no one would notice except a person like me, who has seen modern technology. How can I explain this to them without sounding like I'm making up an unreasonable scheme?* Dacket must have woken from the flickering lights and booms of thunder as she noticed his breathing change. "I keep noticing technology in your city that doesn't fit." There she went, blurting things out again. *The man just woke up. You couldn't give him five minutes. I really need to learn how to control myself better.* She knew that was a joke with her, but it felt good to say it.

Dacket didn't move as he quietly responded, "What does that mean? Do you think more people from your galaxy are here?"

Ziph wasn't sure, but something in her gut told her his suggestion didn't seem like it made sense. "I don't think it's people from my galaxy here. I think it's your royals. I think they've constructed this entire situation with the giant serpents just to keep their own people in line, and I think they're hiding advanced technology from your people. I think a lot is happening that no one seems to notice or talk about except for me."

Dacket rubbed her arm as he explained as gently as he could, "Because when my people begin speaking about these things, they end up missing. Now we at least know where they're going."

Straight to the gut of a serpent. Ziph's heart broke. They were trapped under the control of the Kefale, and there would be no way to escape them. She saw all the acid eaten bodies inside the serpent firsthand and knew the Kefale were feeding the Elarian people to them with growth hormones shoved down their throats. The greatest victims were those being imprisoned and fed to the serpents, and the hunters. *I can't imagine how profoundly these royals have stunted this society. They probably could've had wormhole technology by now if they hadn't been so held back.*

Her hands wrapped around Dacket's forearms over her

chest, and she felt him inhale her scent as he brushed his lips below her ear. "I don't want to stifle your thoughts and dreams, but I am selfish. I only want your thoughts on me right now." Ziph twisted in his arms and buried her face in his neck before he moved to lay on his back so he could pull her on top of him.

Just as Ziph took a long slow breath, ready to return to her slumber, there was a knock at the door and by the sound of it, Trent stood on the other side. Dacket slid out of bed and spoke loud enough Trent could hear him from his bedroom doorway, "Trent, did the serpent light come on?"

On the other side of the door he answered, "Yes, is Ziph with you?" Dacket responded, "Yes," and they heard Trent knock on Whit's door before he opened it and went inside.

Dacket seemed irritated about having to hunt, and it was the first time Ziph had ever seen him have any type of emotion about his job. She and Dacket dressed quickly and met Whit in the hall on the way down to the garage. Thunder blasted above the building, and the stairwell shook as they descended, taking two steps at a time. Ziph felt unease creep in as they pulled away from the garage and onto the road. The downpour made it almost impossible to see anything. The gate lights were flashing the warning they were soon to close, and the guards were all lined up on either side of the gate ready to run for the protection rooms built into the city wall. As they passed through, a few other trucks were already behind them as they turned south toward the open land.

The system star began shining above the clouds, and the sky brightened just enough they could see what was awaiting them. Three serpents were rising from the ground and swaying their long upper bodies in the wind and rain, seeming to beckon the hunters to face them.

Ziph slid over to Dacket and pressed herself against him before asking, "What happens now that there are three?" He released a slow breath before he answered, "There are several hunting houses ahead of us before it is our kill again, but we will need to assist with these kills. These hunters next in line are younger and less experienced, and if an opportunity arises after the first two are down, it is acceptable to jump in and finish the third to help them. If meat is shared when you make a kill out of order, it's still kind of insulting, but it's not a betrayal."

As they reached the stopping point, Ziph's unease became full blown terror boiling in her belly. Nausea threatened to spill over as she leaned over to attach her jets, and she reluctantly climbed from Dacket's truck holding her hand over her mouth. Something felt off, but she couldn't figure out what it was.

The rain had not lightened, and she prepared herself to be soaking wet under her hunting gear. The water seeped behind her collar as she braided her hair back. Whit came up and wrapped a string around her hair to hold the braid, and she turned to thank him, but he leaned in for a kiss instead. When he pulled away from her, he rubbed her shoulders. "You'll be alright. Don't worry Golden Girl. This will be over soon, and we should be back home before midday."

Ziph leaned into him as the first hunting teams began the long run toward the sky belt while the serpents ominously swayed and slithered ever closer. With their team and Gerara's team next to them gathering and readying to move out, Holdu Trep, Gerara's team's new lead approached Dacket. "We are all less than five-year hunters. I know it's not customary, but we discussed asking to join your team on the field until we are ready."

Dacket seemed honored as he answered, "You and your team are exceptional hunters, combining our teams would benefit us all." Whit and the other members of Gerara's former team nodded in agreement before Dacket continued, "I don't anticipate the other teams will secure all three serpents, so we need to conserve energy for the third and ready ourselves as backup."

Ziph swelled with pride at how Dacket commanded the teams. He was a reserved man, but his leadership was diamond strong and unquestionable. When he finished speaking, he slid his mask on, and everyone followed suit. With Dacket in the lead, they ran toward the three massive serpents while they watched the first hunting team slope upward into the air.

Ziph's stomach still churned with anxiety. *Why do I feel this way? This part was always so thrilling before. Now, it feels like we're heading toward our end.* Ziph continued despite her growing apprehension. She was just thankful they could see the serpents. She thought about Gerara briefly, but that wasn't it.

The first hunter teams reached the closest and smallest serpent as Ziph felt gravity release its final hold on her, and she began skating on the air. The engaged team went in for the kill, and she watched them imitate her technique by flying under its chin and making the strike through the neck and into the brain.

The first serpent stilled and began gliding down just as the second set of teams reached the largest of the three serpents. Dacket was still moving toward the largest serpent when two teams began their attack, so with no one else targeting the third serpent, he changed his trajectory to intercept it. Ziph and their new combined team matched his angle, following closely behind.

As they neared, Whit waved his hand to Ziph to offer her his kill since she needed the practice. She accepted and when they reached the serpent, she took the lowest rotation until the beast slowed and she could fly up under its chin. As she rose up toward the serpent's head, she noticed something flash a bit on top of the eye of the snake. She slowed and shook her head to clear the water from her mask before she narrowed her eyes trying to see.

Ziph's heart ripped in half as she clearly saw lashes growing above the eye of the serpent. *It's Lashes, no, no, NO!* Ziph ripped her mask off her face and flew as fast as she could into the line of sight of the serpent. The rest of the team still circling began to slow as they watched her in pure confusion and horror. Ziph screamed at the serpent, "Lashes!"

The serpent closed its mouth and tipped its head down to see Ziph better, and Ziph sobbed as Lashes slowly blinked her big eyes. Nearing the massive snake, Ziph reached out and touched her nose before wrapping her arms over her. Lashes closed her eyes and remained still as Ziph finally turned and faced Dacket who hovered behind her with his mask clenched in his hand. The fury and betrayal written on his face was something she knew she would never forget. *This choice will ultimately break his heart, and she knew that.*

"When I first landed here, this snake found me, and she kept me safe. I can't let anyone harm her. I'm sorry, I won't let anyone near her." Ziph spread her arms out and pressed herself against Lashes nose, feeling her massive warm breaths press against her back.

"You will disgrace our name indefinitely for this." Dacket was as heartbroken as she knew he would be, and he reached up to slide his mask back on, but Ziph couldn't bear his name being ruined either.

"Wait." This was not his fault. He did nothing wrong. He stopped and pulled his mask back off to give her his attention. "I won't come back with you. I won't ruin your name. Just leave me here and go, you can't give up everything because of me." Ziph watched the light drain from Dacket's eyes with her words, and tears erupted from her as she watched his hope evaporate. He squeezed his eyes shut before he turned his back on her and skated to his truck. He didn't break his stride, and Ziph watched every second of it as Whit hovered next to her.

"Golden Girl, I know this serpent loves you, and what you did is truly noble, but you may have just broken our Dacket. I'm not sure where we will be able to go from here, but I'll wait for you by my truck for you to decide. Just know you'll always have a home with us, even if it means we'll lose everything." Whit skated on the air toward his truck as the rest of the team followed behind. Ziph wasn't lost on the fact that the hunting teams heard every word of his speech to Ziph, yet they still followed him.

Ziph wasn't leaving. She knew if she followed them, they would lose their place in the hunting community and their entire livelihood would be destroyed. *Not to mention generations of work for that reputation. I will never jeopardize that.*

Behind her Lashes remained frozen in place and Ziph turned to face her. "Lashes, I know you're hungry." Ziph could hardly make the words through her tears as she tried to explain to Lashes in the simplest way possible. "If you keep moving toward the city, they will kill you. I know they fed you and made you this way. I am so sorry. You don't deserve this. Go that way and stay away from the cities, and don't eat the people they leave out into the wastelands between cities. Just please go there." Ziph pointed to Barren where the green areas were steadily expanding, and Lashes blinked at her twice. Ziph knew Lashes understood as she turned her massive body back into the sky belt and began swimming through the center toward Barren. The giant serpent went exactly where Ziph pointed.

Ziph knew Lashes would not have enough food there, but she might survive for a little while. Maybe without the constant growth hormones her hunger would ease, and she could be happy there. Ziph unsuccessfully wiped the tears and rain from her face before starting on the long journey back to Whit's truck. The rain and her grief soaked her face all over again. Unable to force herself to move quickly, she walked the open space they usually ran, and Whit met her halfway.

"Are you ready to come home, Golden Girl? The rest of the new team agreed to let the blame fall on you if you find a different job and never hunt again."

The sorrow in her was too great to face Dacket, and she shook her head and spoke quietly, "Can I just have your emergency pack. I am not ready to face him or anything else."

"You can't be serious. I don't want to leave you out here." Whit's hands cupped her face, and his thumbs wiped away the tears pouring from her eyes.

"I just need some time." Sorrow filled Whit as he reluctantly nodded, and they walked to his truck for the pack.

When he handed it over, he asked, "Where will you go?"

Ziph looked out onto the open land and answered, "I don't know, I just need to walk." Whit handed her his knife and pack and climbed in his truck before he turned it around and waited for a long while for Ziph to change her mind before he finally drove home.

CHAPTER 34
WHERE'S DACKET?

Whit screamed and pounded on his steering wheel as he forced himself to drive away from Ziph. It was her choice, and he had to fight the urge to turn his truck around and force her to come home. He knew that serpent loved her, it was clearly the serpent she smelled of when they had found her. *She smelled like that damn snake because she was trying to save it. She was distracting us from the baby serpent. Ziph is better than all of us. She's our goddamn queen, and I left her in the sky belt.* Whit's heart felt like it was being sawed from his chest with a dull knife as he pulled in the garage.

Trent noticed Ziph was not with him, and he rushed Whit's truck. In a panic, Trent swung Whit's driver's door open, demanding, "Where the *fuck* is she?!"

Whit couldn't hide his broken heart as he explained through flowing tears. "Ziph protected a serpent and stopped a hunt. She refused to return, she's too afraid to face Dacket. She doesn't want to shame us."

Trent stood speechless for an extended moment and he

shook his head before he finally frowned and his heartbreak filled his voice, "She refused to come home? Where is Dacket?"

Whit was struck with confusion as he asked, "What do you mean where is Dacket? His truck is right there."

Trent glared at Whit as he snapped, "Dacket is not here. I just searched the entire building. I just started my fucking shift early, and his truck was already in the garage, so I looked for him to ask him about freezer maintenance. I'm telling you. He is not here."

Whit climbed down and dread gripped his throat as he asked, "Did you ask Darlow? He had the last door shift." Trent twisted his mouth into a frown and followed Whit to Darlow's apartment.

Whit knocked on Darlow's door, and he answered it still wearing his guard attire. "Is everything alright?"

Whit tried to swallow away the lump forming in his throat. "No. Do you know where Dacket is?"

He seemed surprised, "He didn't tell you? He said he had an important appointment, and he said not to worry that he would return soon." Whit and Trent's mouths dropped open before they tripped over one another rushing for Dacket's room.

"There's no way he was on the fucking list, and we didn't know it!" Whit shouted as he slammed his shoulder into Dacket's door, breaking the hinges and sending the door flying into the wall.

Whit ran toward Dacket's room with Trent one step behind, and when he reached the desk in Dacket's room, Whit yanked the drawers out and tossed them onto the bed in a frenzy. A single tri-folded paper floated down from underneath one of the drawers. When they recognized the Kefale seal on the paper, Whit and Trent crumpled to the floor wrapped around one another. Sniffling away his tears, Whit grabbed Trent's shoulders in a bruising hold and shook him. "I need to find Ziph. I need to bring her home."

Trent helped Whit to his feet as he willed himself to speak, "When she finds out he's gone, she will want to start a war."

Whit shot up and spun to face Trent. "Why the fuck do you think we're going after her first? It's time we start a fucking war."

Whit ran out of Dacket's apartment and jumped all the way down each of the stairwells before he reached Danny's apartment. She was already opening the door with all the ear-piercing racket they made coming down the stairs, "What's happening?"

Whit panted as he rambled off, "You're in charge until I return. I have no time to explain. Send someone to guard the gate and shut down the market." Danny seemed apprehensive but nodded as Whit and Trent ran for Whit's truck.

When Whit went to climb in, Trent stopped and looked out at the road before turning back with desperation in his eyes. "You need to find Ziph and bring her home. I'm no good out there and we both know that. I'm taking my car to visit the Eight Underground, there is a resistance group which meets in a club Ziph and I visited recently."

"Meet back here after you find them," Whit agreed as he started his truck and swung it from his parking space.

Whit soared down the road as if he were late for a hunt. He had to drive quickly enough that the thoughts about what Dacket was facing couldn't catch him. No one believed the palace's lies about the spawning program, but no one really knew the truth of what happened to those chosen for what the palace claimed was an honor, just that they were never heard from again.

Just as Whit passed through the city gate, he pushed his accelerator to the limit and aimed for the little raised bit of land where he knew Ziph would be. It was the place she first landed, and it was where they found her in the rain when Dacket finally came to his senses. She had to be there because he didn't know where else to look. *I can't fucking lose them both. Please, Ziph, please, be sitting next to your pod.* His vision blurred with tears and rage as he forced his truck to its limits. He knew it was stupid to drive this fast, but he didn't care. He had to find her, and he had to find her *now*.

When he finally saw the raised bit of land in the flat, cracked landscape, he shook with dread and anticipation. The thoughts of Ziph not being there were too much to endure. He slammed his hand on his secondary brake and his truck slid to a halt as he jumped from his door and ran up the hill towards Ziph's pod. When he saw the pod, and no Ziph, he began screaming into the fading daylight, "Ziph! Ziph you must be here! Please answer me! ZIPH!" Whit cried out so fiercely stars burst in his vision, and he sat on the ground trying to regain his breath. This was his worst nightmare. How could he have let Ziph go? "Ziphalie, PLEASE! I need you!"

A swollen-eyed Ziph crawled from a deep fissure in the ground nearby and slowly walked toward him. Whit ran for her, and when he reached her, he grabbed her in a bruising hug, dragging her to the ground and crying into her hair. "Whit, what's wrong?" Ziph took his face in her hands and with her own weepy eyes focused on him, asked again, "What is wrong?"

"Dacket is *gone.* They took him for the spawning program."

Through his puffy, swollen eyes, Whit watched Ziph shift from the depths of sorrow to burning rage in the matter of a single moment. With flames flickering in her eyes, Ziph's tone seared the air. "Dacket is *gone?*" Every word was dripping with vitriol as she clenched her fists until her knuckles paled.

The power in her gaze was enough to send a chill down Whit's spine as he admitted in a quiet, careful tone, "I knew you would be ready to fight. Trent is under Eight finding the resistance group."

With a determined glare, Ziph nodded, "We will find Dacket, and I think it's time we found out what else the Kefale are hiding in that castle of theirs. I would rather die trying to save Dacket than allow this to continue."

Whit's smile broke through his tearful anguish, "Me too. I know Trent feels the same."

They quickly made it back to Whit's truck before spending the journey home in silence. Whit kept his tail firmly wrapped around Ziph's leg for the duration of the truck ride. It was the only thing keeping Ziph from losing herself to wrathful desires. *The last thing we need is for me to lose it and rush in with no plan. I need to calm the fuck down before I make a mistake.*

When they returned to the garage, Trent was just pulling in, and he had passengers. When he saw Ziph, his shoulders relaxed, and she felt a sob working its way up her throat as he swung the door open and wrapped his arms around her. "I'm sorry, I just…"

Trent shook his head and interrupted her, "No, you don't owe me any apology or explanation. I don't care. I'm just relieved you're back. Don't ever leave us like that again, and you come to me next time something happens. I don't understand their hunting dynamic. Actually, fuck all their hunting rules. You come first."

Ziph leaned into him and explained, "I needed the time alone. I made a choice to betray my hunting team, and I intended to live with it."

Trent squeezed her close as he whispered in her ear, "I went to Eight, and brought back some people to help us."

Ziph lifted her aching eyes to Trent who had profound sadness hiding behind his gaze, but he smirked at her anyway. "Come into the freezer. We have some meat to chop." He never used that term, *chop. Wait, is he really trying to be covert? He is so adorable.* She grabbed Trent's hand and nearly dragged him toward the market and freezer.

When they entered the freezer, three people she had never met stood around a table with a large paper rolled out and weighted down on the ends. Ziph saw Whit leaning in the corner, and she dropped her eyes as the humiliation ate at her.

Whit was not happy and scowled as he pulled her to the side and whispered, "Look at me." Ziph looked up at him, and she held back fresh tears as he tipped her chin up and spoke only loud enough for her to hear. "No more shame for protecting a living creature you loved, and who clearly loved you. I've hunted for many years, and I've never seen a serpent do anything other than kill and be killed. Is that serpent the same one you smelled of when we took you?"

Ziph knew she needed to admit the full truth. "Yes, I led Dacket away from her when you first found me. She was just a baby. What I mean is, she probably could have still eaten me if she had tried, but she protected me instead."

Whit stared at her with his brow creased as he turned swiftly to face everyone else, who were now staring at them, then turned back to her. "You're joking. It was how long exactly? Could the snake wrap itself around something the size of my truck?"

Ziph shook her head. Lashes was much smaller than that. "She would have been able to wrap around half of your truck, maybe."

Whit's eyes bulged as he spun to address everyone, "The Kefale are growing these serpents from birth to full sized in a matter of months. This could be enough to convince the rest of the hunters to fight with us." Everyone in the room shared nods with looks of approval as Whit continued, "I'll gather the former Grindle team first. I know Gerara has a plethora of prototype weapons in her back room. They're prototypes she was seeking approval from the palace for use against the serpents."

Whit went toward the garage as Trent introduced the three people who were here to help. "This is Copula Killock, Addis Tremor, and Vania Ragi." Copula was a tall lanky man with a long beard. His skin was a reddish brown, and his eyes were bright blue, almost clear. His shaggy grey hair was long and expertly groomed, and he reminded Ziph of a particularly difficult professor she had back on Keru. Addis and Vania both had grey skin with black hair and ochre eyes. She bet they came from the same parents.

The large, unrolled paper was an ancient sketch of the palace, including a basic floor plan of the bottom level. They all spent some time quietly reviewing the plans, multiple routes with job descriptions were lined out, and

Ziph took her time studying each one. She quietly contemplated where Dacket could be, wishing the plans had more information about each room. Copula, clearly the leader, spoke first, and his tone was dripping with passion and power, "We have waited for generations for the sky hunters of Valler to grow weary of the Kefale's manipulations. We call ourselves the Green Line. We aim to dissolve the Sectors and create the structure for a fair, transparent government of the people. We believe the reign of the Kefale Royalty must come to an end, and the Elarian people ought to govern themselves. If you find these plans sufficient, we can move forward."

Ziph was starstruck and leaned into Trent for warmth in the frigid climate of the freezer as she replied, "We will do whatever it takes to help you. If we can regularly battle massive serpents, we can take the palace. What about the other two cities, do you have a plan for them?"

Whit opened the freezer door and came inside with the former Grindle team. They quietly joined the conversation as Copula answered, "The Valler palace controls the other two palaces. There are no Kefale in the other palaces, only egg and offering collection centers, and prisoner storage for serpent feedings."

Ziph's eyes went wide with that last statement, "You knew the Kefale were giving the serpents the growth hormones inside of the prisoners they're fed?"

Copula nodded as he pointed to the plans in front of him, "This line here is an underground tunnel which runs to the other palaces, under the wasteland. It took multiple generations of prisoners to dig the tunnel through the rock, and there is a hub in the center between the cities for depositing the baited prisoners for the serpents. The royals control the entire serpent overgrowth cycle, and they've used it for thousands of years to force our people into submission from their need for protection." He paused to allow everyone to process and nod in agreement with what he explained before he went on, "We have a strong resistance which has spread across all three cities, numbering in the hundreds in Valler alone. We will spread the word. The hunters are ready."

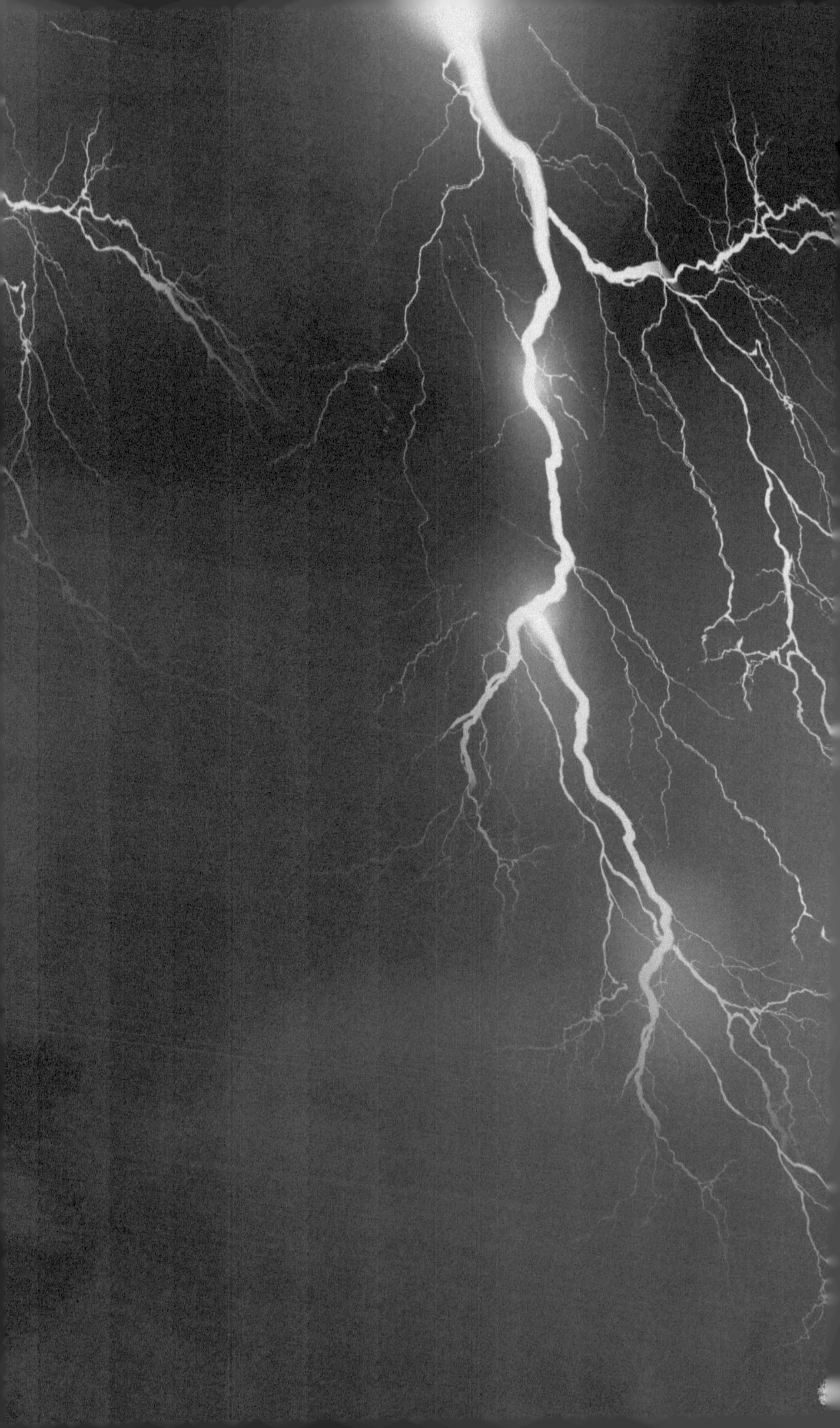

CHAPTER 35
DARKNESS

The cell the guards shoved Dacket into was chilly and bleak. Every time he looked around, the white walls and glass seemed to close in on him as he tried to find a comfortable place on the concrete bench. The keypad on the door shone brightly in addition to the pinpoint lights above him humming with electricity. They were nothing like the lightbulbs he had seen before. Many points of light conversed to create these lights, and something about that made his skin crawl. He rubbed the place on his arm where they had taken blood from him. It hadn't even had time to scab over, and he could already tell they had bruised him. His skin was tender around the puncture site.

Nothing here was familiar. Once he passed across the moat and into the center of the palace, it became a new world. Bright, flat, rectangular devices chimed, and there were movements on them like they were alive.

He wasn't sure how long he had been in the cell, but it was long enough to see three terrified people taken off somewhere and not return. The fresh memory of him sliding the official letter from his mail slot flashed through his mind, and a torrent of emotions flooded him once again. He didn't even need to open it to know what it said inside, but he opened it anyway and read it as he walked up his stairs for the last time knowing he would be forced say goodbye to everyone and everything he had ever known. If he didn't comply, he was jeopardizing everything he loved. He also didn't want the people he loved coming for him, so he hid the letter in his desk under the drawer, like he hid everything he didn't want Whit or Trent to know about.

The last thing he wanted was them coming after him. Hopefully they had not figured out his hiding spot after all these years. Who was he kidding? He knew better than that. He just hoped they had no leads and wouldn't find out what happened to him in enough time to do anything stupid, like try to come after him and get themselves killed in the process. That was his worst nightmare in this moment. He just needed them to stay safe and far away from here.

The air conditioner came on again, and his skin chilled. There was no escaping the vent above him, and his blood felt like ice flowing through his veins. A shout rang out around the corner, followed by sounds of a tussle, a grunt, and then an eerie, lingering silence. He closed his eyes, squeezing them tight. He knew someone just lost their life. He knew his turn was coming. It would just be a matter of time before the guards came for him.

This was no spawning program, and of that he was certain. Something sinister was happening here, but he still would have submitted himself for spawning duties a thousand times over because he knew submission to the royals would keep the people he loved the most out of the

Kefale's sights. *How noble of me after I fucking left her. I left the woman I love out in the wastelands to fend for herself.* He rubbed his sore eyes as regret boiled inside of him. *I fucking left her! What the fuck was I thinking? I hurt her, then I disappeared, and I'm not coming back to fix things. The way I left her will be what she remembers of me for the rest of her life.*

As his heart shattered for what felt like the millionth time, Dacket dropped his head in his hands. *How could I have done this to the woman I love? After all she did was save a life she cared about. Maybe I deserve this. No, I more than deserve this. I earned this end.*

Another man was dragged by the clear glass of his cell, fighting the guard for his life as he neared whatever was on the other side of Dacket's cell at the end of the hall. It had been dark when he was thrown in, and he knew his time was coming because they had cleared out all the other cells, and his was the only one left.

The man shouted 'no' after 'no' and screamed, but his scream was silenced, followed by a thud. A few seconds later Dacket could hear the body being dropped onto a metal surface. He listened closely as he could hear the beeps and tings of devices and tools being used. He held the image of Ziph, Whit, and Trent in his mind, smiling and joyous, as he knew he only had moments of his life left. The one beautiful moment in his truck, when he had them all in one place and the woman he loved underneath him. He remembered the face she made as she broke apart for him, her sweet delight had been music to his soul. In another life, they could have all been happy together.

He imagined Barren was lush with greenery, and they lived in a beautiful home, free from the Kefale, and the danger of hunting. It was a delightful life they could have shared, maybe even a perfect one.

Dacket watched his flawless life with the people he loved evaporate into a nightmare as the guard approached his cell and the clear door slid open, "Turn and face the wall." He complied and the guard took his hands and bound them with some type of mechanical device before grabbing his arm and leading him from the cell.

When he turned and saw what he was being led into, he understood why all those before him had fought so hard. The rumors didn't touch reality as Dacket looked up at easily the most horrifying sight he had ever seen. The doubled headed Kefale kings were laid out on an operating table. The ancient lime green skin stretched over the two faces seemed to be grafts, and his body cavity was split open during what was obviously major abdominal and chest surgery.

All the other people who he watched be dragged from their cells were now in frozen chambers with long sewn up incisions running down their torsos. *They're gutting us and keeping us on ice. They are stealing our fucking organs. The reality of what they're doing is so much worse than what anyone knows.* Nausea and rage burst inside of him, but Dacket was too overwhelmed to fight as he was shoved onto a table face down and a mask was smashed against his face. The air smelled sweet, and darkness overtook his vision.

Please don't let them come for me. Please don't let them come here.

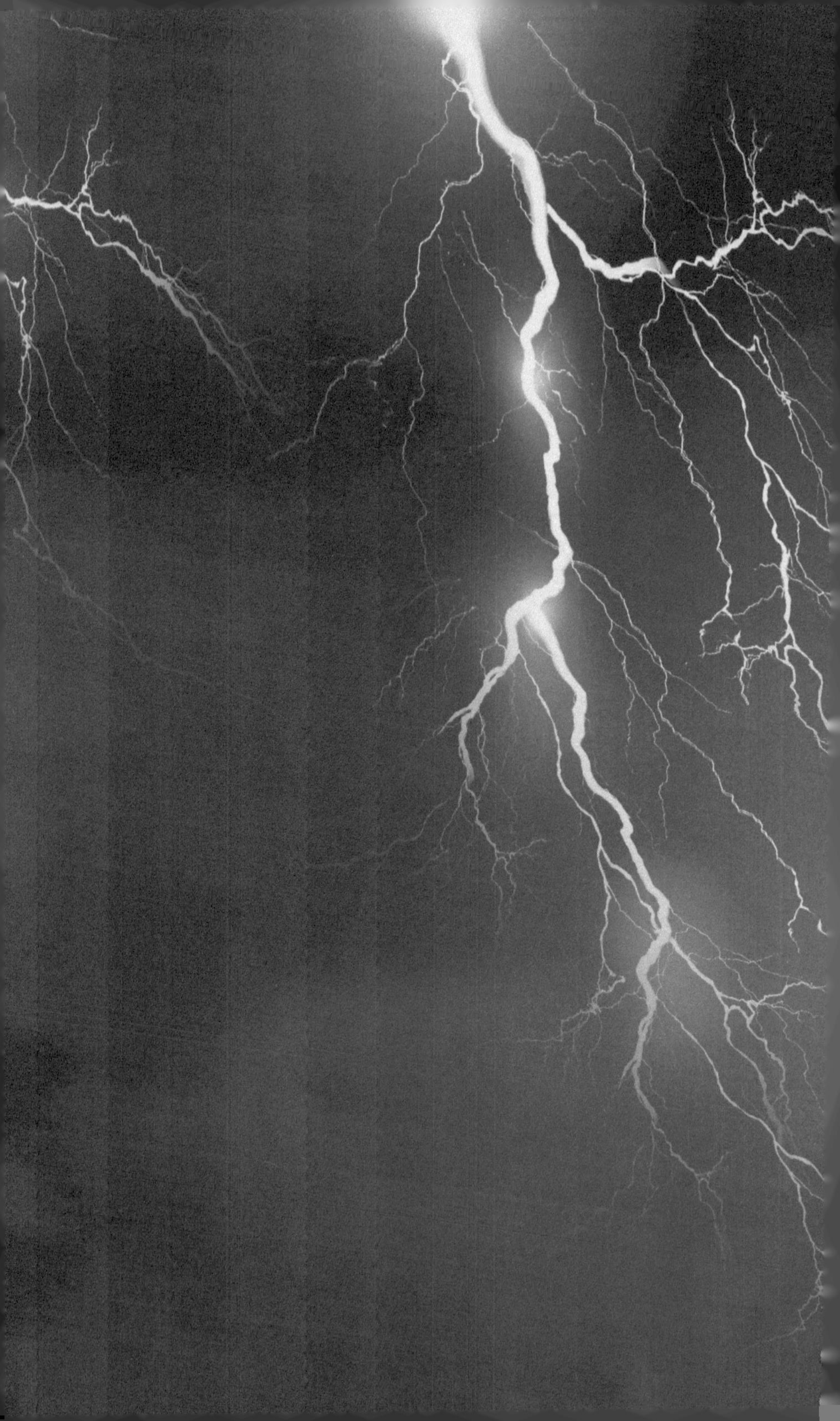

CHAPTER 36
GREEN LINES

Trent, Whit, and Ziph all stood in Gerara's arms closet with their now combined team, all dressed in the reinforced gear Copula provided. He claimed it to be bulletproof, but Ziph had her doubts. It just seemed to be thickened fabric on the torso and thighs.

Her eyes darted around Gerara's living space. The air was thick with apprehension, and she was not spared. No one had outright made amends with Ziph, but not one person questioned why she was with them. Ziph was easily one of the most physically talented people any of them knew. Beside her, Whit addressed the team, "We only have a few more minutes before we need to be in position. Copula has pockets all over the city who will begin gathering to riot, and they will be setting the timed fires any minute. Remember, when the royal guard is sufficiently drawn out, each riot group will set off flares, which will be our signal to rush the palace. Do not move before the signal, or you will be overtaken, and you could scrap the entire plan." Everyone nodded as they strapped themselves with the various guns Gerara had fabricated over the years before they wrapped rain cloaks around them.

They filed from Gerara's front door and spread out in all directions toward their positions. Ziph was headed directly for the gardens facing the palace entrance. Entranced from the long walk in the rain through the streets as empty as her heart, her unfocused mood was interrupted as she was shoved to the side by a group of royal guards running for one of the riot groups. Ziph checked around her before she added some energy to her steps, she needed to snap out of the gloomy, spaced out mood she was in. *I wish I could have slept at all last night.* She had tossed and turned all night and had not had more than a few hours of sleep, even with Trent and Whit in the same bed. She vigorously shook her head, trying to wake up. She had a good man to save, and she knew very well she may end up giving her life in the process. It didn't matter. Nothing mattered after she watched him turn his back on her after she betrayed him. She couldn't force herself to care about her own life in the slightest.

She fought a sob as she realized this was the truth about why he was so resistant to her. *This is the secret he was hiding. He didn't want us to know because he was afraid that we would do what we are currently doing right now, risking our lives for him.* She had silently cried all night, and now she was crying again. She wanted to slaughter everyone involved, and it was hard for her not to fall into her blind rage. She was afraid of who she would become, and what she would do. She loved that man, and she was taking him back.

Ziph looked around her to be sure she was alone, and she rushed her steps as she passed block after block. The shadow of the towering wall behind the palace was just ahead, and she took a left to walk along the back of it. A group of royal guards were running to the left, and she hid behind a thick tree to avoid them before she crossed into the royal gardens to find her hiding place. She casually walked along the paths until she found the line of bushes she was told to hide inside of, then she slipped in and crouched.

It wasn't long before she heard the first flare pop, followed by several more shortly after. The last one popped, and she rushed from the bushes along with Whit, Trent, and the rest of their hunting team coming from all directions. They must have sufficiently lured away all the guards because the hunters were easily able to step into the skiff at the edge of the water, which the guards had left aground in a rush. As they moved away from the edge of the water, they watched Copula's security team approach the palace to assume their positions standing guard for the hunters.

Heavily weighing down the skiff, they furiously rowed the ores into the castle entry and kept rowing until they bumped the boat into the edge of the floor in the interior of the palace. Not one guard was there to meet them, so they climbed off the boat and quietly moved toward a set of double doors. The one thing they knew they had on their side was a rebellion had never occurred before, so they had the element of surprise.

Ziph held her hand up and listened against the crack of the door, and she distinctly heard murmurings and shuffling of boots. She pulled a small, loaded gun from its holster on her side, signaling the team it was time to engage. They followed suit and each armed themselves as Ziph wrapped her hand around the door handle.

When everyone was prepared with guns drawn, she

wrenched open the doors sending them careening into the walls causing everyone in the great room to spin and face them. With guns drawn on the group of four middle aged, double headed Kefale with their hands in the air, Ziph demand, "Where the fuck do you take the people you summon for spawning?"

"They're through that door, down the hall, and down the stairs, but I'm afraid you won't like what you find." The Kefale man sneered at his twin who spoke. As the Kefale were restrained, and Trent assumed guarding the double doors, the one cooperative man continued despite his conjoined twin's contempt, "They're doing despicable things here. You must end this! They've killed many of us for resisting. Almost all of us are trapped against our will by the kings. They're downstairs. You must hu…" He was cut short as his twin reached up to suffocate him, but Whit ended the assault by yanking the man's arm away to restrain him. The rest of the hunters spread out to capture the remaining royals and secure the palace, while Ziph and Whit went to free the prisoners.

"Be quiet," Whit growled at the Eight faces before he turned to Ziph, and they rushed toward the door leading underground. Opening the door, they found a brightly lit hallway with a staircase leading down. They ran the length of the hall before taking several steps at a time to descend the stairs. They approached a swinging metal door at the end with an advanced electric lift next to them, which appeared to be designed for exceptionally wide occupancy. The only place she had ever seen that before was at a medical facility, specifically a surgery center.

Please tell me Dacket is alright. Please be alive. Ziph was nauseous as she pushed the door open, before she even registered what she was witnessing. An elderly Kefale royal lay resting, ancient with stretched skin over his faces, and his torso covered in deep long scars, one being so fresh it was oozing. He was leaned back in a hospital bed, and there were a series of individual freezers with frosted doors lining the wall behind him. The medical staff and doctor stood stunned at the sight of Ziph and Whit. All of them, including the old men, lifted their hands at the raised weapons.

The old men spoke in unison with rough, harsh voices, "We are the Kefale Kings, how dare you interrupt our renewal." With all the machines beeping all around him, Ziph's eye began to twitch. Whit saw it on her face and took a small step away from her. The move was not missed by the medical staff, who began trying to creep away.

With a murderous tone, Ziph shifted her gun barrel and aimed it in the face of the doctor, "Where the fuck is Dacket Critchlow?" He stumbled over his words and shook his head before he pointed at one of the high-tech stasis freezers. Ziph bolted over to the door and swung it open, finding Dacket inside, frozen with a fresh incision down the length of his entire torso. *He's fucking dead on ice. We were too late. My Dacket is gone.* Something broke inside of Ziph, she wasn't sure if it was her morals or if it was her very soul. There was one thing she knew for certain though. *If they can't put him back together, I'm killing everyone.*

Whipping around Ziph pointed her gun back at the doctor's head and in an icy tone demanded, "What did you take, and who the fuck has it?" The doctor's eyes slid to the kings and Ziph followed his line of sight. She whispered, "You, of course," before she turned back to the doctor and extended her arm to point her weapon at his head even closer. "Put them back." Ziph spoke with a brutal ease that gave Whit a frosty chill down his spine.

The doctor seemed horrified as he shook his palms at Ziph, "I can't just put them back. The kings will die!"

Ziph snarled before she pointed her gun at the kings who reared their heads at the threat. Without another thought, Ziph pulled the trigger twice, shooting both of the Kefale kings in the head, and with a lethal calm, she turned back to the doctor and again demanded, *"Put, them, back."*

The doctor, with terror in his eyes, relented, "Alright! I'll do it. I can't promise he will live, but I will try." Ziph took three giant steps toward the doctor and was two inches from his face with her gun smashed in his cheek. She waited, holding her murderous gaze on him until she saw sweat form on his lip. When she spoke, she did so in a whisper, but one loud enough everyone in the room could hear, "You will put Dacket back together the way he was, and then you will give the rest of these people back the organs you stole from them. You'll save *all* of them, or I'll cut you open and rip out your organs with my bare hands."

The doctor panted for air as he nodded and rushed away to prep the king's body for surgery. Ziph moved to a stool in the corner of the room and propped herself up before she finally addressed Whit, who was looking at her with love and a healthy dose of terror, "I'll stay here and supervise this fuckery if you want to finish rounding up the rest of the royals. Send in a hunter for back up once the palace has been taken." Whit nodded to her quietly before he slipped out.

Ziph sat on the stool for several hours as the doctor worked. He began with Dacket, and when the surgeon was returning his heart, Ziph had to muffle a sob. *They took his fucking heart. Even if everyone survives, I may end up killing this doctor after he finishes sewing all these people back together.*

She didn't miss one second and as the doctor sewed Dacket's chest back up, and she moved her stool to be by his side. His monitors all showed he was alive. She guessed it was just a matter of time before she would know if he would truly survive this. She continued killing the doctor and kings in her mind over and over, each murder more violent and cathartic than the last.

Many hours went by, and when the last patient was sewn up, Ziph lead the doctor and the nurses into a cell and locked them inside with a wedge in the door. Whit came in when she went back to sit with Dacket, and Whit wrapped his arms around her as they looked down at him.

"There were fifty-two Kefale, and only seven out of the Eight men we initially caught were uncooperative. They turned out to be the Kings' only supporters. We confirmed everything with the one man who seemed helpful from the start. They have been behind the overgrown serpents. We found advanced technology all over the palace which Copula's team has begun documenting for release. The kings were hundreds of years old, and they have been receiving new organs regularly from the so-called spawning program. Four of the uncooperative Kefale men also had evidence of organ replacements." With her lack of sleep and everything which had occurred to that point, she was trying her best to pay attention but was failing. Ziph reached down to hold Dacket's hand as she pleaded with everything in her that he would heal and wake up, and that when he woke, he would be whole.

Whit allowed the doctor and nurses out to check on the patients periodically over the next two days. Days which

Ziph didn't have more than a few hours of sleep on the floor next to Dacket's bed while Whit watched over them.

Ziph was staring at the moving chest of a woman three tables away as she began to rouse as she fluttered her eyes. A volunteer group of nurses from the resistance group had taken over in the last few hours, and the original doctor and nurses were being hauled away for questioning.

She looked back down at Dacket and nearly fell from her stool when she saw his eyes wide open and focused on her. "You're awake, how do you feel? Are you in pain? Do you remember anything?"

Ziph leaned over him and lay her hand on his cheek as a small smile spread on his mouth. "What did you do?" It was just a whisper, but Ziph could tell he was holding back to avoid hurting himself.

"I killed the kings after we took the palace. They took your heart, and I made them put it back." Tears streamed down Ziph's face. She had held them back for long enough while she waited for him to wake.

Dacket closed his eyes just as they began glittering with moisture, and he breathed, "I'm sorry. I'm so sorry, I should not have ever left you."

Ziph shook her head at him, "Don't apologize for my weakness."

He scowled at her and squeezed her hand. "Your heart is not your weakness. It's why you're here, right now, and it's why I'm alive. It's why everyone else in this room is alive too."

Ziph leaned down and kissed him before sitting back on her stool. "You have another day at least before you can go home. I'm not leaving to find out for myself, but I hear everything is changing outside for your people. There was a resistance gathering, and we joined with them. They had just been waiting for the hunters to have enough of the Kefale to revolt. Now that the resistance is taking the lead, the people are realizing there are enough rodent farms for everyone to eat like they were intended, instead of eating serpent meat. With a coordinated effort from the hunters in the other cities, any remaining overgrown serpents have been eliminated. With the tech the resistance discovered, they confirmed there are no more overgrown giant serpents except Lashes who is now on Barren."

Dacket squeezed her hand again and pulled her to come closer, "I've never seen a serpent yield to anything, or anyone, like she did for you. I should have known you could do anything you set your mind to after watching you with her."

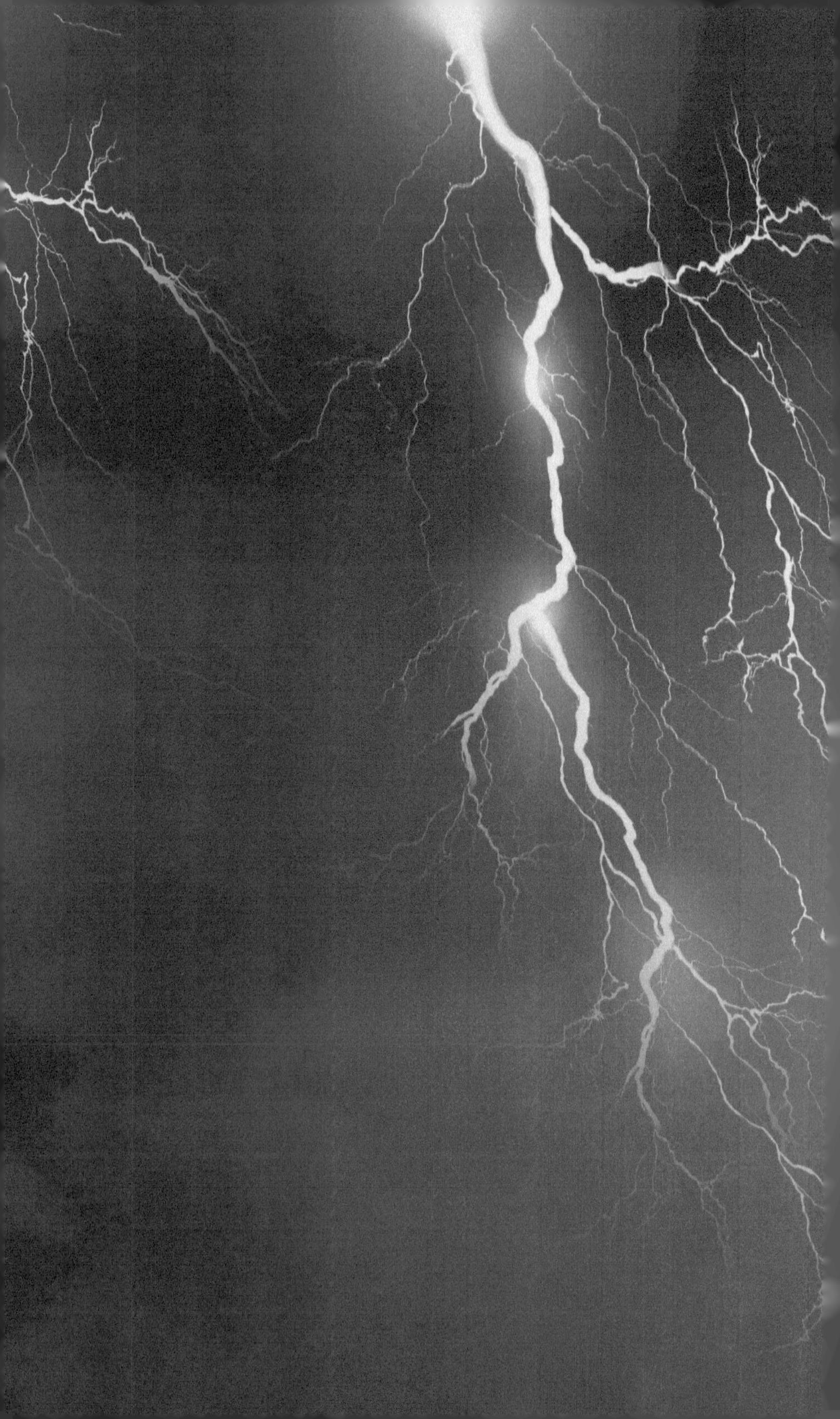

CHAPTER 37

HOME

Dacket groaned under his breath as Ziph and Whit helped him from the recovery table and onto his feet. "Do your people heal like snakes or have you developed quicker healing like mammals?" Ziph asked and Dacket took a few moments before he answered, "We create enzymes which help us heal much faster than mammals. It's part of how we were able to evolve into the people we are today." Ziph was relieved. She knew snakes typically had extensive healing times but could also recover from incredibly damaging injuries.

As they were guiding him out, Trent came up and took over for her, allowing Dacket to use him for support. "Copula asked for you to meet him on level two. He has something to show you in the tech room."

Ziph nodded with her eyes still focused on Dacket and reluctantly went to meet Copula on the second level in the technology room they had been sorting through.

"I found something you may find useful." Copula pointed to what looked like a high-tech communications hub, something clearly not from Binara. "With all our nearby galactic systems without life, and our people so severely held back from progress, we have no use for communication outside of this world right now, but I know you do. This machine seems to be a device that doesn't belong to our galaxy, but possibly yours. If you have use of it, it's yours." He walked into another room, and Ziph stared down at the machine. The First Human emblem on the edge sent a shiver down her spine as she touched the screen.

It was a subspace communication hub, and the antenna read that it was still intact, and in orbit. *Someone with the First Humans sent this here.* The signal showed an open channel available with Melior's United Trusts and Colonies command center which was in the same system as Emendo the planet her mom lived on. *With the new Claudius UTC Empress, I could call home and speak with my mother.*

She moved her hands faster than she knew she could as she searched for a way to dial a private number. When she found the private connection option, and had the digits entered, she swiftly pressed the connect button, and the call sang as it went through.

"Hello? Who is this? Listen, if you are trying to inquire about the reward, it's over. My daughter is gone, and she's not coming back. Please don't call me again." Her mother swiftly ended the call, and Ziph slid to her knees, leaning her forehead against the bottom edge of the screen.

Guilt burst inside of her as she regretted calling at all. *What was I thinking? I can't let her believe I'm alive. She will never stop trying to bring me home. She will fixate with worry if she knows I'm alive. I can't allow her to endure that pain, especially if she's already come to terms with me being gone. I can't contact her again. It would be too selfish. I don't have a choice, I have to let her go.* Her eyes burned as she lowered herself to the floor and drew her legs to her chest. She tried to take a breath, but with tears blurring her vision, all she could do was hold back a sob. *I can't allow anyone from the galactic center to know about this planet, I must destroy this communication hub.* Ziph turned around and reached over to pop the panel from the base before she furiously picked at the soldered connections on the circuit board. She picked them off one by one until there was nothing but a mess of wires under the screen. By the time she finished, the top of her shirt was wet from tears.

"Why did you destroy the hub?" Copula asked with no hint of emotion in his words, but he used a soft tone and held her gaze as she explained, "I come from a place filled with exploitation and pure evil. The unlucky people were routinely starved into slavery, and those who received the worst of it all, were never allowed to exist at all. A recently unseated faction was responsible for the genetic annihilation of over a hundred species developing on worlds all over the galaxy I'm from. I can't allow those beings to know anything more about this place than they already do. Any of this technology you find must be destroyed immediately, and you should never allow communication of any kind. They can track the signals and find this planet. If they sent me, they could send more. We need to be ready."

"I know you dialed your mother. I could hear her speaking. Your refusal to answer her was what drew me back here. I knew there was more to you. Ziph, you are a noble being, and you have more than earned my respect. I will heed your warning, and we will avoid any interaction with, what faction was it?"

Ziph stared at him as she answered, "The First Humans."

Copula agreeably reached a hand out for her before leading her out from the front of the palace where Trent's car was parked. Out front, several resistance members were openly conversing with Kefale who relinquished all power and were happily participating in reform. One Kefale had their pant leg rolled up and was showing several people scars they had covering their legs, which looked like extensive burns. Many of the conjoined twins turned out to be just as much victims as the rest of their society to the Kings and their circle's demands and they had suffered under his volatile control, with ample evidence to prove the cruelty.

"We will hold a celebration in the former royal gardens when everyone has healed. I look forward to seeing you there." Ziph smiled and nodded to Copula as she climbed in the back seat of the car next to Dacket, careful not to disturb him as she sat.

Trent drove slowly as they went home, and Ziph couldn't take her eyes from Dacket as he rested his head against the seat and shut his eyes. He was still in a fog from all the trauma, healing, and pain medication he was on, but he should fully recover. Ziph could not have been more relieved. The journey was smooth, and when they arrived home, there were elaborately decorated gifts piled by the front guard station and more stacked in a parking space in the garage. Many of the gifts were adorned with lovely images of squirrels, and Ziph giggled at the sentiment. Two people were setting more gifts down by the garage as Trent pulled in an open place.

They assisted Dacket from the car and into a chair which Trent and Whit planned to use to lift and carry him up the stairs. Dacket scowled at them when they pulled it out. "I am not being carried up the stairs like some kind of

Kefale Royal." Trent and Whit side eyed one another as they set the chair to the side and grumbled as they helped Dacket up the first steps to reach the door to the stairs.

After he finished taking the first few steps, he had to pause to take a breath and Dacket whispered, "Fine." Trent sighed with relief as Whit ran to retrieve the chair, and Ziph was quiet as she held open the door. Once he was seated and they had him lifted, they easily carried him up the stairs, setting the chair in front of his apartment door, which had been fixed while Dacket was gone. It was obvious Whit had done it, and it was definitely not up to Dacket's standards.

Dacket frowned as he looked at the hinges which were slightly crooked, "You did a terrible job fixing my door." Whit rolled his eyes as she opened the door, and it squeaked a tiny scream until she stopped moving it. Dacket deadpanned him and Whit crossed his arms. "I'm not apologizing. You didn't tell us you were on the fucking list. If you hadn't gone through hell, I would have knocked your ass out when I saw you." Dacket ignored him and hobbled into his apartment as Ziph followed them inside.

Dacket shuffled across the floor to his bedroom, and Whit helped him into his bed as Ziph and Trent prepared his apartment for all three of them to stay with Dacket. Trent prepped a bed on the couch before helping Ziph store the cages of rats Danny had dropped off earlier. When everything was stored away, Ziph changed into nightclothes and crawled into the bed next to Dacket, careful not to jostle the mattress. Whit and Trent were exhausted from all the work they had done with Copula in structuring a plan for voting and assigning jobs to watch the sky belt for any serpent activity. There should be no more overgrown serpents popping up, but no one knew all their hiding places, so the new government forming would keep watch indefinitely.

Whit came in and stood next to Dacket with his hand out, holding a pain pill. "Sit up, I need you to take this." Dacket snarled at the big rough looking pill but complied, leaning his head to sip some water to swallow it. "You're really going to be snappy over swallowing this little pill? Did you forget we eat rats with claws?"

"The pill tastes like a serpent's ass smells." Dacket frowned as he took another sip of water and handed the glass to Whit.

They took turns sleeping with Dacket and assisting him through the nights. It took two of them to help him bathe at first but eventually they made it through the two weeks it took him to heal enough to bathe unassisted. He was quiet for most of the process as he always had been, but Ziph noticed more smiles from him than he had ever given her before. There was something much lighter about him, and she was thrilled for the next few weeks of rest to pass so they could start the life they had been denied.

Copula had assembled a team, and they had carefully calculated the amount of taxes the Kefale still held from each offering day for every person who paid taxes. With the balancing and refunds issued to many of the overtaxed businesses like the meat markets, there would be no need for their former work.

As a thanks, Copula had informed the hunters involved in the rebellion that they would be honored and gifted during an upcoming celebration in a few months. They had just sent word to him that Dacket was healing well, and he responded with a letter stating the celebration date would be selected and announced soon.

Lying awake and trying to be still with her eyes closed

while it was her turn to stay with Dacket, Ziph was thrilled to start hiking a mountain range between Vallor and Adallin and exploring more of the planet, as well as visit the new entertainment being built in the place the palace once was. There had been a unanimous cry to have it leveled, and they did just that days after the last patient was able to leave.

"What are you thinking about?" Dacket was resting on his side and seemed comfortable as he watched her.

Her eyes had been closed, and she wasn't sure how he knew she was awake. "I didn't hear you turn over. Um, I can't wait to go hiking and exploring the mountains and hills between here and Adallin. I heard the mountaintops have snow, and I used to love skiing and snowboarding. Showing your people winter sports would be some life altering excitement for me, and I think that could be our new goal for the future. It was a high demand physical activity back in my home galaxy. We could make it an accessible sport for everyone here."

Dacket gave her a bright, warm smile and she could have melted into the mattress like a blob of Ziph mush. Ziph grimaced thinking about herself as a boneless blob on the bed and Dacket gave her an odd look. "Sorry, I just imagined myself as a goopy blob on the bed. Oh, wow. I realize how that does not make any sense without context. Damn it Ziph, context is important, so, you and your, oh fuck never mind." Dacket laughed as Ziph hid her burning face behind her hands.

"Why don't you go downstairs and run on the machine. You've been wiggling for three hours."

Ziph narrowed her eyes at him, she had not been moving at all, or had she? "No, it's my turn to stay with you. Whit and Trent are away with Copula planning the new routes for the rat pick up lines. Trent turned out to be excellent at planning, but he hated the thought of pitching the idea, so Whit is doing all the talking."

Dacket rolled on his back and laughed, "Fucking typical," before reaching over for his water. He sat up without help and drank a few gulps before he set the glass back down. He started to climb out of bed unassisted, but Ziph was in front of him before his toes could touch the ground. "Don't even think about it. Do you want a rat?" He stared at her blankly, but she knew better than to believe he wasn't hungry. She knew when all of them ate because she was obsessed with how they unhinged their jaws to swallow the rat's whole. *I want to watch you eat the rat, come on, just let me get it. I'll even whack it for you. Come on, please let me whack your rat. Oh, no. Don't say it. Don't say it. Oh gods, I swear if I accidentally say that I may die.* He chuckled as he shifted his attention to the kitchen and back to Ziph.

Oh gods, here it comes. There was a long pause before Ziph blurted, "I really just want to watch." *Don't say it.* "Please, let me whack your rat." *Gods dammit.* Her eyes bulged as she smacked a hand over her mouth. She stared at Dacket for a moment before she continued, "I didn't mean to admit that."

Dacket grinned as he asked, "Is that why you're always right there watching every time one of us eats?"

Ziph nodded as she tried to hold in her embarrassment. Dacket finally relented and moved back to his place in the bed. "You can bring me a rat."

Ziph tried to hold in her thrill as she asked, "Can I whack it too?" Dacket laughed under his breath as he nodded, and she whirled around to fetch him a rat. With the tail in her grasp, Ziph delightfully slammed it into the side table and handed it to Dacket.

"Thank you." Dacket took it from her awkwardly, and he tried not to chuckle while he unhinged his jaw as he watched Ziph attempting not to be obvious as she went up on her tiptoes to see better. As the rat slid down his throat, her mouth gradually dropped open, and when he was finished eating, he reached over and tipped up her chin to close her mouth.

"That was incredible. I am fucking obsessed." Ziph admitted with stars in her eyes as Dacket laughed all over again.

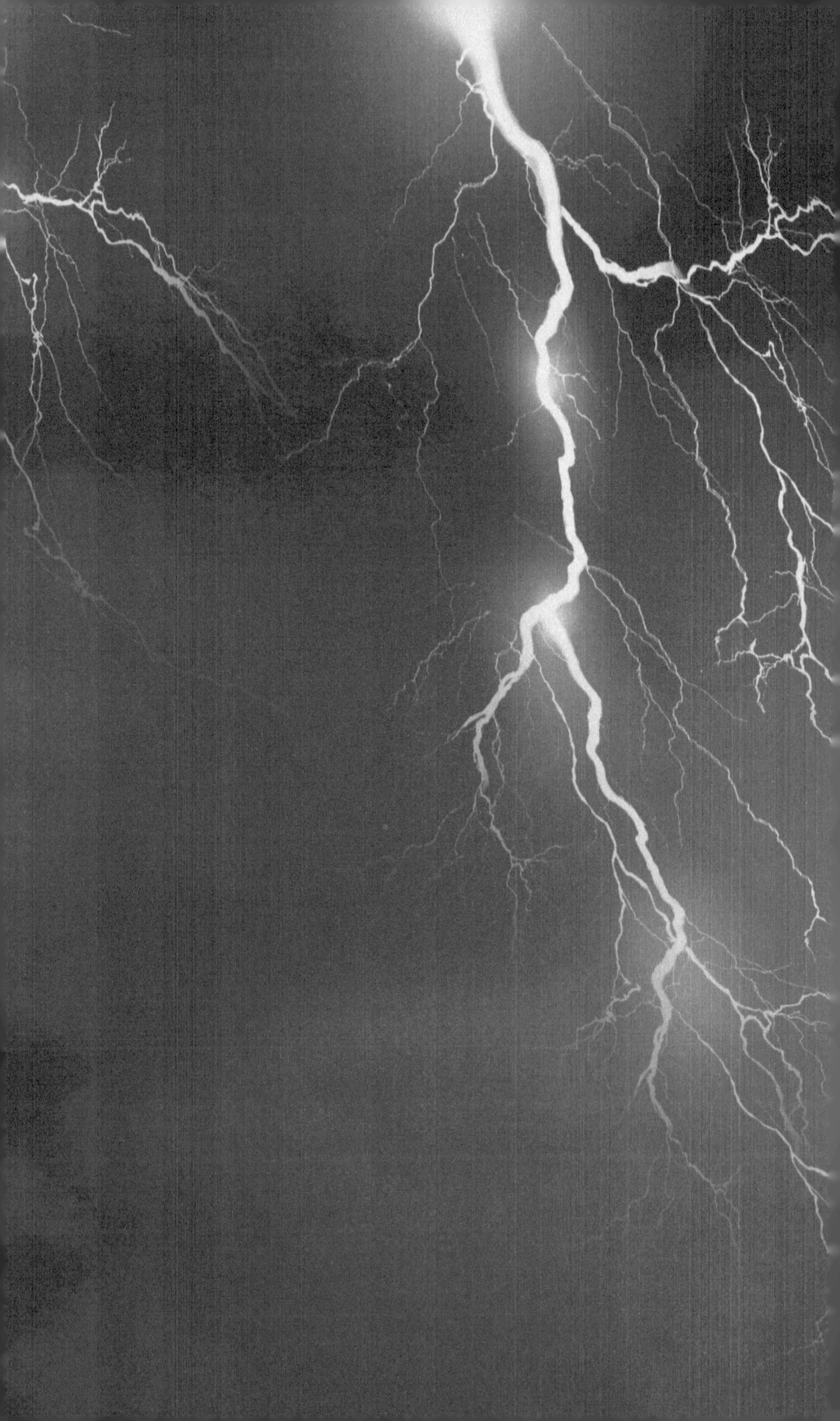

CHAPTER 38

YOU ARE MY FOREVER

After spending some time on the ski machine, Ziph pounded the runner as she worked off her excess energy, and beside her at the weights Dacket had fully recovered and was in the middle of his usual routine. It had been several long weeks of all four of them staying together in Dacket's apartment before they all made plans to reconstruct the top level and extend it over the factory for all of them to live together.

Whit had invited them for a self-care night in his apartment, and Ziph could not wait. Her skin had been feeling dry, and she loved Whit's hydrating mud mask. She did not want to know what was in the mask because it smelled terrible, but it worked, so she didn't complain.

Ziph couldn't help it as she watched Dacket in the mirrors. The way he flexed his muscles as he lifted the bar weights had her zoned out and running much further than she had intended. She had soaked the runner with sweat by the time she started her cooldown, and when she climbed off, her legs were goo. She over did it regularly, but with her energy levels, she bounced back in a few minutes.

She sat on the floor, and Dacket brought her some water before joining her. "At some point after the celebration next week, we should go hike the mountains and decide on a place to build your ski resort."

Ziph stared at him. They had only spoken about the idea a few times, and she half expected him to be joking. When it was clear he wasn't, she blurted out, "I want to go right after the celebration is over."

Dacket laughed as he agreed, "We can do that if that's what you want. I'm back to normal according to my last exam, and I feel great, so I would love to do some hiking. Plus, I received a letter from Copula with a generous land allotment in the mountains as our gift."

Ziph's mouth dropped open, and she couldn't help it as she admitted, "I want to go right now."

Dacket gave her one of his beautiful smiles before he leaned in and kissed her. "We can't go right now, but I have photos of the land we can choose from for us to review tonight. The letter also added that with the new technology dispersed from the palace, we should have mobile video communication in weeks as well as plans for community transportation flights and railways. The Kefale kings were hoarding years of advancements from our society. They have plans to reveal it all at the celebration. I am sure you miss some of the technology you had before."

Ziph remembered when she said his society was primitive and cringed internally. As usual her moment of embarrassment started a cascade of her embarrassing moments rushing through her mind. She squeezed her eyes shut. *Say something! He's sitting there, waiting. Oh, I should try to explain my feelings, right?* "I still feel bad for the primitive comment."

Dacket's smile went slack as he admitted, "Did you forget how we met? I bit you."

Ziph stopped her spiral, and stared at Dacket, "So, you did. Good point. Trent bit me too."

Dacket scowled deeply at her admission, and he reached forward to grasp her leg, "What? When?"

Ziph warmed to his concern. "It was a while ago when you had to wake me up at his apartment."

After staring at her for a long while, Dacket huffed before he narrowed his eyes, "He didn't say anything else, did he?"

Ziph reached up and lovingly tapped Dacket in the center of his chest. "Yes, he did. I know all about why Whit has a bondage kink, Mr. Bitey." Dacket deadpanned her and Ziph laughed again as she continued, "Using exposure therapy to face trauma is very effective."

"If you bite Whit, he will bust all of our eardrums with his scream," Dacket shook his head, as he frowned.

Ziph smiled at him and rubbed her finger along his collar bone, "That was not where I was going with that. I just meant, for me, Trent biting me was quite therapeutic after you fucking paralyzed me for what, two whole days?" Dacket cringed, he had exceptionally potent venom and hated how second nature it felt to reach out and sink his fangs into flesh. Sometimes they ached so badly, he would sink them into a cold piece of raw meat from his ice box, just to empty his venom into something. The thought of it made his mouth water.

"Why are you two on the floor?" Trent came in and stood over them with his hands on his hips.

Dacket scowled up at Trent. "You bit her?"

Trent laughed as he put his hand out for her. "You know my venom doesn't do anything. She liked it and I will definitely be biting that juicy ass of hers again." Trent lifted Ziph and smacked her ass before he went over to the runner and began walking on it.

Ziph went upstairs to clean up and change before she met Dacket in their living room. Her hair was wrapped in a towel, and she went to Whit's apartment as Trent was just opening Whit's door to bathe. He had been staying in the second room since Dacket had been taken by the Kefale. They all gathered around Whit's table in his kitchen with the files and Dacket spread them out.

"These are the land segments we can choose from, we are to decide and then pass this along to the former Grindle team before the end of tomorrow, so they have enough time to select one before the celebration," Dacket explained as they all focused on the different maps, some elevation and some were arial photographs.

"You weren't joking when you said Copula released updated technology, these images are fantastic. We need an area with a good range of slopes for skiing, and we need somewhere to have a lodge with a separate place for a home. We don't want to live at the lodge. We should hire Danny to be the resort manager. She would probably love it," Ziph explained as she imagined Danny shining in the leading role at the resort. *Danny loved being in charge when we were all away. She is going to scream at this offer.* Whit agreed and pointed to a map he had been studying. She had truly forgotten what advanced technology was like, and there was something about these advancements which were making her feel so much more at home within the Elarian society.

Whit pointed to one of the information packets and

tapped the corner. "This place has everything you mentioned, and it's the highest elevation. There is even a spot for a home off to the side."

They all agreed and Whit took the pen and made their selection before running the paperwork down to the guard for delivery to the Grindle home where Gerara's team now lived. Trent went to clean up and dress while Ziph and Dacket found a comfortable place on Whit's couch as they waited. When Whit returned, he sat on the other side of Ziph with a book in his hand. Ziph pulled the towel from her damp hair and tossed it in Whit's laundry bin before returning to her place on the couch with a plop.

Ziph rested her head on Dacket's shoulder as Whit flipped through the pages and they waited for Trent to come out from the bathroom, Whit rose from the couch and pulled out his basket of facial creams and masks. After passing them around and everyone applying them to one another, Whit stood up and began reading a story about a boy who built a boat and took a long journey down a river to escape a giant bird. It was one of many books distributed when the palace was cleared out for demolition. Whit had shown up with a wagon, and they allowed him to fill it until it was overflowing. It took him four trips from the garage to his apartment to move them all upstairs. Most of the books had been confiscated works from people who had been arrested or taken for spawning, and some were quite controversial for the former royalty. The story he was reading had been one of Whit's favorites of all the books he had found, and he had been insisting on having a reading night.

While he read, Dacket slipped his hand around Ziph's waist and pulled her toward him until she was nearly on his lap. Dacket's tail slipped around one of her ankles while Trent wrapped his tail around her other calf. Trent noticed her movement away from him and inched along with her, and he ended up right next to Dacket with Ziph half on his lap and half on Dacket's. With Dacket's arm around her, he lifted her shirt and slid his hands to her breasts to begin circling his fingertips around her nipples.

Trent noticed and nudged Dacket to move her hips to his lap, and Dacket reluctantly moved her ass over to Trent who had his hand down her pants before she could think. She gasped softly as he pushed her legs apart and found her clit with his finger and thumb. *Whit might throw that book at us when he looks up at us not paying any attention.* Trent pinched her clit too perfectly, just in the right place, and she squeaked, causing Whit to stop reading and frown at them.

He noticed how disheveled and heated Ziph was, which made him lower the book. When he saw Dacket's hands up Ziph's shirt and Trent's hand down her pants, he snarled his lip and put his hand on his hip. "When was someone planning to tell me to stop reading? When did it become time to fuck? You realize we all still have mud masks on!"

Ziph fell over onto Dacket's lap and the three of them laughed as Whit glared at them. He tossed his book on the table and grabbed several cloths. He wet and threw them at Ziph, Trent, and Dacket, nailing all three of them with soggy slaps.

They wiped their faces clean before Whit, who stood in front of his rope chair and hooked his finger at Ziph. "I've been waiting way too long for this. Ziph come here." Ziph walked over to him, and he lifted her sleep shirt off and dropped her loose pants to the floor. Trent and Dacket surrounded her as Whit lifted her into the woven chair in an upright position before he wrapped the ropes above her knees and ankles, securing her legs wide open. He finished by taking her hands and tying them above her head at an angle forcing her breasts forward before he stuffed the ball in her mouth.

Trent moved between her legs and knelt down before running his forked tongue from her asshole to her clit, making her heat deep inside her belly as she wiggled as much as she could. Dacket grabbed her hips and positioned himself behind her, and she could already feel him pressing his lubed cock against her tight ass. Their tails were like roaming hands, and she shivered when one of them slipped inside her pussy, hooking the tip forward and making her desperate.

Trent moved himself where her thighs were over his shoulders, and he used his fingers as he devoured her to find her clit, and when he did, he gently bit down on it, holding it between his front teeth. Ziph whimpered as she felt Trent flick at her clit with his tongue while Dacket caressed her nipples, only stopping when she could hear Whit behind Dacket kissing and whispering to him. She felt their tails wrap around her legs and waist as she grew closer to her pleasure cresting.

Dacket was hard as a rock pressing against her ass when Trent sucked down on her clit, causing her to fly over the edge. She squeezed his head between her thighs as she thrashed against the ropes, moaning around the gag. Trent took his fingers and spread her leaking wetness around to her asshole before lining himself up with her pussy. Dacket and Trent both slid into her at the same time, and Ziph released a soft cry as they filled her so completely, she felt like she couldn't possibly handle any more.

Behind Dacket, Whit had his cock lubed and he pressed into Dacket before they began moving together. Dacket's heated panting at her ear and Trent's pleading eyes with the way she was filled could have sent her into explosive bliss right then, but she knew what was coming, and she braced herself for their cocks to split.

When their cocks split into four and began rolling, Ziph was thankful she had that ball gag in as she cried out around it as Dacket and Trent began to flutter and roll their tips inside of her. Behind her, Dacket kissed down her neck and gently pinched her nipples as the grinding and thrusting continued just long enough for Ziph to feel a perfect heat spreading and gnawing at her as it prepared to burst. All it took to tip her over was Trent releasing the bruising hold he had on her hip long enough to pinch her clit. She saw stars and gasped as she came, crying out and shivering with her pleasure blasting through her body like lightning. Whit shot cum into Dacket first, which caused Dacket to cum at the same time as Trent. Ziph was unprepared for the second jolt of pleasure from the jets of hot cum, and she yelped as her hips shook and fought the hold.

When everyone slid free from one another, Dacket and Trent untied Ziph before Trent carried her into Whit's bathroom to clean up the evidence of their activities. Once everyone was clean and ready to sleep, they all piled onto Whit's bed in an entangled heap. Ziph was in the center with Dacket and Trent on either side, and Whit behind Trent. She wasn't sure how she could sleep with so many bodies crowded in one bed, but when she was prying heavy arms from her in the middle of the night for a bathroom break, she giggled to herself thinking about her pre-sleep assumptions.

Ziph went for a glass of water before she grabbed a blanket and went to the roof to admire the stars. She wasn't quite ready to return to bed yet. She curled up on one of the plush chairs and wrapped her blanket around her tightly in the chilled night air.

A few moments later Dacket came up and lifted her before sitting down and setting her in his lap. He leaned his head against hers before he kissed her temple. "I've never felt hope before you, it feels like you are my forever. I can't seem to ever have enough."

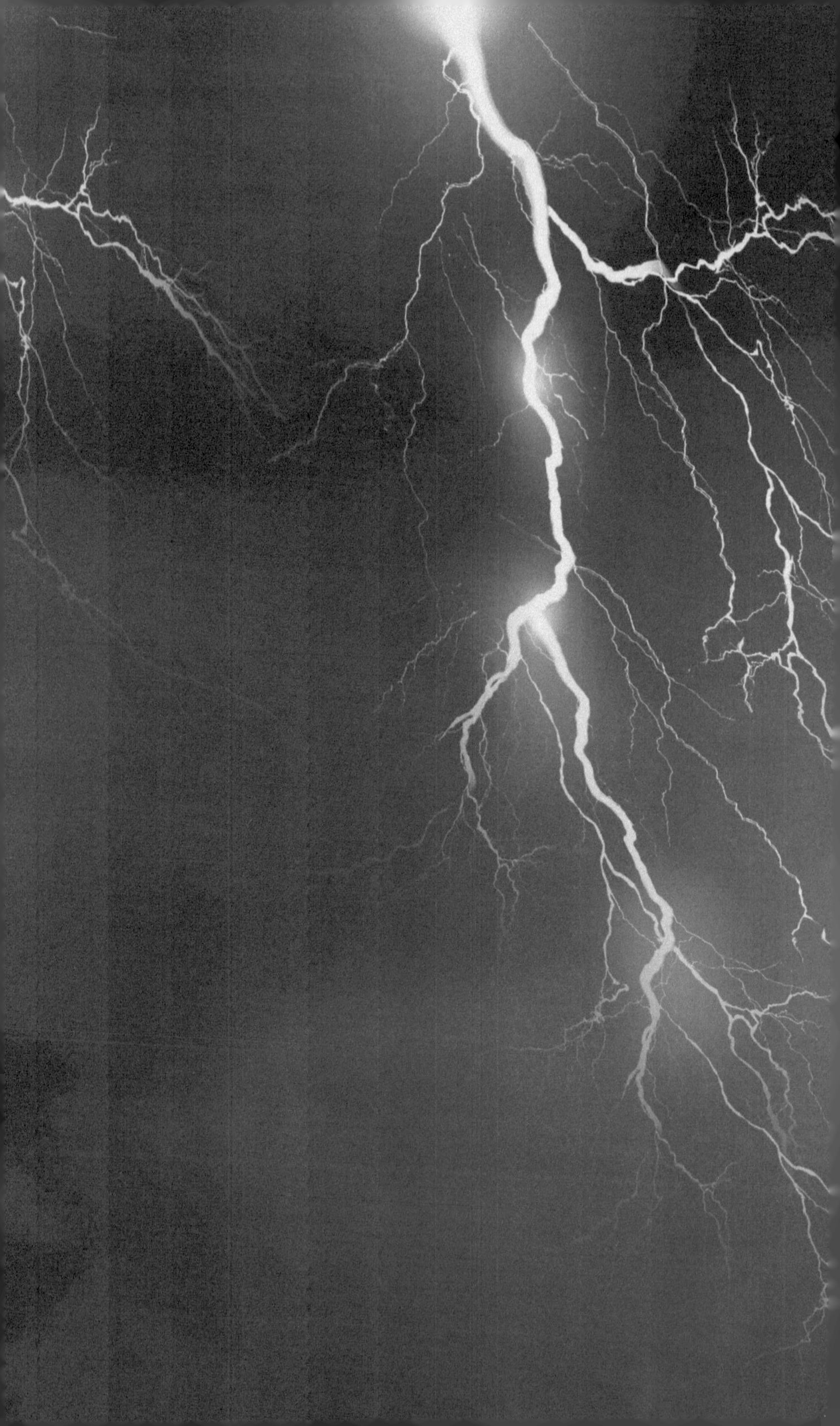

CHAPTER 39

CELEBRATION

Ziph, Whit, and Danny had spent hours on makeup and hair as they prepared for the celebration and open questioning of the remaining former Kefale Royals. Ziph couldn't wait knowing the people would interact with the former royals and question them all night. It was the highlight of the nightly events.

Slipping on her backless floor length shimmering ruby red gown with a high slit and deep v cut neck which was perfectly coordinated with her red lipstick and smoky black and brown eye makeup. Whit wore a sharp black suit and Danny had on a black halter mini dress that would surely show her ass if she bent over.

Whit opened the door when they were ready, meeting Dacket and Trent in the hallway. Ziph loved seeing them dressed up, Dacket looked perfect in his slate grey suit and Trent was beaming in his new black suit.

Ziph linked arms with Dacket and Trent before they descended the stairs and started on their long walk through the city to the royal gardens. As they walked, Ziph was awestruck at the beautifully painted banners and colorful lights strung along the streets. People were mingling everywhere, and she could already see the beginnings of street commerce. Her heart could have burst when she saw a little girl selling cream and orange roses as they stepped into the gardens, and of course Whit went flying over to buy them all for far more than the girl was charging, sending her squealing in delight and showing off her handfuls of coins as she ran to her graciously waving parents.

Staying true to his words of humility and servitude, newly elected Copula was modestly dressed and greeting anyone and everyone who wanted to approach him. Ziph watched as he interacted with the people, and she was thrilled to see he had all the contents of the Kefale Royal Palace on display along with explanations written in thorough detail with volunteers nearby for verbal explanations. Each piece of advanced technology had an accompanying sign up for free education on the tech, as well as potential job offers for an attempt to develop the tech for broad use. He was taking transparency and societal growth seriously, and she knew the Elarian people would support him with the level of dedication he was providing.

Copula saw Ziph, Dacket, Whit, and Trent and came over directly, politely excusing himself before excitedly addressing them, "I am thrilled to see you. Please join me for a photograph." They all moved toward a beautifully arranged background of foliage and roses in a mixed rainbow of colors before turning and posing with Copula in the center, who was grinning like he had won the friend lottery.

Ziph guessed they *had* won the lottery in another sense as well. They had made it through with no permanent harm, and that in itself was a priceless win. The moment the picture was snapped, Dacket wrapped his arms around her and whispered, "There are enormous apples growing on a tree behind us."

Ziph yanked Dacket by the hand and rushed toward a low branch of the apple tree as Whit and Trent went with Danny to look at all the new tech. Ziph reached up and plucked a pink and yellow apple from the tree before biting into it and juice trickled down her chin. *I'm glad I spent extra time setting my makeup.* More liquid trickled down her chin, but this time on the other side of her mouth, *I wish I could eat and not wear half of it!*

Dacket chuckled a bit under his breath as he reached in his pocket and handed her a napkin. "I can tell when you're talking to yourself in your head."

Ignoring him, Ziph dabbed her chin before she handed it back. "Did I wipe my makeup off?" She angled her face to what she thought was the light for him to see better but just ended up making an odd face as she jutted her chin out.

Dacket bit his lips together holding back a laugh and shook his head as he angled her face where he could see. "You look perfect." He pulled her in for a kiss and slowly backed them up to the apple tree's wide trunk. With her back to the tree and Dacket hovering over her with his amber eyes lit on fire, Ziph felt her skin burning in antici-pation. He reached up and brushed a bit of golden hair from her face.

"All the gold in the universe comes from the stars, and that goes for you too. A lovely golden squirrel dropped on a world of snakes. It sounds like a horror story, yet you charmed us all. Now our world is forever changed for the better. How can such a gift of the stars ever be repaid?"

Ziph stared at Dacket stunned as she tried to respond but failed and frowned, trying not to cry.

Dacket smiled and kissed her forehead. "You don't sneak around and look through people's things at all, do you?"

Ziph shook her head as she blinked away the tears. She hated having her privacy invaded and would never do such a thing. "No, never. I despise that."

Dacket kissed her forehead again before he explained, "I've been writing off and on since I was a child. I don't know if I'm any good, but I would like for you to read some of my favorite stories and poetry. Writing was heavily regulated before, so I never wanted to bring it up. It hurt too much to talk about."

Ziph waved her hand at her burning face. *What the fuck did this man just say?* "When the fuck, what, I am *fucking* flustered. That was so hot. I need *air*!" Dacket moved back a step to let her by and Ziph twirled around to face him. "Is writing what you want to do now that you won't need to hunt anymore? You are very good, and I would love to read what you've written." Realizing her translator didn't extend to her eyes, she continued, "Actually, I'll need you to read it to me because my translator doesn't work for reading, just speaking and listening. I should probably learn how to read your language in case my translator ever stops working." In her head, Ziph had undressed him, and they had sex against the tree about three times in the last few moments. *We need to rejoin the party happening behind us before I do something stupid like suck his dick behind this tree. He would need to close his eyes because we don't need him laughing. Oh gods, I need to get out of here.*

"That would be wise. I would be happy to teach you while I read to you. Your core is becoming very hot."

Dacket shot her a knowing grin, and Ziph reached over and grasped his open suit jacket to pull him to her. "Let's join the party before I have any more dirty ideas." Dacket linked his arm with hers and led her from the trees, just as they emerged Ziph spotted a Corvus man with an Elarian woman on his arm, and gasped as she squeezed Dacket's arm before hopping in excitement. "That man is from my galaxy!" Ziph nearly yanked Dacket's arm from its socket as she pulled him over to the dark haired man with giant black bird wings. "Hi, I'm Ziph, and I'm from the galactic center too! Were you taken to a lab and transported here too?"

The Corvus man burst with excitement as they both yelled, "In a drop pod!" He continued as he gripped the smiling, reddish toned woman's hand he stood next to. "I am Lodock Grewin, and I was visiting Emendo to pick up an order for my company when I was sent here. I've been here for about a year, and when I heard about what they call an elsewhere woman, I had to drag Hanalia to Valler to see if I could meet you. I can't believe you're from the center. I wonder how many other people have been abducted and transported to planets in this galaxy? There were eight pods open when I was sent here."

They started with nine pods or more?! Ziph felt nauseous as she responded, "When they sent me, I was in the last pod." The group grew silent as the party bustled around them before Whit came up and broke the silence by handing Ziph and Dacket a small electronic device.

"Copula wanted us to have these communication devices. They record video and have these things called screens." Dacket opened it up, snapped it shut, and slipped it into his pocket without looking at it. Ziph remembered the screens in the Kefale Palace and wrapped her arm around him, understanding seeing a screen again may have been upsetting. He seemed calm about it, but Ziph knew he had a lot of trauma to work through after enduring being cut up for spare parts.

Dacket continued to lose his gleeful mood, and Ziph was not having that at all. She pulled him aside and whispered, "I saw all of that. Do we need to go home?"

"Please." Dacket stared at her like she had saved the world all over again.

She would save the world as many times as she needed to for Dacket, Whit, and Trent to be safe. Ziph had not lost one moment of rest over anything she had done, in fact, it gave her a bit of joy to recall pulling the trigger and killing the kings. *I don't think I'm ashamed to admit I would kill a lot of people for these men and not lose a wink of sleep over it.*

She all but dragged Dacket away from the crowd and waved to Whit who waved back at her with a wink, seeming to wordlessly understand Dacket needed to be whisked away. They may have revered him as their leader, but Dacket, by far, had the kindest heart, and they all endeavored to protect him whether they were fully aware or not.

Once they had broken away from the crowd, Dacket's shoulders relaxed, and he was able to slow his speedy gait. After a few blocks, he broke the silence with a quiet, "Thank you," as he reached over and took her hand in his.

Ziph wasn't sure how to respond without stressing him out again, so she changed the subject. "How about we go to the roof and look at the stars." She knew that always made him happy before. He seemed to love that idea and began to return to his cheerful mood. Eventually, when he was ready, she would tell him all about the shows she used to watch when she was in school on Keru, and she expected that the Elara would develop some digital entertainment soon. Giving him a way to find meaning in a screen after what he went through should help him cope with the connected trauma, or so she hoped. It all depended on him.

When they eventually reached the rooftop after their long walk through the city, Dacket pulled Ziph into his lap and wrapped his arms around her before resting his head against hers. "My heart used to skip a few times, and sometimes it would make me dizzy. There were times I had chest pains too. It hasn't happened once since I woke in the palace with you, and I wonder if I had a mild heart condition before, and that doctor fixed it."

Ziph scowled, remembering the gun she had smashed at the doctor's cheek and how she whispered to him about ripping his guts out with her hands. "What if it was major and he saved your life? It was so hard not to kill him when I saw what he did to you. I'm so glad I didn't let loose on him, and I'm so relieved you're better. Are you having more scans done soon?"

Dacket scoffed under his breath, "I hate it. They make me stand in a tiny room. I can't move for several minutes, and there's a lot of obnoxious banging, but yes, I'll go back and have another one soon. The last one came back perfect, and they explained the palace doctor agreed to share all his medical knowledge in exchange for his life since he was only one of three palace surgeons. He and the other two will be teaching permanently from the prison they're building though, they assured me. I don't know if Trent shared the letter which came earlier. Copula's new council agreed that although those at the Kefale Palace were coerced, they still agreed and complied with orders. Anyone without evidence of resistance was ordered to trial, and that's expected to happen soon."

Ziph hadn't been sure Dacket was ready to talk about any of that yet, but she was wrong, and that gave her hope for his emotional healing. She leaned in to kiss him and he was already focused on her, his eyes full of warmth and love.

As their tongues intertwined, Ziph shifted to straddle Dacket's lap, and he kneaded her ass with his strong hands. Dacket's hands moved over her dress and brushed against her nipples before he pinched them causing her to squeak.

Ziph yanked her dress off her shoulders as fast as she could, and it pooled at her feet, Dacket smiled when he saw she wore nothing under her dress. He leaned up and removed his jacket before unbuttoning his shirt. Ziph was eternally impatient and knelt before him to unbuckle his belt and help him step from his pants.

When he was finally out of his clothes, she crawled onto his lap, and they resumed kissing, but it didn't last long as Dacket hauled her up so he could flit his tongue around her nipples.

He stopped and looked around before he lifted her and lay her out on the table, Ziph tensed with the cold metal against her skin, and her nipples tightened in response. Dacket rubbed his thumbs over her hard nipples and kissed her between her breasts before he parted her legs and used his knuckles to force her clit to the surface.

He smirked at her squirming desperation before he leaned down and gave her exactly what she was yearning for, taking her flesh between his teeth, nipping and sucking. He took his time and brought her to a steady rhythm before quickening and lifting her higher. With the chill at her back and the heat between her legs, it was a fiery rush of pleasure as her orgasm raced through her. She arched off the table and moaned loudly into the night as she wiggled her toes. Dacket reached down and squeezed the arches of her feet briefly, just how she liked, before pulling them, and her, down the table and back into his arms.

He sat back in the chair and lowered her onto him. As his cock slid inside, Ziph felt him fill her up and with the first thrust, he broke into four parts. His tail slipped between her ass cheeks and began pressing inside. She relaxed onto him as he pushed her down onto his cock and tail with his hands firmly on her waist.

When he began to roll and flutter inside of her, the way she responded to him was like a switch, and she burst with a second wave of intense all consuming pleasure, leaving her sweating and whimpering as he emptied inside of her with a groan.

He grabbed her face and brought her in for a kiss before he whispered, "Ziphalie, I believe you made the Kefale return my heart just to steal it for yourself."

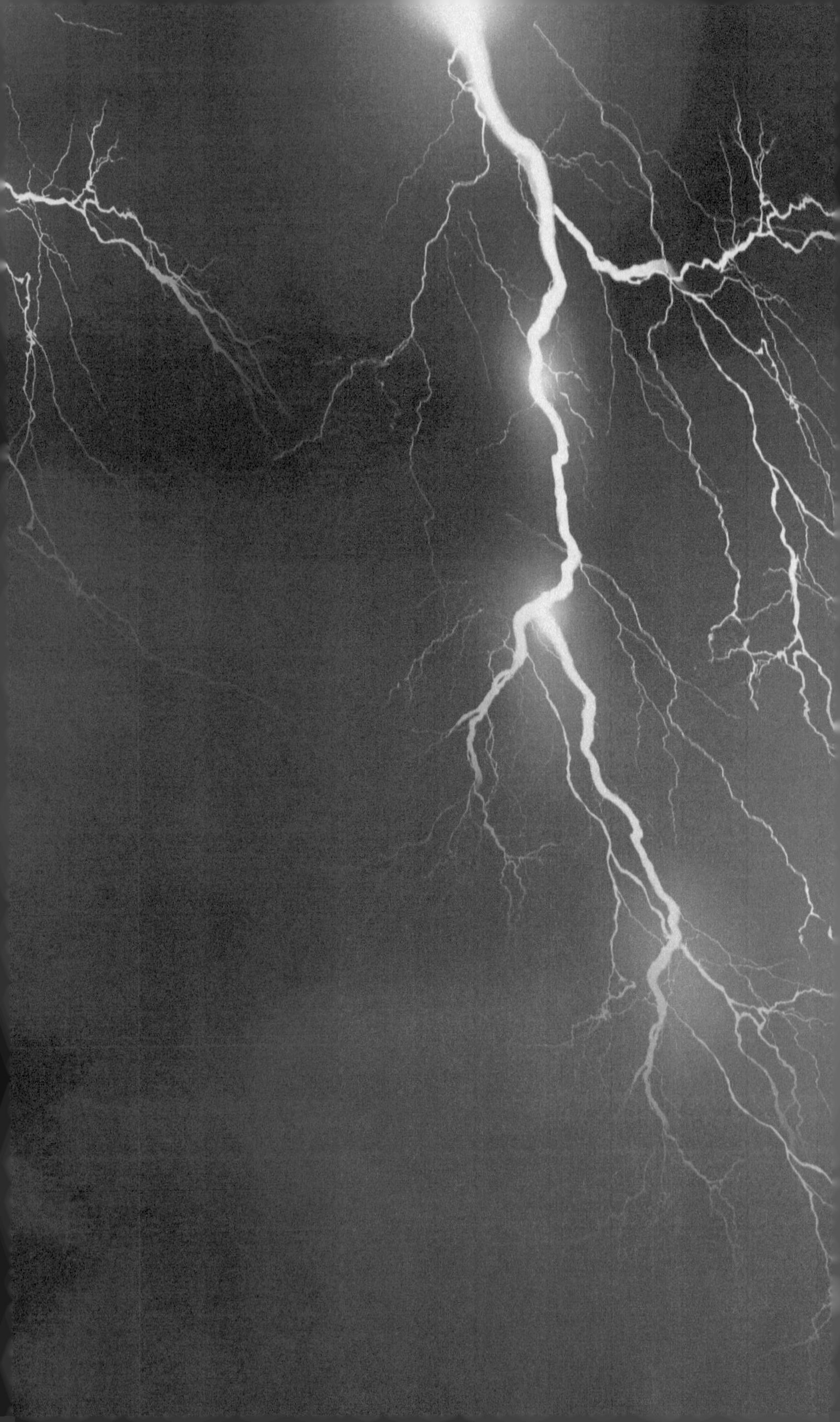

EPILOGUE

The fire crackled in the stone fireplace as Ziph dried the glue on her pheromone nodules in her mouth as she rested on the rug naked. The day of snowboarding at the resort she owned with Danny, Dacket, Whit, and Trent had been enough excitement for her for the day and she had skipped dinner with her men after Danny went back to work as the resort manager.

It had taken her a while to become used to calling Dacket, Whit, and Trent, *her men*, but they insisted on it during their first hike of their property. They had all surrounded her on their knees and pledged their lives to her, and she in turn pledged her life to them. It was the happiest moment of her existence, and they had made each day after that more beautiful than the last. Just a few months later, they signed the documents for their new home on Barren, which was over eight years ago. It was completed shortly after they had begun building their ski lodge in the mountains of Binara.

Since the fall of the Kefale, the Elarian people had populated their second world Barren after they had discovered an extensive underground water system. The technology developed in the last eight years had allowed them to explore the rest of their planet, which was mostly lifeless other than masses of algae in a vast northern ocean. An immense ice cap topped the other side of their world, and it turned out the only reason they had any warmth in the south was the magnetic fight between gravity pulling and the fighting opposite poles of Binara and Barren. It made sense with all the massive fractures in the ground, reinforcing there was clearly a gravitational tug-of-war occurring between the planets.

Space flight was now commonplace, and they were even considering terraforming another world in their system of multiple rocky, livable worlds. Ziph walked over to the wall of windows and looked up at Barren, and down to the giant spiderweb of gardens surrounding the Elarian People's Capital. There was a small winding design in the gardens, and she spent time each day searching for it, if only to admire it for a moment from her windows at their ski lodge home. The waved design was the memorial for Lashes, the last of the great serpents. *My sweet girl.*

Lashes had been memorialized when she passed away a few weeks after Ziph had saved her life from her own team of hunters. The determination for cause of death was natural causes, but Ziph knew she had starved, it was the entire reason the serpents ever dared to approach the cities. They had ended the Kefale feeding the serpents the Elarian people pumped with growth hormones between the cities, and Lashes had been the last of their victims.

The serpents which came after Lashes had been substantially smaller, and although still large enough to consume a person, the size difference was monumental. The discovery that the serpents were naturally docile, came at a devastating blow to the Elarian people, especially the former hunters, and there was a collective effort to protect the serpents indefinitely. They were now considered the official Elarian animal, and many other animals which developed in unique ways in the sky belt were being set up with protections. Most of them had webbed toes or winged limbs to aid in movement in the no gravity environment with a thick atmosphere, and Ziph had been heavily involved in the biology project to document them.

Copula was finishing his second five-year term, and a new council leader was stepping in, a younger woman, she was a long time student of Copula with progressive ideas to elevate their society even further. Ziph thought she was perfect if anyone were asking her opinion.

She smiled thinking about Danny screaming as she went down a hill too steep for her, Ziph giggled knowing Danny would likely talk about it for a week. She and Danny had developed the kind of friendship she could describe better as a sisterhood. Danny had become her family just as Dacket, Whit, and Trent.

She dropped her towel and opened the glass door to access the balcony overlooking the mountains. She knew her men would be stomping through the snow down the path any minute, and she hadn't surprised them naked on the balcony in a while, so she crawled over the edge to dangle her feet.

Trent was the first over the snow drift to see her, and he whistled before he informed everyone behind him, "She's naked on the balcony."

She could hear Dacket from behind the trees before she could see him. "Why the fuck are you walking so slow then?" They were shoving one another from the path when she finally saw them all roll down the hill fighting in a ball of limbs and tails through the fresh snow. Their home had an additional few inches of snowfall while they had been away at dinner.

Whit held a paper box up above his head to keep it from being crushed as Trent and Dacket pulled him back down the snow drift with them. She knew that box was her dinner. *Maybe they'll actually let me eat before they fuck me this time.*

When Trent reached the ground in front of the balcony, he jumped and grabbed the bottom of the ledge to climb up instead of using the stairs inside. Dacket pulled Trent's boot off as he passed underneath his swinging legs, and he and Whit went inside for the stairs.

Only wearing one boot, Trent had her in his arms and was setting her on her feet before Whit had finished shutting the door downstairs. "I know you're hungry. Do you think it's funny to tease us like this? Are you planning to eat naked too? You'll be lucky if you get any of this food down before I make you cum."

She pursed her lips defiantly and batted her long lashes at Trent as she could hear Whit and Dacket coming up the stairs. "Why would I dress when you're just going to take it off? You better let me eat. I'm hungry." Trent tipped his head to the side as he thought about it like it brought him pain and reluctantly agreed while behind them Dacket and Whit came in their bedroom. Whit brought Ziph her box of mixed steamed vegetables with a personal fruit pie.

"You will probably cover yourself with this like you do all your meals, but that's part of what you think is so funny isn't it? I fucking hate butter."

Ziph laughed and scowled at him, "I'm honestly just feeling lazy." Ziph plopped down in front of the fire on the plush cream rug and began devouring her meal. She fully ignored the men as they chatted behind her, as well as ignoring her manners as she dripped buttery sauce all over her chest and stomach.

By the time she had finished her pie, she looked down to find a chunk of fruit splayed over the top of her breast. She looked up and Whit stood with his hands on his hips glaring at her audacity. "If you drip on that rug, Dacket will make us redesign this cabin like a rental so you can't mess it up again. I do not want that. It took time to find all these items. Now you're wearing half the meal. Did you even manage to get any butter in your mouth?"

Ziph looked up at him just as a bit of fruity syrup dripped from her chin onto her breast, and she heard Dacket huff behind her. She narrowed her eyes. *He's about to throw me in the water. Fuck, it's already running. Damn, I bet Trent is already in there.* She reached up and began licking the butter sauce and fruit syrup from her fingers. *I honestly don't think I could love it anymore that they hate butter.*

Dacket hauled her up by holding her under her arms as Whit grabbed her feet and they carried her to the bathroom as she'd protested, "I can fucking walk!" but Whit scoffed at her, "Not without dripping your nasty butter juice!"

Dacket made a "Bleh" sound behind her, and she looked up to him as he scowled down at her. "Butter is the nastiest thing I've ever experienced, and it's all over you. You know we *hate* butter." *WAIT. Are Dacket and Whit naked? Where did Trent go?*

Ziph did know how much they hated it and ignored it because butter was delightful, and she was just lucky she had found a bovine creature to give them milk for her buttery needs. It wasn't perfect, but it was close enough to what she had at home, and she was more than happy. It was also really fun, slathering butter on her nipples and not telling her men about it. *The way they lift their heads up and shake because they can't stand the taste is absolute perfection. I want to see it about a million more times.*

Trent came back in the room, naked with an additional bottle of soap as she was thrust in the warm stream. When Whit set her down, she was at chest level, and she quickly realized *she* wasn't the only reason they were in the shower. They had been snowboarding all day and she had been the only one who had a bath at that point.

"You complained about me, and my butter boobies?! The three of you smell like dead fish!" Ziph slapped a hand over her mouth and nose as they all started soaping up, finally cutting the scent of their sweaty odor. Ziph reluctantly soaped up again before she rinsed and wrapped herself in a towel.

She didn't make it far as Trent yanked her towel away and grabbed her by the waist before twisting her around and setting them both on the heated bathroom floor with her in his lap. *Damn, we didn't even make it out of the bathroom. We never make it to the bed.*

Whit and Dacket dried and tossed their towels away, joining Trent on the floor. Whit moved next to Trent and together, they moved Ziph between them on the warm tile before wrapping up her limbs with their tails. Dacket crouched between her legs and lifted her ass up so he could find her clit with his teeth. Ziph whimpered and whined as he bit down gently and slightly moved his teeth as he slipped his tongue along the sensitive flesh. He knew exactly how much pressure she needed, and where, to send her straight into dazzling waves of dancing pleasure. Ziph broke apart with a rush and moaned on the warm floor at her back while she was surrounded by the men she loved, and her nipples were as hard as rocks as a result.

Trent lifted her to her feet and leaned her back to suck on one of her pierced nipples before Dacket turned her, and he grasped her hips and lined up his tip with her pussy so he could angle her down onto his hard cock. Whit moved behind her and lubed himself before he slid into her ass. Trent positioned himself behind Whit he sank his lubed cock inside of Whit's ass with a sharp breath.

When they were all joined with their tails and arms wrapped around her, Trent and Dacket thrust at once, filling Ziph and Whit at the same time. The heat and thrill of always having her men surround her during sex was so enthralling. She was at the precipice of a scream when their cocks finally split in four parts inside of one another.

Dacket covered her mouth sensing her mounting pleasure, and as she released her delighted cry into his hand, he pulled her back against his hard chest. He ground against her pussy, making her break apart again, and this time her delicious waves were so thick they made her feel as though she was in a boat on the ocean of Keru.

The warmth flowed through her as they burst with cum inside of her and Whit. She was spent and gasping when they pulled themselves free. They cleaned up and all climbed into their enormous bed before wrapping all around Ziph to sleep.

Whit cleared his throat and sat up before he announced, "I was planning to wait until tomorrow morning, but I can't do it. We have been offered something I cannot live without." They all sat up and gave him their undivided attention, Whit never spoke like that, and they knew it had to be important.

"There is a young couple who has just laid fifteen eggs.

They are panicking at the number of eggs, and they have offered us one of the female hatchlings. Actually, I'm lying, she said Ziph would be a wonderful mother and *begged* me to take *at least* one." Whit explained with a shaking voice, and Ziph reached over to take his hand. Elarian birthrates had skyrocketed when they discovered the serpent growth hormones were causing the fertility problems. She knew the young couple, and the young woman had just started working with Whit in the Elarian defense department. The whole reason for the department was solely based on the threat of humans from the galactic center making it to their planet. Ziph knew Whit was thrilled with the woman's work, and she and Whit had been talking about wanting children for a few years.

"I love the idea," Ziph blurted out. She had decided years ago if they were offered a child there would be no question. Trent and Dacket agreed right away, and Whit was so thrilled he jumped on top of them with his arms spread out to squeezed them all together as he cried tears of joy.

Venus, you sneaky bitch, maybe you're not so bad. Ziph understood a bit of beauty in that moment. Venus had not ruined her life after all. *I was sent here, but I made my own little piece of paradise. Maybe heaven isn't somewhere you go. Maybe it's something you create.*

ABOUT THE AUTHOR

Lauren Logan is a neurodivergent, disabled science fiction romance author from North Texas. After high school and junior college, she attended the University of North Texas and studied Psychology and History. She met her husband in 2008, married in 2010, and they now have two little boys. They all enjoy watching science programs about astronomy as well as staying caught up on the latest Star Trek episodes.

In 2015 Lauren developed a passion for hair and began a journey that would lead her to hair school in her thirties. She specialized in vivid color and within a year and a half she had been nominated as a top 100 pastel colorist in the

Behind The Chair global hair awards. Unfortunately, the ultimate hair honor had come too late. A few months before her nomination was announced, Lauren had been forced to quit her dream career as a vivid hair colorist. The loss was devastating and she fell into a dark place.

November of 2020, Lauren was formally diagnosed with an autoimmune disease, Rheumatoid Arthritis. The disease course is aggressive and effects nearly all of her major joints, as well as both hands and feet. She has developed deformities in her fingers, making any chance of regaining her former hair career impossible. On rainy days you can often see her walking with a cane because the changing weather can bring on a flare. Since her diagnosis, she spends much of her time unable to leave her bed due to the constant pain and fatigue. The medication she is prescribed leaves her immunocompromised as well as having many difficult side effects.

Refusing to let her disability steal her ambition and kill her determination, Lauren began writing at the beginning of April, 2022. Over the course of one year, she completed writing two full length Sci-fi novels. Since the completion of the Reticere Series, she is now working on several stand alone novels in the same universe. Writing gives her hope and being an author gives her a future. She pours everything she is into her stories and she hopes you love them as much as she does.

For more information visit:
www.AuthorLaurenLogan.com

facebook.com/authorlaurenlogan

instagram.com/laurenloganart

tiktok.com/@lauren.logan